To a Lovely Young Girl, and Thank Her For Reading my Story

Chasing
SHAKESPEARE

by

R L K

DORRANCE
PUBLISHING CO
EST. 1920
PITTSBURGH, PENNSYLVANIA 15238

Dorrance Publishing Co
585 Alpha Drive
Pittsburgh, PA 15238
Visit our website at www.dorrancebookstore.com

ISBN: 978-1-6480-4399-4
eISBN: 978-1-6480-4564-6

Chasing
SHAKESPEARE

CHAPTER ONE

Peter Jameson stood watching the small home from the tree line; even as the cold began to freeze his feet, he remained undeterred. A man of 30 having a young wife of 23, who had lost interest in the marriage. Yet she was his by law, even the endless beatings could not prevent her from seeking other companionship. Throughout his life, he despised those having more than he possessed. As he continued to think, his head began to ache. The pain continued, not from the cold wind that began but the very thought of someone wanting to take what was his.

His thin bony fingers tightly wrapped around the knife that fit to his warn belt. The longer he waited, his head continued to pound against his small skull.

Suddenly, he noticed a rider approaching, and a young man wearing the blue coat with pure white trousers given by the British was now in plain sight. Stopping in front of the cabin, the young man quickly dismounted and, without fear, tied his horse to the post and entered.

Jameson, in a burst of energy, ran to the edge of the cabin and, after noticing the long sword attached to the man's saddle, took it from the sheath. Slowly opening the door, he found the two in an embrace, while the pounding in his head consumed him with rage.

"You traitor!" he said, pointing the blade toward the young man who stepped in front of the young woman. "Now you wish to take what is not yours?"

"She does not love you and will no longer stand your beatings," the young man replied, showing no fear while using his body to shield her. "She'll be leaving this night with me."

"Hand over that pistol." The blade touched the handle of the pistol. "We'll talk of this once you've given it up."

"Don't my love," she cried out, "he's evil."

"Maybe so, but he'll not harm a British soldier." As if assured by this, he slowly handed him the pistol, in fear of being hung.

"Soldier," he began to smile while taking the pistol and cocking it. "You're nothing more than a traitor to the people."

"Peter, I don't love you," she said, stepping away from him, "and I'm begging you to leave us."

"A whore begging," Jameson said, stepping closer to the two, "so that she can lay with such fifth."

"I demand you retract that," the young man blurted out while attempting to remove his white gloves from his belt, "or face me in a field of honor."

Instantly placing the pistol against the side of the young man's skull, he pulled the trigger.

"You killed him!" she cried out in grief. "You'll hang for this."

"No. After having killed you…" He plunged the blade into her chest. "He shot himself."

Within minutes, he placed the bodies where it would appear a murder/suicide occurred. Walking out, he understood he would have to leave the state, knowing the British soldiers would be looking for him and, in their fury, would force him to tell the truth.

The following morning Colonel Hockman of the British army entered the cabin by request of the local authorities.

"Colonel, sorry having to call you out," said the man standing over the young woman who had the sword still sticking inside of her, "but do you know this soldier?"

"I've 1,000 men under my command," he said, examining the young man's body, "but he wears the insignia of American Volunteer… British sword," he said, touching the handle then pointing toward the floor, and pistol. "Yes, both are British." Walking past the two bodies toward the bedroom, he asked, "Is the young woman married?"

"Yes, she is, he followed him inside the room. Can't find him, but we're looking."

"You are assuming the young soldier killed her," the Colonel said, looking toward the bed, "and then took his own life."

"It appears so, sir," he added.

"Interesting he would come all this way to kill the young lady," he said while opening the shudder, "who carefully had packed for a journey."

"Just four dresses," said the policeman as the Colonel opened the chest, "and personal things."

"Along with a missing husband," the Colonel added.

In the year of 1781, Colonel Hochman stood looking at the large map on the wall, as his aid Captain Willard entered the office without knocking.

"Sir, all patrols report no activity," he said while standing at attention in his bright red uniform, "and they brought deer and elk."

"Six months ago, came here to this God forsaken place," he blurted out, "a fortress built to stop the Americans' use of the river. Then having to watch a British army leave to do battle elsewhere, while I sit here doing nothing."

"We have denied the American forces from using the river," the Captain attempted to ease his thoughts, "and it must be important enough for us to remain."

"We control nothing but the ground we stand, turning toward the man, while the American army is camped a day's march from here. We are captives, allowed to fend for ourselves but not to leave."

"Sir, having lost the Carolinas," the Captain said as if reminding him, "we cannot abandon Pennsylvania. Our armies could not defend New York, if we were to leave. Besides, by remaining here the American army cannot leave either."

"The American army is just waiting for us to leave, sitting behind his desk, knowing we must take the road toward New York. I've studied the terrain, and can see at least a dozen places where they could ambush our columns. They watch and wait, and if we were ordered to leave we'd all end up prisoners of war or dead."

"Sir, if the American army wished us dead…" The Captain was now at ease. "They would have attacked us long ago."

"General Dodd is no fool," the Colonel said, giving a small chuckle. "He has an army of 800 to 900, and no intention of wasting his men by attacking this fort."

"Captain Hughes of the American volunteer army," he replied as if reminding him, "has suggested we should attack the settlement. It is his belief they are supporting the American army, with supplies and weapons."

"I despise the man and trust nothing he says," Colonel Hockman said almost in an angry rage. "You've been in this war for less than a year but know nothing of him."

"He does have 300 volunteers," he cautiously replied, "willing to fight."

"I've cursed the day he came here," he began, "never a man so despicable."

"Sir, I don't understand," the Captain said, showing his lack of information. "They say he was a hero during the battle of three rivers."

"Let me tell you about the man," the Colonel said leaning back in his chair. "He wants to attack the settlement because it's where he lived before the war. The people know all his men, and if captured will help place the hangman's noose around all their necks. He's no hero, only a mad dog that should have been put down years ago."

"You're saying he wants to destroy the settlement…" The Captain was shocked at the very thought. "So no one can identify him?"

"Precisely," the Colonel responded, leaning forward. "At three rivers, Hughes and his 700 men were on the right flank. Only when the British soldiers broke the American line did he attack, they claimed killing over 90."

"Yes," said the Captain, remembering the story, "the newspapers reported their victory."

"What they failed to report," continued the Colonel, looking him in the eyes, "64 soldiers of the 90 were the wounded, and his losses were over 100. Many wanted him court-martialed, but the politicians felt such an action would create concerns among the volunteers wanting to join."

"Do the Americans know what he did?" The Captain sat down as if exhausted.

"Yes, which is why I ordered his men to remain inside the fort," he added, "if General Dodd ever learned of it…"

"He would attack," the Captain said, realizing the situation they faced. "But you said he had over 700 men."

"At Fox Meadow," he continued, "his men were placed in the center. It was thought having British by their side, his men would stand firm. After several volleys, the American army attacked. Hughes's army retreated; had it not been for the bravery of our fine soldiers, the battle would have been lost. Command couldn't over look this: 100 of his men were court-martialed and shot for desertion in the face of the enemy. Which is why only 300 are here, wish they had shot all of them."

"Sir, if the American army does come," the Captain questioned what could happen, "will they run or fight?"

"If the Americans come," said the Colonel, relaxing in his chair, "those 300 will be forced to fight. They understand what will happen to them if they're captured, all be hung."

"I hope so, sir," he said, standing up, "but with powder supplies so low…"

"Doesn't matter," Hockman said, taking a deep breath, "their 12 reported cannons out range our six, and their army isn't supplied by the settlers but by the French."

"Which means," Willard said, swallowing hard, "well-armed and supplied."

"Exactly," he admitted, "which is why we cannot give them any reason or excuse to march against us."

For the following week, Willard made his report to Colonel Hockman, but listened with little interest to Hughes's daily complaints.

"Sir," Willard replied in a soft tone while tapping on Hockman's door. "Please open."

"Captain, are you aware of the time?" Hockman asked, looking out into the darkness.

"Yes, sir, but it's quite important," the Captain said, looking toward the man dressed in a gown. "A gentlemen has arrived with a dispatch from General Cornwallis."

"Bring him in." Without further discussion, he walked over to the table and lit the lantern. "Immediately."

The strange looking man wearing buckskin clothing entered without speaking, then slowly bowed. He began speaking in French, while Willard translated each word.

"Name is unimportant but know only," Willard paused for a moment, "and he is Canadian that has come here with a letter. Furthermore, he has little interest in the war."

"Just where is this letter?" Hockman demanded to know.

"He wants five gold coins for the beaver pelt," Willard blurted out as the man removed the fur from his belt. "It is of fine quality."

"Captain, go to my desk," the Colonel said, pointing to it, "and find my coin box."

After counting out the five gold coins, the strange man handed Willard the fur and started toward the door but turned.

"What is he saying now?" Hockman asked while he spoke.

"Says the road is heavily guarded, repeating his warning, many wait."

With the pelt and warning given, the strange man left.

"What am I to do with this?" Hockman asked, examining the pelt.

"Believe the letter was sewn in the pelt, sir," Willard responded.

After tearing the pelt open, Hockman examined the wax seal. Quickly opening the letter, he silently read the information.

"General Cornwallis's forces are surrounded in New York," he began speaking. "He's requesting all available forces to join him. He believes with sufficient forces, he can attack the American army. Time is short, and such an attack be made before the French Fleet arrives."

"Sir, if the Americans are watching the road," he asked, "how can we proceed?"

"We give them an army to fight," Hockman said, taking a deep breath, "one they will more than happy pursue."

"Hughes's blue coats." Willard understood the logic of his thoughts.

"In the morning, request that the Captain is to meet with me," the Colonel said, rubbing his hands while speaking. "He'll finally get his wish to attack the settlements."

The following morning, Hockman sat looking over toward the man who stood only six feet with large cheeks that reminded him of a large hog.

"Captain, I'm giving you an order to attack the settlements," Hockman said, looking into his light dull grey eyes. "Your forces will burn crops and all military supplies found. "You're to begin your attack on the first settlement in two days."

"Why now, sir?" he asked. "After all these weeks of confinement."

"We've been ordered to withdraw from here," he began. "We need to destroy the American army's supplies, so they cannot follow. Once you complete your assignment, continue toward New York. My forces will leave here in four days by road, and without sufficient supplies, the Americans will be unable to move against me."

"My troops are to attack the three settlements," Hughes said, standing up and pointing to the map, "then proceed over rough terrain that will take us weeks to arrive at New York?"

"All supplies you'll need will be provided by the settlements," he calmly replied. "Besides, that terrain is well suited for light infantry."

"When are we to leave?" he asked. "And my written orders?"

"Tonight after dark," he answered, "and all written orders will be issued once we've reached New York. Understand, use only what force is necessary. Your main objective is fields and supplies."

"What if they resist?" he asked as if knowing the answer. "And by defending ourselves, would such be covered under necessary force?"

"If such were to occur," Hockman said, attempting to hold back his temper, "use good judgment."

Captain Hughes along with his 300 slowly slipped out of the fort unobserved and quickly entered the vast forest. Guiding his men for over 20 miles, he stood on top of one of the many hills and simply waited.

"Sir, why are we stopping?" an elder man of 40 having captain bars on his collar asked. "If we're to be at the first settlement by tomorrow, we need to move."

"The Colonel thinks me a fool," said Hughes in an angry tone, "wanting us to attack a settlement where an American army is within a day's march. We'll attack alright, once that American army has moved to crush Hockman."

"Sir, I thought once we've destroyed the supplies," the elder's tone revealed confusion, "the American army would need time to resupply."

"Nonsense," he blurted out. "Hockman is using us as the bait to lure the Americans to attack us while he escapes."

"But if we fail to attack on time," he said as if thinking about the instructions given, "the entire American army will march against the Colonel."

"Yes, the poor Colonel will fight a superior force," Hughes said with a slight smile, "and in three days, we'll follow his order to destroy the three settlements."

"So we're waiting three days," asked the elder Captain, "then attacking?"

"Yes, Captain. We remain hidden for three days," he quickly answered,

"We've only enough food and water for two days," the elder Captain reminded him.

"Then tell them to miss a meal," he ordered. "The settlements will provide."

While Hughes carefully placed his men, the American army was alerted to the fact that the entire British garrison had marched out of the fort with wagons.

"Gentlemen, we've waited and trained for this moment," General Dodd addressed the officers. "All have been issued orders, so let us begin."

"Sir, if all goes well…" An older man wearing buckskin clothing stepped up to the General. "My boys will be waiting for you in five days."

"You've a long march through heavy forest, Tye," General Dodd said, taking his hand, "but knowing the quality of your men, you'll not disappoint me."

"Have my men in position for a perfect ambush," Tye said with a smile while looking over toward the 400 frontiersmen. "Now don't you be late, sir."

"Can't start a shooting war without a General," Dodd said, releasing his hand. "Don't worry, my troops will be there."

"Sir." Colonel Hiram Schroeder, a man in the late forties, rode up on his black stallion. "Ready to move out."

"You seem eager to leave your daughter and grandson," said Dodd, giving a slight chuckle. "Thought you'd want to stay behind."

"Been waiting a long time to rid this land of the British," he immediately replied. "Once they're gone, I'll have all the time in the world to be with them. Besides, left 30 good men behind, just in case."

"Those men will no doubt wish they had come with us," Dodd said with a smile, "but their families will be happy."

"Colonel, just give the order." His frail body barely covered the saddle.

"Have the men proceed, Sergeant Peters," he replied as he turned to the man.

In columns of 10, the American army marched out, all looking forward to face off with a British they despised. On the afternoon of the fourth day, General Dodd halted his troops, having marched within striking distance of the British.

"Let the men rest," he said, taking his spyglass out and looking toward the empty road ahead. "Tonight we'll march, and by morning, be prepared to attack."

"Our scouts have reported the British have made camp," a young Lieutenant said after leaping off his horse. "They're within four miles where Major Tye waits."

"Hockman can sense trouble," Dodd said, taking a deep breath. "We've done little to slow or stop him, so he knows something waits him."

"Sir, if we move by night," the Lieutenant assured him, "our cannons could be in place to attack once his army enters that open field."

"Send a runner to Major Tye," he began slowly. "I'll have instructions for him."

"Yes, sir," the Lieutenant said, saluting the man. "I know the perfect person who will carry it."

As the men rested, a young man riding an animal covered in white foam entered.

"Need to speak with General Dodd," he said out of breath, "please."

"Alright, what's this?" Dodd asked while walking through the crowd of men that gathered around the man. "Speak up."

"Sir, the Blue Coats are attacking the settlements," he blurted out, "ya need to help them cuzz they're killing everyone."

"Slow down and explain," Dodd said, grabbing the boy around the arms. "Take your time."

"Several hundred Blue Coats attacked the settlement, the boy, taking a breath, quickly began. "We spotted them in the woods and began putting the children and women in wagons. They came down so quickly, the men tried to slow them but had no chance. I drove one of the wagons with the children, When I got them far enough away, went back alone to see what I could do."

"What of the women?" several yelled out. "Did they leave?"

"Church was on fire when I got back." Tears began to flow. "Heard the screams but saw them shooting the men."

"Go on," Dodd ordered. "What happened next?"

"Found the town constable wounded," the boy said, composing himself while wiping his eyes. "We found horses. I was ordered to come here while he rode to warn the other settlements. He was bad off, can't say if he reached them."

"Sir, let me take 100 men back to the settlement," Hiram said as if demanding rather than asking. "I'll assemble men along the way and attack them."

"Impossible," Dodd said, shaking his head. "We attack a British army in the morning, and I'll need every man."

"But, sir, the people," Hiram began to plead.

"A massacre has occurred," he blurted out, "and we can do nothing about it."

"They were with the British all the time," men began shouting, "and ordered to attack the settlement."

"I'm ordering all of you to rest," Dodd shouted out. "We attack a British army in the morning, so prepare yourselves."

"Colonel Schroeder?" Sergeant Peters walked toward him. "You're not goin' to let them Blue Coats get away with this?"

"No," he was defiant, "and when we're finished with them, no one wearing a blue coat will be safe."

"Be making sure the men understand," he said, his thin lips exposed his blackened teeth.

The following morning, Major Tye watched from the trees as the first wagon entered the open field.

"Alright men wait for the rest of them," he whispered.

Suddenly, the driver whipped the animals to speed up, while several soldiers lifted the canvas.

"Open fire," Tye yelled out. "Drop the horses on that first wagon."

In seconds, the four animals lie dying, forcing the other two wagons to stop.

From both sides of the woods, the frontiersmen began firing into the wagons filled with supplies and soldiers. Colonel Hockman now ordered columns of soldiers on foot to join the fight, and within minutes, all began firing.

"Keep firing, men!" Willard shouted out as the men knelt down in front of the wagons. "Mark your target by the smoke."

"Captain Willard, have the men remove that wagon," Hockman ordered. "We must break out."

"Yes, sir," he said as the wagon he stood by exploded.

As the smoke cleared, Willard stood looking toward his missing arm and his red coat shredded by shrapnel. Trying to speak, he simply fell to the ground.

While the soldiers began lining the road to fire, a single horse on the second wagon was shot and killed. The three others attempted to pull away but could not.

A young soldier without regard to his own safety stood, and began cutting away the leather restraints. His body seemed to protect the three frightened animals, but his efforts were successful when the three fled in terror down the road.

The soldiers watched as the young man turned, and collapse. All knew it was a noble but foolish act; such a pity and waste of life.

Cannon fire began to rain down on their position, along with the accurate rifle fire from the woods. As explosions erupted, body parts flew high into the air while others simply fell dead on the ground while attempting to maintain a formation.

The third wagon was wet ablaze when struck by cannon fire. Several soldiers under it were consumed in flames causing further panic.

"Form square, men," Hockman shouted from his horse, "and move out of this field."

"Column one, fire!" Peters shouted while five columns of soldiers stood ready.

As one column fired into the forming British square, the next stepped up and fired. Then someone yelled, "No quarter, no quarter!" became the rallying call.

Stepping over the dead, the American soldiers, column by column, fired toward the now helpless British soldiers.

"Strike the colors," Hockman shouted as his men fell, but his words never heard as a single rifle ball entered his neck.

Seeing their leader fall, the soldiers began throwing down their rifles. But the American soldiers were in a blood rage and continued to fire. Without stopping the mayhem the British soldiers continued dying, even as they tried to surrender.

"God damn it!" General Dodd, riding up, began shouting. "Cease firing! And that's an order, and by God, you all best obey!"

Within seconds, the firing stopped, and each soldier began looking around as if in a trance and unaware of what had happened.

"Tend to the wounded," he shouted as his men stood waiting for orders, "and place those British soldiers under guard."

"Sir," said Tye out of breath from running across the field once the battle had ceased. "Sorry, we didn't hear the order to stop shooting but heard no quarter."

"No such order was ever given," he snapped, "but if I were to find out who gave it, he'll be charged."

"Sir," a young Lieutenant came running up and saluted, "17 prisoners and 31 British wounded. Believe many of those will not survive the night; injuries are far greater than our medical staff can manage."

"Understand," Dodd said, returning the salute. "Just do what you can for them."

"I've wounded and several dead," Tye spoke up. "Permission to tend to them."

"Yes, of course," Dodd said, taking a deep breath while looking toward the many bodies of both American and British. "When finished, meet with me."

"Yes sir," Tye said, saluting him while walking away.

"Sir." Hiram walked up after watching Tye leave and saluted. "Request permission to return to the settlements."

"Colonel, you've wounded and dead," General Dodd said, his voice showing anger. "I'd suggest you care for them first before requesting to leave."

"Yes, sir, but my daughter and grandson," he said, repeating his concern. "I must know."

"Tend to your wounded," he demanded, "then meet with me at my tent."

After several hours Tye and Hiram stood outside the large tent, waiting for permission to enter.

"Gentlemen," an older Major began while opening the flaps, "you may enter now."

"General." Tye was the first to speak up. "All the wounded are being treated."

"Having defeated the British forces," he began, "we now must consider the force which attacked the settlements. We've two options, one to return to the settlement knowing we've no chance to seek them out. The other is to continue on this road, and with luck reach New York before they arrive."

"Sir, we don't know the situation at the settlements," Hiram spoke up for the first time. "Let me and 100 men go."

"They could be needed," Tye seemed to agree, "for all we know, they still could be in the area. Then allow me to take my men toward New York, using the road. We'll take only what supplies needed, and force march."

"Very good," he agreed. "Once we've cared for the wounded I'll march the army to New York."

Leaving the tent, Tye stood for a moment while looking over at the burnt wagons.

"Tye, you've something to say?" Dodd came out as if to breathe the fresh air.

"During the battle, I watched as a young British soldier saved three horses," he began. "No concern for himself but for those horses."

"One brave soldier trying to save defenseless animals…" Dodd looked toward the field of battle. "While another murdered innocent women and children."

"You believe Hockman ordered it?" Tye asked.

"No," he admitted.

"Nite, sir," he said walking away.

CHAPTER TWO

Hiram and his 100, after a five day march, entered the settlement, finding all buildings and cabins burnt to the ground. Riding toward the church that was totally destroyed, Hiram noticed several older men and women standing in the cemetery.

"Ya come too late," one of the men said while walking toward him. "Damn ya all for leaving them."

"We battled the British," Hiam said, dismounting, "having no idea of the Blue Coats."

"Makes no difference to them that died," he continued.

"Excuse Brother Sid." An elderly man approached. "He was one of the first to arrive and see what terrible things done here."

"My daughter and grandson," Hiram said, looking as the people began to surround him.

"How old was your grandson?" an elderly woman stepped out to ask.

"Less than a year," he quickly replied, "daughter 20."

"Found her with child in the church," her voice began to quiver, "along with 27 others. We buried them together. She clung to the child."

"Them bastards boarded them in," the man blurted out, "then set the church on fire."

"Let me show you where they lay," the elder, in a calm tone, said while touching Hiram's shoulder. "Placed them together in a proper box and said words."

Standing over the mound of ground, having a wooden cross, Hiram was unable to shed tears, for rage consumed his soul.

"Colonel," Peters said walking over to him. "Real sorry about ya losing them, but might need to speak with the elder."

"They were my life Peters," Hiram said, taking a deep breath. "My reason for living, and now, all I feel is hate. I'll not stop until every Blue Coat is under the ground, no matter how long."

"Which is why ya need to speak to the elder," he continued.

Walking away, he noticed the elder waiting outside the small broken gate.

"Your Sergeant said you came to find the men who did this," he began. "They were here for three days, looting and burning before moving on. The constable was able to warn the other settlements and had the word passed about this to the local farmers."

"We all came with our children," an older woman walked over to explain, "and all the young men with rifles left to find them."

"The old ones stayed behind to bury the dead," the elder spoke up, "they didn't want to slow the young ones up."

"My two boys knows them woods good," another man said as he walked up. "They're fast of foot and will find them."

"We've no word of the other settlements," the elder continued, "but maybe they had enough time to get the women and children out."

"Peters, have the men ready to march," Hiram ordered. "How far is it to the next settlement, and can we use this road?"

"Twenty-six miles," the elder replied, "and the road will lead you there."

Force marching the men to the next settlement, they found the remains of 16 men stripped lying by a wooden barricade. Entering the empty town where every structure was burnt down, they found another 12 men hanging from trees.

"These men were left here to slow them up after they evacuated the town," Hiram spoke up, "and no doubt made a fight of it."

"Elder said they never found any Blue Coats," Peters said while looking toward the tree line. "Must be taking them and burying them later."

"Peters," Hiram shouted. "Have the men check the burnt out cabins for bodies."

Within an hour, they found over 40 stripped bodies, all in different cabins as if they belonged there.

"Burn them," Hiram said, "so no one knows how many have been killed."

"Let others bury them thinking they was good people," Peters added.

"Leave a note," Hiram ordered, "tell whoever discovers these bodies that they were Blue Coats."

"What about the men hanging?" Peters asked while looking toward them.

"Leave them," he said, turning his horse toward the road. "We'll find others to come back to bury them."

"You heard the Colonel," Peters yelled out as the sun began to set, be marching all night so start moving.

Before the sun began to rise, the 100 arrived at the third settlement.

"Sir, everyone's gone," Peters reported after having rode into the settlement with three others. "No bodies and just a couple buildings burned."

"Colonel, they left toward the hills," one of the men began, pointing toward the forest, "in a big hurry."

"Have the men find somewhere to sleep," Hiram ordered. "I want them ready to leave before nightfall."

"Checked most of the buildings," said another soldier as he walked up to him. "Everything is gone. Must have had time to pack up, left nothing for them."

"Sir," Peters said, walking up to him as he unsaddled his horse, "know them Blue Coats are long gone, and we ain't fast enough to catch up."

"Regardless," Hiram said, turning toward him while dropping the saddle to the ground. "We need to try, and remember others are slowing them down."

"Then we'll do what we can," he said while turning. "Be ready to move when ordered to."

Tye and his frontiersman, using the road, arrived at a makeshift camp of volunteers, some 30 miles from New York.

"Names?" said Colonel Tye, walking up to a sentry that looked no older than 16. "Under orders from General Dodd."

"Be wantin' to speak with our commander," he said looking toward the other three men who stood watch, "was shot and is staying in the medicine tent."

"My men are tired, so have someone show them where they can rest," he ordered.

The young man, without speaking, signaled for the three to help while he escorted Tye to the medicine tent.

"Colonel Tye, is it?" asked a young man lying on a wooden cot with bandages covering his chest. "Can't say I've heard of ya but glad having your men here. And name's Hamptin."

"You've quite a camp," Tye said while stepping beside the cot. "Where have all these men come from?"

"Farmers mostly," he replied while trying to sit up. "Came in from all over when hearing about the massacre."

"Good to see so many," he admitted while the young man found a small stool and placed it beside the cot, "but why aren't they out looking for the Blue Coats?"

"Six days ago, 30 of us found them." His breath was labored. "Set up a series of ambushes. Had them fire one round, then move on to the next spot. Working good, until they moved around us and got myself shot."

"So they're gone?" he asked.

"Not hardly," Hamptin said with a slight smile. "I started with 30."

"I don't understand," he admitted while sitting down on the stool.

"Farmers from all over started showing up," he continued, "any man that could carry a rifle. Last count, over 100 men up in those hills, searching and killing. Most know every inch of those hills, and making them pay for what they did."

"Who's in charge?" he wondered.

"Can't say," he blurted out, "but they're up there doing what needs to be done."

"Then how on earth do you know what's happening?" Tye was shocked by the man's apparent lack of concern. "For all you know, the Blue Coats have slipped by and are now in New York."

"Three days ago, a runner came here," he replied, taking a deep breath, "said they were leaving their wounded behind. Seems they're running low on powder, and just running."

"So how many wounded have they brought down?" he asked.

"None," he said leaning toward Tye. "Haven't had any come down."

"Why not?" he inquired. "Need to know what they're up to."

"Set my own runner up there," he said laying back down, "told them to bring the wounded here."

"And…?" said Tye, knowing there was more to the story.

"Runner came back with a bag," he continued, "having five heads."

"You need to send runners up there," Tye said, as if demanding him to do so, "and tell them to bring the wounded back alive."

"First off, can't say where any of them are." Hamptin was using all the strength he had. "And won't do that."

"Why not?" Tye demanded an answer.

"Cause I ain't about to find the head of my runner inside one of them bags," he said shaking his head. "Those farmers know only one way to end all this. They believe in the feud, and having killed them families, they all swore retribution. Now, I ain't stopping you from going up there to negotiate, but they won't listen. They just might make you and yours part of the feud, get people killed."

"Then what would you recommend I do?" he asked with interest.

"Let them folks be." He added, "Then find General Washington and join 'im."

Hunted for weeks, Hughes and 26 others finally entered the fortress of New York.

"Send the man in," Colonel Francis Watts ordered as if disgusted having to meet with the man.

"Captain Hughes of British American forces," he said, standing at attention while addressing the man, "reporting."

"I am quite aware of you, Captain," Watts said, standing 6'3" with graying hair, "and have read your account but wonder what you omitted."

"Don't understand, sir," Hughes said, unaware of what he referred to.

"Attacking American settlement without written orders," he began, "and rumors of women and children murdered."

"All lies, sir," Hughes said, defending himself. "It was rumor only, started by the Americans that wish to divide us. Concerning orders, Colonel Hockman assured me they would be here once I arrived."

"Colonel Hockman ordered you to attack the settlements," Watts said, testing his explanation, "and why would he do so?"

"The settlements were supplying the American troops," he calmly answered. "Once we cut that support, they would be unable to move."

"I'll discuss your report with General Cornwallis," he said, stepping away. "You're free to go, but I'll have further questions."

"Well you spoke with him," General Cornwallis, dressed in his best uniform a,sked while sitting behind his desk. "And your opinion?"

"He's a liar and should be shot," he began. "Twenty-six men and having only two wounded. Denies all reports of the murders, and furthermore claims Colonel Hockman ordered him to attack the settlements."

"Five weeks ago," Cornwallis said, standing up and walking over toward the window, "with reinforcements, I could have broken out of this elaborate birdcage."

Watts waited for his general to begin by saying nothing.

"That man," his words burst out, "has lost the war for me. Colonel Hockman's entire command wiped out, and now Washington's army swells with men wanting revenge. Now he comes forward to impugn the good name of a British officer, believing we're fools and easily convinced."

"His presence does concern me," Watts added.

"Once that French fleet arrives," he turned toward the man, "and the Americans learn his cohorts are here, they'll be no stopping them."

"Many British soldiers will be killed," the Colonel spoke out loud, "and any dialogs would be impossible."

"Had I the authority to court-martial each one of them…" Cornwallis said walking back and sitting down behind the desk, "but they're protected by the King's rule."

"Even with such a display, it would not prevent the American army from attacking," Watts said finally, sitting down and facing the man. "I believe a more severe action is required."

"Colonel, would you care to explain what severe action is necessary?" Cornwallis said, leaning toward him. "I'm listening."

"Sir," Watts said in a calm but controlled tone, "I believe as Commanding Officer with overwhelming responsibilities such matters be left to me."

"Colonel Watts, I cannot allow you to jeopardize your outstanding military career," Cornwallis said, looking him straight in the eyes, "when dealing with these mad dogs alone."

"I've fought many a battle with you, sir," he said, standing up. "This I do for the good of the service and will not allow such men to tarnish my general's reputation."

"Yes we have fought many battles," Cornwallis said with a smile. "Do what you think is best, but understand I will never abandoned you."

"Always have known that, sir," Watts said, saluting him. "A few minor details to work out, but rest assured, this matter will be handled discreetly."

Two days later, Captain Hughes sat across Watts, who seemed preoccupied at the time sitting behind his desk.

"Captain, your arrival here has come at a most inopportune time," Watts said, sitting up straight and giving him undivided attention. "Though unverified rumors persist, the American army believes them to be true. If reports of the French fleet are true, and they arrive this garrison will fall."

"What does any of that have to do with us?" Hughes asked, as if unconcerned.

"If the American commanders negotiate a surrender," he continued, "they would most certainly demand that you and your men be subject to their military justice."

"We are loyal British soldiers," Hughes said, quickly standing, "protected by the King."

"Which is why," Watts said in a calm tone to placate his anger. "We've decided to remove your men from this garrison."

"How is that even possible with the American army so close?" he asked while sitting back down.

"We still hold three miles of beach," he began, "and with the assistance of an Italian captain commanding a fast schooner can be done."

"Can he be trusted?" Hughes asked with interest.

"The man takes no sides in this war," he assured him, "and has taken several of our wounded officers for a price to Canada. He speaks little English, so any of your men…"

"None of us speaks Italian," Hughes said, quickly admitting his shortfall.

"Then I will write instructions for him to follow," Watts said, opening a drawer, "and provide the necessary funds to ensure they are followed."

"When do we leave?" he asked while standing up.

"Tonight, 1:00 in the morning," he said taking a parchment out. "He'll meet you alone on the beach where you'll give him the funds and instructions. Understand: no weapons, he allows only his crew to carry."

"Makes good sense," Hughes agreed. "These days it's best to trust no one."

"Besides, his vessel is small," Watts explained, "few crewmembers but enough room for your men. Understand this, once in Canada, your men are to be discharged and no longer British soldiers."

"Understood," he blurted out, "we'll go our own way once we've reached Canada."

"Alright," Watts stood up, "prepare your men for their journey."

As requested, Hughes and his men carefully left the fortress, using a small sally port door as clouds began to cover the bright moon.

"Follow the cove," Watts said as they began filling out, "to the beach where your meet with the Italian captain."

"You're not coming?" Hughes asked as if surprised.

"I've more important matters to contend wit. Besides, you've the instructions and coin, just give them to the captain."

Once beyond he door, Hughes led his men out of the small cove toward the open beach.

Watts walked through the tunnel that led to the main parade ground and quickly found the duty officer.

"Lieutenant," he said walking into the small office where the young officer sat, "I've been informed several American British troops have deserted and are now attempting to escape by sea."

"Yes, sir," the young officer stood up as if confused by what to do. "Ah."

"Lieutenant, assemble 40 armed men," he demanded, "and march them to the sally port."

"Understood," the young officer said, saluting him, "and then…?"

"Just assemble the men," he said, shaking his head, "I'll take charge."

"You not British," the Italian captain said in broken English while pointing his pistol, "I go."

"Hold on," Hughes said running toward the man that stood only six feet but having a large belly, "got this."

Seeing the large coin bag, the man turned away from the edge of the water.

"Told to give you these," Hughes said, looking toward the small boat waiting with four oarsmen, "and have you read the instructions?"

Cautiously, he placed the pistol under his large black belt and quickly took the coin bag then the parchment.

"You read?" he asked after having studied the words.

"Yes," as if ashamed knowing he knew nothing about the instructions, "you're to take me and my men to Canada after having been paid. Do you have enough boats to carry all the men?"

"Si," the Italian captain said with a smile as he placed the bag of coin in his large pocket and rolled up the parchment, "I read."

"You need to hurry," Hughes said, trying to rush the man along, "maybe I go with you."

"Me go," he said, pointing to the craft while trying to communicate the best he could. "Stay, I tell crew."

"Alright," Hughes yelled out while the man entered the craft. "Hurry because we can't stand out here in the open for very long."

"Captain, what's happening?" One of the men walked up as the small craft moved away. "Are they coming back?"

"Yes," he said walking toward the group of men, "and in a few days, men, we'll be drinking ale in some Canadian town."

"Never been there," several blurted out, "they say it's real cold."

"Which is why you find a good woman," Hughes replied as if keeping their minds off the situation, "along with heavy fur blankets."

"Sir, the tide is going out," one of the men shouted, "and that ship is setting sails."

Suddenly, two massive explosions from American cannons came close, making it clear they were seen.

"We've been betrayed, men!" Hughes shouted as two more explosion erupted much closer, back to the cove.

Running for their lives, as three more explosions spread sand and water in the air, but none of his men struck. Entering the small cove that led to the sally port, they found several British soldiers on top of the rocks waiting.

"Colonel Watts," Hughes began shouting as he ran toward the sally port door, "Please open up."

"Desertion in the face of an enemy," Watts began, "is punishable by firing squad."

"But," he screamed out as the door opened and five riflemen opened fire.

Three of the five rounds struck his chest, killing him immediately.

From the cliffs, the soldiers opened fire on the entire group, which had now crowded around the door.

They could do nothing; each fallen body made it impossible to move. Within minutes, all 27 men lay dead or dying.

"Sergeant," Watts, from inside the sally port, yelled out, "pull these bodies away from this door and place them in the cove."

"Yes, sir," the Sergeant said, standing at attention.

"They're traitors and deserters," he continued. "Let the morning tide have them."

"Understood." He was about to turn.

"However," Watts continued, "bayonet each man to ensure he's dead."

"Throats will be cut, sir," the Sergeant said with a slight smile. "Never have liked them."

By midafternoon, the cove was cleared of bodies, washed away by the sea. Three days later, the entire French fleet had arrived, joining the American forces.

Sir, several American officers watching the bombardment of the British fortress, I've a strange message from an Italian captain.

"Take it to General Washington's headquarters," one of the men replied. "I'll be along shortly."

Colonel Tye, standing alongside of others, could not believe he stood looking at the man that had defeated the British.

"What are you doing, Brad?" Tye asked in a whisper while looking down at the sketch of General Washington he had drawn. "You know the General doesn't like posing for artists."

"This is a historic moment," he whispered back, "besides I'm doing it by memory."

"Well don't let him see you doing it," he ordered. "Just what do you plan doing with all those drawings you've done over the years?"

"Maybe publish them," he continued to whisper, "show my children and others what this war was really like. Besides we need some record of what we did, and why for future generations."

"Well, can't say it's a bad idea," Tye said with a smile, "but I just wonder what the future will say of us even if you were to get that published."

Within weeks, the fortress of New York fell to the American army, and the people began to realize the war was coming to an end.

"Well, General Dodd, now that we've New York," Tye asked, "while were celebrating the victory, what shall we do now?"

"British army may have surrender here," he explained, "but the war goes on. Now what we need to do is bring all scattered forces here."

"Should be easy," he calmly replied, "just send out runners with orders that New York has fallen and all men are needed here."

"Colonel Schroeder and his forces are reported on the border, rolling out a map of the area, take several men and find him. I'll provide orders, but want him back here."

"As you wish," Tye said, saluting him, "shouldn't be any problem."

While Colonel Tye and several officers searched to find Schroeder, his force were busy stopping wagon trains attempting to cross over to Canada.

"Sir," Peters yelled out while looking toward 15 wagons, "another bunch heading toward Canada."

"Alright men," Hiram yelled out from the hillside, "you know your duty, so let's make sure not one Blue Coat escapes."

His entire force came charging down toward the slow moving wagons, having mostly women and children.

"Sir." An elderly man walked out as Hiram's forces surrounded the entire group. "May I ask why such a show of force toward peaceful people. We've no weapons and wish only to go our own way."

"Count 12 men," one of his men shouted out, "16 women and six children."

"Peaceful," Hiram yelled out to his men, making it more of a joke. "Heard that from just about every loyalist trying to escape to Canada."

"We're just poor families tired of war," the elder began, "and wish only to escape this madness."

"Sergeant Peters," he yelled out, "begin your search of the wagons, and round up the men, so they won't give us any trouble."

They placed the men in a circle while the rest began searching the wagons.

"For poor families," Peters yelled out as he threw a piano onto the ground, smashing it, "got mighty nice things."

"You've no right destroying our things," said a heavy set lady who came running out to examine what remained of the piano.

"Shut your mouth, lady!" One of the men rode up to her and pointed his rifle. "We got every right, so step away."

"Well lookie here," Peters said while throwing a large open chest out of the wagon that emptied on the ground. "Got a Blue Coat."

"My dead husband," the woman blurted out, "killed six years ago."

"Sir, found three more Blue Coats," another soldier said as he rode up and threw the coats on the ground, "two shotguns and a British pistol."

"We need the shotguns for hunting," the elder quickly explained, "but you must believe we're not loyalists."

"Oh, I believe you," Hiram shouted out, "with the British army surrendering everywhere that you're no longer loyalist."

"So what shall we do with these turncoats men?" Peters shouted out.

"Kill them!" they began shouting. "And burn the wagons!"

Out of fear, or foolishness, one of the men began running from the circle. It was all his men needed once the man was rode down and killed, they began slaughtering all the other men within the circle.

"Burn the wagons!" someone yelled out as the women began crying and holding the few children in their arms. "Let 'em walk to Canada!"

As teams of horses fled, they watched the wagons burn.

"You tell others what will happen if they try sneaking away," Hiram said, turning his horse around, "and that they'll never be safe no matter where they go."

Without further words, his men followed Colonel Schroeder, knowing they would wait for the next wagon train trying to escape. After four long weeks of searching, Colonel Tye and his men rode up the spot where they found the remains of 12 men and 15 burnt wagons.

"Any idea, Colonel?" Brad asked as he rode up and pulled out his sketching pad. "Not Indians but maybe highwaymen."

"Captain Clark," Tye said being formal and tolerant with the man, "know any highwaymen to kill all the men and burn wagons?"

"God, I hope it's not what I think," Brad said, quickly drawing the scene. "For if it is, how can this be justified?"

"It can't be, Brad," Tye said, taking a deep breath, "never."

Within three days, Colonel Tye and his men discovered Colonel Schroeder residing in a small town where the people were afraid to deny him anything. Entering the town, the people stood silent as if afraid to welcome them.

"Was wondering when someone would show," Hiram said walking out of the hotel wearing his uniform. "Been keeping the border safe."

"On whose authority have you taken to take over this town?" Tye asked while dismounting. "And what arrangements have you promised?"

"My authority," he replied, as if it were enough, "and the people have been gracious enough to give us what we ask. I was about to dine, would you care to join me?"

"You've been ordered to return to New York," Tye said, ignoring his invitation, "and join with General Washington."

"Is that so?" Hiram said, almost defiant. "And who's going to protect the border against British loyalists trying to escape to Canada?"

"Not my concern or yours," Tye said, walking up to him and standing in front of the man. He handed him the written order. "Obey, or be considered a deserter."

"Sergeant Peters!" he shouted. "Assemble the men for it appears we're needed elsewhere by order of General Dodd."

"Peters." Tye stepped aside and looked carefully at the man. "Have we've ever met like before the war in Carolina?"

"Can't says ever knowing ya." His expression changed and the blood seemed to leave his face. "And never been to Carolina."

"Now that's been cleared up," Hiram snapped while placing the order in his coat pocket. "Can we move on?"

"Passed a burnt wagon train three days back," Tye continued to confront the man. "Your handiwork?"

"Loyalists trying to cross the border," he added, "found Blue Coats and British weapons in the wagons."

"They resisted," he asked.

"Of course," Hiram replied while turning around and entering the hotel. "Now about dining with me."

"My men and I will help assemble your troops," he answered. "I think it best we leave within the hour."

"Colonel, he's lying about those people resisting," Brad whispered while watching him mount. "None of them were armed and grouped together."

"I know," Tye replied, sitting straight on the saddle. "By the way, Brad, did you get a good look at that Sergeant Peters?"

"Yeah," he replied, "a nasty looking man."

"Draw him for me," he asked. "And keep it to yourself."

"Sure," Brad said with a smile. "Any reason why?"

"Tell you later, Captain," Tye said, tuning his horse around.

As they left the town, it appeared most, if not all, were happy having them leave and hoping they would never return.

CHAPTER THREE

The war would last for another two years, when the British government seceded and signed the Paris Acord, giving the American people freedom.

"Well, Tye, now that the war is finally over," General Dodd said, sitting behind a large desk in a room that could fit 20 men. "What are your plans?"

"Going back to Carolina," Tye said, sitting in one of the many comfortable chairs. "I was a constable and farmer, so think I'll take it up again."

"Then marry a beautiful woman, of course," said Dodd with a chuckle. "And have many children that will listen to your many adventures."

"Seems the thing to do." He added, "What about you?'

"Resigning my commission," he began. "Been asked to come to Washington and help with rebuilding the country. Could use a man like yourself there. Nation is broke and needs good men willing to help."

"Not for me," Tye said with a smile. "But thanks for the offer."

"Have asked your Captain Clark to come along?" he added. "Need men like him to document what we've done and will do."

"He'll fit right in!" He laughed at the very thought of the man doing such a job. "Sees everything as a historic event. But if you ever need me, know where I'll be."

"Hope I'll never call on you," he said standing up and reaching out his hand. "But it's good knowing I can."

"Heard Colonel Schroeder resigned weeks ago and left," Tye said remembering the wagon train. "Was told he was asked."

"Hiram changed," he said, taking a deep breath. "Hatred has taken him, and he's unfit to have a command. He poisoned his men against our government, believing we allowed loyalists to leave the country without punishment."

"Saw what he's capable of," Tye said, without explaining further, "and his sergeant is no better and might need watching."

"Captain Clark said you wanted a drawing of the man," he replied. "Any reason?"

"Just a feeling we've met," Tye responded, surprised Dodd even knew about the drawing, "and when I get back might show it around to anyone who might remember him."

"Good luck, my friend," Dodd said with a smile, "and I will keep you in mind."

While Tye had returned to Carolina and began his new career as constable along with farming, other events were taking place. Schroeder and Peters were busy inspecting gold buttons in Boston, Massachusetts, no longer confined to military rules or regulations.

"Well, gentlemen, do my buttons meet with your approval?" an elderly man wearing thick wire-frame glasses asked. "The Pettrie button company is proud knowing you've chosen our factory to manufacture such fine quality merchandise."

"Perfect." Hiram picked up one of the buttons and allowed it to shine by the sun. "Could blind a man if he looked closely enough."

"However," questioned the man, "the initials HS is highly unusual for military use."

"Local militia," Hiram answered, "supported and trained by me."

"God bless you, sir," the man said, taking his hand. "A true patriot for America."

"Yes," Hiram said taking out several gold coins. "One-day people will say Colonel Hiram Schroeder is a true patriot and hero."

"My family and company will be proud knowing we helped," the man said while taking the coins from the table.

"Well, what now, sir?" Peters asked as they left the company.

"Twenty of our officers are waiting," he said while they entered a carriage, "to be fitted with green uniforms having gold buttons. Each one will bring back 20 volunteers, and when ready, march to Kingstown settlement."

"Will the weapons be ready by then, sir?" Peters asked.

"Spent a fortune to arrange everything," he replied. "Plenty of everything, including cannons, just in case."

"Having each group enter Canada at different locations and time," Peters praised him. "Brilliant idea. So no one takes notice."

"Two hundred British loyalists just 140 miles from our border." His expression changed. "Thinking they're safe being in Canada."

"Kill them all," Peters blurted out. "Be heroes when people find out what we did."

"Destroy the entire settlement," Hiram replied angrily, "just as they did ours."

"Cross the Niagara," Peters began rubbing his head as if the pain returned, "then follow the river to the settlement."

While their plans moved forward, others began noticing, and they, too, decided on a course of action.

"General Dodd, I said I'd help when needed," Tye said sitting in an overstuffed chair in a room filled with books and other treasures, "but your letter said for me to get here fast, even knowing the war's been over for almost six months."

"No longer general, Tye, sitting behind the desk, here in Virginia I'm just another man working with others trying to make something of this country."

"Heard you've gathered people to document the history of the country," Tye said with a smile, as if letting him know he, too, is well informed, "along with giving my opinion on how we should proceed when forming a new government. However, you didn't ask me to come here for that, so tell me the bad first."

"Newton Young, a man whom I've relied on during the war wrote me," he said reaching into his desk, "has been following some 29 men heading to Canada."

"For what purpose?" Tye understood the danger.

"Not sure," he admitted, "but the name Hiram Schroeder has come up."

"I know he's rich enough to pay for an army," Tye began, "and angry enough having been relieved of his command that he could consider a revolt."

"Newton only said the men were well paid," he quickly informed Tye, "but has no other information as to why."

"Think Schroeder wants to start another war?" Tye asked. "Only this time in Canada?"

"No idea," he continued, but whatever he intends will not be good for us. As you know, the French settlers want to divide Canada, but with France having financial trouble, they may be looking for outside help."

"So what can I do for you?" he asked, knowing the general had a plan.

"Tye, you were asking about Schroeder's sergeant," Dodd began, "about some murder that happened before the war."

"Man went by Peter Jameson," he said, removing a poster of his likeness. "Wanted for questioning only. Problem is that Carolina was hit hard by the war. People killed or scattered, which made identification hard. Most couldn't remember, while others thought it might be."

"Tye, I would like you to travel to Canada, "he said, looking over the poster, "get with the Canadian Rifles rather than the British army and ask them to help you locate this man. You'll find they may be willing, and it is a within their authority as constables."

"Sir, this poster is for questioning," he pointed out, "and I've no authority there."

"I'll give you proper paperwork, including extra posters." He added, "And tell them everything we know about the man, and include Schroeder."

"If they're wanting to train and arm the settlers," Tye replied, "it would be something the authorities would want to know. I'll show the poster, hope to find out more."

"Use that poster when necessary," Dodd pointed out. "People talk."

"So, when do I leave?" he asked.

"I'll have all the paperwork within an hour," Dodd stood up, "and have you on a fast ship this afternoon."

Two days later, Tye found himself waiting for word from the Colonel, having given all the paperwork to the man. Then he spoke to the man and others for over two hours.

"Constable Tye," said a middle-aged captain who walked toward him, "Colonel of the Royal Rifles will speak with you now concerning yesterday's meeting."

"Mr. Tye." The Colonel, an older man having a large red mustache, sat behind a desk that showed age and use. "After lengthy discussion, we decided to use diplomatic approach rather than threat of force."

"Sir," he said, standing in front of the man, "with all due respect, these men are extremely dangerous."

"We understand completely," he continued. "Captain Zachery Pendle will assist you to locate the two if they are in fact here."

"Constable Tye." He stood over six feet, having broad shoulders and thick blond hair. "Tomorrow I am to meet with the French delegation. They've been appointed to represent the French settlers and will register complaints with me."

"What has that to do with locating Peters and Schroeder?" he asked.

"Everything." His bright blue eyes seemed to sparkle while he spoke. "Because I intend asking them about the two."

"Of course they would never lie to a Captain from the Mounted Canadian Rifles," Tye said in sarcastic tone.

"Certainly they would," Zachery said with a wide smile, showing his white teeth, "but not now."

"Constable Tye," the Colonel spoke up. "The French don't want to start a revolt knowing there are over 7,000 British soldiers here."

"Most are waiting to return to England," Zachery informed him, "having fought in your insurrection."

A slight chuckle came from the Colonel, who seemed amused by the comment.

"Constable Tye," the Colonel seemed interested in his effort to arrest Peters. "What proof have you that this man is responsible for these two murders?"

"The commanding officer, to avoid any suspicion of a cover up," he began to explain, "authorized a board of inquiry to investigate. The young man by the name of Howard Deanery was left handed, yet the wound was on the right side of the skull. His scabbard was still on his horse, tied outside. The young lady had packed, as if preparing to leave. The husband, Peter Jameson, vanished without a trace. I testified during that inquest, and too many unanswered questions were brought up. The entire inquest was properly documented for everyone to read, then ruled suspicious in nature. However, case would remain open, for further inquiries."

"If an inquest was conducted," Captain Pendle pointed out, "all documents would have been sent to England."

"Yes," the Colonel concurred, "understand, Constable, if these men are not located, Captain Pendle will escort you to the border."

"Understood." Tye knew he could not argue.

"Be leaving first thing in the morning," Zachery replied, "which is 5:00 AM."

"Five it is," Tye said, looking into his broad face that showed small scars for having to enforce his will on others.

Having been given shelter at the general store, he slept well but woke before Zachery entered alert and ready to go.

"I've taken the liberty of having your animal saddled," he said, walking into the room without being asked, "a fine looking mount if I may say."

"Noticed all your men on fine looking mounts," he replied rolling up his blanket. "Guess that's something we have in common."

"Yes," he said with a slight smile. "Men such as us must rely on such animals."

"Life or death," Tye said walking toward him, "in our line of work."

Leaving the small settlement, he noticed a great deal of activity with men on duty and others preparing food.

"You people ever sleep?" he asked.

"When necessary," he chuckled. "We are few, less than 150, but protect our country."

"So these Frenchmen you're meeting..." As they rode, Tye decided to make conversation to pass the time. Just what do they want and how can you stop them from just taking it?"

"All of us have sworn a duty to enforce the law, Mr. Tye," he began, "and we take that oath serious even if it means our death."

"Was just curious how so few intend stopping so many," he pointed out, "with so few in such a large country."

"Yes, Canada is very large, with pride, but we are all Canadians who wish only to obey the law. Contrary to your belief, the majority of people support us."

"Then why are you meeting with these Frenchmen," he again asked, "if so many support you?"

"Understand these men represent a small but very vocal group," he began explaining, "that can and at times create distrust. Therefore we must consider what it is they're telling the people, and attempt to resolve those issues."

"What are their issues?" he asked, now wanting to know.

"First they wish to divide our country," he began, "one ruled by England and the other a free French territory. Of course, it is unacceptable. Canada must always be one country, ruled by England."

"I'm sure there's more," Tye said, understanding the complexity he faced.

"They wish to avoid paying British taxes," once again he began, "along with free land. French demand total control over all resources and trade, excluding any British involvement. Such a demand is unthinkable, allowing vast territories yet to be discovered without British assistance."

"Especially if gold or silver were to be found, knowing the cost."

"Mr. Tye, giving up the vast forest would be unforgivable," he said shaking his head, "but mostly it is their insistence that only French law would oversee them."

"No British tax or law," Tye said with a slight smile, "you know that sounds mighty familiar."

"You Americans, believing that taxes will not be imposed," he began to chuckle, "and laws many learned from England will be applied. You're a small country, and will learn by your many mistakes. Remember the sun never sets on British soil, and one day, your fellow citizens will come to appreciate England."

"Enemies today," he said in a low voice, "friends tomorrow."

"Yes," Zachery replied when hearing his words, "and America will be thankful."

"By the way," Tye began, curious about where they were going. "This place where the meeting will be, what's so special about it?"

"It's 30 miles from a British settlement," he began to explain, "the only one within 100 miles. Thirty miles south to the Niagara belongs to the Seneca tribe, no white settlers allowed. Forty miles west, are the French settlements. The meeting place is neutral land, belonging to no one."

"So this British settlement is your first line of defense," Tye said, understanding the importance of the settlement, "French would have to take it first."

"Yes, they are British subjects," Zachery noted the fact, "and yes, if an attack would come they would be first."

"The Senecas…" Tye wondered about the tribe, "They friendly?"

"Their numbers are fewer since the war," he continued, "but quite friendly."

"They fought with the British?" he asked.

"Yes," he continued to answer all Tye's questions. "Unfortunately few returned."

"Many Americans never returned home either," he added.

"In all wars," Zachery said, looking beyond the trail, "such things happen."

"Is that why you volunteered to meet with the French delegation?" he asked, trying to judge the man. "To avoid a war and killings?"

"I belong to the Canadian Mounted Rifles," he explained, "entrusted to enforce all laws. I care only about protecting the people, which include the French."

"Even those that don't want your protection?" he asked.

"Don't judge all French settlers," Zachery said, taking a deep breath, "most only wish to raise a family without fear from those who wish to take what is not theirs. The few that demand so much, fail to understand what most want."

"Peace," he quickly replied, "and be left alone."

"Precisely," he said with a smile, "and I'm here to see that it be so."

"Well, let's hope the delegation will see it your way," he said smiling as he spoke, "and make reasonable demands."

For two days they traveled over hills and open country, barren of cabins.

"Well, they're here already," he said, looking over toward several tents, "and in time for a meal, I believe."

"Smells good," Tye added, "whatever it is they're cooking."

"No doubt they brought servants," he said, guiding his horse toward the campsite, "and enough food and wine to enjoy."

Entering, Tye was surprised how well they were equipped: large tents with barrels of wine and hanging assorted meats.

"Thought you said only five men were coming," he said as several men came out of the tents to escort them, "must be 50 or 60 people here."

"Probably brought beds with them," Zachery chuckled as a young man wearing a servant's uniform came forth.

"Sire," he said, standing in front of the animals that were held by two others. "We welcome you, and if you wish, I'll show you to your tent. Your animals will be tended to, and whatever your needs, just ask."

"We'd like to freshen up first." Zachery dismounted while speaking. "And if possible meet with the delegation."

"Monsieur Basile has invited you gentlemen to dine with him," they were told in a calm and polite tone, "and the others at six."

"Please inform Monsieur Basile we'd be honored," Zachery said, giving the servant a quick head bow, "and that Mr. Tye from America will be joining me."

Having cleaned up as best they could, the two were escorted to the large tent where five men all wearing respectable suits sat.

"Gentlemen may I introduce you to Constable Tye," Zachery in a very formal tone, began addressing the men, "from American."

"Monsieur Geraud and Hultot," Basile began introducing the men, "Mathis, and last Benoit. We represent the will of the French people, all who have settled here."

"Gentlemen, pleasure is mine," Tye said while waiting for the men to sit first.

"Captain Pendle," Basile began first while sitting, "before discussing any matters, let us have a toast and dine."

"Viva La France!" was shouted around the table as they all drank.

Once toasted, all allowed the servants to serve the many dishes of food along with fine wines.

"Mr. Tye." Benoit looked toward him. "Your opinion of our table?"

"Food along with the wine," Tye said, picking up the glass and sipping it, "exceptional."

"You are an American sheriff," he continued to question him, "of some importance."

"To the people I serve," he said, placing the glass down, "yes."

"You have come to Canada," the man continued to probe his intent, "to arrest someone you believe murdered his wife?"

"Along with a British soldier," he added.

Captain Pendle was kind enough to reveal the poster.

Hultot now spoke up: "It only suggests questioning."

"Questions that must be answered," he immediately spoke up, "such as why would a husband not come forth after learning of his wife's death?"

"One could assume he might have been frightened," Benoit suggested.

"Too frightened to learn where she was buried?" Tye countered his suggestion. "And then change his name?"

"Quite true, these questions should be addressed," Basile spoke up, "but you've no poster or charges against Mr. Schroeder."

"True enough," Tye agreed with the man. "But his hatred of the British is contagious."

For the next half hour, Tye informed the men of what he knew of both men. Afterward, the five men adorned for several minutes, discussing all they had heard and a solution.

"Constable Tye, in that we have no knowledge of either men," Basile began as if being their spokesperson, "however, if they were to come, we will not in any way assist in their arrest. We will, however, escort them to the border."

"I am sure Constable Tye would like time to consider your proposal," Zachery quickly spoke up while noticing the expression on his face. "In the meantime, let us discuss your concerns."

While the servants cleared the table, leaving only the wine they openly spoke of their demands. For over an hour, they insisted on having their demands met, while Zachery remained silent but writing down each point.

"Now that you've heard our proposals," Basile calmly began. "May I ask your opinion, Captain Pendle?"

"I've no opinion, Monsieur Basile," he said, folding the written pages. "I am here only to listen and consult with my commander of this meeting. Your proposals will be listed and sent on to much higher authority."

"Mr. Tye?" Basile turned to him. "As an American having broken away from British rule, what is your opinion.?"

"Got no authority to speak," he admitted, "but all of you should be thankful having a man like Captain Pendle, who is patient enough to listen. But I will say as an American, if you were to demand such from us, we'd run you out on a rail or hang you."

"Your country did ask our King," Basile reminded him, "which was freely given."

"Was appreciated," he said pouring himself a glass of wine, "but when the war was over, never asked them to stay."

"As an American," Basile continued, "you must understand we share a common cause to be free of British rule."

"Maybe," he replied, taking a large gulp of wine before answering, "but America has no quarrel with Canada. You start something, don't look for help from us."

"You can now speak for your government?" Benoit spoke up in angry tone.

"No, just for me," he said, laying the glass down, "and hundreds just like me. But know this, if you break your promise about Peters or Schroeder, we don't forgive or forget."

"I think we should call this meeting to an end," Zachery quickly spoke up. "Your demands will be submitted to the proper government officials, and we thank you for the kindness shown."

After shown to their tent, Tye watched as Zachery opened the folded papers and began reviewing them.

"You didn't approve of my comments," he began. "Not diplomatic enough."

"On the contrary," he replied, folding the papers. "They needed to hear the truth from someone that has no interest in the matter. England would never approve but will take them serious in order to keep enough soldiers in Canada."

"They were telling the truth about Schroeder," Tye admitted. "He hasn't made contact with them."

"Yes, I know," he said removing his coat. "And if he were to arrive they will keep the promise made."

"They'll take him to the border alright," he said, sitting down on the large cot provided, "with instructions on when he can return."

"Unfortunately," he said, laying down on his cot. "I must escort you to the border."

"Well, if anything," Tye said, laying down himself, "your government knows about the two and can be on the lookout."

"Tye," Zachery gently nudging him as he slept, "time to leave."

"What time is it?" He quickly sprang to his feet. "Why didn't you wake me?"

"It's after 8:00," he replied. "Met with the delegation as they prepared to leave."

"Could have woke me," he said grabbing his clothes. "I'm assuming no coffee."

"I managed to have coffee and breakfast made for you," he said, pointing to several metal containers, but wanted time alone with the men.

"Thank you," he said, dressing quickly, then walking over to the prepared meal, "so this is how you say goodbye to me."

"Orders are orders," he said with a smile, they will keep the promise given, and our troops will be watching for the two."

Having drank the coffee and eaten the meal, the two walked out of the tent, where several men disassembled it.

"You Canadians really do like to start early," he said, seeing that almost every tent was gone, "but I appreciate you letting me sleep in."

"Gentlemen your horses." A porter came over with the animals.

"Thank you," said Zachery, taking the reins from the man, "and advise Monsieur Basile my compliments for a wonderful meeting."

Riding out, Tye looked back and noticed all tents gone.

"Been thinking," he began after several minutes. "The British settlement wasn't on any of my maps."

"Kings settlement," Zachery replied, "is relatively new. When the war in the colonies turned, the loyal families to England fled here. Most with only the clothes on their back, came to Canada seeking refuge."

"Captain, you should kick my butt all the way to the border," he said, slapping his forehead, making you chase the wrong varmint.

"What are you saying?" Zachery blurted out.

"Schroeder isn't here to meet with the French," he explained, "he's here to attack that settlement."

"Constable, I know you wish to remain here in Canada," Zachery said with a slight smile, "but it will not work."

As they rode along, Tye explained his thoughts and the reasons why the settlement would be in danger.

"Small groups of men crossing the border," he insisted, "unnoticed."

"You've no proof," Zachery replied.

"I know," he admitted, "but feel I'm right, and these posters will come in handy."

After three days of riding and in Seneca land, both knew they were being watched by those unwilling to be seen. Suddenly from a tree line, four shots rang out, Zachery's horse fell to the ground, throwing him violently against a large boulder. A bullet pierced Tye's leg, while another struck and killed his animal.

Thrown from the animal, Tye crawled over to Zachery.

"Well lookie who we got here." Peters came riding up with three others. "A spy."

"Lieutenant, this one is some kind of soldier," one of the men said while dismounting and looking down at his body, "and dead."

"You three take the saddles off," he ordered, "then take them to the river and dump them in."

"Several miles to the river," one of the men reminded him.

"Just do what I say," he commanded. "I'll stay here and see what this one knows."

The three following his command stripped the two animals of the saddles and rode away only to throw them in the tree line.

"Lieutenant," Tye asked, sitting beside Zachery, "so what army do you belong to now?"

"Colonel Schroeder's army," he replied. "Came here to finish what they wouldn't let us do during the war."

"Destroy a British settlement," Tye said, realizing he was correct. "Mostly of women and children, right?"

"Traitors," he snapped, "that murdered our own."

"Do they know about you," he said, holding his leg, "having murdered your wife and a British soldier?"

"You mean a whore?" he asked, holding a pistol while kneeling. "And a no good trying to take what wasn't his? So is that what brought you all the way here, looking for me."

"Yes," he said, looking the man in the eyes, "then taking you back to hang. But think the British will do it for me. This man belonged to the Canadian Rifles."

"Don't matter what he was," Peters said with a smile. "Colonel's got it all figured out."

"Massacre the settlement." Tye now understood. "Blame the French."

"Start a war and let them do the killing," he answered, "while we provide the weapons and training. When it's all over, we become heroes and in charge."

"No, just murderers," he said as if defying him, "like you. Do they know about your past, or is that something you left out."

"Don't need to know," he blurted out.

"Wonder what those men will think when they hear about it," he said looking over toward the lifeless body of Zachery and Tye.

"Won't be around to tell them," he stood up then pulled the trigger.

"Thought ya was taking him prisoner," one of the men said while riding up to him, "and letting the Colonel talk with them."

"Came here to spy on us," Peters said while mounting his horse. "Going to warn the settlement and army, so we couldn't take a chance.

"That one looks to be a soldier," another pointed out, "could mean trouble."

"What are ya goin to tell the Colonel?" the taller of the three asked, as if unconcerned. "Don't matter to me 'cause my brothers came here to kill British."

"Colonel has more important things on his mind," Peters reminded them, "be telling him we killed two British hunters that came snooping."

"Should we bury them?" the youngest of the three spoke up.

"Leave them for the wolves and bears," Peters ordered. "Won't be nothing left in a week or so."

"Yeah, they got some big ones around here," the older brother now replied with a laugh. "Be gone in no time."

"Let's get back," Peters said, happy they followed the older brother's rule.

"Lieutenant, we heard shooting," Schroeder said, walking up to the men as they entered the camp. "What happened?"

"Found two British hunters coming this way," he replied while dismounting. "We took care of them. Don't worry about anyone finding the bodies; all the varmints will take care of them."

"The longer we have to stay here," he said as if concerned, "the more likely we'll be discovered."

"Half are here now," Peters added. "In four days, the rest should be here."

"Got no choice but to wait," he admitted. "Need all the men to march on that settlement of British. But you're sure no one will discover those bodies, can't let something like that disrupt our plans."

"We'll widen our patrols," Peters recommended. "Make sure no one comes close."

"Good idea," he said, turning around. "I'll leave it to you."

"Yes, sir," Peters said with a smile. "I'll take care of everything."

Satisfied by the lack of concern for the two men killed, eight Seneca braves were examining the bodies after having watched the entire incident quietly.

"Swift Wind, we must leave," Little Ox said while looking around, "before soldiers return and find us."

"We leave, but take bodies and saddles," he ordered. "They leave, so others find and bring trouble to village."

"No good take bodies and saddles." Little Ox attempted to stop him. "They kill with rifle and all know we not have."

"Soldiers here on Seneca land," he explained, "want only war."

"Maybe they go away," he said as if hoping for it. "Not come to village."

"They come," Swift Wind assured him. "Others follow when find bodies. We take all, let council know, and wait for them to speak."

"I go get branches for travois," Little Ox agreed. "We take to village."

CHAPTER FOUR

Traveling for six days and nights, they entered the village of the Senecas. Swift Wind walked to the man standing by a younger woman.

"Why you bring dead white men here?" Without further comment, he moved slowly to reveal his slender but muscular body. "Does Swift Wind bring war to tribe?"

"I not bring war," he replied, defending himself, "but many soldiers come to make war. I bring dead, so war not come. Soldiers kill with rifle and leave."

"Why soldiers kill their own," he asked while looking down at the wounds, "then leave for all to find."

"Kill horses and hear only loud words," he admitted. "Not to speak English, kill white man who not wear red coat."

"Where soldiers now?" he asked, looking toward the horizon. "They come?"

"No, they wait," he answered, "but have many rifles and thunder rifle with wheels."

"Have wagons," Little Ox finally spoke up, "see many barrels and bags."

"Soldiers come to make war on village," Swift Wind blurted out as several began to crowd around. "Red coat find bodies and make war on all Seneca."

"Swift Wind wise not leave white men to be found," he said, looking over at the many people that had assembled. "Not want war with red coats, but if soldier comes then we fight. Take bodies to sacred cave, bury as white men."

"I go back to watch soldiers," Swift Wind began speaking, "give warning when they come to village."

"You now eyes of village," he said, taking the man by his shoulders. "Council come, and we make plans."

"I Swift Wind return," he said, taking a deep breath, "to warn all."

Within an hour, the young brave had gathered what he needed and began his journey back.

That night air was stagnating from the long day of heat, even the watchful dogs that stayed alert to warn the village of danger refused to bark or move. His small tribe would come to know it as the year when rain had not come, and the once green forest started turning brown before it's time. Having been born with two large front teeth, his father, the chief of all the Senecas, had named him Longteeth. Throughout his 48 years, none had ever belittled his name, gaining their respect by his bravery battling tribal conflicts that led others to follow him as their chief.

However, this night, he walked around the many teepees wearing only a small frontal and back leather cover. Having woken by the heat, he quietly raised without disturbing his wife of two years and pondered the omen given to him four years ago.

As he looked out into the silent forest, he remembered that not so long ago there were hundreds of campfires with the smell of full cooking pots preparing to feed the people of the different tribes. Now only his small tribe remained, and always wondered why so many left the land that offered so much. Miles of forest with enough game for food, and in the winter, they could move the 20 miles to the caves along the Niagara river for shelter.

"My husband is once again troubled by his thoughts..." She walked to his side wearing a light tan deerskin gown inlaid with small seashells and colored stone, which distinguished her as his wife. "I wish I could unburden you of such thoughts, but I cannot for you are my husband and chief."

"Little Sparrow, I have asked the great spirits to show me which path I must take." He looked down at the young girl of 18 with long, black hair and shinning brown eyes. "And if Tenskwatawa words were true. Night after night, they do not speak, they know I have heard the words from the prophet so the great spirits say nothing or maybe they, too, have left."

"The great prophet spoke of the omen many seasons ago," she reminded him as her thin body eased under his arm, "and it has not come to pass."

"But now a vengeful army comes and if they blind all those who look upon it by the sun," he began to repeat what Tenskwatawa predicted, "even in death, they will destroy what remains of the great Seneca tribe. For many seasons, I have waited and watched, for an army I know nothing of or seen."

"The great spirits have not abandoned you, my husband," she insisted. "They have protected us from those who have wished us harm, and for more seasons than I know, our people have lived alone in peace."

"When my father left with 500 warriors to fight against the Americans in the Great War, for the first time he began to speak of the past, I said nothing and watched him leave with the British soldiers. I said nothing when only six came back, and watched as half my people died from the white man's sickness carried by those warriors. The great spirits have abandoned me, for not speaking the truth and allowing our people to enter into the white man's world."

"Your father did not listen to the great spirits." Knowing he carried the burden, she went on, "And you could do nothing as the son of a great chief. No longer do I hear the cries of the women having lost husbands, and all the children laugh with full bellies. No, my husband, the great spirits watch and protect us, and if they do not speak, it is they know what a great chief you are, and need no such help or words of wisdom."

"If I need no words of wisdom, Little Sparrow…" He smiled pressing, her closer to his warm body. "Then why have I sent Swift Wind out to watch for such an army to come?"

"Because my husband will never stop worrying about his people." On her tiptoes, she kissed him on the cheek. "So that the people sleep well at night."

"Your husband is now tired and his fears gone." He returned her kiss. "And it is good me speak from heart."

With each passing day, the land began to wither by the hot sun. Small streams began to dry up, and even the forest animals began to move away. On the seventh day of the drought, a lone runner appeared, his thin body covered in sweat and feet bloody for having run the many miles without stopping.

Within minutes the entire tribe surrounded the young man Swift Wind, who collapsed from exhaustion. The men gently lifted him off the ground as the women began cooling his body with water.

"Carry him to one of the teepees," Chief Longteeth said walking through the crowd that had assembled, and examining the young man's condition said, "Give him water and have the medicine man come to care for his feet."

"My Chief, they are coming," he struggled for breath and continued to repeat his words. "They are coming."

As they carried him to the first teepee, Swift Wind continued to repeat the words of warning, and once they had laid him down on several deer pelts, began leaving.

"Swift Wind," one of the older warriors walked over to him and spoke into his ear, "you sent him to the end of our world and now he returns. I fear he cannot say all he saw, the sun has touched his head."

"I will speak with him." Longteeth bent his 6'2" body down in order to enter into the darkness where the young man laid. "Swift Wind, tell me what you saw."

"My Chief, the great white man's army comes," he replied to his voice as the medicine man began placing leaves and ointment on his feet after having been washed by the lone woman that assisted. Their bodies shined so bright by the sun that I could not see faces."

"How many come?" he pressed for answers. "And when will they be here?"

"Many as leaves on tree, and two thunder rifles pulled by ox." He was becoming coherent as he continued, "They move slowly, but in four moons, they will come."

"Rest now, Swift Wind, and we will speak later." He smiled at the young man, knowing the pain he accepted in order to report such news. "And forever people will speak of your bravery around the campfires of the warning you gave."

"When they come, I will be ready to fight," he promised looking down at his tattered feet. "And I will not fail to protect our people and land."

"Rest my young warrior," he said as he left the darkness into the light.

"What shall we do?" Several that surrounded the hut asked when he appeared. "Should we go to the caves and hide?"

"Have the women and children prepare to go into the caves," he announced to those standing around, "and the warriors ready themselves for battle."

He watched as the women began packing food for the journey, and the men began making arrows and painting their faces for war. As darkness fell, the women of the village made large fires, so that the work could continue, but now he had to leave and go to the sacred place of the dead where the great spirits gathered.

"Oh, Great Spirits, I ask only for a given sign." He stood naked in the middle of the burial grounds that generations of his people used. "If this is our end, show me what I must do."

After hours of standing, he finally collapsed from fatigue and by the heat of the night, and when he awoke, the sun was just starting to rise.

"Over here, he has fallen," Little Sparrow screamed to those searching the forest. "My husband, all night we have looked for you."

"The Great Spirits have not abandoned me," he said, leaning his body on hers. He slowly lifted himself off the ground. "They came to me and showed what path must be taken."

"It is good," she admitted, walking him toward the village as the others gathered behind them, "but first I will clean and prepare you for the council."

Unlike the village of teepees that allowed the people to disassemble them quickly, the supreme tribal council hut provided permanence to the land. Placed in the center of the village and built of stone and mud, all knew of its importance, and only 12 men of importance or influence had the right to enter. The entrance was large enough that no one had to bend down to enter. The members stepped down into the hut that had been dug three foot lower, allowing milder temperatures for those who attended the meetings.

Entering the hut, he found only six members waiting. The war council was now made up of three warriors and three elders all sitting to form a circle. The eldest wore a faded red British officer's coat with long buckskin trousers. In contrast, the young warriors wore only animal skins to cover their front and painted faces.

"Our people must not prepare for war," the eldest began as he allowed Chief Longteeth to stand in the middle of the circle, "for an army that has not come, and if it comes it too powerful to fight."

"Stone Eyes, the army comes…" He looked at the man with dark brown, almost black eyes and his face covered in wrinkles but still made his presence known by his forceful voice, "and may be powerful, but the Great Spirits have spoken to me and have shown how we can crush them."

"If the Great Spirits have spoken, then we must listen," one of the young warriors yelled out, "and follow their words."

"Are they the words of the Great Spirits," the elder continued, "or the prophecy of Tenskwatawa that haunts your every thought?"

"His words are in my thoughts, so I can choose the right path for my people." He chose his words carefully. "But if this is the army that will end our people, then let them say we fought a good fight."

"You are as wise as brave." The eldest looked around the room with his eyes that seemed to look one in the soul. "And I am an old man who thinks little of himself but thinks of the young that will suffer. If it is war, then let no enemy leave our land alive."

"Death to all those who come!" the young warriors began chanting and whooping. "It is war."

"Tomorrow we prepare for the white man army," he continued. "The Great Spirits have shown me what needs done, and death awaits them."

By first light, the entire village had assembled, where he immediately gave instructions for the women to cut all the long, dry grass down. The men using the six steel hatches given to the warriors by the British were to cut down dead trees, and then chop them into smaller pieces.

"Have the women continue cutting the tall grass to those trees," he said pointing to a row of trees that were almost two miles away, "and then bring the grass to our sacred burial grounds."

"You cannot let the white man to enter the sacred ground," one of the older women began to protest.

"The Great Spirits have spoken that death awaits them there," he reassured her, "and our people will rise from the great beyond to kill the evil men who come."

"Some of our people speak to themselves that by having the soldiers enter the tribal burial grounds you will anger the Great Spirits." Stone Eyes came to him with the misgivings of several. "But I see wisdom in making this our battleground."

"When the six warriors returned I listened to their stories of how the armies fought," he began, "always in the open and never in woods. The women will spread small pieces of wood on the ground, then cover it with the dry grass, then wood and more dry grass. When done they will walk over it, give wagons the path they must take."

"A path taken to death." Stone Eyes realized what was in store for the approaching army. "And the weapons will turn against them."

"Those who speak will listen to you." He looked at the man with respect and admiration. "Silence their tongues."

For three days, the entire village worked to complete the path, and when finished, he allowed a victory dance that gave the people confidence but was cut short when a runner entered the dance circle.

"They are here," he announced the warning for all to hear, "and they camp by river they follow."

"Little Ox, you will take your warriors to the south woods." Having already shown each his plan of attack, he said, "Let the army enter, then use 30 warriors for a fast attack on the men at the end and then run back to the woods. Blue Sky, the north woods, and with 30 warriors, fast attack the front then run back to the woods. Stone Eyes will be in the west woods, and I in the east. The soldiers will prepare for battle; let them see and hear you. Remember do not attack. When they make ready for our attack, we light the fire arrows."

Once all the planning seemed complete, he asked the medicine man to conjure up a concoction, which once given would make the warriors invincible.

Finally, the sun began to rise as the warriors began moving toward their assigned areas, each ready and prepared for the battle to come. By early afternoon, he saw the army that had haunted his dreams, dressed in olive green coats with white pants and bright green buttons. The gold buttons shined brightly by the sun's rays.

They marched 10 abreast into the field without scouts or concern, most unprepared for battle; had their muskets tied to the large backpacks they carried. The entire column talked and laughed as they marched, showing they had no fear or knowledge of the tribe's existence. The entire army was led by a man who seemed older than most of those who followed, riding on top of a black stallion; he said nothing and showed little interest in the surrounding land.

As predicted, the army chose the path created by the women and continued toward the ancient burial grounds. From the south, Little Ox's warriors struck first with such violent ferociousness that the soldiers began to panic. The entire column crumbed as their fear began to spread.

The leader, Colonel Schroeder, turned his black stallion around and galloped toward the fleeing soldiers just as Blue Sky made his attack.

Men began shouting orders to assemble, and as if guided by fate they began forming a protective square precisely where he wanted them. Quickly the oxen and all the supplies along with the cannons were place in the center of the square, three separate lines of 100 men composed the outer defense and capable of continuous firing at any attacking enemy.

He heard the men shouting orders but could not understand the language. He watched as Lieutenant Peters instructed the men from each line on when to fire. It was a formidable looking square, all sides protected as one row of soldiers stood with rifles in the ready while the other two rows knelt behind those standing. His mind immediately grasped the concept of the formation: the front row would fire on the approaching enemy then kneel down to reload while the second group fired and followed by the third. Such firepower would certainly destroy all his warriors on the first charge, leaving the village defenseless.

All the warriors had returned to the safety of the trees as they began moving the cannons among the men, while others placed several powder kegs and steel balls next to the wooden wheels.

Watching as the men prepared the cannons to fire, he decided it was time to torch the ground, and with one movement of his hand, several warriors raced out from the woods with flaming arrows.

Understanding the danger from those attempting to set the field on fire, the first row of riflemen opened up on the warriors. The sheer numbers of rifles firing began taking its toll; of the 20 warriors sent out, only two survived, but others came out to fire their arrows. The unremitting rifle fire from those in the square struck them down.

Immediately the two cannons began blasting those who stood ready in the woods, repeatedly the warrior's defied death by charging out with lit arrows. How many were killed, he could only wonder. Finally the field began to smoke, and within seconds, the entire ground was covered in flames. When the flames reached the first row of soldiers, their powder horn began to explode, creating more panic by the flying debris of body parts and animal bone. Seeing the carnage from the explosions, the men began throwing their horn away, but many exploded in midair, making the situation more dire. Suddenly, the powder kegs resting by the cannons ignited, and every man within 20 feet lay dead or dying.

Longteeth strained his eyes to watch the chaos within the square as the soldiers screamed in agony when the flames overwhelmed them, then watched in amazement as the leader Colonel Schroeder placed his pistol against the black stallion's head and put the animal down. As he reloaded his pistol, there was a tremendous explosion that engulfed him, and those who still stood. The entire field was now covered by a heavy black smoke, so powerful was the explosion that it smothered the fires.

As the wind cleared away the smoke, he saw a huge crater filled with bodies of both man and animal. Burnt bodies still smoldering were everywhere, what was once uniformed soldiers were now just hideous looking figures with black flesh and crushed bones.

The large wagon carrying the many barrels of powder had destroyed his enemy, so enormous and violent was the explosion that even his warriors seemed mystified by what had just happened.

As the flames seemed to reach the sky, several soldier on fire came running out as if attempting to flee. One was Lieutenant Peters, consumed by fire and having two arrows in his chest. Within seconds all lay dead, their uniforms bloody and blackened.

Leaving the safety of the woods, Longteeth walked toward the crater but had to turn back when his moccasins began to burn from the heat of the ground.

By nightfall, the ground had finally cooled and with the use of torches, the entire village was able to see the carnage close up, broken muskets still in the hands of those burned to death, a sight that sickened both woman and warriors alike.

"It is a very good day for our people," Stone Eyes said picking up one of the muskets without a wooden stock. "Forty-six brave warriors killed, but we destroyed our enemy and their thunder rifles."

"We must never speak of this and bury all, so no one will ever know." He walked over to the large crater. "By making such a hole, the Great Spirits have shown us what we must now do."

"This we must not do," Stone Eyes claimed in anger. "To win such a battle and say nothing. We must send runners to all the tribes, and once they know, we will unite to defeat any army."

"No, my friend, they will seek revenge." He looked toward the man holding the useless weapon. "The Americans and English will come with an army so large and prepared that our women will sing the song of death forever. They must never know or see what has happened here. Put their bodies in the burial hole. We must cover the body with dirt, and then bury the animals on top of them. All their weapons, take, and throw into the Great Niagara, and let no warriors take one even powder horns."

As ordered, the warriors carried all weapons to the river and began throwing them into it. One of the rifles wedged itself on a rock shelf, resting as if hung there.

"A good fight that we must never speak of." Stone Eyes gave warning, "The warriors will wonder why after such a great battle they must become frightened women who are afraid of the wind."

"I have heard and obeyed the words of the Great Spirits," he replied, understanding the frustration by concealing such a victory, now the warriors must listen and obey my words for the good of the tribe."

All the following day, the people without question followed his every instruction; no one spoke, nor did anyone openly defy his words.

By the end of the two days of work, all remnants that there had been a great battle fought were gone. Once again, Mother Nature with rain could reclaim the land, to grow whatever it deemed appropriate.

Again, Longteeth's thoughts denied him sleep, for hours he would seek the comfort of darkness and solitude to think. He sensed danger, not from an army, but from a harsh winter that would come early. In that moment, he made the decision: the entire tribe would move to the caves on the shore of the Niagara.

Expressing his concern of an early winter, all the people followed him to the Niagara Lake and entered the large cavern that served them for generations as winter quarters. It was an ideal location for the tribe, 30 miles from the great fall. The huge rocks rose 60 feet and having only one entrance that only he knew made it a perfect place to spend the winter. Inside, a rock path led down to a chamber large enough for 5,000 or more to live, and with a series of caves allowed younger families privacy.

On the walls of the rock, past generations engraved their history, showing great hunts and war parties raiding other tribal villages. As he studied the etchings that only his people ever saw, he felt it was here that the story of those brave warriors killed in the battle might be preserved. Summoning those with the skills and tools to make such a story on stone, he permitted them to etch a permanent record of the battle, which included the two men killed, and to show the soldiers committed the act.

Fall winds came with cold rain and sleet, then as he foretold the harshest winter ever. Once the snow started, it concealed the sun for weeks at a time. Every morning, the women would dig out the snow that cover the entrance, and then use it for water once melted.

By mid-January, the snows became less frequent, allowing the people to leave the cavern for a brief time and enjoy the winter wonderland but under the watchful eyes of the warriors. For precaution, the elders decided to place the tribal bow and 20 arrows in the tribal flute near the entrance, in the event of any possible attack. This small token of protection allowed the children to play on the snow until their cheeks were bright red, and once exhausted, they returned to the warmth of the cooking fires within the cavern.

Many nights he stood by the entrance looking out, wondering about the world they left behind and the new land in Ohio the people wished to go. On one such night, Little Sparrow joined him, and together they sat under a heavy buckskin blanket without speaking.

Without warning, the entire cavern began to shake, and then the entire formation of rock began falling toward those who slept. The two jumped from under the blanket, a rock struck Little Sparrow and pinned her under it. Even with all his strength, he was unable to move the rock from her legs. As he covered her body with his, he watched the falling rock crushed and covered his people. The entrance disappeared as the stones smashed against his body, and then he looked down at her frightened face and gently kissed her. The screams of the dying would go on for only minutes, as the entire mountain began to collapse on all inside.

As the mountain collapse, the etchings on the wall repeated the omen,

A vengeful army will come and blind all those who look upon it by the sun, and even in death, they will destroy what remains of the great Seneca tribe.

CHAPTER FIVE
(PRESENT DAY)

"Got a minute, Samuel?" She entered the small office of one of three broadcast stations in the city. "If you're not busy."

"Never too busy when it comes to you, Janice," he said, standing up from behind the metal desk and showing his large body. "Please take a seat and tell me what you need."

"Need to take some time off," she said while gently sitting in front of his desk, "maybe two, three weeks."

"You're not planning to quit or looking for another job?" he asked, holding his chest as if experiencing a heart attack. "Couldn't run this television station without you."

"Nothing like that." Her thin but full lips said with a smile, allowing her perfectly white teeth to show. "Just needing time to do some research. It's what you pay me to do, right?"

"You're thinking I'm holding you back?" he asked, looking over her slender but well-built body. "Making you do the research while others that rely on it are in front of the camera."

"Well, I have been here for a year and half," she said in a coy manner that charmed most, "and you always said I'm the best."

"Janice, when I first met you," he said, wiping the small droplets of sweat that appeared over his black forehead. "I said to myself, there is one of the most beautiful women I've ever laid my eyes on."

"Heard you say that to any young black females that enter this office," she began to laugh, "but I know you mean no harm."

"May have said it many times," he said, taking a deep breath as if trying to shrink his growing stomach, "but only meant it with you."

"Thank you for that," she said in a charming tone.

"Janice, I've been in this business a long time," he said, sitting back down and leaning toward her. "I know talent and beauty when I see it. Yes, I've been holding you back, wanting you to understand how important getting the story right."

"I've always tried to get the truth out," she replied. "I don't want anyone to have to apologize for a mistake I made."

"And you've done a wonderful job," he admitted while relaxing back in his chair. "All the people broadcasting the news rely on you. They know any story you researched is factual, not opinion of third party blather. You're unique because it's truth you seek, a rare quality in today's news world."

"I just do what you ask," she said, downplaying her importance. "Find the truth and double-check all my facts."

"Over the many years I've been in this job," he said, looking toward the single window, "I seen so many come and go. Even been around some of the best and brightest, but there's one thing I have learned."

"What's that?" she asked with interest.

"Watched careers built," he began. "Hundreds of great news stories that made them famous. Then that one story that wasn't true or accurate, and no matter how many good stories they broadcasted, it's that one story that becomes their epitaph."

"You think it could happen to me?" she asked, wanting his opinion.

"No," he said, turning his eyes back to her, "because you know why truth is so important. One day, you will be the face of the network. People will say they watch because they trust and adore you."

"Samuel, I'm not looking to be the face of the network," she admitted, "but someone who from time to time reports a story."

"You're young and beautiful," he said, shaking his head as if she already knew it, "and when you finally sit in front of that camera, you'll be there forever. When you're rich and famous, I'll sit back and smile knowing I played a very small part."

"No small part." Her voice quivered as she spoke. "A very large part."

"Now about the time off," he said, clearing his throat as if attempting to avoid showing emotion. "When your mother passed, we allowed three weeks but you came back to work after a week."

"Mother had made all the arrangements," she explained, "and being alone in the house only made me miss her more. Besides, she wouldn't have wanted me to sit around doing nothing, she was so active all her life."

"Taken so quickly," he replied, as if remembering the time, "and a picture of health."

"Sometimes at night," she said as tears began to flow, "I can still hear her humming."

"So tell me the truth," he said in a stronger tone. "What are you researching?"

"I've information where I might be able to interview a famous author," she admitted. "He might be staying at some fancy estate for a couple days."

"You're not talking about that Shakespeare fellow, are you?" he asked, shaking his head. "So many have impersonated the man that you can't trust any information on him. Hell, just last month, an entire camera crew said they found him."

"Yes, I know," she began to laugh, "had to spend days apologizing."

"Cost them more than money," he said as if cautioning her. "Reputations were more than bruised."

"I'll be careful if you allow me the time," she said, giving him an expression he could not ignore. "Just have to trust me."

"Two weeks," he said in a firm tone, "and come back here prepared to work."

"I will," she said standing up with a smile, "with either a great story or tail between my legs."

"Just promise me to enjoy the time off," he said standing. "Not all work."

"Thank you, Samuel." She started toward the door. "For being there."

Looking out the stained windows of the Greyhound bus, one could only wonder why any person of prominence would want to come here with so many empty buildings of failed businesses. The streets appeared unused, the railroad tracks rusted, and weeds covered the wooden trusses, and it was obvious the town had accepted its fate of obscurity because of hard times and neglect.

The two men watched as she stepped gracefully off the large bus and waited for the driver to retrieve her single suitcase. Her light tan skin and expensive clothes revealed a person out of their element, but her beautiful face showed a certain amount of determination to accept and overcome whatever obstacle placed before her.

"Excuse me, young lady," he called over to her as the bus pulled away, spewing a light blue smoke behind. "You sure this is your stop?"

"Well, this is Hopeland," Janice said, looking over to the two men who seemed more interested with the small pieces of wood they whittled.

"Yeah, we're all Hopeland things will get better," he said in an amusing tone.

"Now that was a good one, Frank," the second man said without looking up. "Have to remember that one."

"Apparently, I've found the town's jester, and he has an audience." She looked over at the two odd men who looked shocked by her words.

"Seems like she's got your number now, Frank," he said, laying down the knife to face her.

"Might be, but at least I know where I am," he snapped back as he studied her from head to toe.

"What are you two a salt and pepper comedy team?" Her tone showed a little anger. "Or maybe the town's official welcoming party?"

"Leone, I think she just called you black," he looked over to the man wearing a sport shirt and jeans. "Might even say that's a little racist."

"It's alright 'cause she's black," he reminded him after giving her a quick glance. "Besides, I am black, right?"

"Well, if you're fine with it," he said, folding his knife and placing the piece of wood down on a small table. "but should I be a little offended by her calling me white?"

"Don't think she meant much by it." His brown eyes shined as he spoke. "'Course she could be one of them troublemakers from down south."

"My God, what have I got myself into?" she said picking up the one suitcase and carrying it toward them. "I must be in the Twilight Zone."

"We're just funning with you, young lady." They stood up and walked over to her. "Haven't had anyone getting off that bus in months. Let me carry that bag for you, my name is Frank Ehlert, and this here is Leone Pegasus."

"I'm Janice Gardner." At first, she hesitated handing the man, who wore jeans and a freshly pressed, white, short-sleeved shirt, her bag.

"Pleased to make your acquaintance, Miss Gardner," Leone's large brown hand reached out and took hers. "Meant no harm, like Frank said. So what brings a beautiful young lady like yourself, to our little town?"

"I'm a reporter and told an important person will be visiting here." She looked at the man who wasn't much taller than herself, but his thin face showed hard time and having several light brown scars on his neck, revealing he may have been involved in an accident at some time. "And I'm hoping to have a chance to interview him if possible."

"Don't know about no important person coming here." Frank carried the bag to the front of the little empty store where they had been sitting. "But if you want to interview a real life hero, then Leone is the one."

"Now, Frank, she's not here to interview no broken down soldier," he said, showing his off white teeth as he smiled, "besides who'd want to see the face of a wrinkled old black man on a color television?"

"Might not show now, but one time, old Leone was a fine looking man," he said offering her the chair to relax in. "Got himself a Silver Star plus Purple Heart, and those shrapnel scars go to proving it."

"Sounds like a great story, but I don't think my boss would approve." She suddenly realized why he looked familiar. "You know, you look a lot like an older David Brinkley. I should know because I did research on his career, remarkable career."

"Come to think about it, Frank..." Leone looked at him carefully. "With a little more hair and taller maybe."

"So who is this important person coming to our little town?" Frank asked, deciding to change the subject, believing he looked nothing like the man.

"I'm here hoping to interview Shakespeare," she blurted out, "one of the most popular authors we have today."

"Yeah, but he's dead," he said, puzzled by her announcement. "'Least that's what we been told that by everyone that should know."

"It's A. Shakespeare," she corrected him. "And after seeing this town, I can understand why you haven't heard of him."

"Know William, because we got ourselves a library," Frank said as if defending the town, "but never heard about A. Shakespeare."

"I'm sure everyone in town has read that single book you have," she replied quickly, "and just for your information, A. Shakespeare has written seven novels."

"WOW, she is good Frank," Leone began, laughing. "No use trying to outwit her cause she's out of your league."

"Well, no mind 'cause neither one of us heard of him, and don't think most folks have either," he continued, "but what makes this person so interesting?"

"For one, he's never given an interview." Her soft brown eyes lit up speaking about the man. "Because no one has ever met or seen him. Got a call he was coming here to relax, staying on an estate near here."

"The Universe World Corporation owns the only estate around here," Leone informed her, "a real fine mansion about 15 miles from here. But you can't go out there by yourself. A high wall surrounds the entire area, and the county sheriff arrests all trespassers that try climbing over it."

"What am I going to do? Because I have to get that interview." She appeared shaken by the news and paused for a brief second, could rent a car and wait outside.

"Or you could just ask Frank real nice like to take you out there," Leone suggested as he gave a quick glance to both.

"You know the rules." Frank's tone showed how serious it was. "No strangers allowed on the property."

"You work there?" Her voice showed excitement. "Please say you'll take me."

"Look, my wife and I clean the place," Frank began to explain, "but no one is there when we do it, and you can't stay outside the gate because the deputies will arrest you."

"Why not take her along as a helper?" Leone suggested without waiting for further discussion. "You said earlier Linda was feeling poorly, and I'm sure Miss Gardner would be more than happy to take her place."

"Let me think over it cause we have another 20 minutes before having to leave." He sat down in a huff. "But if I decide, you go prepare for a long hard day of cleaning, and I mean cleaning."

"I'll do anything you ask." Her heart leaped as Leone gave a quick wink to her. "So how long have you two known each other."

"Both born and raised here," Frank pointed for her to sit in the third chair, "I've never left, but Leone joined the Army and stayed away for a lot of years."

"No need to go talking about two old men when there's a beautiful woman present." Leone seemed interested in her. "So tell us a little about you."

"Not a whole lot to tell really." She seemed a little embarrassed by his inquiry, been a New Yorker all my life and raised by my mom. With a scholarship, I was able to attend college, and majored in journalism and broadcasting. For the last year and half, been working at a local television station, doing research."

"You never said anything about your father," Frank asked.

"Never knew him," she answered. "Mom said that he left when I was born and was killed going to fast in his car. She once showed me his grave, and he had no other relatives. Made it easier on both of us, not having others reminding us about the man."

"Sorry for being so nosy." His tone showed that he was sorry for having asked. "And if you still want to leave, its time."

"I'll explain everything to Linda," Leone said, standing up, "so she won't worry."

As they drove out to the estate, he told her how once the little town was a thriving city, and how the railroad making almost hourly stops allowed visitors to purchase food or other essentials. But when the railroad cut services and the super highway by-passed the town, factories shut down and the businesses left with them. Even the mansion on the estate suffered, built by a movie studio in the early fifties as a hideaway for the movie stars, who by the sixties wanted nothing to do with it because they wanted seen, not forgotten. Luckily, the corporation bought the studio and with it the estate, which they restored to its original condition. Now they used it to conduct business meetings, and from time to time, an important person who didn't need or want exposure stay there.

It was everything she imagined, walls covered with rare paintings or sculptured statues and rooms filled with comfortable furniture for those fortunate enough to use. Every room, including the bathrooms, had a television and stereo; signed pictures of movies stars hung on walls in the movie room that had a huge screen plus 12 padded seats. The oak dining room table sat 12, and a hutch contained fine china plates and gold eating utensils.

"You know there's even a bowling alley in the basement," he continued to explain all the comforts of the mansion, "and a three hole golf course in back."

"This place is a palace," she said. As promised, she worked as they spoke. "I would have never known such a place exists if you hadn't brought me here. Do they tell you who stays here? I mean, have you ever met anyone?"

"Some, but mostly by accident," he admitted. "Some have come earlier than expected, and I see them arriving. However, the corporation doesn't want anyone to know who comes and goes. Most are just looking for privacy and are not interested with those doing the cleaning."

"So, you really don't know whose coming here today?" She showed disappointment. "But we can hope he'll arrive a little early."

"Tell you what I'm going to do." He stopped working while he thought about what he needed to say. "Stay with my family tonight, and if by chance I learn something, then you'll be told. Understand I'll only give the information to you; what you do with it is totally up to you."

"Deal." She snapped at the offer. "So what other rooms need cleaning?"

By the time the sun began to set, he looked over the rooms that she cleaned and was completely satisfied she fulfilled her obligation.

When they arrived at his home, she saw three children huddled around the television that immediately jumped up and ran to him when he entered.

"Well, have all of you been listening and obeying your mother today?" he asked after taking one into his arms. "Because I don't want to hear from her that you haven't."

"I have Dad," the tallest of the three spoke up, "but they haven't been nice at all, and Mommy sent Frankie to the corner."

"Frank, we'll talk later, but in the meantime," he said, placing his young daughter down, "I want to introduce someone to you. Please say hello to Miss Janice Gardner, who will be our guest tonight."

"Hello, my name is Susan, and I'm six," she said with a large smile on her face. She looked at the other two. "These are my brother and sister."

"I'm Frank," he said, upset knowing he would have to explain why punishment was necessary, "and Lisa is too shy to say anything to you."

"Lisa is three, and let me warn you," he bent down and kissed each one on the forehead, "once she warms up to you, she won't stop talking. This beautiful woman is my wife, Linda."

"Miss Gardner, it's a pleasure to meet you." Linda walked in holding a towel but wearing a dress and high heels. "Leone stopped by earlier and spoke quite highly of you."

"Thank you, Linda," she looked surprised by her voice and had the loveliest green eyes she had ever seen. "Hope I'm not imposing."

"Of course not," she said with a genuine smile, "we're real happy having you."

"You know most men will never admit this," he walked over to her, grabbed her trim waist, and kissed her on the lips, "but I certainly married up."

"Excuse my husband, but he shows off whenever there's company," she winked as he stepped aside. "He's still in training, but I've got a good feeling he'll do."

"Let me say how beautiful you look." She looked toward her and couldn't understand how trim she was after having three children, and so young.

"Well, thank you very much." She brushed her long brown hair away from her face. "Not often I get such compliments."

"I tell you every day how beautiful you are," he said as the three children began laughing at his words, "and I've even heard Leone say it."

"The two of you don't count," she continued to smile, "but don't stop saying it. Now the kids have already eaten, but I've made extra and kept it warm."

"Leone said earlier you weren't feeling well," she said. "I hope that I'm not making extra trouble."

"May I call you Janice?" She asked, looking her in the eyes. "You're no problem. It will be so nice having someone besides this big lug, and three little ones to talk with."

As they ate, she remembered the times when she was younger having such dinners with her mother, and the food was just as good, in fact, better than she had for months having to cook for herself. After eating, she helped with the dishes as the two young girls sat at the table watching with interest.

"Hon just talked with Frank, and he said it wasn't his fault for breaking the lamp." He walked in with the young boy following. "Said that the girls wanted to play catch with him. Said when he threw the ball to Susan, she didn't even try to catch it."

"Oh, you little tattle tale," Susan blurted out, "besides mom says I'm a lady who shouldn't go around playing catch."

"Now you can see why I wanted you to stay." She finished putting the dishes away. "I put Frank in the corner for listening to Susan. Frank is old enough to know she never intended to play catch, but had every intention to get him into trouble."

"Well, son, she has you there." He looked down at the young boy. "It's time you start thinking about things before going along."

"But Dad, she promised," he spoke up in his defense.

"Son, promises can be broken because they're words," he explained. "It's actions that determines who that person is."

"It's still not fair I got punished," he replied, defiant to the end.

"Fair or not, its bath time, and then bed for all of you, she said, placing her small hand on their backs, "and I don't want to hear any more about it.

"You have a beautiful family Mr. Ehlert," she watched as they paraded up-stairs, "and you've been kind to me, and I want to apologize for saying you look like an older David Brinkley."

"Come to think about it," he said pouring himself a cup of coffee from the stove, "that might have been one of the nicest things you said to me. Let bygones be bygones, would you care for a cup?"

"No, thank you," she said while motioning with her hand, "it's been a real long day, and I'm a little tired."

"Of course, you're tired," he laid the cup down, "and we already placed your suitcase in the spare bedroom."

The room was large enough for a queen size bed with nightstands, and an old console television having both radio and record player. On the walls were pictures of all the children, but one was a picture of Leone with the en-tire family.

"Finding everything you need?" Linda knocked then opened the door slowly. "The bathroom with a shower is through that door."

"It's a wonderful room," she turned around to face her, "and I was just looking at the pictures of your family and saw Mr. Pegasus in one."

"Leone's like family." She walked over and looked at the picture as if re-membering the day they took it. "Godfather to the children and a true friend. Even though he has his own home, he spends most of his time here and the children love him."

"Mr. Ehlert seems fond of him," she mentioned, "I mean in a normal way."

"Some women might be a little jealous when their husband spends time with another person," she began to explain, "but you know Leone brings out the best in people and just having him around makes you thankful."

"Except for my mother, of course, I've never known anyone like that," she admitted, "but it's nice to know such people are out there."

"No doubt someone as beautiful as you are," she said as she turned and started to leave, "will one day meet and know such a person."

Once alone, she turned off the small lamp on the end table and immedi-ately fell asleep under the warm comforter and soft pillows. At first, she thought it was only a dream of a telephone ringing, but soon after, she heard a soft tapping at her door.

"Janice, may I come in," he asked from outside the door. "Sorry to disturb you, but you might be interested in what I have to say."

"Yes, please come in," she quickly, and turned the lamp on, but stayed under the comforter, "is there something wrong?"

"No, well, maybe..." He walked in fully dressed and saw Linda standing by the door in a robe. "Just got a telephone call asking me to pick up the person who's going to stay at the estate. Now, it's not that Shakespeare fellow, but Linda and I decided you might want to meet the person."

"So he's not coming?" she asked, showing disappointment, "but who is this person?"

"No, hon, he's not coming," Linda replied, holding the robe firmly around her body, "but I think you'll do just fine meeting her."

"Understand I can't tell you who she is," he said looking down at her, "and if she doesn't want you there, then we have to respect her wishes."

"Is there enough time for me to take a quick shower?" she asked pulling the covers down.

"Make it quick," he said, looking back at the door to ensure Linda had left, "there's one more condition."

"Name it, but it has to be within reason." The answer revealed suspicion.

"I'm sticking my neck out by doing this," he began. "Could lose my job, and in this town that could be fatal. I'll get right to the point, if I ask a favor of you in the future, you'll do it without any excuses."

"What kind of favor are you thinking about?" She stood up and looked him in the eye. "Because there are limits."

"It will be within your power to do it." He crossed his heart as he spoke. "So do I have your word?"

"You have it," she answered without thinking, "and I'll be ready in 10 minutes."

"Meet me outside." He continued to speak walking out, "You'll take the family truck while I drive the van."

Walking out of the room, she found Linda looking out the front door and holding a travel cup filled with coffee.

"Might be a long night, so take this." She handed the cup to her. "Be careful and good luck."

They drove on the highway for 30 minutes when he turned into a brightly lit truck stop. Leaving her alone for what seemed hours, she began to wonder who the person was and why meet here of all places. Deep in thought, she was startled when Frank opened up her door and motioned for her to leave the truck.

"I'll be driving the truck," he began. "Told her about you, and she's agreed to meet with you but will decide on an interview once we've reached the estate."

"So I'm driving the van," she said walking over to it.

"Yeah," he said opening the van door to a young woman holding a child. "You can put him in the child's seat."

Snapping the seatbelt around the child that appeared no older than four years of age, she quietly entered the driver's side and closed the door.

"Mrs. Planterson, this is Miss Gardner," Frank said while holding the door for her, "the reporter I told you about earlier."

"You said nothing about how young she is." Her tone showed concern and apprehension. "I take it she's unaware of the situations."

"You're Mrs. Planterson, wife of Senator Planterson." She turned to see her face. "He was just on the news asking for help in locating you. He said you suffer from depression, and that you've taken his son."

"That's just like Michael," she said, staring out the window. "Either telling people I'm careless or depressed. When will the lies stop? I've let them go on for so long, I could almost believe them."

"He's one of the best-known and powerful men in Washington," Janice said without hesitation. "The press loves him."

"Yes, they certainly do," she added, "which makes me wonder why you'll willing to go against him."

"I didn't know I was against anyone." Her answer was honest. "And right now, I'm not even sure what I'm doing here."

"You're here to listen to what she has to say," Frank spoke up as he was about to close the door, "so that people can learn the truth."

"The truth is, I've left my husband, and it isn't because I'm depressed." She turned around and gently pulled up the coat sleeve of the sleeping child. "Michael almost broke his arm because he was angry and drunk."

"He did that?" she asked, looking at his small arm wrapped with a bandage from the hand to elbow as she followed Frank. "Can you prove it?"

"Doctor Cider wrote that he sprained it while playing." She covered the arm with the coat. "Even knowing what really happened. For the last three years, I've endured his drunkenness and cruelty, but it stops now with this. Doctor Cider is a friend and business partner to Michael. He's treated me six times. Three times for broken ribs and once for nose, and each time he says it's my fault."

"Other than Doctor Cider," she began to think about the story, "did you ever go directly to the hospital or see someone different? Doctor Cider has residency at three different hospitals, and many friends."

"Once I went by ambulance, and another time I went by myself," she said as if reliving each visit, "but each time, Doctor Cider came. Yesterday when the attendant treated my son, another doctor began yelling at Cider about his obligation to report child abuse."

"We need to see those hospital records," she spoke aloud, "and what about being arrested for drunk driving?"

"The police don't stop senators for anything." She almost laughed at the question. "And if they ever had, I can only say may God help the poor officer."

"We're here Mrs. Planterson." Frank walked back to the van after opening the automatic front gate of the estate. "And you'll be safe for a while. Now I'm leaving, wrote the codes down that you'll need."

"Thank you, Frank," Mrs. Planterson said while taking his hand. "I know you're taking a big chance by helping."

"Ain't doing nothing but what's right," he said, gently releasing her hand, "but know you're in good hands with Janice."

Inside they put the small child quickly in bed, and for the next four hours, she gathered whatever information needed from the at times frightened woman.

"Well, I need to get back to town." She walked out of the study where the two talked. "I'll try to verify some of this, but I'll need a camera man."

"Can he be trusted? " she voiced fear.

"Yes," she said with a smile, "but no need to tell him everything."

"If my husband finds out I'm here," she reminded her, "he'll have you and your camera man fired for sure."

"Then I'll do the interview in the morning," she continued, "and after I do a little research on the hospital records, we'll broadcast maybe day after tomorrow."

"Michael did say something about an important meeting," she added, "and would be away for three maybe four days."

"Perfect. I'm almost relieved having the time to do the work, just leave everything to me, and I promise it will work out.

"So until tomorrow," she said, walking over and giving her a hug. "Thank you.

"Remember no phone calls," Janice reminded her, "but before I leave, are you sure this is what you want?"

"Yes, I must," she said with a slight tremor in her voice, "but if you think I'm wrong…"

"No," Janice replied with a smile. "I believe you're very courageous and concerned for your child. But I must warn you, once an investigation begins there may be things that come out that you're not aware of."

"I know Michael has dealt with many people," she admitted. "Some that are dangerous, but I must do this. My only hope is that you'll stand by me, no matter what happens with all of this."

"Well, when the arrows start flying," she said with a laugh, "I'll be standing there with you."

Saying her goodbyes, Janice left after entering all the proper codes in the house and gate. Driving several miles away from the estate, a dark sedan drove behind her and began flashing a blue and red light.

"God please tell me this isn't Planterson," she thought as she slowly pulled the van over.

"Madam, there's a rest stop about a mile from here," a large man wearing an overcoat spoke through the window, "please proceed to it."

Following his directions, she drove to the small deserted rest stop.

"Alright I demand to know who you are," she said, exiting the van and walking toward the sedan, "and are you working for the Senator?"

"Ms. Gardner, we ask the questions," the same man said while climbing out of the vehicle, "and I need to know what business you have with Mrs. Planterson."

"You already know who I am," she said, standing firm as if to defy him, "a reporter, and I do not intend to say more."

"Then you'll be going to jail," the man said, taking out handcuffs.

"Brock, that's enough." Another man, much smaller but thinner stepped up. "I'll handle this."

"So who the hell are you?" Janice demanded. "And what do you want?"

"FBI," he said, showing his badge and identification, "Carson Hayseed, Senior Agent in Charge, and Brock Olyermine is my partner."

CHAPTER SIX

W "So why are you stopping me?" she continued to question the man. "Are you working for the Senator?"

"No," he immediately replied, "we don't work for the Senator, but we need to know what Mrs. Planterson told you and how you came to know she was here."

"Agent Hayseed, I have my sources," she began, "that I will not reveal. About Mrs. Planterson, she's scared, and for good reason."

"I see," he said, taking a deep breath, "and she told you about his meeting."

"Yes the three-day meeting," she said, knowing nothing more but pretending to know all.

"What are you planning to do with the information she gives?" the agent asked, showing distress, "And please be frank."

"My cameraman will come here by tomorrow," she said with conviction. "I'll interview her, and you can watch it at 6:00."

"She knows." Brock came walking over to him. "We need to keep her from making that interview."

"If I don't do it," she was defiant, "someone else will. But if you tell me what you know, I might reconsider."

"Alright," Carson said, walking her over to the picnic bench, "have a seat."

"Fine," she said, sitting on the bench while he sat on the table, "go ahead."

"Senator Planterson is staying at a beach house," he started as Brock stood watching, "of a businessman and wants no one to know it. In two days, two other executives will arrive, and hand him $10 million."

"A bribe," she blurted out, "a lot of money for what."

"Planterson is sitting on contract they need," he continued. "Over the last few years, these men have received insider information on future government contracts. Using that information, they purchase stock, and then wait for the contract, which makes them rich. They found out about this contract, but Planterson has held it up in committee."

"So for $10 million..." she understood. "He releases the money."

"Worth over $100 million," he added, "now I'm not interested so much in the Senator but the businessmen I want. Figure with everything, he'll be through."

"You want to find the leak," she surmised, "and the businessmen."

"These are bad people," Brock spoke up, "paying someone to give them information on future contracts and low bidders."

"Along with bribing others to keep the contracts in committee," Carson added, "or in this case, release it."

"You're asking me to sit on a story until you make the arrest." She stood up and walked around the table. "That will make my story useless and jeopardize Mrs. Planterson where she could get hurt."

"Lady, this case is more important than anything you have," Brock replied as if disgusted by her reluctance to cooperate, "so get with it."

"You know about the Senator hurting the child," Janice could see it in their faces, "and did nothing."

"Yes, we know about him hurting the child," Carson admitted, "but if we got involved, our entire operation would have fallen apart. If you were to broadcast an interview with Mrs. Planterson, his career would be over."

"Which means they'd walk away with the $10 million," Brock explained, "and get the contract they wanted."

"They would be more than happy letting you destroy his career," Carson added, "and within weeks would be business as usual. It would also jeopardize one of my men, and an informant whose willing to help."

"Planterson doesn't realize how dangerous these men are," Brock said, shaking his head. "If they thought for a minute we had these men working, there's no telling what they might do to them."

"We've an agent inside the house," Carson informed her, "and an accountant who will come forward once we've made the arrest."

"Well, if they're that dangerous…" She sat back down as if to think. "I want your promise to give them protection."

"Done," Carson instantly replied. "Besides she could be helpful. But what do you want? I know there's something."

"I would want to be there when their arrested," she asked rather than demanded, "and you give me a five-minute interview."

"You'll hold off interviewing her," Carson looked down toward her, "until after we make all the arrests."

"No," she quickly replied. "I'll do the interview tomorrow like I promised her and broadcast it after the arrests."

"Deal. Carson jumped off the table and brought out his small notebook. "I'll keep my promise. Now, after your interview, call this number, and I'll tell you where you can meet us."

"Tomorrow is Friday," she stood up, "and I'll call you Saturday."

"Understand one thing," he warned her, "tell no one and concerning that five minute interview, nothing about how we came to make the case."

"I'll prepare questions for you," she said with a smile. "Now can I go?"

"Yes," Carson said finally, taking a long deep breath. "See you Saturday. By the way, there's something you need to know, and it concerns Mrs. Planterson."

"So tell me," she insisted.

"The Senator is planning to have her committed, as if ashamed having to tell her, then with this money he'll divorce her and marry his secretary."

"How does he expect to get away with that?" she asked.

"He'll, of course, resign from the Senate," he continued, "then work for the men that gave him the money."

"Then you best finish what you started," Janice said as if demanding.

When she returned to Frank's home, she noticed several lights on.

"Where have you been?" Leone came out first to greet her. "Frank said you were coming right back, but it's been hours."

"I'm fine," she said, climbing out of the van, "but can't talk about it."

"Ms. Gardner, you came here asking for our help," Leone began as Frank joined him, "we could lose our jobs helping you, so we think you owe us an explanation."

"Fine," she finally agreed, "but need your promise not to tell anyone."

After hearing their promise, they sat around the table with coffee listening.

"Well, Frank, guess we got no choice," Leone said after pushing the cup away, "think we have to call Bruno."

"Dangerous men," Frank replied while looking toward Linda, "and knowing all about hospital red tape, I think you're right."

"Whose this Bruno?" Janice blurted out.

"Ooh Mommy and Daddy are going to call Uncle Bruno," the three little ones began laughing from the bedroom door.

"What are you kids doing up this late?" Frank said, turning toward the laughter. "Get back to bed now."

"We were thirsty," Susan said, slowly moving into the kitchen, "and wanted water."

"Mommy, is Uncle Bruno coming?" little Frank asked as if excited.

"Children, go into the bathroom and get your water," Linda said, standing, "and we're just talking."

"But we like kitchen water better!" Lisa said walking toward the sink.

"Kids, you've had enough to drink today," Frank said, standing up, "come along."

"We'll be right back," Linda said with a slight smile while looking toward the three little ones that surrounded her.

"Bruno is a great storyteller and brings gifts for the children," Leone explained, "but one tough attorney that you'd want sitting beside you."

"But I can't tell him anything right now," she said, remembering the promise given.

"Don't say anything," Leone suggested, "give me a copy of the interview, and I'll send it to him."

"Leone, I don't know you that well," she admitted, "but somehow I trust you, but getting a lawyer involved might create more problems than it solves."

"She's going to need someone like Bruno," he assured her, "especially if things go as planned."

"I can't speak for her," Janice said, exhaling as she spoke, "but maybe he could meet with her and let her decide."

"Fair enough." He gently patted her hand. "Trust me, she'll agree."

"I've got to call my cameraman and get him here with all the equipment," she jumped to her feet.

"Phone's right there," Leone said, pointing to it.

The following morning, a white van having the call numbers of the station on the side pulled up to the house.

"Janice, a young man of 25 having long red hair came out of the van yelling, 'my cousin said he'd kill me if anything happens to this van.'"

"You and your cousin have been keeping that van in his shop for over a week," she said walking out to him, "while you film some music video."

"How did you know about that?" His jaw seemed to drop. "Can't fix a transmission in less than a week, so we've been using the equipment."

"That transmission was fixed two days ago," she continued, "so when did your cousin promise having the van back?"

"Wednesday," he admitted, "but how did you know?"

"Randy, I do research," she said with a smile, "and have sources. So let me introduce you to the others, and control yourself."

"Easy for you to say." His freckles seemed to get darker as he spoke. "Get myself fired and killed all in a week."

"Trust me, Randy," she said, standing in front of the husky, 6'2" man. "If everything goes right, the station will be giving you the van."

"Yeah, 'if,'" he said, following her toward the door, "and if not, we go to jail."

After introducing him to all, she grabbed him by the arm and led him out.

"Janice, I've been up all night driving," he blurted out, "I'm tired."

"After this interview," she said, opening the van door, "you can sleep for a couple hours before having to leave."

"What have you gotten me into?" he asked, climbing into the driver's seat.

"A wonderful adventure and future," she said.

Entering after giving the code to the metal gate, the two entered the mansion and found Mrs. Planterson waiting in the kitchen.

"Good morning, Ms. Gardner," she immediately replied with a smile while looking over toward the small child that sat in a high chair. "And this must be your cameraman. We just finished breakfast, but I made coffee if you would like some."

"This is Randy," she said without responding to her request, "and this is Mrs. Planterson, but you already know."

"Mrs. Planterson, I'm honored to be here." His voice revealed sincerity and a little fright. "I've seen so many pictures of you, but you're so much prettier…"

"Thank you," she said, interrupting him as he began to blush, "you're so kind."

"Where would you like me to set up my equipment?" he asked as if afraid to say any more. "I mean, which room."

"Library," Janice quickly recommended, "great room, and maybe later the living room if we need more."

"Give me 15 minutes," Randy said, turning to leave, "and I'll have everything ready for the interview."

"Mrs. Planterson, while he gets ready," Janice said, walking toward the coffee pot, "I need to tell you something that concerns you."

"Is it about Michael's affair with his secretary?" she blurted out while sitting down at the table, "I've known about it, and we've argued."

"You know about her," Janice said, as if relieved, knowing she already knew, "but it's about the people he's meeting."

"They're dangerous," she replied, looking down while shaking her head as if trying to hide the tears, "am I right?"

"Yes, I'm afraid they are," Janice said, sitting beside her, "but do you trust me?"

"Of course I do," she said, wiping the tears from her eyes and taking her hand.

"I'm arranging for you and the baby to be placed in protective custody," she began, "and may have an attorney to represent you."

"If you think its best," she answered in a soft tone, "I do have a law degree but unfortunately haven't used it in years."

"I just want the two of you to be safe," Janice told her, gently squeezing her hand, "and have someone around when I'm not."

"Janice." Randy came into the room. "Everything is ready."

"Mrs. Planterson," Janice began, "I just want you to know this interview doesn't have to be all negative. You can talk about the happier times, which I know you had."

As the interview began, she spoke of the good times when they first began campaigning. How Michael listened to the concerns of the people, but after the first term, the frustration. He came to realize the burden of office, dealing with powerful men or lobbyists and special interest groups. His promises would go unfulfilled, and his drinking began and never stopped.

"Michael came to understand his position in Washington," she said looking into the camera, "to keep the status quo. He began believing I was responsible for not being the wife that supported such a life, and even pointed out his failings. He became distant, and when he drank, angry. In many ways, I reminded him of all the broken promises, and our marriage began to crumble, even after the baby."

Janice questioned her about the many injuries, noting date and times. She avoided naming the hospitals or even doctors, knowing such information may be libel and challenged by the courts.

Every question asked was well thought out, making it easy for Mrs. Planterson to answer without hesitation. After an hour, Janice turned to Randy to end the filming.

"Very little to edit it," Randy recommended, but they have to show it."

"No editing," she insisted, "show it as we filmed it. I don't want anyone to claim we doctored the interview, or left things out."

"Alright," Randy said with a smile as he began taking down the equipment, "but truthfully I think it went great and really doesn't need editing."

"Make a copy," she said while walking over to Mrs. Planterson. "Now you'll be safe here, and I'll be back Monday."

"Janice," she said, taking her by the hand while standing, "how can we thank you?"

"Just keep being the mother I know you are," Janice responded, gently squeezing her hand, "and after the people see this interview, they'll come to know it."

"Janice," Randy said while carrying the equipment out to the van, "we're going to be famous after this."

"We just got started Randy," Janice said with a smile, "by Monday, we'll be front page famous."

"Great!" Randy said, almost shouting. "But promise from now on I'm your cameraman and that you'll tell me what you're doing."

"You're stuck with me," she said, climbing into the van, "but can't promise much more."

Once they arrived at Frank's home, the two found most sleeping.

"Shh," Susan with her finger over her thin lips whispered as she opened the door, "Mommy and Daddy are sleeping."

"What are doing up, Susan?" she whispered. "You should be sleeping."

"I heard you," Susan said silently laughing, "I wanted to open door and say hi."

"Well, hi," Janice said, giving her a quick kiss on the forehead while handing her a copy of the interview, "now when everyone wakes up, give this to your father."

"Okay," she replied, taking the cartridge and holding it against her body.

"Now promise me you'll go back to bed."

She replied with a smile, "Alright."

"Why can't we stay here for a few hours?" Randy asked as they walked back toward the van. "Catch up on some sleep."

"Need to keep going," she said, walking over to the driver's side door. "I'll drive while you use that blow up bed in the back."

"My God, what else do you know about what my cousin and I are doing?" he asked, surprised she knew about the bed.

"If you're planning to work with me," she turned to face him, "I don't want to see your name on any porn film made by your cousin."

"It's not a porn film, for your information," he exclaimed, "it's a zombie film with a few love scenes."

"Nonetheless," she said, opening the door. "Keep your name off the credits, okay?"

"I'll be in the back," he responded, showing frustration, "what else are you expecting from me?"

Ensuring he was safely inside the van, she began driving, but from time to time checked her smart phone.

"Hello," she answered the small phone as it began vibrating and chiming.

"Ms. Gardner, I assume your interview went well," Carson on the other end began.

"Think it went very well," she replied, "so now what?"

"Sending you directions," he replied, but he sounded tired. "You'll be shown where to put the van and follow my people's instructions."

After a long, eight-hour drive, she pulled unto a large industrial building.

"Madam, please pull your van inside," a gentleman wearing a polo shirt and blue jeans said, pointing to a large open door, "and wait."

Following his request, she drove into the building where three people waited as the door closed.

"Ms. Gardner, where is your cameraman?" a young woman asked while opening the door. "We were told he traveled with you."

"Sleeping in the back," she replied, turning to see him curled up on the bed. "I'll wake him."

"Please do," the young woman said, showing dissatisfaction by her presence. "We've arranged accommodations for the two of you."

"Randy, get up," she yelled out, "we're here."

"Where is here?" he quickly asked while rubbing his eyes to focus.

"Not important," she blurted out while sliding out of the driver's seat. "Just grab your equipment and follow me."

"There is no need for equipment," the young woman replied, "we'll let you know when the time is right."

Ms. Gardner." Carson came out from one of several doors to greet her. "Glad you made it, but nothing for now, so I recommend you get some sleep because it might be a very long day tomorrow."

"You no idea about what she considers a long day," Randy said stepping by her side, "wonder if she even sleeps."

"Guess we'll find out," Carson replied with a slight chuckle. "Angela take them up to their rooms."

"Fine, sir," she said, walking toward another door, "please follow me."

After climbing a staircase, she found herself in a small room having no windows but with bed a sink and shower.

"All the comforts of home," she said turning toward Angela.

"Agent Hayseed has instructed us to wake you," she said, taking a deep breath while shaking her head, "when needed."

"You don't like me being here?" Janice asked as if interested.

"Frankly, no, I don't," she immediately replied, "you're a reporter, and I've never known any that can be trusted."

"It's good to know how you feel," Janice said, sitting down on the bed. "Makes me want to work harder to gain your trust."

"Ms. Gardner, you can work 24/7," she answered while closing the door, "and I still won't trust you."

"Well it's always nice to know who your friends are," Janice said in a sarcastic tone, "and those that aren't."

Without further discussion, Janice felt the need to rest and within minutes was fast asleep.

"Ms. Gardner," Carson softly spoke, "it's time."

"Oh my God," she said, trying to wipe the sleep dirt from her eyes, "I can't broadcast looking like this."

"The businessmen just arrived," Carson said with a smile, "make yourself presentable and come down stairs to watch."

"You've camera's on them now?" she asked, rushing over to the sink while speaking. "Why didn't you tell me?"

"We document every crime," he explained while watching her washing her face and combing each out of place strand of hair, "it's used for court, not for the public."

Looking into the mirror, she seemed satisfied by her efforts and followed him downstairs to a room having several television monitors.

"Now we wait," he explained. "When they come out, my man will give us the signal the money has been transferred."

"Where do you want me and Randy?" she asked while reviewing the monitor.

"You'll be behind us," he continued. "Say nothing to anyone, is that clear? Afterwards you can say what you will, but you must make it clear the Senator is under suspicion of bribery pending further investigation."

"What about after the arrest?" she asked while Randy came running up to her with camera on his shoulder. "Your promise?"

"Five minutes," he answered, "but no names and nothing about how we came to be here, alright?"

"Agreed," she said with a smile. "I'll write up questions for you to look at before starting."

"That would be nice," he said, giving her a look of appreciation.

"Looks like we might have a little time," Randy said putting the camera down. "Here, you might want to use this."

"A complete makeup kit," she said while taking the black leather case from his hand, "with toothpaste and brushes."

"It goes along with our movie," he said with a smile, "the ladies like to look good while filming and have fresh breath when kissing."

After finding a sink, and with the help of Randy, who helped with the makeup, she was ready.

"So how do I look?" she asked, breathing into her hand to smell her breath.

"Perfect," Randy said while placing the final touches of makeup on her face.

"Alright everyone," Carson called out, "the cars have arrived, so they're coming out."

Following closely behind, she was startled to find they were within walking distance of the home. Carson stopped everyone by the side of the building, as several men, including the Senator, left the residence,

"Now," he said, taking out his radio and speaking.

"Randy, please get this right," she said as agents swarmed around the group of men, "and make sure you show them handcuffing the people."

"I know my job," he blurted out as he continued to film the entire event. "Now get in front of the camera and start talking."

"This is Janice Gardner, and as I speak, Senator Planterson is being handcuffed on suspicion of bribery," she quickly began while Randy continued to show her face along with the men being detained. "It's a sad day for America."

For several minutes, she went on to speak to the people, making sure each minute of the arrest was on film.

"My God, Janice," Randy said as the agents transported the men away and the entire street was empty, "you were fantastic! I've never heard anyone speak like you."

"Don't know what came over me," she said, blushing somewhat, "but when the camera came on, and they were arresting them the words just came."

"I'm getting this to our station," he said, turning to leave, "and having them hear you."

"Tell them there is more coming," she said, "an interview with the agent in charge."

"It'll take me about 10 minutes," he said jogging off, "and I'll be there."

As she walked toward the building where they had started, she began to think of the questions needed.

"Well, you'd be happy to hear we got the money," Carson came walking over to her, "and been told one of the men has already confessed and is willing to cooperate."

"What about the Senator?" she asked. "How much trouble is he in?"

"Got him carrying the money," he answered, "and witnesses that heard the promises given to accept the bribe. By the way, heard some of the things you were saying, I was impressed."

"Thank you," she said, almost embarrassed to accept the compliment.

"Now about that five-minute interview," he spoke while looking for her cameraman and taking out his pen and small notebook. "Take a little time to write them down."

Within minutes, she wrote down the questions, then handed the sheet of paper.

"Good questions," Carson said after reading each one. "Off the record, can tell you more arrests will be coming once we've issued search warrants on the offices and homes of the businessmen."

"So you're going to tell me it's an ongoing investigation..." She realized what he was saying. "Nothing more?"

"Can't say more until my commander has a look at things," he admitted, "and once we've got the search warrants. However, if you stick around until nine, where a press conference will be held, I'll allow you the first two questions."

"Room will be crowded," she reminded, "with a lot better reporters."

"Ms. Gardner," Carson said, taking her hand, "none will ever be better than you."

As promised, she was given the first two questions during the conference, and immediately afterwards the two headed back to Hopeland.

"Look at this," Randy said while opening his computer. "Our story was the first to break and has tripled the ratings."

"Anything from the boss?" she asked, knowing all was unauthorized.

"Haven't gotten that far," he admitted. "Wanted to see the good news first before finding out we've been fired."

"Well, find out," she demanded. "We've one more story before the ax falls."

"Oh God," he said, thumbing through the many folders. "Corporate wants to meet with us immediately. What do you think they want? Maybe they found out I took this van."

"Think the van is least of their concerns," Janice responded with a smile. "Probably having their lawyers writing up all the violations."

Arriving at Frank's home, they noticed a large chauffeured limousine sitting in front of the house with the driver standing outside. Entering, they noticed all three children sitting on bikes or tricycles, and the adults sitting around the dinner table.

"Lookie what Uncle Bruno brought us." Susan came running over to her as if finding her long lost sister. "And he's wanting to meet you."

"So, you're the child that brought down the house of cards." He stood only six feet but had broad shoulders and sandy brown hair. "Got to admit, one helluva story."

"Bruno, not in front of the children," she stood revealing a slender but beautiful body and lovely face. "You know how they love to imitate you."

"Uncle Bruno is in trouble now," little Frank began laughing. "Be sitting in the corner."

"Ms. Gardner," his voice seemed to carry throughout the room as he approached. "My wife Kathy is my guiding light and always right."

"Kathy," Randy blurted out, "you were in all those movies and Broadway."

"Along with being a model," Bruno proudly spoke up while taking Janice's hand, "and honoring me by being my wife."

"Ms. Gardner," Kathy said walking over to her. "Last name is Wyatt and so happy finally to meet you."

"They're like family," Linda said walking through the door carrying a large planter of food, "and they spoil our children."

"Oh, Linda," Kathy with a smile spoke up. "Ours are all grown, and we so enjoy doing it because they're so perfect."

"Frank isn't, Aunty Kathy," Susan spoke up. "Mommy had him sitting in the corner."

"Susan," Linda turned toward her with an expression of displeasure.

"Well, he was," she said in a soft tone.

"Reviewed your interview," Bruno spoke up as if changing the subject, "knew right away Ms. Planterson needed me."

"We were talking," Leone spoke up, "and thought maybe it best you and Bruno go out to the estate alone."

"Sounds like a mighty good idea," Bruno spoke up. "No need all of you joining."

"Van or limousine?" Janice asked.

"What do you think?" Bruno said walking over and kissing his wife on the cheek.

As they sat in the back of the spacious vehicle, Janice looked over toward the man who seemed just as interested in her as she was to him.

"You've known Leone and Frank long?" she asked, not waiting for him to start the questioning.

"Leone while he was in the army," he said, opening the small cabinet as he spoke, "and Frank when he was town marshal."

"Sounds like there's a story there," she quickly replied.

"Yeah maybe," he answered, bringing out two glasses and a bottle of wine. "Sure someday the two will tell you about it. Now, would you care for a glass, or would you rather ask questions that I'll not answer?"

"Too personal," she continued to pry.

"Some," he said, pouring the wine. "Mostly good memories that I care not to share with others I just came to know."

"I'll have that wine now," she said, taking the glass from his hand.

As they entered the grounds of the mansion, they had nearly finished the bottle.

"Wish now I had refused the wine," she said, sitting back trying to compose herself, "and asked questions."

"Come along," he said taking her hand as the vehicle came to a stop, "just try to keep up with me."

"Ms. Gardner," Mrs. Planterson came running toward the two as they entered, I been watching the news. What's it all mean?"

"Means your husband is in a whole lot of trouble," Bruno said standing behind Janice, "which is why I came."

"I sorry not having told you," Janice began her apologizes, "but the FBI made me promise, but none of this has anything to do with you."

"But if what they say is true," she began crying, "he'll be going to jail and what will happen to the two of us."

"Which is why I brought Mr. Bruno Wyatt with me," she said, stepping aside. "He's an attorney who is here to help."

"Now, there, Ms. Planterson," he said, stepping up to her while trying to comfort her, "from here on out I'm here for you and the child."

"I've no money," she replied trying to compose herself. "Where can I go?"

"Having reviewed the interview," he began in a soft tone, "first thing is clearing your name. We'll start by talking to this Doctor Cider, then pulling hospital records."

"I've spoken with the agent in charge of the investigation," Janice began, "they'll place you in protective custody."

"Ms. Planterson, you let me deal with them," Bruno quickly spoke up. "Meantime, you're here, and I'll see that all needs are taken care of."

"But Bruno," Janice objected, "the agent said they'll help."

"Of course, they will," he said with a smile, "but under my terms. Once we start our inquiry into Doctor Cider's involvement, think the hospitals will be rather anxious to settle..

"Settle?" Ms. Planterson spoke up as if confused, "I don't understand."

"You were an abused wife of a prominent public figure," he pointed out, "and Doctor Cider covered it up by falsely accusing you of being a threat to yourself. No doubt the hospital had to know, and by doing so are culpable."

"But how can you ever prove it?" she asked while exhaling.

"Once we start our inquiry," he revealed with confidence, "people will line up to help you."

"Ms. Planterson." Janice stepped toward her. "I trust him, and if you trust me…"

"I do," Mrs. Planterson said, taking her hand, "but please don't forget us."

"Never happen," she said, squeezing her hand.

"Mr. Wyatt." She looked toward him. "Is there anything you can do for Michael?"

"I could," he admitted, "but you're my client, and I'll be closely working to protect the two of you. Mr. Planterson's troubles will be his alone. My only concern is to see that none of it comes to you."

"There will be things you're not aware of," Janice warned, "just let Mr. Wyatt handle them for you."

Will it get nasty," she asked, "and hurt our child?"

"Might get messy," Bruno spoke up, "but that's why I'm here."

"Along with me," Janice spoke up.

CHAPTER SEVEN

For a week, they watched as Bruno did his magic, even allowing her to interview him, and he spelled out his concerns. But it was the second interview of Agent Hayseed that convinced her that all would be made right, especially when confirming her claim of being the victim of abuse.

With the story fading in the news cycle, Janice decided it was time to leave and face management.

"Well, thanks for everything," she said to the sad looking group after placing what little she had in the van, "I wish there was a way…"

"Just promise to come back," Linda said while giving her a hug, "the children adore you, and you know how we all feel."

Bruno said, "If you have any trouble…"

Leone walked over to take her hand.

"I know," she said, giving him a hug instead of a handshake, "just call."

"Same goes here, Janice," he whispered in her ear.

"Take care of yourself, girl," Frank walked over as Leone stepped aside. "We think of you as family."

"What about me?" Randy asked, as if trying not to be forgotten.

"Same goes to you," Linda said, giving him a hug while the others a handshake.

"Well, look who finally came back," Samuel said, standing in the doorway of his office. "Thought I asked that you come back immediately."

"Our work wasn't done," Janice said while walking toward him as others stood clapping, "so if we're fired, tell me now."

"Got a dozen requests for interviews by other stations," he said with a smile, "and we've captured the attention of all the networks. The Plantersons interview was a smash hit, and breaking the story of the Senator's arrest has made ratings through the roof and beyond what we expected."

"Truthfully," she admitted, "I had no idea about any of this when I started."

"Sir, about the van," Randy spoke up, "sorry having taken it without getting your approval or go ahead."

"Yes, about that…" he said, looking toward the man. "I gave my approval, but in the future, no more joy riding."

"So what now?" Janice asked with interest.

"Not sure," he admitted. "Come tomorrow, you're going to meet with the President of the corporation, who's flying down here. Guess he has questions and wants to meet with you in person."

"Is that good or bad?" she continued to question him.

"Find out tomorrow," he said, being truthful, "but you did great."

Arriving at work early, Janice disposed of the nightly coffee and made fresh.

"Maybe they decided not to come," Randy said, walking through the door at 9:00.

"Mr. Acorn, may I introduce you to Janice Gardner and Randy Kemp," Samuel said, walking beside a middle aged man wearing a polo shirt and blue jeans.

"Well, what do you think, gentlemen?" Acorn turned around to face four others wearing suits and having briefcases. "Just what are we going to do with this lovely lady?"

"Hollywood," one of the men suggested.

"No," he immediately snapped, "too good with such a fine looking ass."

Immediately, without thought or reason, Janice slapped the man's face.

"You can fire me now," she said, stepping back after the attack, "but I'll not let anyone think it's my ass that gets work."

"It's about damn time," he said, looking toward the four men who appeared shocked by her action. "Now that's what I've been looking for."

"Sir, are you alright?" one of the men walked over to speak.

"Fine," Acorn said, finding a desk and sitting on top of it. "Ms. Gardner, for two years, I've told three female reporters that very line and a lot worse to the men. None objected, until now. No, you are not fired, but promoted."

"Where to, sir?" another asked while opening his briefcase.

"There's a highly classified base in the Middle East," he began, "the troops are doing a valuable service, but my reporters give me nothing but official reports. Want you there, and do your job to get me what I want."

"Firsthand accounts," she replied, "to show our viewers."

"Reporters claim the officer in charge won't allow them to leave the base," he explained, saying, "He'll not allow them to risk their lives under his watch. In six months, I'll know if you were a one hit wonder, or a reporter."

"When do I go?" she asked. "And can Randy come?"

"Tonight." He stood up. "Pack what you need for a few days, the rest make a list. Your camera operator can go, if he wants."

"Sir," one of his men said, closing his briefcase. He walked over and whispered in his ear.

"Make that in two days," he corrected himself. "Have to see a doctor about some shots and paperwork."

"Shots?" Randy blurted out. "What kind?"

"Ms. Gardner," he said, ignoring Randy's question, "I expect good things from you, so find a way to make it happen."

The two days turned to three weeks of doctors with needles, and paperwork with interviews along with background checks.

"Man is it hot," Randy said, leaving the Humvee, "can't believe we left air condition for this."

"Stop complaining," Janice ordered while taking out her luggage. "I'm just glad to get away from all those doctors."

"Speaking of doctors," Randy begrudging said, taking out the large camera, "Did I tell you how my arm swelled up after one of those shots?"

"Yes, I believe you mentioned it 30 or 40 times on the plane," she said while waiting for someone to tell them where to go, "but it looks alright now."

"Had I lost it," he said, walking toward her as the vehicle moved away, "what would you do about that."

"Find another cameraman," she said with a smile, "now hush."

"Madam, I've been asked to show the two of you to your quarters." She stood no taller than 5'10" with blond hair but muscular. "Please follow me."

Entering a small wooden structure with air conditioning, she found two rooms, each having beds and shower along with folding chairs.

"This will be your sleeping quarters," he explained. "We'll attempt to provide further comfort once you're settled."

"Sergeant, I'll take over." He entered the room where she quickly stood at attention.

"Very good, sir." Without saluting, she quickly left.

"Lady, I'm here to go over some of the rules," he began while removing his cap that revealed the thick black hair and bright green eyes along with a slender body.

"You're a lieutenant," Janice began while noticing the black fiber bars on the collar. "Right. So just what do you call this base? I'm sure it has a name."

"Nowhere," he said with a smile.

"I don't quite understand," she said, puzzled by his comment.

"This base is nowhere on any map," he admitted, "and classified as not being here."

"So if you're not here," she replied, continuing to question him, "what is it you do?"

"Convoys," he said while standing, "we take medical and food to a local sanctuary hospital some 30 miles from here."

"I noticed females soldiers," she once again began, "how many and their jobs?"

"Numbers classified," he answered, "but they are soldiers doing their duty."

"So tell us about the rules," she said, taking three of the folding chairs. "Sitting's allowed right?"

"Of course," he said, opening the chair and sitting. "First, we're in a combat zone, so no names. Please when speaking with us, use rank: sergeants, corporals, and privates."

"No saluting," she added, "but why?"

"This will avoid our families from possible harmed," he explained, "or exposed to unnecessary harassment back home. The enemy we face has influence, and with computers and a following."

"Understand completely," she immediately replied. "Don't we, Randy?"

"Yeah," he spoke up while sitting.

"Now, for your safety, lady," he began to relax somewhat, "I'd suggest you wear uniforms rather than civilian clothes. They watch us, and might think you're important, so it might be best blending in. Finally, the Colonel will brief you, twice a day."

"I didn't come all this way to be briefed," she said, standing.

"Colonel has issued orders." He stood up. "You're not to leave the base."

"And I don't intend sitting around doing nothing," she blurted out.

"Take it up with the Colonel," he said, placing his cap on.

"Colonel has already taken it up," he strolled in with a perfect uniform of a combat officer having gray hair. "You will not leave base. No harm will befall you, not under my watch, is that clear?"

"I came here to report a story," she said, walking over to the man who would be perfect for a poster of what an officer should look like, "not your report, but mine."

"Lieutenant make them as comfortable as possible," he said, turning to leave, "and you have your orders."

"Yes, sir," he said, again without saluting.

"Lieutenant, it can't be that bad," she said, as if attempting to flirt with him. "I mean, we can at least discuss the possibility."

"Happily married, lady," he replied, showing her the gold band, "besides, the colonel is right."

"WOW," Randy said, shaking his head, "even your feminine charms didn't work."

"Shut up," she snapped.

After three weeks of watching several convoy's come and go, Janice began to think she would be no better than the other reporters.

"Randy, I intend getting on one of those trucks," she began while watching the troops loading the trucks, "and see where they go and make it a story."

Without warning, explosions began peppering the entire base, and soldiers began scrambling for cover. However, many fell to the power of the blast.

"Randy, keep that camera going," she yelled out over the loud explosions while running toward a young soldier exposed and screaming for help.

"Damn it, Janice," Randy yelled out as he followed her, "you're going to get me killed, and I'll be no use to you."

"Think we best get you out of here," she said, kneeling beside a young female sergeant and ignoring Randy's comment, "and move you behind that wall."

"How bad is it?" the young girl asked while Janice pulled her behind the wall. "Am I going to die?"

"Got a pretty large piece of lead in your leg," Janice answered her while looking over the rest of her body, "but otherwise you're okay."

"It hurts so bad," she said, grabbing her leg, "please pull it out."

"Don't think that would be such a good idea, Sergeant," Janice said, trying to calm the young girl. "Let's keep it there until a doctor pulls it out."

"Look over there," Randy yelled out while pointing toward the Colonel exposing himself to the explosions while helping the wounded and pulling them to safety, "can't believe it."

"Colonel, over here!" Janice yelled out. "And Randy, you better be filming this."

After pulling the last soldier to a safe place, he ran toward the three.

"How are you doing, Sergeant?" he asked while sliding beside her.

"Colonel, I would appreciate it if you would get someone up there," Janice began while looking toward the hills that surrounded them, "and get this nonsense stopped."

"Got three squads moving up there now," he replied quickly.

"Might want to send a few more up there," she recommended, "and she could use a doctor for her leg."

"Get right on it," he said while getting ready to run. "You'll be alright here?"

"Be taking care of the sergeant," Janice promised.

"Can't believe you," the sergeant began, "I'm so scared, and you're talking to the Colonel as if nothing happened."

"Every bone in my body is trembling," Janice said with a smile.

"You'd never know it," she answered.

"It's the uniform," she continued to keep the conversation going while looking around as the explosions continued.

"Be truthful," she asked, as if begging, "am I going to lose my leg?"

"No," she quickly replied, "but when the doctor takes that hunk of junk from your leg, tell him that you want it."

"Why would I want that?" She seemed confused.

"In a few years from now, while your children sit around you," she began, "you'll tell them a mighty good story how you came to have it."

"You're wonderful," the sergeant said, and for the first time, she began to smile. "I forgot about the pain."

"The Colonel told me to get over here." A young man with two others having a stretcher came running over as explosions and rifle fire began around the surrounding hill. "Shrapnel in her leg, so be careful."

"Tell the doctor I want it," the sergeant yelled out, "not to throw it away."

"Alright," the young man replied as if shocked by her insistence. ."I'll make sure he knows to keep it for you."

After several minutes of intense rifle fire, the bombardment ceased.

"It's about time," Janice said while standing up and looking toward Randy, whose face was pale white. "Tell me you got everything on film."

"Not that you're concerned," he blurted out, "but I'm fine."

"Good," she replied while walking toward him, "but…"

"Yeah, I filmed it all," he said, shaking his head, "nearly got myself killed doing it."

"Before broadcasting it," she said while dusting her clothes and straightening her hair, "I want to make a brief statement."

"Ready when you are," he said, placing the camera on his shoulder.

"Today, Randy and I experienced an attack by the insurgents using rockets," she began in a soft tone, "we both witnessed the Colonel risking his life to pull the wounded to safety as the shells burst around him. I now understand why the men and women are so devoted and loyal to such a brave man."

"I'll get this out right away," Randy replied while running toward their room.

"Got wounded," the young Lieutenant yelled out as he came walking in and looking over toward her, "need stretchers and medics. Glad to see you're not hurt, lady."

"Is lady my official rank, Lieutenant?" she yelled out.

"If you insist," he replied in a joking manner.

Later after sending the entire film to the networks and giving the Colonel a copy of the day's action, she sat quietly, wondering what tomorrow might bring.

"Lady," the Lieutenant said, entering the room, "Colonel thought you might want to know that the Sergeant is doing well and transported out."

"That's wonderful news," Janice said with a smile. "What about the others?"

"A couple in a bad way," he admitted, "but all transported out alive. Oh, the doctor wanted you to know, the Sergeant kept her trophy."

"Appreciate you telling me," she said in a sincere tone.

"One more thing," he continued, "Colonel ordered that you're allowed to come with us in the morning. Convoy leaves at 6:00, won't wait."

"Be there promptly at six," she said, wanting to hug the man but knew better.

The following morning, the two were placed inside the armored vehicle and traveled the dusty roads toward the sanctuary. Entering the large compound having four separate areas with barbed wire, there were with hundreds of people in tents.

"We're here," the Lieutenant said as the vehicle came to a stop. "While they unload, I'll introduce you to the doc."

Entering another guarded gate, they entered one of several tents having 30 to 40 people laying on cots.

"Doc, want you to meet someone," the Lieutenant yelled out, "a reporter."

He stood 6'2" with short black hair, and his dark brown skin seemed to shine as he walked toward them.

"A reporter," he said in a soft tone, "how did that happen?"

"Had a little trouble at the base yesterday," he began, "calm as ever ordered the Colonel around."

"Never ordered," she interjected, looking into his handsome face and noticing how he stood so proudly. "I just asked."

"Even treated wounded while under fire," another soldier spoke up, "helluva lady."

"I'm honored having you here." He gently took her hand where she felt a soft warmth. "You must tell me about it."

"Got a copy of it, sir," Randy spoke up, "if you care to watch."

"This is my cameraman, Randy," she said, trying to catch her breath. "He was the brave one, not me."

"Would enjoy reviewing it," he said, releasing her hand, "and while doing so please look around, and if you have any questions…"

"Doc, got paperwork for you to sign," the Lieutenant said while they started toward the door, "and we've been hearing rumors that the insurgents have themselves a new leader, which might help explain what happened yesterday."

"They've replaced leaders before," he reminded the group, "and we've given no reason for them to attack us."

"Just passing it along," he responded as they entered his office.

Looking over the many patients, Janice wondered how so many seeking medical attention learned of this place. Within 10 minutes, the small group came out of the office, most laughing.

"Be checking on the unloading," the Lieutenant said as they walked over to her. "I'll hand you over to the Doc."

"So, Doc, tell me about this place," she asked while studying his strong handsome features. "How many patients, and where are they from?"

"Classified," he replied, "we give them numbers, not names for their protection. Now you can interview anyone inside the hospital, but no one outside."

"I don't understand," she seemed puzzled.

"We segregated the four groups outside," he explained, "if you choose one over the others, it appears preference. Our security is local militia, no threat to anyone."

"Well, what about you?" She decided to change the subject. Where you're from, or married with children?"

"Classified," he repeated, "but off the record, Arkansas."

"WOW, a doctor from there…" she began.

"Might be surprised that there are many black doctors," he said, interrupting her with a smile, "and lawyers, along with other professions."

"I didn't mean it the way it sounded," she said, attempting to apologize.

"Sure you didn't," he said, as if making her feel bad, "lot of that going around."

"You must think me a horrible person…" Her chin rested on her chest.

"No," he said, taking his hand and lifting her cheek up "I find it amusing. You're forgiven, remember I am from the Bible belt that attends church."

"A true believer?" she asked.

"A believer, but not a fanatic," he said looking toward the many patients, "seen my share of miracles. Take number 138: should have died when he lost that arm."

"Looks healthy enough," she said while looking at the young boy of 12 with his mother beside him, "what happened?"

"Insurgent took his family and made him a soldier," he explained, "he handled the fuse to the land mines and fell. Took his hand, and they left him to die. His mother escaped the camp, found him. and brought him here. Couldn't save the arm, but somehow, he survived."

"Mother's love," Janice said, remembering her own experience. "Now they're both safe."

"They shot the father," he added, "as example on disobeying their rules."

"Have to go, lady," the Lieutenant said while sticking his head inside the door.

"Lady," she said, turning back to him, "My rank, but it's Janice."

"You plan to return?" he asked. "If so, maybe we could have a meal together."

"Yes, I'm coming back," she promised, "and a meal would be nice."

"Then I'll look forward to it, Janice," he said, taking her hand and kissing it, "and the name is Russell Greenland when we're alone."

"Doc is real nice," she began as she entered the armored vehicle, "and handsome."

"Yeah, real nice," the Lieutenant replied, "couldn't say about handsome as a man."

"As a women," she immediately corrected him, "he is. When can I come back? Would like to talk with some of the patients."

"Ask first, lady," he turned around in his seat to confront her, "remember rules."

"There are nothing but rules," she blurted out.

"Lady, all of us obey the rules," he said, giving her a warning, "otherwise people get hurt or even dead, understand?"

"I'm sorry," she responded, realizing he was trying to make her understand. "I do understand."

"Good," he said, turning around and relaxing.

"Can I ask if he's married?" she said, changing the subject. "Or is that classified?"

"It is," he answered without turning, "but heard him say he was."

When they returned to the base, her thoughts immediately turned to the man, maybe out of loneliness or that he was both kind and gentle.

"Janice," Randy came running in, "got some great news."

"Tell me," she said, snapping out of her daydream.

"First, the rating on our film broke all records," he began, "and everyone wants an interview when we return."

"Well, that won't be for a while," she reminded him, "so what else?"

"They arrested the person supplying the information to the businessmen," he continued, "a low level typist. FBI said he wasn't paid in cash, but heroin. They even made a case against the dealer, drugs and insider trading."

"A typist," she said, shaking her head, "unbelievable."

"Man, we're going to be famous when we get back," he said sitting down and exhaling. "Two major stories, and we're just getting started."

For the next two months, she returned to the sanctuary five times. Each time, she and Russell spent together either with quiet meals or walking through the hospital or all the different outside groups. With each meeting, she began to sense emotions that she could no longer control or hide.

"So, each time you greet the people," she asked while walking with him, "you have to meet with all the different groups?"

"Show no favorites," he said as they entered the first group of refugees, "we treat everyone the same. No doubt, the insurgents have come here for help."

"People back home aren't quite sure what to make of all this," she replied, "and all wonder why you do it."

"Someone has to," he said, holding her hand as they walked. "If not me, who?"

"Russell, before leaving," she looked toward him, "is there somewhere we could be alone for a few moments?"

"I've a small sleeping room," he said as if knowing how she felt, but...

"Please say nothing," she said, holding his hand and pushing him along,

Once inside they began kissing, without words they quickly disrobed, and for the brief moment made love on the small bed.

"I have to go," she whispered while hearing the Lieutenant shouting her name, "but maybe next time, we skip the walk."

"There's so much I wish to tell you," he whispered, "and yes. We skip the walk."

"Finally. Where were you?" the Lieutenant demanded to know after she slipped out of the room unnoticed. "Looked all over and thought about leaving you behind."

"Needed to be alone," she said while walking past him, "being married you should know why."

"Oh," he replied, "well, next time tell someone. Now let's go."

"Lieutenant!" Doc came out running toward him. "Got a few more items I need for the next supply drop."

"Candles?" the Lieutenant asked, looking at the list. "And pillows?"

"Our generators from time to time stop," he replied, "and for the ladies."

"I'll see what I can do," he replied, folding the list and placing it in his pocket.

"What gives?" Randy asked, sensing her quiet demeanor. "You haven't ordered me around since leaving and now you're just staring out the window."

"Just tired," she in a soft tone replied, "and thinking."

Once they arrived at the base, Janice avoided the dinner call and decided on a long warm shower. As nighttime fell, she laid in bed thinking of the moment they had.

"Lady, may I enter?" the Lieutenant asked after knocking on the door.

"Please," she immediately answered.

"Noticed you skipped dinner," he said, handing her a heated MRE meal, "thought you might like this."

"Thank you," she said, taking it from his hand while he sat.

"You know he's married," he began. "One of rules is not to get involved."

"How did you know?" Her hand began shaking. "It was the first time."

"My duty to look out for my people," he began, "which includes you."

"I care for him," she said as small tears began to form. "He's…"

"Handsome and kind," he remembered her words, "but you're not in America, and here, the conditions are challenging for everyone."

"Are you going to inform the Colonel?" she asked.

"No, you're both over 21," he calmly replied, "just wanted you to be aware."

"Thank you," she said, laying the package down.

"You're both good people," he said as he stood up. "Just don't let it be a problem with me or why you're here. You might suggest to the Doc that he zips it up all the way.

"Lieutenant…" she wanted to say more.

"See you at breakfast," he said, walking toward the door, "and enjoy the MRE."

For three days, Janice anxiously waited for the convoy to start, and when notified, even helped load the supplies.

"How long will you be today?" she asked the Lieutenant, who seemed to play with her emotions. "Well, if you're so anxious to get back, 30 minutes if you help."

"Thirty minutes," she said, shocked by his comment, "we were planning to do interviews with those in the hospital."

"Well, in that case," he said, chuckling as he spoke, "tell the men to take their time and give you four hours."

"We're doing interviews today?" Randy asked as if hearing it for the first time.

Once they arrived, the two quickly entered the hospital, while the others began to unload the trucks.

"Hello Doc," Janice said in a soft voice, "like to interview a few patients, with your approval, of course."

"Certainly," he said, agreeing without questioning. "If I might recommend three."

Calling each by their number, he allowed them to use his office for privacy. Within two hours, they had interviewed all three, and two others.

"The people are serving lunch to the men," he began, "to show their gratitude for bringing in the supplies. If you're hungry, please go out and join them. I'm sure you'll enjoy a fine hot meal."

"Starved," Randy blurted out as he picked up the camera.

"Go on and have lunch," she insisted, "I want to talk with some others."

"You sure?" he asked, starting to the door.

"Take your time and enjoy," she replied as he fled the office.

"Think we have time?" he asked while giving her a kiss.

"We better," she responded, removing her uniform shirt, "because it's all I've been thinking about over the last few days."

It seemed the good Lieutenant gave them time to be together, and when finally entering the room, shouted out to avoid embarrassing them.

"Doc, need your signature," he said, walking in and finding them sitting quietly on the bed, "and got one case of candles and just six pillows as you ordered."

"Thank you, Lieutenant," he said, standing up and walking toward him.

"Lieutenant, we were talking…" She quickly stood. "Would it be possible for me to stay here until the next convoy? I'd like to speak with some other patients, just in case."

"Janice, we used the last of the film," Randy said, walking in, "and I need to order more when we get back."

"Perfect," she replied with enthusiasm, "I'll stay and set up the interviews while you go back and order the film."

"Colonel might not like it," the Lieutenant said, but he noticed how the two waited for his approval. "Doc, can you promise that no harm will come to her?"

"Oh yes," he eagerly answered, "I promise."

"Fine," the Lieutenant said, shaking his head. "May be four maybe five days before coming back."

"We'll be fine," Doc said, taking the paperwork from his hand.

"Doc," the Lieutenant said as all left the room, "depending on you to keep your word and not let her out of your sight."

"Four or five days together," Janice said once they were alone, grabbing him around the neck, "and remember not to let me out of your sight."

"I don't have rounds for another hour," he said as he unbuttoned her uniform.

That night neither slept, but made passionate love many times.

The next morning, the two up already, walked out to perform morning rounds.

"I've agreed to stay here another three months," he began speaking while removing a bloody bandage from one of the many patients, "they're having a hard time trying to find another doctor to come here."

"You didn't do that for me," she asked while watching him work.

"Had I known," he said with a smile, "maybe, but no. I agreed five weeks ago."

"I've less than two months," she added, "maybe a week or two more."

"When my wife learned of it," he continued, "she wrote to say she was meeting with a divorce attorney. Married five years, first two maybe three happily, but the last two we began drifting apart."

"You still love her," she said, almost afraid of his answer.

"When I first came here, it was her hope I'd come back to her," he explained, "never to leave again. Her family is very wealthy and influential, and I was able to build a nice practice, making millions. She wanted a luxury social life of parties, and I just wanted my life to mean something and help people like these. When I returned here, we both knew our marriage was over. But do I still love her, can't say."

"I just don't want to be the one that ends a marriage," she added.

"Funny," he said, standing up after redressing the wound, "if anyone is responsible it's me and everyone here."

Over the days together, he spoke of his childhood, without television but books and board games with his parents. A geek in school who never achieved greatness in sports but academically awarded scholarships.

On the morning of the sixth day, the Lieutenant arrived with Randy.

"Lady, you got two hours," he said, walking in, "for those interviews."

"Randy, set your camera up here," she asked while looking over toward the Doc. "He's the one I want to interview."

"But I'm not very good with interviews," he explained.

"Let me handle it," she said, touching his hand, "just be yourself."

For over an hour she asked the questions, and he surprised himself by explaining every detail in ways all could understand.

"WOW, now that was a great interview," Randy said when she ordered cut.

"You did great, Russell," she said as Randy left the room, "and I want you to know that I love you."

"You've stolen my heart," he said, giving her a kiss.

CHAPTER EIGHT

While alone, her only thoughts were of Russell, remembering the warm candle lit nights with the soft pillows as they made passionate love. She had never known such romance or the tenderness he showed. Now all she wanted was to return to be in his arms once again.

She was suddenly thrust from the fond memory when the Lieutenant knocked on her door and asking to be allowed entry.

"Come in, Lieutenant," she replied while walking toward the door.

"There's a convoy leaving in the morning," he began, "can't allow you to go."

"Why not?" she asked, exhaling sharply while speaking.

"Been training replacements for the last month," he explained. "Most of us are short timers now, and I need to see how they work together. Be sending five regulars with them, just as observers to see what mistakes they make."

"You're not going with them," she said, surprised to hear that he was staying behind.

"No," he admitted, as if having been ordered, "Colonel thinks they'd be waiting for me to tell them what to do. Once they return, I'll go along on the next convoy to correct the mistakes. You can come along then. Just be patient; I'll get you back.

"Lieutenant," she asked, seeing an opportunity, "would you care if I interviewed the short timers that are planning to leave."

"I'll speak with the Colonel," he replied, pausing for a moment, "but don't see the harm."

As requested, she began interviewing the young men and women, who spoke highly of their mission and officers.

"Janice, everything we do is like solid gold," Randy said while checking his equipment after having completed several interviews. "We're pulling in ratings they haven't seen in months."

"It's why we're here," she calmly answered him, as if unconcerned with the ratings. "Just hope it does some good."

While having dinner with the troops and discussing the interviews, alarms began to sound and the entire rooms cleared.

"Whatever is happening," she yelled out as Randy sat looking confused, "we need to get out there and find out. Hurry and get your camera, might need it."

Outside, she saw several of the convoy trucks riddled with bullet holes, and corpsmen removing wounded.

"Lieutenant," she ran over to him as they continued to remove the wounded from the vehicles, "what happened?"

"Insurgents ambushed the convoy," he said while watching the commotion. "Three dead and 11 wounded, but they didn't leave anyone behind."

"If you order me," she began, "I'll not film."

"No, won't order it," he said as he began walking away, "people need to know."

Within minutes, he along with others, carried the wounded inside, allowing the two to film the event.

"Never saw so much blood," Randy said while pointing the camera inside one of the bullet-riddled trucks. "Can't believe anyone survived this."

"Just do your job, Randy," she insisted. "Film it all?"

As Randy filmed, Janice spoke of the terrible tragedy that befell the brave men and women, pointing out they carried only food and medical supplies. That night, helicopters came and went, transporting the most critical patients to hospitals aboard American naval ships. By the following afternoon, the base was back to normal operations; however, the Lieutenant was absent from the daily inspections and meals.

On the second day, trucks with supplies began to arrive that seemed to fill the entire compound.

"Something's going on," Janice said while looking over toward Randy, "and we need to find out."

Walking out of the room, she heard the sound of jets passing over and circling the hills, as if looking for any sign of trouble.

"Lady, just what are you doing," the Lieutenant asked while standing next to her.

"Damn, you scared the life out of me," she said turning, "and how do you get so close so quietly?"

"Soldier's secret," he said with a smile as he looked toward the sky where the jets had just left. "They're scanning the hills for any insurgents."

"Planning to send another convoy?" she asked while two more trucks arrived.

"Biggest one yet," he replied, "since the last one didn't arrive, we decided to send double supplies. Figure the spotter watching will be reporting our progress, but the sanctuary needs the food and medicine."

"Can't you just find the spotter," she asked, "and stop him?"

"In time," he said, exhaling while looking over at the trucks, "in time."

"Will I be allowed to go along?" she asked. "With so many, I won't be any trouble.

"No, not this one," he answered. "Maybe if all goes well next time."

"Lieutenant, sir," a young corporal called to him as he appeared near a truck. "Colonel is requesting your presence."

"Be right there," he yelled back. "Well, nice talk, lady."

"They're planning something big," she said, walking in and finding Randy brushing out the camera. "Be ready to leave in an instant with that camera ready to film."

For two days, she watched every move made by a particular Sergeant, who seemed close to the Lieutenant.

"Look," she said while peeking through the small window, "that Sergeant is putting something in the Lieutenant's vehicle, and it's covered."

"So?" Randy walked over and gave a quick glance.

"Grab the camera and what you need," she said while continuing to watch. "We're going on a little trip."

"What are trying to do," he said, grabbing his camera and supplies, "get me killed, or even arrested?"

"Just follow me," she said, waiting for the man to leave, "and be very quiet."

"Opening the door," she said as she ran toward the vehicle with Randy closely behind. "Get under the tarp on that side," she added, pointing to where she wanted him to hide after opening the rear door. "I'll be on this side hiding—and be quiet."

"Sergeant, they all understand the order?" the Lieutenant asked as Janice listened from under the tarp.

"Everyone knows what to do," he reassured him, "be leaving 20 minutes after us. Take alternative routes, and make plenty dust."

"Good," he replied as if satisfied.

After 30 minutes under the tarp, Janice slowly rose her head up.

"So what's the plan Lieutenant," she asked while appearing in his rearview mirror.

"Sergeant, how did she?" he blurted out.

"Had nothing to do with it, sir," he said, surprised by her appearance.

"Have a mind to turn this vehicle around," he said, slamming on the brakes and turning around in his seat, "and cameraman?"

"Here, sir," Randy finally appeared.

"Lieutenant, we came this far," she reminded him, "and whatever your plan, you just might need us."

"This mission is dangerous." He turned and leaning against the steering wheel. "And people could end up dead."

"What's the difference between me and those soldiers following?" she asked. They have families and want to live. They may have been ordered to go, but mostly they trust you and know you'll do whatever it takes to get them back alive. I go because it's my job, but I know no harm will come to me because you're here."

"You keep close to me," he said, pressing down on the gas pedal. "Colonel's going to demote me for sure."

After another 20 minutes of driving, he pulled the vehicle over.

"Alright," he said, opening the door. "Come on out."

"We're going on foot?" she asked.

"No," he replied while opening the rear door. "About a mile from here the Colonel believes is where the insurgents will be waiting."

"Dolly here," the Sergeant said as he opened the large crate hidden under the tarp, "will spot them and send back a picture of what they have."

"A drone," Randy blurted out, "WOW, it's one of those new models."

"Quiet and starts recording movement within a half mile," the Lieutenant explained. "They won't even know their being filmed."

"By the time Dolly confirms target," the Sergeant began. "The convoy will be here with us waiting."

"Waiting for what?" she asked.

"Just have cameraman ready," the Lieutenant replied as they readied the drone and equipment, "and you'll see."

Under the steady hand of the Sergeant, the drone flew toward the area where they suspected the insurgents waited.

"Now we watch the monitor," the Lieutenant said while looking down at the small screen. "Go a little higher, Sergeant."

For several minutes, all they saw on the monitor was desert.

"Right where we thought they'd be," he yelled out, "and look at the equipment they brought with them."

"Rocket launchers," said the Sergeant, giving it a quick look. "Mortars and machine guns."

"Take it over to the others side," he ordered. "See what they have."

"Looks to be the same," the Sergeant yelled out as he guided the drone to the other side of the road. "Figure over 100 men."

"Time to radio in the codes, so the Lieutenant paused for a second as if thinking, "Cameraman, be ready."

From the front seat, he began repeating numbers then coordinates. After several minutes of listening, he heard the voice confirming his order.

As the convoy drove up and stopped, four jets roared overhead. The first two jets began dropping cluster bombs on both sides of the road, then flew off to allow the next two to continue the bombardment. Explosions and fire engulfed both sides of the hills, and Janice could feel the heat of the fire from where she stood as Randy filmed.

"What was that?" she asked while secondary explosions filled the air.

"Their rockets and equipment exploding," the Lieutenant explained, "and vehicles."

"Alright, Randy," she said, getting herself ready to be filmed. "Camera on me with the hills in the background."

"Ready when you are," he said, pointing the camera at her with the required background.

"I'm standing here less than a mile from where the insurgents attempted to attack a convoy," she slowly began, "that provides food and medical supplies to the sanctuary. Only days before, they attacked another peaceful convoy, killing and wounding many. Today, given no other option, our brave soldiers retaliated, but it was not out of hate or vengeance. Such action is required to prevent starvation and unnecessary suffering. The brave men and women that travel with these convoys know the food and medical supplies they carry are not for war, but for the good of those who seek freedom."

"Perfect," Randy said, turning the camera off.

"Could anyone live through that? she asked while looking toward the hills that were now covered in smoke.

"Probably not," he calmly replied, "but we need to see for ourselves."

"Only one way to prove it," she answered. "Film it."

"Be nice to show the Colonel the equipment they used," the Lieutenant said, looking toward the hills, "and where it came from, but this must be classified. Just can't, not for the public viewing."

"If I promise you'll have the only copy," she began, "never shown to the people?"

"You can give and keep that promise?" he asked.

"Randy, are you up to it?" she asked. "If not, I'll do it."

"I'm the cameraman," he blurted out, "seen blood and wounded."

"Got your promise," he said, looking straight into her eyes.

"Yes," she said, crossing her heart. "Randy will stay while I go with the convoy and stay there until you come to get me."

"Be three or maybe four days," he said, shaking his head. "But no argument about coming back with me."

"Promise." She again crossed her heart, then whispered, "Thank you."

"Randy, you'll find a jar of Vaseline and mask," the Lieutenant said, turning toward him. "Put some in your nose and use the mask."

"Is it going to be that bad?" his voice quivered.

"Yeah," he answered. "See you in four days."

Entering the first truck, they followed as the Lieutenant led the way. Slowing as they passed, she watched as two trucks stopped and unloaded armed soldiers wearing masks. Without further trouble, the convoy finally arrived at the sanctuary, where the women greeted them with unusual cheers.

"Janice, are you alright?" Russell came running out when noticing her. "We saw the smoke and wondered what happened."

"I'm fine," she said, giving him a quick kiss. "But what's with the ladies."

"Called Ululation." She received her kiss as he spoke. "It's a high pitched sound or chat giving praise or thanks."

"If anyone deserves thanks, it's those soldiers," she replied. "Tell you all about it."

"What are we waiting on?" he asked while taking her hand then leading her toward his quarters. "My every thought has been of you."

"Been thinking of you," she said in a soft tone, "and don't ask what they were."

Within minutes, they clung together in unbridled lovemaking, but it seemed as if it were the first time. As their bodies dripped with sweat, she never felt so alive. With every touch of his gentle hand, her body responded. So many times she could hardly catch her breath, but refused to allow him to stop.

She hungered for every moment of passion; never had such experience overwhelmed her soul. Never had she known love, nor a man like this.

"I've good news," he said, holding her tight while listening to her heartbeat. "My wife sent me divorce papers that were signed. She asked that I sign them and send them back."

"So, she knows about us?" she asked while exhaling,

"No," he answered. "I didn't want you involved and think somehow you were responsible. The decision was hers alone, and one that will make her happy."

"I don't want anyone to get hurt because of me," she softly began. "I do love you, but if you think there's any chance…"

"Her letter made it clear she was not willing to wait," he said, touching her lips. "And that I was committed to helping these people over those more deserving."

"Where does that leave us?" she asked, feeling his warm body on hers.

"Means she'll file the papers with the court," he whispered in her ear, "and 30 days later, it will be official. Be returning to the states a single man, free to do what I want, and with whomever I want."

"So what do you want to do?" she asked with a slight smile.

"Plan to reserve a room for three days at the finest hotel in all of New York for us," he continued, "and never leave and have a dozen red roses brought in each day."

"Might get hungry," she said, teasing him with her tone, "or bored."

"Room service," he answered, "and promise we won't be bored."

Every day seemed to bring them closer together. While making his daily rounds or his surgery schedule, Janice would stroll among the different groups. All accepted her as Russell's lady, and that gave her status to listen to all those willing to speak.

The stories told of harsh conditions, having little to eat with crop failure or the insurgents stealing what little they had. But life at the sanctuary showed them kindness, where all were treated the same as a free people.

When apart, her thoughts remained of him, yet she understood his life would be devoted to helping others, which is why she made every precious moment with him important, allowing those thoughts to sustain her until his return.

On the fourth day, she could hardly breathe when noticing the Lieutenant's vehicle passing through the gate followed by several trucks.

"Morning lady," he said, parking the vehicle and climbing out as he spoke. "Is the Doc around? Because I need to speak with him."

"He's on rounds," she replied, "but be here once he knows you're here. How did Randy do with the filming, is he okay?"

"Did better than I thought," he admitted. "He only threw up twice."

"Lieutenant, it's always good seeing you." Russell came running over to him.

"Doc, is there somewhere we could talk," he asked while looking around, "in private?"

"If you want," Janice said while looking toward the two, "I'll stay out here."

"Might as well join us," he replied. "You'll hear about it when we return to base."

"Alright, why all the secrecy?" Russell asked. "Janice told me about the battle, and no doubt the insurgents were hurt badly."

"Yes, they were," he admitted, "lost equipment and men. But for the last few days, we've been listening to a lot of chatter. They're planning something."

"There's no reason to believe they'd attack us," Doc said, attempting to reassure him. "We pose no threat to anyone."

"Lieutenant, you know if they attack here," Janice said, voicing her opinion. "The world would be outraged and would react."

"Maybe or maybe not," he replied with a slight smile, "but I still worry, which is why they pay me the big bucks. Now I've asked your security to patrol outside the compound in the hills. They won't do it, mostly because there are so few."

"Their responsibility is inside the compound," he answered, "with so many people…"

"The Colonel has agreed to send you 50 armed troops," he continued, "to patrol the hills around the compound."

"That would give them the excuse they need to attack us," he quickly pointed out, "and it would prove we're under American military rule not a sanctuary."

"Just a suggestion," he replied, "but please give it some thought."

"Promise I will," Doc said, taking him by the shoulder. "Now about my supplies?"

"Need your signature on these," the Lieutenant said, handing him the paperwork, "and while you look them over, I'll check on unloading."

"Any idea how long it will take to unload?" he asked with interest.

"Two hours tops," he said, looking toward the two as he walked toward the door. "Have to get back."

"I so dislike letting you leave," Doc said while waiting for the Lieutenant to leave. "When we're not together, I think of all the things I want you to know. But when together, I don't wish to waste a moment to speak of my thoughts."

"Soon we'll have a lifetime to speak of our thoughts," she said, wrapping her arms around his body. "But for now we've only two hours."

By the time the trucks were unloaded and ready to leave, Janice and Russell stood outside waiting.

"See you in a week, Doc," the Lieutenant blurted out while walking toward the two. "Everything neatly packed away."

"One thing." Russell came over to him. "Could you bring up more candles?"

"More candles?" he asked, looking toward Janice. "Fine."

"Love you," she whispered while following the Lieutenant to his vehicle.

"Could use a nice, warm shower," she said as they entered the base. "Feel as if I've half the desert on me."

"Be joining us at dinner?" he asked while stopping the vehicle. "Been missing your face and conversation."

"Thought you were happily married," she joked.

"I am," he said with a laugh, "but like having you around."

"Like having you around, too," she admitted. "Be joining you and the others for dinner."

"Come in." She decided to look in on Randy before entering her quarters.

"I'm back," she said walking in and finding him lying in bed. "You okay?"

"Yeah," he said, slowly getting up. "Doctor said I got a sunstroke and need to drink water and rest."

"Was it that bad," she asked while sitting on the side of the bed, "truthfully?"

"Yeah, it was," he finally admitted. "Burnt body parts everywhere."

"I should have never asked you," she said, knowing she had made a mistake.

"No, it's my profession," he said, exhaling as he spoke. "I'm a cameraman and must film it."

"I just don't want you hurt," she said, giving him a hug. "You're so important to me."

For over an hour he spoke of the scene, and when finished, he seemed calm by having shared the event with someone.

"Randy, whatever happens in the future," she said, taking his hand while speaking, "we will do it as a team."

"It means a lot," he replied, squeezing her hand.

"Let's get ready for dinner," she said, kissing him on the cheek. "I'm starved."

"Oh, by the way," Randy replied as he stood up and walked over to his small bag. "Gave the Lieutenant the original copy of the film, but you're in charge of the backup."

"You know what I have to do with this," she said, taking the small unit from his hand. "Gave my promise."

"It's your decision," he said as if reminding her, "but I'll back you."

"See you at dinner." She began walking toward the door.

As she entered the dining room, everyone stood up to greet her.

"Got a lot of fans, lady," the Lieutenant said walking over and escorting her to a place at the table.

"Thank you," she spoke up, "but truthfully, all of you are my heroes, and that includes my wonderful cameraman."

"Lady, you always know the right things to say," he replied in a soft tone.

"By the way, she said, handing him the backup unit, "we always make a backup in case the original is damaged. Randy hasn't authority to give it away, only I can."

"Thank you," he said with a smile. "Promise kept."

For two days, she waited with Randy, who continually cleaned his equipment.

"They haven't gotten any supplies in for the convoy," she said while watching Randy working. "What are they waiting on?"

"You know they deliver supplies at different times," he responded, assuring her they would come.

"I know," she admitted, "but I just hate being idle. But for sure I'm getting plenty sleep and food."

"Nothing wrong with that," Randy said while peeking through the blackened window. "It's getting late, and maybe tomorrow the trucks will come."

"Let's hope," she said, walking toward the door. "See you in the morning."

"Lady," the Lieutenant calmly woke her from a deep sleep. "Need to wake up."

"What's all the noise?" she immediately asked. "Guess I was more tired than I thought."

"Helicopters coming in," he replied, "got a report by a commercial airline. Pilot reported seeing flashes he said were explosions, and fires. He gave coordinates. Has to be the sanctuary, and we've lost communications with them."

"So what's going to happen now?" she asked, removing the blanket revealing her naked body.

"Four attack helicopters are enroute," he began. "I'm taking 60 men up there to assess the situation."

"Can I come with you?" She began dressing. "I'll get Randy."

"You're to remain here," he continued, "but once we've secured the perimeter, you'll be flown in. While waiting, get your equipment ready, and once on the ground, keep low."

"Promise me you'll find Russell," she implored him, "and see that he's safe."

"I'll find him," he said, patting her on the shoulder, "and bring him to you."

"Thank you," she said as he turned and left.

For over an hour, she and Randy waited when suddenly several helicopters began landing.

"You two," a young gunner inside the helicopter yelled out, "time to go."

"Have they reported anything?" she asked while entering the fully loaded helicopter. "Damages or casualties?"

"Can't say," he admitted while pointing to the many crates. "Ordered to bring medical supplies and you two."

No sooner had they landed, she jumped off and began running toward the gate.

"Lady, I'm here," the Lieutenant shouted out while walking past the smoke and fire.

"Where is he?" she screamed. "Please tell me he's alright!"

"He's gone." His voice quivered as he spoke. "Was in surgery when the attack began. They targeted the hospital ward and surgery building, then communications."

"No no no," she bawled loudly while falling to her knees. "God, not now."

"Ms. Gardner." The Lieutenant knelt down and gently took her by her arms. "He's gone, and no amount of tears will bring him back."

"I need to see him." The tears continued to flow, but she realized it was the first time he called her by name. "Please, take me to him."

"No," he said in a stern tone. "I won't allow it to be your last memory of him. Please, do what I ask."

"But I loved him," she responded, unable to control her crying.

"I know," he said, taking a deep breath and looking around at all the carnage. "But look around. He was one of hundreds killed and dying. If you truly loved him, show the world what evil men do."

"I can't," she said, pressing her head against the legs as she continued to cry. "I just can't."

"You must," he told her, speaking softly, "for you're the only one to speak for him and all the others that can't."

"Randy, are you filming this?" She leaned back to speak with him. "Give me a moment to get ready."

"Need to find somewhere different," he yelled out, "higher."

As she spoke and remembered the description Randy had given about what bombs and rockets do to the body, she realized the Lieutenant had shielded her from seeing it.

"Here you need this," the Lieutenant said, taking out his handkerchief and handing it to her. "I'll get back to my duties while you do yours."

"Lieutenant, promise you'll take care of him," she said, standing up and wiping her swollen eyes. "Don't let anyone else do it."

"Promise," he said, standing up, "and I'm so sorry."

"Randy, we need to get up on one of the buildings," she said, still attempting to control her crying using the handkerchief, "to show all the fires in the compound."

Once situated on top of one of the few remaining buildings, she began speaking.

"This is Janice Gardner and Randy Kemp reporting," she began as her voice quivered and tears continued to flow, "from what was once the sanctuary. The cries you hear come from the wounded children, pleading for help or mothers. These people harmed no one. They came here to seek medical attention and food. Yet they became the victim to evil men that wish only to enslave or murder. Can the world leaders turn a blind eye to such tragedy? For they are us. Some might say this isn't our battle or war; if not here, then where or when."

She paused for several seconds, as she could no longer speak.

"We came here to report a story of the doctors and soldiers," she continued, trying to hold back the tears once again, "that devoted their lives helping the people. However, we came to know them as proud parents and friends wishing only to live in peace. I have always believed such organizations as the United Nations would never accept or allow evil men to continue murdering the innocents of the world. We must demand that such evil cannot be tolerated, and restore peace to this land."

"That was great," Randy replied while he finished scanning the entire compound.

"We need to film the soldiers helping the people," she said, regaining her composure, "and all the damage."

"Right," he replied in a weak tone. "Just lead the way."

For over two hours, she guided Randy around the compound, speaking softly when watching the soldiers removing the dead or wounded.

"We've more than enough footage." Randy in a soft timid tone spoke, as if afraid. "Maybe we should call it a night."

"Never enough." She continued to wade through the rubble that was once the buildings. "I want people to see what they did."

"Janice, we have enough," Randy said again, making a stand. "There's nothing more to film."

"Then you leave," she ordered in an abrupt manner, "just give me the camera."

"The camera is my responsibility," he said, holding the camera against his chest, "and I say we've enough footage."

"It's my responsibility to say when there's enough," she said, showing further anger, "and if you don't like it, then quit or get fired."

"Then fire me," he responded, showing anger himself. "I'm not filming any more."

"Fine, you're fired," she snapped. "Just leave me alone."

"If that's you want," he said, turning around. "I'm taking the first helicopter out of here."

"Go!" she screamed as he walked away. "Just go. I don't need you or anyone."

Alone and surrounded by the burnt out building, she fell to her knees while pounding her fist against the hard ground.

"You men," the Lieutenant and several others came toward her, "take her to the copters and see that she leaves."

"No!" She began resisting. "Leave me alone; I'm staying."

"I'm ordering you out," the Lieutenant said in a stern tone. "Now don't give these men any trouble."

As if exhausted, she fainted.

"Go on," he ordered as he looked down at her. "Pick her up. She's done here."

Having arrived at the base, she remained alone for two days.

"Lieutenant," Randy came running to his side. "Janice hasn't left her room in two days and I'm worried."

"Let her be," he ordered, "I've been checking on her and know she's still hurting."

"She's not eating," he reminded him. "I put meals outside her door, and they weren't touched. We really need to do something. I worry about her, even after she fired me."

"Forget whatever she said to you," he said looking over toward her door. "She didn't mean it and probably won't even remember saying it. By tomorrow afternoon, if she doesn't come out, we'll go in."

"Been hearing rumors that the base is closing," he asked, "any truth to it?"

"Rumors only," he said, exhaling while looking him in the eyes. "Command will be letting us know in writing not by rumor."

The following day, Janice stepped out, holding her hand over her eyes.

"How are you feeling?" The Lieutenant walked over to her, as if waiting. "You look like hell but no worse for wear."

"I look like a mess," she said looking down at the dirty uniform, "but don't know how I feel. Emotionally totally drained, and all cried out."

"Maybe after a warm shower and clean clothes," he began while handing her a package meal, "and eating will help."

"Thank you," she said, taking the meal from his hand, "and if I did anything…"

"Talk later," he interrupted her. "Shower first, alright?"

CHAPTER NINE

For a week, Janice spoke very little to anyone, but listened to the soldiers as they spoke of going home to loved ones or how many were planning to spend the extra money they made one on liberty.

"Well, I'm all packed," Randy said after entering her room. "Wonder what's going to happen when we get back."

"Randy, I know I've apologized 100 times," she began, "but I just want you to know I didn't mean anything I said. I can't do without you, and need to know you'll be there with me."

"It was a terrible night," he said with a smile, "and truthfully, I can't remember what you said."

"Liar," she said, kissing him on the cheek, "but thanks. I don't have much, but maybe you could help me pack."

"Be happy to help," he said, walking over to her small closet.

"Heard you got your orders," the Lieutenant said as he walked toward her.

"Yes," she replied, sitting on the porch as if enjoying the cool afternoon air. "Headman wants us out as soon as possible, so Randy just left to check on it after helping me pack."

"How ya feel about leaving?" he asked while sitting beside her. "Looking forward to going home?"

"Mixed emotions," she admitted. "Heartbroken, but have only myself to blame."

"How so?" he continued to question her.

"You warned me about Russell," she explained, "and I didn't listen."

"Whoa," he blurted out as if remembering what he said, "warned you that the Doc was married, which was true. But nothing about falling in love, big difference."

"Thought they were all the same," she said, surprised by his comment.

"Not hardly," he explained. "Doc was my friend, and we talked a lot before you came. He came to find something he needed, a purpose. Then he discovered something he wanted even more: you. You made him happy, and I knew whatever challenges, the two of you would be okay. It's the reason I let you stay with him. You made a nice looking couple."

"Never thought you felt that way," she said, a little embarrassed, never knowing.

"Know he's gone," he said while looking directly in her eyes, "but he left you the gift of knowing true love. Now I can't say if you'll ever feel it again, but if it were to come, that same emotion will return."

"Thank you," she said, leaning over and giving him a kiss on the cheek, "for everything."

"Still happily married," he said, touching the spot, "but was nice."

"So what about you?" she asked. "Where to?"

"Don't know," he said with a smile. "Go where the army orders. However, it's likely we'll be ordered to leave this the way we found it, just sand."

"Can I ask you something," she said in a charming manner, "which breaks the rules?"

"Go ahead and ask," he said in a serious tone.

"What's your real name," she asked, wanting him to reply honestly.

"Danny Lee Navor," he replied, as if proud having told her. "Oklahoma born."

"Danny Lee Navor," she immediately repeated his name, "I'll never forget you and the kindness shown."

"Back at you, Janice." He stood up while reaching into his pocket. "And I got you a little something."

"A nametag," she said, taking it from his hand. It was inscribed with the word "Lady" with a star.

"Never know when we might find ourselves in some jungle or desert paradise," he said with a wide smile, "like this and might need it."

"What's the star for?" she asked, looking at the nametag.

"You're a reporter," he said, chuckling as he walked away. "Figure it out."

"Hello, Lieutenant." Randy came running up.

"Randy, where have you been?" she asked as he sat down.

"Over in the communication office," he said as if out of breath, "bringing in a helicopter tomorrow especially for us. Be home in three days. Isn't that wonderful?"

"Yeah, wonderful," she replied, looking around at all the soldiers walking around.

"Oh, by the way," he said, reaching into his pocket. "Look what the Lieutenant gave me. My own nametag, with the word 'Cameraman' with sergeant strips."

"Gave me one, too," she said, showing it to him.

"He made you a general," he blurted out while looking at the star. "Now that's really not fair."

"No, it isn't," she began laughing, "not fair at all."

The trip back to the states was long and tiring, and neither slept well on the jet.

"Miss Gardner and Mr. Kemp?" Aa young woman entered the aircraft wearing a well-fitted suit. "I'm Molly Rains from Corp and here to escort you there."

"Who are those people waiting for?" Randy asked while looking out the window at the group of people. "Is there a celebrity here?"

"Oh my, you really don't know?" She turned to him with a surprised expression. "They're here wanting to interview you two. Over the last several months, the entire country has been watching your broadcasts."

"Ms. Rains, we're both tired," Janice in a calm tone spoke up, "and neither of us want to speak to anyone."

"Why I'm here," she said as if assuring them, "just follow me, and I'll be doing all the talking, okay? Ladies and gentlemen of the press," Molly yelled out while walking through the long corridor. "There will be no interviews at this time. Ms. Gardner and Mr. Kemp have had a long journey and need private time to adjust to the time differences."

As Molly directed them to a side door, she heard a familiar voice shouting her name repeatedly.

"Susan?" Janice noticed the young girl attempting to move through the crowd.

"I told Mommy you'd hear me!" Susan said, running to her side and grabbing her legs. "But there were so many people."

"Susan, where did you come from?" Janice asked, leaning down and giving her a hug.

"Uncle Leone and father thought it would be good if we came," she began as Janice lifted her up. "They're waiting over there."

"I'm so happy all of you came!" She began moving through the crowd.

"But you're crying," Susan said while wiping the tears from her cheeks,

"Happy tears, Susan," Janice assured her, giving her a quick kiss on the cheek. "Linda!" Janice blurted out while handing Susan to her then giving her a hug. "You don't know how wonderful it is seeing all of you here."

"Been watching all those terrible things that you went through," Linda said, returning the hug. "Couldn't let you show up without us."

"You alright, Janice?" Leone asked while walking up to her. "Broke my heart watching what you went through."

"Oh, Leone, I'm fine, but it's all good now," she said, giving him a hug, "so happy you're here."

"Well, what about me?" Frank came over. "Don't I get a hug?"

"Of course!" she replied, grabbing him and giving him a hug while looking down at the other two, and Frankie and Lisa.

"Ms. Gardner," Molly said while Janice leaned down and began hugging the two other children, "we need to go."

"Not going anywhere without my family," she said while brushing back Frankie's hair with her hand, "just go without me."

"Randy," Leone said walking over to him. "Did one fine job over there, son."

"Thank you, Mr. Pegasus, means a lot hearing it from you."

"Randy, you can go with Molly," she said standing up as the others began greeting him. "I'll be fine."

"Was told to bring both of you," Molly blurted out, "and I've a limousine waiting."

"How many fit in the limousine, young lady?" Linda asked while releasing Randy.

"Believe eight, maybe nine," she answered.

"Frank, you go get the van and follow us," she ordered, "while we take a nice ride in the nice big car."

"Really Mommy?" Susan yelled out while grabbing Janice's hand.

"Wonderful idea," Janice said while looking toward Linda. "Thank you."

"If you want company, Frank," Leone spoke up,

"No, you're coming with us." Linda was defiant. "Frank can drive by himself."

"Come on, old man," Janice said, taking him by hand. "You're with us."

The vehicle was perfect for all. Susan sat on Janice's lap while Lisa on sat on Linda's. It was like a family reunion for all, the children asking questions about the where they were going while all laughed at all the unanswered questions.

"I'll show your husband where to park," Molly said as the vehicle stopped in front of multi-floor skyscraper, "and meet all of you at the elevators."

As they walked toward the large doors, the children began running, which allowed Janice to speak with Leone.

"I know you were in the service," she began while holding his hand. "Don't know what you saw, but having spent time with the troops opened my eyes."

"Watching you with them..." he stopped for a moment. "I'm certain they feel the same about you."

"Even got my own nametag," she said, pulling it out of her pocket.

"A sign of respect and admiration." he examined the name. "I'm impressed. Even made you a general."

"You noticed that?" she asked with a wide smile while squeezing his hand.

After passing through security and with everyone accounted for, Molly swiped her card as the elevator door opened.

"All aboard," she yelled out as if happy having delivered them all.

As the elevator climbed to the top floor, the door quickly opened.

"Ms. Rains." His voice showed shock seeing so many.

"Mr. Acorn," Janice stepped forward. "I'd like you to meet my extended family."

"Pleased to meet one and all," he said, coughing as she introduced him to everyone, "and forgive my cough it flares up now and then."

"A spoon full of honey each morning," Linda replied as he took her hand, "might help with that cough."

"Seen my share of specialists," he said, looking into her lovely face, "none have ever recommended that, but I'll try it."

"Free advice," she commented with a smile, "and can't hurt."

"Janice and Randy, I need a private moment," he began. "In the meantime, Molly will escort your family to the cafeteria."

"We appreciate your offer," Frank stepped forward, "but we'll not take up any more of your time."

"Mr. Ehlert," Edgar Acorn stepped over to him. "Please accept my hospitality. I'm pleased having all of you here, it's good knowing Janice has such people that care for her as I do."

"In that case," he said, looking down at the children who appeared disappointed, "we could get something to drink."

"Nonsense," Edgar immediately replied. "We've a fine selection of foods. Molly, see that they get the royal treatment, anything."

"I could show them the broadcast room," she mentioned.

"Fantastic idea," he blurted out. "The children would enjoy that."

"Meet you in the cafeteria," Leone whispered in Janice's ear, "when you're finished."

"Appreciate all you're doing for them," Janice said to him as they left the room.

"For you," he said looking toward her, "I'd do anything, so just ask."

"Then Randy and I would like to have a week off," she asked. "Been a trying time."

"Unfortunately, it's the one request," he said, walking toward his large desk, "which I cannot give. Your story has touched the hearts of the nation and others, and now they wish to see you in person. We must make the most of this opportunity because our affiliates are demanding interviews."

"I'm drained," she admitted, "and wouldn't be up to such interviews."

"You know in the 24 hour news cycle," he said as if reminding her, "the story will be cold and forgotten in a week. It's imperative you try, for those that cannot speak for themselves. Besides, there is the political component, the United Nations, and of course the United States Senate."

"I don't understand," she quickly replied while sitting down and looking toward Randy, who also seemed bewildered.

"The film you sent the army," he began slowly, "film that I've never seen or heard about until two days ago. Apparently, it's been shown to our Ambassador and other members that represent certain countries, and some have accused the two of you of doctoring it."

"That's a lie." Randy immediately stood up, making his point clear. "All they have to do is check the backup."

"Yes, a backup that should be in our possession, making it clear rules were broken, but it's not."

"I alone made the decision to give the army both copies," Janice said, taking full responsibility. "I gave them my promise that it would not be shown."

"Oh, you did?" he said, looking her in the eyes. "All film, including backup is the property of the corporation and cannot be handed over without authorization from me."

"I gave them my word," she continued to explain. "Besides, the public may not enjoy seeing torn charred bodies. Randy had nothing to do with it. If you wish, I'll resign but please allow him to remain employed."

"Sir, I knew what she was doing," Randy said, sitting back down. "I'll resign to."

"That film you so eagerly gave away was priceless," he said, looking toward the two, "but keeping a promise is worth much more. Tired or not, you must meet with these people."

"How long will we be on the road?" Janice asked, surrendering to his wishes.

"Starting tomorrow," he quickly replied. "Be here at 10:00 for wardrobe and makeup. We've arranged a private meeting with the American Ambassador and others at 1:00, then back here for an interview by Mr. Munson. It will be in two parts, broadcasted at 11:00 to all our affiliate stations."

"WOW," Randy blurted out. "Private meetings."

"The following day, you're meeting with several Senators," Acorn continued, as if making them aware of the importance of their schedule. "Another private meeting repeating the same questions already asked, Afterwards, 10 cities in two weeks, giving interviews."

"Two weeks, maybe three?" Randy seemed excited by the idea. "Yeah, we're ready."

"Now the interviews at the United Nations and Senate," he began while opening a drawer, "will be important but mostly intelligence gathering. Afterward, the interviews will be more on the human side, what you observed."

"Whatever they want to know," Janice spoke up, "we've nothing to hide."

"Good," he said, handing each an envelope. "I've taken the liberty of advancing each of you $6,000. Arrangements and expenses are taken care of while touring, but you might need a little mad money. For tonight, I've arranged for the two of you to stay at the Grande, where you can relax."

"If you wouldn't mind, Janice said taking the envelope from his hand, I'd like to spend the night with those that came with me."

"In that case," he said, handing Randy the envelope, "guess you're on your own."

"Thank you for the money," they both repeated.

"Remember, be here by 10:00, he said as they started toward the door.

The two joined them in the cafeteria and enjoyed laughter and a meal. Later, Janice returned with them to the motel, and for over an hour explained the obligation she had agreed to.

"Are you really up to such a strenuous couple of weeks?" Linda asked after listening to her. "So many cities in such a short period."

"Especially after what you've been through," Leone replied.

"I'll be fine," she said, looking toward Leone who expressed concern.

"You know I could use some fresh air," Linda quickly spoke up as if sensing something in her tone. "Janice, come along for girl talk."

Outside, Linda took her by the hand and led her to a small wooden bench.

"Janice, you're like a daughter to me," she began while holding her hand, "and I have a sense when my daughters are hurting."

"I fell in love," she began crying while speaking of Russell and their time together.

"Mommy, why is she crying?" Susan came running out from the room. "Don't you want to be with us no more?"

"Oh my dear," Janice said, taking her into her arms. "I love you like a little sister and one day hope to have a child just like you."

"Mommy," Susan said, looking toward Linda, "she wants a little white girl like me."

"No dear," with a slight smile. "She means to have a beautiful little girl of her own that is kind, like you."

"You think I'm beautiful?" Susan asked while wiping her tears. "And kind?"

"Oh, Susan, I think you're the most beautiful girl in the whole wide world," she said, kissing her on the cheeks, "and very kind."

"Hear that, Mommy?" she shouted out for all to hear. "She thinks I'm the most beautiful girl in the world!"

"Yes, we all heard," Linda said, standing up, "Now go back inside and finish packing."

"I'll come in to say goodnight," Janice promised.

"Don't cry no more," she calmly replied while slipping down. "I love you, and so does Frankie, even if he is a boy."

"I know," Janice said, gently holding her face, "and I love all of you."

"Wish there were words to ease the pain you have." Linda gently placed her arms around her. "But there are none. Just remember we're all here for you, family."

"Just having you here," she said as if a heavy weight of loss had been lifted, "it means so much to me. You've given me a family, that I so dearly needed."

"For sure," Linda said in a gentle tone. "You've a little sister that truly loves you."

"Would you buy the children something?" she said reaching into her pocket. "I'll be so busy but want them to have a memory."

"Three thousand dollars," Linda blurted out, as if shocked, "I can't."

"Please," Janice said, insisting while pushing the bills toward her, "maybe just this once."

"Tell you what," she said with a smile, "something little and the rest to be placed in the college funds we've arranged."

"Thank you." A smile came to her face.

"Janice, we all love you," Linda said in a firm tone, and you are family. When all these interviews are over, promise to spend time with us."

"Promise," she said, crossing her heart. "Now maybe we should go in and make sure everyone is packing."

The following morning the staff prepared her for the meeting with makeup and the perfect dress. After entering the building, security escorted them a private room, and there, they met with the American Ambassador.

"Now I don't want either of you to be nervous," she began explaining. "They're wanting to know about the film you made."

"We're here to tell them the truth," Janice replied, "that's all."

"Excellent," she replied with a smile.

Entering the large room, several members sat around a table. After introducing each member to them, the ambassador sat down to allow each one to question the two.

"Ms. Gardner," one of the men in a black suit stood up. We have concerns about the film you've submitted. We're interested in the film given to the army, apparently taken after an attack."

"What concerns have you?" Janice asked while sitting down beside Randy.

"That is was quite possible altered," he continued.

"Impossible," Randy blurted out. "Backups can't be altered. The backup unit is a onetime recording, cannot be altered."

"Please explain," he said, as if demanding to know.

For 20 minutes, Randy explained the technical aspects of the backup and why it could not be altered.

"So, if you compare the original film with the backup," Randy finally added. "They would match in time and content."

"May I ask why you permitted the army to have both copies?" Another rose to question them. "And why Ms. Gardner, you failed to be included?"

"I promised to classify this film." Janice rose to her feet. "And believed people need not see such horror. Also to prevent it being used as propaganda, or excuse to attack the sanctuary."

"But they did attack the sanctuary," another member rose.

"Yes, they did," she admitted, "but not because of the film, which they knew nothing about and have never seen."

For over an hour, the members asked questions, concerning the people and needing to know if they ever saw weapons delivered.

"No weapons were ever delivered." She stood up and looked each member in the face. "And I'll call anyone who says otherwise a liar."

Finally, the members thanked the two for their insight and left them with the American ambassador.

"That was great," the ambassador claimed, "and Randy we did verify the film, but thank you for explaining to technical aspect to them."

"Got the feeling some of them," Janice spoke up, "didn't much like what we said, even knowing it was the truth."

"You're a force to be reckoned with, Ms. Gardner," the ambassador said with a smile, "and that isn't what they expected. Your passion and honesty, it overwhelmed them."

"I decided no one would destroy a good man's character," she admitted, "and the humanitarian work that was done."

"You accomplished that goal," she spoke as if relieved, "and more."

Returning to the station headquarters, the two given new attire and makeup.

"Ms. Gardner," Munson entered the small room used for hairstyling. "Can't tell you how thrilled I was when asked to interview you."

"Mr. Munson, it's our extreme pleasure…" She tried to stand but was quickly asked to remain seated, "having such a distinguished figure as you to conduct it."

"Been watching your reports," he said, taking her hand, "and must say never have I seen such a professional reporter. One day, you'll outperform even the best of us, and I'll be proud knowing I had an opportunity to interview you."

"You don't know what it means hearing such from you." Her voice cracked. "I've admired you for years."

"Let's not mention just how many years," he chuckled. "See you on the set."

For an hour, Munson conducted a fine interview, allowing both Janice and Randy to share the time.

"Good interview," Edgar strolled out as the interview concluded, "but before we call it a night, we need to review it. So why don't you two go down to the cafeteria, relax, and we'll be down shortly."

"Think we did okay?" Randy asked while the elevator took them down.

"Did fine," Janice said as the door opened.

Within a half hour, Edgar entered as the two sat together.

"Janice, may I speak to you alone," he asked in a polite but firm tone.

"We've no secrets," she began, "so please speak freely."

"Randy, you're a fine cameraman," he began, "and if I wanted to learn the trade, you'd be the one I'd come to. However, you slowed the interview down, by giving technical information. Janice, you allowed him equal airtime, time that would have clarified your opinion further."

"So what are you suggesting?" she asked.

"Randy will remain here working," he began, "while you alone do the interviews."

"Absolutely not," she protested. "We go together or not at all."

"He's right, Janice," Randy admitted. "People don't care about film or lens and camera angles. What they want is watching you, explaining what we saw."

"But you're my cameraman." She was shaken by his comment. "Together."

"Cameraman," he said with a smile, "always behind never in front.

"Mr. Munson has agreed to reshoot the interview," he advised her. "If you're up to it."

"Go," Randy insisted, "and don't worry about me."

"Every interview," she said, taking his hand then crossing her heart, "I'll mention your name, so no one will forget who was there with me."

As requested, she alone made a second interview, and all agreed it was one of the best ever. Before midnight, Janice had flown to Washington, and by early afternoon, she began meeting several senators who occupied the great institute.

"Ms. Gardner, we are so pleased having you attend this meeting," one of the men said while taking her hand. "We've all heard of your remarkable interview with the members of the United Nations."

"I'm afraid some had different opinions of my appearance," she said, removing her hand, "but I spoke the truth which may account for their reservations."

"Told you we'd like her," he said to the others. "Now let me introduce them."

After making the introductions, they led her to a large room where refreshments were available.

"Ms. Gardner, would you care for anything?" the man who seemed to be the spokesperson asked. "We've a wonderful selection of fruit and drink."

"Water please," she replied while sitting down on one of the many comfortable chairs that surrounded the table.

"We know the film given to the army," he began, handing her a bottle of water, "was never altered. However, we wish to hear your opinion concerning the sanctuary, and is it necessary? We believe your insight would be most important, an outsider's view."

"May I ask why private meetings," she asked, "not public."

"The public only now knows about the sanctuary from your reports," he began explaining. "Many countries are willing to support countries with money that wish to wage war on foreign land having fragile governments."

"Many are members of the United Nations," another spoke up. "Wolves in sheep's clothing watching the slaughter."

"Private meetings such as these allow us to form allegiances," their spokesperson continued, "without their knowledge. We wish for you to continue your quest, to allow the people to make up their minds without our involvement."

"Well, ask what you will of me," she said, taking a sip of water.

The meeting seemed to go better than anyone believed. The senators expressed their heartfelt appreciation for her open and honest opinions. Leaving Washington, she began the schedule planned out, from city to city and many times meeting with supporters or admirers.

Having conducted an interview at one of the stations in Los Angeles, Janice returned to the luxury hotel for a quiet in room meal and sleep. Having finished the prepared meal, she heard a soft knock on her door.

"Alright, I'm finished," she began, wheeling the cart toward the door. "You can take the cart back."

"Ms. Gardner," a very attractive woman of 30 stood as she opened the door. May I have a moment of your time?"

"Sorry, but I cannot give interviews," she said wheeling the cart out, "but you can contact Mr. Edgar Acorn."

"I'm Mrs. Greenland," she quickly spoke up, "Russell's wife."

"Please come in," her heart pounded while catching her breath. "May I get you something to drink or eat?"

"No, thank you," she strolled in as if on a runway to reveal her slender body. "I will not be staying long."

Janice looked into her face as she slowly sat, so soft and perfect, that would make many a man look twice.

"May I say, you're very lovely," Janice said, attempting to make small talk, "and can see why he cared for you."

"Very kind of you," she said in a soft and alluring tone, "but having seen the interview between Russell and you, I noticed a connections."

"A connection?" she said, never realizing it showed. "He was kind to everyone and showered all with concern."

"Yes, but his mannerism and body language was completely different," she explained. "His soft tone and eyes revealed more. He spoke in a way I had never heard, and listening to his laugh that I had not heard in years. Ms. Gardner, were you and Russell in love? I sense you were."

"I'll not answer," her heart began to ache as if attempting to rip from her chest, "for he is dead, and it will do neither of us any good."

"When Russell first went overseas to that God forsaken place," she began, explaining her life, "I allowed it, hoping to disillusion him of such notable intentions. However, it only encouraged him, ignoring a worthwhile practice for those people."

"Mrs. Greenland," Janice said, defending him against such unrealistic beliefs. "Russell's work was important, and he saved so many."

"For the first two years of our marriage," she continued, "he established himself among the finest surgeons and socially known. Then it all changed, maybe I never understood his passion but having turned his back to all we built… When I sent him the signed divorce papers, I had hoped he would return to me. However, I misjudged him, and received his answer with his signature."

"Maybe he wanted you to come to him," she replied, knowing it was not the case.

"No, I knew our marriage was over." Her voice began to quiver. "And having seen the interview, concluded he felt the same. When I learned he had been killed, my first thought was that I wouldn't need to submit the divorce papers to the court. How could anyone be so cruel, knowing he was a better husband than I was a wife?"

"You no doubt were in shock," Janice said, attempting to ease her pain.

She reached into her handbag, brought out an embroidered handkerchief, and gently touched her eyes and nose.

"Our last meeting was in anger," she continued, "but watching the interview, I saw the kind man I loved."

"He was very kind," Janice admitted in a tender tone, "and generous to all."

"I'll not bother you further." She rose while opening her hand bag. "I'll never know what took place between the two over there. But no doubt you made him happy, for he once looked at me the way he looked at you."

"Russell was a remarkable man," her voice cracked while speaking, "who touched so many with his kindness and loving manner."

"Ms. Gardner," she said, handing her a printed card. "Russell requested to be laid to rest in Arkansas next to his parents. I believe he'd want you to know, so you could visit."

"Thank you," Janice said, looking down at the card revealing the location.

No sooner had the door closed when she leaned against it and began crying in silence.

CHAPTER TEN

Recovering from her encounter with Mrs. Greenland, Janice never regretted not answering the one question, which brought her there. However, she followed the agenda given, going from one city to another and meeting with hosts who wished only to be seen with her.

"Ms. Gardner, that was a great interview," he replied after all the cameras were tuned off and crew began leaving. "If you're hungry, I know of a nice Italian restaurant where we could discuss maybe getting together tomorrow."

"I'm so sorry," she began while walking toward the door. "Haven't you heard they corrected my schedule and I leave tonight?"

"No one told me," he replied, shocked by her announcement. "I had hoped we might spend time together getting to know each other."

"Well, that's the curse of broadcasting," she said with a smile while opening the door. "Schedules change, and marriages saved."

She walked out alone, leaving him standing.

When she finally arrived at the last city of St. Louis, the schedule allowed for a two-day stay with only one interview. Having given the interview early morning, she walked out to the waiting limousine where two men stood.

"Gentlemen," she approached the two very large muscular men wearing black suits while reaching inside her handbag. "Are either of you familiar with Arkansas?"

"Well, we know where it is," one of the men replied, as if joking.

"I wish to go here," she said, handing the man the card given to her by Mrs. Greenland. "Can you drive me there?"

"Drive?" he began to laugh. "I know the town, but it's over 400 miles away."

"Oh," she said, taking the card from his hand. "Then just take me back to my hotel."

"Now, we've been ordered to take you anywhere you wished," he said walking over to the rear door. "Won't drive you, but if you care to fly…"

"Fly?" Her tone showed eagerness. "A jet?"

"No, helicopter," the other man finally spoke up, "used for morning traffic conditions."

"I'm the pilot," the man said, opening the door for her, "and she's a beaut."

"Is it possible without getting you into trouble?" she said, holding onto his hand.

"Ms. Gardner, I volunteered to be here," he began, "told to treat you like royalty and if you want to go."

"Besides," the other man spoke up again. "We don't do traffic on Saturday, and Bernie's just about the best pilot you'll ever find in these parts."

Fifteen minutes later, the large vehicle pulled up to a large hanger, and inside sat the helicopter.

"Beautiful, isn't she? Bernie said walking over touching the craft. "Handles like a dream and love every minute I'm controlling."

"It is beautiful," she admitted. "Once flown in an army one."

"Yeah, they're just plain Janes compared to this," he said, opening the door. "Frankie, go down to the tower and make out the flight plan. Also, have a car waiting at the airport when we land."

"Will do," he shouted, walking toward the car. "Let me know when you're coming back, so I can be here waiting."

"All gassed and ready," he said while flipping several switches. "You ready?"

"Yes," she said, climbing in with a wide smile.

As he flew the helicopter, he spoke of the timeserving in the army and having learned the trade.

"Flew many a mission," he replied into the small microphone attached to the helmet. "Some rougher than others, but these beauts always brought me home."

"I can see it on your face," she replied while listening to his every word, "that you love flying."

"Yes'um, I do," he said with a wide smile. "How I met my wife who's a pilot. She flies for the fire department and emergency services. Can I ask what you're needing to do in Arkansas, if'in you don't mind telling?"

"Just visiting someone I once cared for," she said while looking into the clouds that floated around, "and tell him all the things we never had a chance to say."

"Believe words are important," he admitted while shaking his head, "but it's how we treat each other that need no words."

Relaxing in the large seat, she couldn't help closing her eyes and falling asleep.

"Ms. Gardner," his calm voice spoke into her ear, "we're here."

"Oh my Lord," she said, waking and somewhat embarrassed. "I'm so sorry having slept."

"No need," he said, taking his helmet off, makes me proud knowing you slept while this beaut of a machine carried you into the heavens.

"Guided by a true angel," she replied, removing her helmet and giving him a smile.

"Ride is over there," he said, pointing to a large man wearing a colorful Hawaiian shirt and shorts. "I'll refuel and be here waiting."

"Thank you, Bernie," she said, gently taking his hand. "Won't be too long."

"Ms. Gardner." He stood over six feet and weighing more than 300 pounds, "said you wanted to visit a cemetery?"

"Yes," she said, looking into his face, which had several small scars and a nose that had been broken many times. "Is it far?"

"Twenty minutes," he said, opening the door for her. "Just sit back, and old Hector will get you there safely."

"Would you mind if I sit in front?" she asked the large man.

"Be pleased having you sit up front," he said, closing the rear door and walking around the large limousine. "Been watching ya on TV."

"Hector," she began as he opened her door, "I hope this hasn't interfered with your daily plans."

"Never much on watching news," he said while she slid into the seat, "but after listening to them interviews, come to trust ya."

"Thank you," she replied as he closed the door.

"Don't want to pry none," he said, sliding under the steering wheel, "but I know a florist on the way."

"Please stop there," she quickly spoke up, "I'd like to pick up a dozen red roses."

"Be my honor." He began driving.

"You been driving long, Hector?" she asked, wanting to know more about him.

"About two years now," he began. "Professional boxer retired after fought in over 100 bouts. Wife saved my winnings, and got tired of fixing my nose and cuts. Collected a lot of money with over 80 wins, but nothing beats just coming home to the family."

"Must have taken a toll on your body," she asked, looking at the man as drove along. "You don't have to answer."

"No, it did," he admitted. "Many of man I fought have passed on, and thanks to the good Lord I ain't one of them."

"Maybe one day I might come and ask you about that," she said with interest. "Not to disparage the profession, but to let people know the hardships."

"Be pleased having you ask," he said, agreeing.

After stopping at the florist and entering the large cemetery, he drove slowly around until finding plot number.

"Believe we're here, Ms. Gardner," he quickly exited the vehicle.

Not waiting for him to open her door, she quickly started walking toward the grassy area holding the roses.

"Hello Russell," she said, looking down at the headstone having the logo of the foundation and that he was a member. "I brought a dozen red roses."

Tears began to flow, and her legs weakened where she knelt down, and for several minutes, she could only weep.

"Ms. Gardner." Hector came running to her. "Any way I can help?"

"No, but thank you." She wiped the tears away. "Just…"

"Take all the time ya need," he said, never allowing her to continue. "I'll be by the car."

After composing herself, she placed the roses by the headstone.

"I miss you so," she began, speaking as if he were there.

For over an hour, she spoke of the changes, the interviews, and even about meeting his wife. But always reminding him of her love and missing his gentle manner.

"Russell, I must be going," she said, wiping the tears as she spoke, "but know I loved you and would have said yes to marriage."

Walking back to the car, she noticed Hector wiping tears from his eyes.

"Are you alright, Hector?" she asked while handing him a tissue.

"Could feel your pain?" he said wiping the tears. "Sorry."

"It's okay," she said, looking back toward the headstone. "More love than pain."

Without further ado, she rode back to the airport, and thanking Hector with what she referred to as a "generous donation," walked toward the awaiting helicopter.

"All good?" Bernie asked as she approached. "Need anything?"

"It's all good," Janice said with a smile. "Very good."

"Just came over the radio," he began while walking toward the helicopter. "Navy stopped a Korean vehicle trying to run the blockade. Seized over 50 million in weapons, everything from rocket launchers to small arms. Of course, the government has no knowledge, but hate to be the owners of that vessel."

"You seem to be familiar with that part of the world," she asked, as if interested in his views.

"Six years in the army," he explained. "Two years in Korea flying these beauts all over the country. Rumors mostly, but it's said that those who fail aren't around long to speak of it."

"Well, what is important?" she began to relax. "Those weapons will never be used."

"You do know," he turned to her while guiding the helicopter higher, "had it not been for you, those weapons may have been delivered."

"Wasn't me," she almost whispered into the attached small microphone, "but those wonderful people that were killed or wounded."

"However, you became their voice," he reminded her, "and shamed the world for allowing it to happen."

"So what will happen to you once they know about our little trip," she asked, changing the subject, which they didn't authorize?"

"Was told my boss got a call from Mr. Acorn," he blurted out, "saying how pleased he was that we went above and beyond. Got a nice bonus out of this, and there be a letter congratulating everyone on a good job!"

"That was really nice of Edgar," Janice said, looking out the glass as she thought of the man.

"You know the man?" he asked, surprised by her words.

"He arranged all of this," she explained, "and I'm to meet with him now that this was the last interview."

"Ms. Gardner let me say, in a solemn tone, you're the genuine article.

Genuine, she began to laugh at his comment, no just me.

You're so much more, he explained, honest and trustworthy but mostly a person who really does care.

Really appreciate what you said, tears began to flow as she whispered, just maybe too much.

When finally arriving back at the network's headquarters building, she walked in wondering if anyone would even notice her.

"Ms. Gardner," several uniform officers came running toward her. "We've been worried sick about you when they told us you weren't aboard the airline."

"I took an earlier flight," she said as the men surrounded her. "I hope it didn't create a problem for you."

"No, Ms. Gardner," one said, taking a deep breath. "We were ordered personally by Mr. Acorn to pick you up and bring you safely here."

"I'm sorry having not told anyone," she said, a little embarrassed by all the attention.

"Not your fault," he said, making a path for her. "We should have thought ahead and been there waiting no matter what time."

"Be honored if you allow us to escort you upstairs," another officer spoke.

"If you insist," she said, smiling as the men opened the elevator door for her. As the door finally opened, she noticed Edgar walking down the long corridor.

"Gentlemen," she said turning the officers, "it's been a pleasure, and thank you for all you've done."

"Ms. Gardner," Edgar shouted out as if surprised by her appearance, "so glad you finally arrived."

"Well, you can thank these wonderful men for helping me," she said, allowing the door to remain open.

"Great job, men," he calmly replied to the men, "and thank you."

"Ms. Gardner," one of the men stepped forward as the door began to close, "never will any of us forget you, and God bless."

"What was that all about?" he asked.

"Just following your orders," she said turning toward him, "and being nice."

"My dear, can I get you anything?" he asked while walking toward his office. "Can't tell you how pleased I was with the interviews and there ratings."

"Was tiring," she admitted, "but satisfied having told their story."

"By the way, learned the Lieutenant is now a captain," Edgar said, walking behind his desk, "and the Colonel a general. They're somewhere in Texas, training a new division."

"Oh, that is good news," she said while standing in front of the desk.

"Please make yourself comfortable," he said while relaxing in his overstuffed chair. "You're practically a household name. So I want you to anchor the 6:00 national news in Chicago. What do you say to that?"

"Sir, with all due respect," she said, knowing the great opportunity presented her. "I'm not ready for that because it's a prestigious position. People have spent years in the field, before anchoring."

"I think you are ready," he said, pressing the intercom button. "Have coffee brought up with Danish."

"So maybe send me back?" she asked knowing he seemed disappointed.

"Out of the question," he quickly snapped, "Army and I believe you're too well known and would be targeted by the insurgents. You'd jeopardize anyone around you, and if hurt or killed make for great propaganda."

"I'll take a week off," she began, "if you've nothing for me."

"Hold on," he began shifting through a stack of papers. "Got a request from your FBI friends asking for help."

"Agent Hayseed," she said, quickly remembering his name.

"Oh, here it is," he said while removing a sheet of paper from the stack, "you know this Quartman?"

"He's one of the businessmen that attempted to bride the Senator," she answered.

"Mr. Quartman was sentenced two weeks ago," he explained, "refused to cooperate unlike his two business partners. Was given 10 to 15 years, the other two five because they testified against him."

"So why does he want to meet with me?" she questioned him. "He's been sentenced, and the cased is over."

"Don't know," he answered, "but he asking that no camera's or surveillance be used when you meet."

"Certainly, the FBI or federal prosecutor would never allow that," she added, "and I can't help him."

"The case against the senator begins in two months," Edgar began to explain, "and the prosecutor needs to know why he asked for you. It's his opinion Mr. Quartman may be willing to testify on behalf of the Senator and claimed he was coerced."

"Nonsense," she blurted out, "Senator Planterson was well aware of what they wanted and took payment."

"Just a thought," he said with a smile, "but if you decide to talk with him, I'll make the arrangements with the authorities."

"Where is he being held?" she asked, then pausing for a brief moment. "Maybe?"

"Federal prison, 20 miles outside of Washington," he added.

"Arrange the meeting," she finally agreed, "for tomorrow morning. After I meet with him, a week off, okay?"

"I'll have transportation waiting," he said as she stood up to leave.

"Let you know if there is a story," she said while walking toward the door.

The following morning, Agent Hayseed, who seemed happy having her there, escorted her into the prison.

"It's good seeing you again," he began as his face began to blush. "Lovelier than ever, may I say."

"Compliments are always welcomed," she said, giving him a smile.

"Understand you can't promise him nothing," he warned, "and even without cameras, I'll be watching, so be careful."

"He's not dangerous," she reminded him, "but he'll be told whatever he says will be shared with you."

"Honesty," he blurted out, "maybe why he wants to talk with you."

Entering the door that led to a fenced in grassy area, she saw him handcuffed to a picnic bench.

"Ms. Gardner," he said, turning toward her. "Would stand but…"

"I told them that you weren't dangerous," she said, sitting on the other side of the bench.

"Rules are rules," he began. We're to sit and behave."

"Understand, Mr. Quartman," she quickly began, "I cannot do anything for you."

"Totally agree," he said, smiling. "I'll do my time without asking for help."

"Then why am I here?" she seemed puzzled.

"How would you like a story about human trafficking and drugs?" he began. "Many underage. Now before you answer, the person is powerful and prominent."

"Of course," she immediately replied. "Underage human trafficking is an important story that needs told."

"Now there is a price to be paid," he continued, "if you want the information."

"If it concerns having your sentence reduced," she replied, "or being moved, I am sorry I cannot help."

"Nothing like that," he said, chuckling. "I'm prepared to serve the time. The one pleasure I miss, is my pipe tobacco."

"Pipe tobacco," she said, surprised by his request.

"It's a special blend," he explained, "found only in little Havana at a little shop called Silver Leaf."

"Why ask me to purchase it?" she asked. "The officials would allow you to order it."

"Yes, they will," he admitted, "but its $500 a tin, and I don't have the money."

"Five hundred," she said, totally taken back by the cost. "What's it made of? Gold?"

"Called mixture four," he continued. "Leaves are rare and a perfect blend of tobacco. When working I smoked it, and now I would like to have that pleasure again."

"So what are you asking?" She knew there was more.

"Two tins a month," he answered, "for three years."

"Thirty-six thousand," she said, figuring the cost, "and what am I getting in return?"

"Name of the person," he calmly replied, "and background, along with the name of a man who knows everything about the operation."

"Here's the deal," she said, standing. "Need time to consider this. If I accept, you will have the first two tins. However, if you try making me a fool, you will regret it."

"No intention of making you look like a fool," he admitted. "Watched your interviews and was impressed. You're a fine reporter that I'd trust, unlike those other vultures."

"Mr. Quartman," she said, reaching down and touching his hand. "Trust works both ways."

"I know," he said with a smile. "And I promise you will not be disappointed."

As she walked out of the prison, Janice explained to Hayseed what had transpired and the conditions given.

"So he'll give you the name of the person," he seemed puzzled by the request, "for three years of tobacco?"

"Very expensive pipe tobacco," she reminded him. "So what do you think?"

"Well, we could partner up," he added. "Split the cost and see what happens."

"Then see what your prosecutor says," she continued to walk while thinking of all she needed to do. "And I'll speak with Mr. Acorn."

"I will," he promised. "In the meantime, I'll run a total background on Mr. Quartman and see what pops."

"I've a week off," she said, walking toward the limousine. "So until then, I'm unavailable for anything."

"See you in a week," he said while watching her enter the vehicle. "Be good."

"You know where I'll be," she said while sliding in.

Arriving at Frank's home, she found Susan waiting on the porch.

"Mommy! She's here!" she said, running toward the car while shouting. "She's here."

"Hello beautiful," Janice said, taking her into her arms. "Said I'd come."

"Mommy bought me a new dress," she blurted out. "Been waiting forever to show it to you."

"You look like a perfect lady," Janice said, releasing her and looking toward her.

"Janice," Linda came out running. "Susan refused to come in, but we're so happy that you came."

"Week off," she said, giving her a hug, "and wanted to be with family."

"It's so good hearing that, Linda said, returning the hug, "and you are family."

"So Frankie, have you been good?" she asked, kneeling down to face the young boy. "Listening to your parents."

"Yeah," he said in a sheepish tone, "but Susan tries to get me into trouble."

"I'm sure she does," Janice said, giving him a hug. "It's a sister thing."

"Well, hello," Frank and Leone spoke up while watching her hug little Lisa. "Do we get any hugs?"

"Of course!" She stood up and quickly grabbed both around the neck. "I'm so happy that you're all here."

"Got your room all ready," Frank replied. "Leone even made room in his home for you, so you can come and go as you please."

"Just want to spend time with all of you," she said, taking a deep breath, "and relax."

"Came to the right town for that," Leone said, walking toward the car. "Go on in, and we'll bring in the luggage."

"Daddy put up a swing in the back," Susan said while taking her hand, "and says we all can swing on it."

"Then why don't we all go back there," she said, looking down at the child, "and try it out?"

"Go on," Linda said with a smile. "We'll put your things in the room, and I'll bring out tea and lemonade."

As she pushed the children on the swing, Janice realized this was home.

"Alright, guys," Linda came out holding the tray of filled glasses. "Let Janice have some time to catch her breath."

"So, Janice," Leone asked while spreading a large blanket on the ground. "What's next for you."

"Not sure," she said, sitting down on the blanket with Susan beside her.

As they sat, she explained the strange meeting she had with Quartman and his unusual request.

"Little Miami," Leone said, looking toward Frank, "if you decide to go I might know someone there that could help."

"Alright," Linda snapped, "there will be no more talk of work. Tomorrow, we go to the local pool, and then out to eat."

"No talk of work," Janice said, crossing her heart.

As everyone readied for bedtime, Susan came out holding a large book.

"Will you read me a story," she asked, handing her the book.

"Susan," Frank spoke up, "you haven't let her out of sight the entire day. Maybe you should let mother read it, and let Janice relax."

"Of course, I'll read you a story," Janice replied while looking toward Linda, "if your mother helps."

Once in bed the two began reading the fairy tale, each voicing a different character. Before the story even ended, Susan was fast asleep.

"Now that's teamwork," Linda said, taking her by the hand.

For the rest of the week Susan became her shadow, going shopping or to the library where she found three books by A. Shakespeare that she never mentioned to anyone, including Frank or Leone.

"So, you're leaving in the morning," Leone asked while she stood outside alone. "Have you decided what to do?"

"Called Mr. Acorn," she began. "He's agreed to finance the entire matter if I decide to proceed. Thinks it better we do it without FBI help, make it easier for people to speak with me."

"People do have a tendency to shy away from FBI," he admitted, "but they can be of great help."

"Yes I know." Tears began to flow. "I know the agent in charge, and he's a good man."

"So, why are you crying?" he said while taking out his handkerchief.

"I hate leaving," she said, taking the silk cloth from his hand. "Haven't felt this way in years."

"My dear, you're not leaving," he said, taking her into his arms. "Just going back to work. But know we're always here, because were family."

"I love all of you so much," she said as she continued crying.

"We feel the same," he said while he continued to hold her.

The following morning the mood was as dreary as the weather; tears and rain flowed down.

"Will Susan be alright?" she asked Linda, who looked back at the child crying on the porch. "I told her it's work time."

"She understands but cares so much for you," she said with a smile. "She'll be fine if maybe you call now and then."

"Once a week, I promise," Janice said, giving her a last hug, "and tell her how much I'll miss her."

"I've written down a number," Leone said handing her a folded note. "If you decide to go into little Havana, he could help."

As she waved goodbye to all, she made the decision to travel to Florida. After landing at the busy airport, a gentleman of Cuban descent wearing a well-made white suit approached her.

"Ms. Gardner," he said, giving her a slight bow, "I am Ainslie Rall and have the honor to assist you."

"Thank you," she said, a little embarrassed by his charming ways. "Leone said I could use your help."

"So how is my friend?" he asked while taking her luggage. "It has been a while since we last talked."

"He's fine," she replied while following him. "Never complains."

"Just like Leone," he began to chuckle, "walk 100 miles to help a friend but never speak of his injuries."

"Injuries?" Janice said, taking his arm and stopping him. "What injuries?"

"Shrapnel," Ainslie responded, surprised she didn't know, "when he was wounded."

"How?" she insisted. "Please tell me."

"Come, I'll explain on the way," he said, leading her outside to the awaiting vehicle.

"Nice car," she said, looking over the limousine that had been waiting for him.

"I am, after all, a lawyer," he said, opening the door for her, "and state legislator. It may also be that I am running for Congress, next year."

"I had no idea Leone knew people like you," she said, totally taken by surprise. "I'm sorry and met no disrespect."

"None taken," he began laughing, "and you might be surprised the many friends our friend knows."

"No doubt," she said with a smile. "Now about his wounds…"

"Leone was staff sergeant overseas," he explained. "He was truly a good leader. He had an instinct where trouble might be, and following his advice saved many men. However, we got this reservist captain, who needed combat for a promotion. Got word that a village was under attack, Leone said we needed to go in slow and cautious. Captain order speed, and that led us into an ambush."

For several seconds he paused, as if to remember the day.

"Two mortar teams blasted us, killed three and wound four others. While moving the wounded, an explosion peppered Leone. Once the wounded were safe, he ordered the men to follow him. They took out both mortars, and ended the ambush."

"While wounded," she said, amazed by the story.

"Spent two months in the hospital," he continued. "Learned later that they couldn't remove all the fragments. Everyone knows those fragments move, and one day might kill him unless by some miracle they can be removed. They awarded him a Silver Star, but most of us thought it should have been a Medal of Honor."

"Because he was a Black man?" she asked.

"No," he quickly answered. "Undeclared war that wasn't popular."

"Oh," she said, remembering the many demonstrations. "My mother and I watched television as the people took to the streets."

"Well, here we are," Ainslie said, changing the subject as the vehicle pulled into the parking lot.

"What did you get out of it?" she asked, looking into his face. "If I may ask."

"A nasty scar," he said, laughing to himself, "and a Purple Heart."

"Entering the tobacco shop, she could smell the pungent smell of cigar, and other tobaccos that were on display."

"Hector," Ainslie yelled out as he entered. "Where are you?"

"Right here," he said, removing several long strands of beads that covered the doorway. "Just checking my inventory."

"More like counting your money," he said walking over and taking his hand. "Got a customer interested in mixture four."

"Why, yes, we just happen to have a couple tins of it," he said with a wide smile, "but the cost is expensive."

"A couple...?" Ainslie stepped beyond the open beaded doorway. "I count twelve."

"An order that the customer never picked up," Hector said, defending himself, "or paid for. Six thousand dollars plus tax, collecting dust."

"This is my friend Janice," he said, introducing her to him, "and she might be interested in purchasing the 12 along with others."

"I'm so pleased to meet you, young lady," he said, taking her hand and kissing it.

"She's a good friend, Hector," he said as if warning him, "so how much for the 12?"

"Five hundred," he instantly replied, "it's fair."

"Said she is a good friend," he repeated, walking over to him. "Now what about a discount?"

"Alright, $400, but that's the best I can do," he finally admitted.

"Deal," she immediately replied, "and I want you to sign a contract to furnish two tins every month for the next two and half years."

"I cannot do it for less than $450," he began, reading the contract that was hand written by her, "and the tobaccos are rare and hard to come by."

"Write $450 per tin," she said, pointing to the line, "and sign it. I'll take the 12 tins today, using credit."

"This card is a corporate account," he said, looking at the card. "Now I recognize you, Ms. Gardner."

"Hector, just sign the contract." Ainslie stepped in front of the counter.

"Gladly," he said with a smile. "But why all this tobacco?"

"A story," she said, taking the contract from his hand, "and if true, I will send this back all signed."

"Well, you got your tobacco," Ainslie said, carrying the 12 cans out to the vehicle. Hope the story is worth what you paid for these."

"Can't say." She turned to him. "But it was worth having met you and listening to the story you told."

"You know, there's something about you," he said, looking at her hard. "Can't say what it is, but you remind me of Leone."

"Apparently, you haven't seen Leone is a long time," she said, laughing at his remarks, "and no doubt miss him."

CHAPTER ELEVEN

Entering the prison while being escorted by Hayseed, she felt a little uneasy having purchased the tobacco without knowing why.

"Now," Hayseed said while gently taking her arm. "Give him nothing unless the information is valid."

"Carson, I know what to do," she said, for the first time addressing him like a friend. "He'll not play me for a fool."

"My only concern is watching after you." His tone was calm. "And to ensure no harm comes to you."

"Good to know you're here," she said, turning toward the iron door. "Open please."

"Oh, Ms. Gardner," Quartman stood up from the bench. "You came bearing gifts."

"Not so fast," she said, sitting across from him. "Let's talk."

"Please, I brought my pipe," he said, taking it out to show her. "Let me have a little."

"Fine," she replied, opening the canister and allowing him to fill the bowl.

"Now this is heaven," he said, lighting the tobacco and inhaling.

"Kept my part of the bargain," she said, handing him the unsigned contract. "You keep yours."

"There is a war going on in Mexico," he began while continuing to inhale, "between the Mexican drug cartel and Columbians."

"Everyone knows about that," she said, dismissing the information. "They're fighting among themselves for control of the drug trade."

"Precisely," he said,, taking the pipe from his lips, "which will allow you to work, unnoticed."

"Just what are you talking about?" she asked, now interested in his explanation.

"Are you familiar with Mr. Robert Zone?" he asked, pointing the pipe toward her. "Operates his own production company in California."

"Never heard of him," she admitted.

"Several years ago," he said, puffing on the pipe as he spoke. "My company dealt with him on a movie we would finance. Twelve million, on paper a sound investment, but a catastrophe. I spent three months out there, learning the business."

"So what does he have to do with drugs and human trafficking?" she inquired.

"His studio is a front for the Columbian drug cartel," he said in a calm manner, "which is why his accounting books looked perfect. Using the backlot warehouse, where the drugs and the people can stay unnoticed."

"What happens to the people once they leave the studio?" she asked.

"That I don't know," he instantly answered, "probably sent to sweat shops or prostitution around the country."

"That's not enough," she said, sliding one can over to him. "You must know more."

"Like I said, was out there for weeks," he said, taking the can in his hand. "The movie we invested in was to be directed by Fred Jabra. Saw some of his work, and was impressed by his ability. However when the filming began, he was replaced."

"Did they say why?" she interrupted him to ask.

"Claimed he was on the needle," he explained, "and unreliable. However the replacement director was a complete buffoon, couldn't direct himself out of a bag. That's when I went looking for Jabra, and after a week found him suffering withdraws in a flophouse. Had no choice, bought him the fix he needed."

"You should have taken him to the hospital," she said, somewhat condemning him.

"Maybe should have," he said, admitting his liability, "but afterwards, he told me about Zone. Warned me to get far away from him, unless I was willing to partner up with the cartel. He claimed any profit would come with strings attached, and just write off the money invested as a learning experience."

"Therefore, you did what he asked," she said, realizing his situation.

"Painted a real bad picture," he continued, "wanted nothing to do with any of it. We gracefully walked away losing everything, and the cartel left us alone."

"So, where can I find Jabra?" she asked, hoping he knew.

"Don't know," he admitted, "but with your connections, you could find him. He'll be able to tell you everything, and maybe names. Before leaving him, gave him what money I had, a little over $500."

"Was nice giving him money, but you're wanting Zone." She wanted to know the reason. "It's can't be about the money, so why?"

"You're right. It isn't about the money," he said with a slight smile. "Several weeks ago, he did an interview. Sat there claiming he never knew we were corruptible, and said had he known no respectable businessperson would have taken a dime from us. Now I accept what they say about me, but that bastard is a murderer, and people need to find out what he really is."

"What makes you so sure?" she said, questioning his information. "He's still in the business."

"Why wouldn't he be?" he said, looking her straight in the eyes. "Never been arrested and can be interviewed on television."

"For now," she said, handing him the second tin of tobacco, "the rest will come once I've confirmed the story."

"Just keep in mind who you're really dealing with," he warned her. "Play it nice and slow so no one notices."

Walking out, she found Hayseed waiting.

"See he earned the tobacco," he said, noticing she no longer carried the tins.

"Earned maybe all of them," she said then explained what he revealed.

"Columbian cartel," he said, whistling as he repeated the name. "Going to need our help."

"Be needing to talk with Mr. Acorn," she admitted, "and I'm sure you need to talk to your superiors."

"Call me in two days," he said, handing her his card with a private number. "Put our heads together."

"Two days," she said, taking the card from his hand.

Within hours, she was in the office of Mr. Acorn and waited as he thought over the information she had finished.

"The key is this man Fred Jabra," he slowly began, "but don't like the idea of sending you out there knowing the Columbians are involved."

"I agree Jabra is key," she admitted, "but if the story is true, we can't just do nothing."

"FBI willing to help?" he asked, leaning forward. "And you'll want Randy."

"Agent Hayseed will be there," she said, knowing he was interested, "and Randy."

"Alright," he finally agreed. "But you'll need someone who knows Holly-wood and all the players. Jeffrey Knows."

"Who?" Janice asked, surprised by the name.

"Our man in Hollywood," he explained. "Best reporter we have out there. His name says it all. Nothing happens out there that Jeff doesn't know. Wanted you to go there to learn how he does things, but he's temperamental and might quit if he thought we were trying to replace him. Great opportunity to meet him, where he won't feel threatened."

"Can you have Randy and I on the first flight out?" she asked while standing up.

"Of course," he said, chuckling, "with a nice expense account. However, promise me that you'll be careful. I'll have money and credit card delivered. Ten thousand enough?"

"Plenty," she said, turning toward the door, "and I'll be careful."

"Oh, one more thing," he said, standing up. "Today, the United Nations announced they will reopen the Sanctuary with more doctors and nurses. The leaders of all the ethnic and religious sects have agreed to put their differences aside. They intend to work with the government, and raise an army. Pledging 500 troops to protect the hospital."

"That is wonderful news," she said with a wide smile. "I just wish…"

"Wish what?" he said, interrupting her.

Nothing, holding back her feeling as she left.

Before climbing aboard the jet, Janice called Hayseed and explained her intention of leaving to find Jabra, which he reluctantly agreed with.

"We're back, Janice," Randy almost yelled as he climbed aboard the jet, "and I've learned so much more. You won't believe what I can do with a camera."

"Together again," she said, giving him a kiss on the cheek, "but this time we're going against the Columbian cartel."

"Oh, Hell you say," he said, stepping back and looking her in the face. "Well, boss, follow you anywhere, so lead on."

"Equipment on board?" she said with a smile.

"Everything we need," he answered, "and I know where we can get more."

When they landed, two men escorted them to a private entrance, then to an awaiting limousine that had already picked up their equipment and luggage.

"Sorry for all the secrecy," he said, rolling down the window that divided them from the driver, "but we felt it necessary to avoid any undo publicity."

"Are you Mr. Knows?" she asked as the man began to laugh.

"No, Ms. Gardner," he explained, "he asked me to escort the two of you to him."

Within minutes, they arrived in front of a small building, which seemed to be in the very heart of Hollywood.

"I'm delighted having met you," the young man said as he opened her door.

"Maybe next time you could tell us your name," Janice said while looking into his eyes while exiting the vehicle.

"Only important that I know who you are," he said smiling as the driver began taking luggage and equipment inside. "Have a wonderful stay. Good day, madam." The driver tipped his hat after having placed the last of the equipment inside.

"Ms. Gardner and Mr. Kemp," a voice shouted from inside, "please come and make yourselves at home."

Entering, they found Mr. Knows, a man in his fifties having a gray handlebar mustache with a small goatee under his lower lip.

"Mr. Knows," she looked into his bright green eyes and a protruding belly that the vest seemed to hide. "I have heard so many good things of you."

"You've a fine reputation yourself," he said, extending his large but soft hand toward her.

"May I ask why all the mystery?" she said, taking his hand and was surprised how gentle he was with her. "Why all the secrecy?"

"Was informed of your mission," he began to explain with enthusiasm, "which may involve the FBI or others. I'm in a peculiar position, many of my friends are reluctant to share information with those agencies."

"So to maintain your friends or sources," she said, understanding his situation, "we've never met or know one another."

"Taken years to build trust," he continued, "if they knew the FBI was involved, I'd lose many of my most loyal friends. However, my services are at your disposal, as long as you not mention my name to anyone."

"Promise," she said, crossing her heart. "However, Mr. Acorn will be informed."

"Granted," he said with a wide smile showing his perfectly white teeth. "Now, what is it you need from me?"

"Need to find Fred Jabra," she quickly announced while sitting down in one of the many comfortable chairs. "We believe he was a director that once worked for Zone studios."

"Haven't heard that name in years." his expression changed as he spoke. "Someone who showed promise at one time. However, it is said he had taken to the needle, then disappeared without a trace."

"You said he showed promise," she continued to inquire, "how so?"

"Mr. Jabra arrived, like so many, and he began while making himself comfortable, claiming to be a director without reference. However, the Zone studio hired him, as an assistant director. As luck would have it, a brute and drunk for a director was cast out. Jabra replaced him, and having listened to the people corrected the script when needed. A modest success, film critics noticed and approved of his work."

"Just one film," she interrupted him as Randy sat quietly.

"No," he continued, "a second with further adulation but the third a disaster. The rumor mill was relentless, claiming he was high failing the cast and himself. It was then that he disappeared, never to direct another film.

"I've been told he was last seen in some flophouse in a bad way," she said, informing him of what she knew, "would that help locating him?"

"Might," he said, pausing for a moment before speaking, "but people that find themselves in such conditions are most likely long gone."

"Could you try?" she said, attempting to encourage him to begin the search.

"Yes, I'll make inquiries," he said with a slight smile.

"Thank you," she said, taking a deep breath. "Is there anything you can tell me about Mr. Zone and his studio?"

"Mostly rumor," he began. "The man is a scoundrel that produces third-rate B movies with poorly written scripts. He does have some talented actors and actresses under contract, which I've been informed he claims is his stable. Some have suggested drugs used as payment, but nothing proven."

"Then you know why I'm here," she said, testing him to see if he'd co-operate.

"Yes, I've been informed," he admitted. "If he is the monster you've sus-pect then my services will be available. You will find the accommodations ex-tremely comfortable," he said while standing and looking around. "Mr. Kemp could use the second floor that has been prepared. Both refrigerators stocked, and there are many fine restaurants in the area. Once I have learned some-thing, you will be informed."

"Then we will wait here to hear from you," she said, standing as she spoke, "and again I wish to thank you."

"Good day, Ms. Gardner," he said, taking her hand and gently kissing it. "Let us part with the knowledge that right will prevail."

For two days, they waited to hear from Knows, but enjoyed the many pre-pared meals placed in the refrigerators.

"Tell you what, Janice," Randy said as he walked down the staircase from the second floor while eating one of the meals. "Food here is great."

"Person could get spoiled staying here," she admitted. "Comfortable and the entertainment center…WOW.

"I know!" he said with excitement in his voice. "Like being in a theater."

A knock came to the door, and when opening the door, they found the same man who had escorted them from the airport standing.

"Ms. Gardner," he quickly replied. "I have arranged transportation if you're ready."

"Of course," she said, looking toward Randy. "We're ready."

"Please, no camera," he insisted, "be best."

Driving an older model van having limited accessories, they arrived in a part of town that was not on any tourist map.

"Begin your inquiries here," he said, pointing to the old stone building. "I'll be here."

"May I be of assistance?" a young priest walked toward them as they entered. "You are welcomed to remain if in need of confession or seek salvation."

"We didn't realize this was a church," Janice in a soft tone replied while looking toward Randy, who was likewise surprised.

"People gather here to worship," he explained, "this is their church."

"Father, were here looking for a gentlemen by the name of Fred Jabra," she began, unable to lie or pretend. "It's quite important."

"I know of no such person," he explained. "However I must admit our policy is that no last names be mentioned. Admittedly, I've been here a short time, six months. However, I've not heard that name."

"He may have come here seeking help," Randy spoke up, "for addictions."

"As you know," the young man continued, "the cost of such treatment tripled. Due to cost, the church suspended the program over a year ago. However, we do refer them to other treatment programs. Our primary mission is for the homeless."

"Well, thank you," she said, reaching inside her small handbag, "I'd like to contribute."

"Contributions are appreciated," he replied when noticing her placing a $100 in the wooden box.

"You are Ms. Gardner," a young, slender Latino lady approached the two as they stepped out into the bright sunlight, "looking for Jabra?"

"Yes, we are," Janice responded, showing her excitement when hearing his name. "Can you help?"

"Please come," the young woman stepped down.

"We mean him no harm," Janice explained, following the young lady who appeared in her early twenties but attractive, even with oversized clothing.

"No one can harm him." She turned to face the two.

Within minutes, they entered a small cemetery, where the young woman stood over a small stone marker.

"You may speak to him now," she replied while sitting beside the grave.

"He's dead," Janice could hardly breath when speaking.

"Nine months," she said while picking out the weeds that surrounded his grave. "He was my husband for very short time."

"I am so sorry," she said after composing herself. "We came hoping he could tell us about the Zone studio."

"What is it you wish to know?" she said, looking up as tear formed in her lovely brown eyes.

"Did he tell anything about the studio?" she quickly asked.

"It is how we met," she replied, wiping her tears. "The Columbian gangs who work for Mr. Zone stole me from my family."

"Ms...." she began but hesitated by not knowing her name.

"I am Sofia Antonia Jabra," she replied.

You were his wife," she said, surprised by her announcement.

"Si," she simply replied. "He saved me from them, and I tried saving him."

"We have an apartment not far from here," she began, "and we can speak freely there if you were to come with us."

"I must not leave the church," her voice quivered, "for I've no papers."

"But if you married Mr. Jabra," she began, "you become an American citizen."

"He was not a citizen of this country," she responded, looking toward the two as she spoke, "but a Mexican citizen."

"Sofia, you must not speak with her," the young priest giving her warning as he walked out. "She is a reporter that could bring the authorities here."

"I promise not to reveal the mission of your church," Janice said, as she now understood why all the secrecy. "Please allow her to come with us."

"No authorities," he replied, "then bring her back."

"I will notify Agent Hayseed of the FBI," she answered. "No harm will come to her, but we'll make things right."

"Sofia," the priest said, kneeling down repeating a prayer, "it is your decision."

"I have prepared myself for this day," she replied. "It is time to go."

"May God go with you," he said, giving her the sign of the cross as he spoke.

"We will wait as you pack," Janice said, taking her by the hand. "I promise no harm will come to you."

Having packed what few possessions she acquired, she said her goodbyes.

"So you're here to help?" Janice asked the young man who escorted them to the church. "Think you could buy her some clothes?"

"It's what Mr. Knows asked," he said holding out his hand. "Get her what she needs until you can take her out."

"Two hundred enough?" she asked.

"This is Hollywood," he said with a smile. "Four hundred be a good start."

"Fine," she said, handing him the bills. "Comfortable clothes for now."

Once inside, she showed her to the spare bedroom, then had Randy leave to bring back dinner.

"Sofia, while we wait for dinner," she said, sitting her down, "can you tell me how you ended up at the church?"

"When I was taken," she slowly began, "they placed me with others in a steel container and taken aboard a ship. They would open the top to give us water and food. We spent many days in the dark, but there must have been a terrible storm, for the ship rocked from side to side. Some of the containers broke loose, one struck ours, making a hole that I could see out of. The storm must have damaged the engine, for I saw a helicopter with the Mexican flag circling. We could hear the sailors yelling about needing a tow."

"Would you mind if I write down what you've said?" she asked, knowing Hayseed would need to review all she witnessed. "And how is it you speak English so well?"

"My father was once an important man in our country," she replied, "and taught me English, so one day I could come here."

"You learned well," she replied with a smile. "Please continue."

"The harbor was very large," she began again, "they placed us on trucks, and we passed through many Mexican cities. We traveled for five days, where they took us to a tunnel, and it was there we heard that five had died."

"Any idea what they did with them?" she asked.

"I do not know," she admitted.

"What did you do for bathrooms," she continued to inquire, "and food?"

"A toilet with a hole in the bottom," she explained. "Each night, they would stop at large empty buildings and give us food. Inside the container was water, and each morning they gave us a bag with sandwiches."

"Disgusting," Janice blurted out while writing, "treating you like animals."

"After leaving the tunnel, I saw a sign," she continued, "saying W-286. Then we ran through a cornfield to a farm having red and green lights, they made us entered his barn. They opened the floor, and we went down into a cellar."

"Did you hear anything?" she asked.

"Yes an argument with the farmer," she quickly answered. "Showers were given and food. I heard one man say he wished there was more money, and did not like having to leave the women alone."

"They never tried raping anyone?" she asked, surprised by what she heard.

"The farmer was a very large man, and reminded him that the last one who tried…" she paused for a second before speaking, "they found with his balls in his mouth. He reminded the man they paid him well to transport only, but offered to make a call. The man said he understood, and wished no further discussion. As the man walked away, the farmer reminded him Americans paid top dollar for virgins."

"What happened after that?" she continued to probe her memory.

"Three trucks came," she answered, "and for three days drove us only during the day to a warehouse on the property of the Zone studio. When they were unloading, I ran through many buildings where I found my Fred working. He hid me in the editing room, and later took me to the church."

"So that's how the two of you met," she said, surprised by such a freak meeting, "but how did you become man and wife?"

"I found him passed out in the courtyard." She paused as if remembering the day. "He was very sick, so we took him in. I tended him, and we fell in love. So little time together, he was so frail that God took pity."

"So sorry for your loss." Her heart seemed to ach for her sorrow.

"The drugs destroyed my love," she reminded her, "and I will help stop it from happening to others."

"Then together we will," she said, standing up. "I must make a phone call, and Randy will be back shortly…

"Finally," she said as Randy entered the building with food. "Need to have you stay with Sofia."

Within minutes a cab pulled up, and Janice, without explaining, ran out. She was dropped off in the middle of a busy shopping center, where she saw Agent Hayseed standing by his car.

"Why all the mystery?" he asked as she approached him. "Get in, and I'll drive."

"I was worried you had not arrived yet," she said, climbing into the vehicle.

"Bureau chief wasn't happy about this," he chuckled, "but after told him I'll take a vacation, he gave me a week to look into it."

"Well, here is what I have," she began to read him from the interview.

"That is quite a story," he admitted while he listened to her, "but first we need to verify some of it. Now if the vessel suffered damage and towed, there will be a record of it. I know people that can verify it, and can be trusted. The sign reported is mile marker, and we can track that down very easy."

"She wants to help," Janice replied as he drove, "and if all she says is true I have a request that you can help with."

"Name it," he quickly answered.

"Green card for now," she began, "and later, citizen status."

"WOW," he said, slowing down the car as he spoke. "Might need to call in a favor, but I have someone in mind that could help."

Finding a safe place to pull the vehicle over, Hayseed slid out of the car and made his call without her listening.

"Alright," he began when finally entering the car, "here is the deal. I must meet her, and explain what needs to take place."

"Fine," she agreed, "but under no circumstances are you to act like an FBI agent."

"How should I act?" he asked.

"Like a gentlemen," she told him with a smile, "meeting a young lady who needs our help."

Entering the building, they found the young nameless man enjoying conversation, and having eaten with the two.

"We set aside food for you," Randy replied as he stood up. "Hello, Agent Hayseed."

"You said—" Sofia blurted out while standing, "You said…"

"Ms. Jabra," Carson strolled over to her and in a calm tone took her hand. "I'm here to help, just like everyone else. Now, I'm working on a green card for you, but first we need to find you a sponsor."

"No problem," Janice said, walking over to the couple. "I'll sponsor her."

"Need someone who has the authority to hire her", he explained, "or provide support while she attends college."

"Let me make a phone call," she said, walking into her bedroom. "Who would he need to call?"

"Here," he said. writing down a name and number. "Use my name when he speaks with him."

"All finished," she said walking back out and entering the kitchen. "Know you must be hungry," Janice replied after placing several items out on the table, "so let's eat."

"Could eat," he said. walking over to her as his small phone began to vibrate. "It's my friend, so I'll take the call outside."

After several minutes, Carson reentered the building, having an expression of disbelief on his face.

"Ms. Jabra," he slowly began, "your green card is coming."

"You're not arresting me?" she said, almost fainting as she rejoiced.

"Arresting? No," he admitted while looking toward Janice, "and you never mentioned her sponsor would be Mr. Acorn, head of the network."

"Said you needed someone with authority to hire," she said, laughing as she spoke, "and he has that right."

"Scared the living you-know-what out of my friend," he said, finding the humor in his words, "but the card's good for a year and renewable. It also gives you the right to apply for permanent status, citizenship."

"Thank you," she said, giving both a hug. "I'll come with you to show you farm. Prove I will be good American, and help others."

"Not necessary," Carson spoke up, "too dangerous."

"Think we need her," Janice spoke up. "She knows the ranch, and we can't afford to get it wrong."

"Well I'm out of here," the nameless young man said as he started toward the door. "Oh, by the way, spent all but $30 that Randy has. Now if you need anything, gave Randy my number."

"Just who is he?" Carson questioned as the young man left. "An interesting character, no doubt."

"Yes, he is," she said with a smile, "but someone who knows the town and can get us anything we might need, including information."

"Now that we got the green card," Carson began as he started toward the door, "need to get to office and make some phone calls."

"The people you're calling," she began, interested and concerned about those he needed to call, "can they really be trusted?"

"Yes," he said looking her straight in the eyes, "especially when they know it's the Columbian cartel we're after."

"If you trust them," she finally agreed to stop questioning him, "then so be it."

"Might be a day or so before I come back," he said, opening the door while speaking, "but with any luck have something we can use."

For two days with the new clothes and no fear of arrest, the three strolled the streets and shops.

"It is like when I was home," Sofia said, entering the building after having bought several articles of clothing, "going to the market with father."

"Answer the door," Janice yelled out while preparing the nightly meal.

"It's Agent Hayseed," Randy yelled back.

"Just in time for dinner," she yelled as he entered the kitchen.

"Got good news," he said opening his jacket and bringing out a small note-book, "and bad."

"Start with the good first," she said, placing the food on a platter, "then the bad news after we eat."

"Good news is we've identified the name of the ship," he began reading from the notebook, "Night Star owned by a Columbian corporation. Also located the mile marker, which has four ranches near it."

"Alright, everyone," she shouted for them to come to the table. "Dinner's ready."

After they had eaten, Carson pushed himself away from the table.

"Great meal," he said, as if congratulating her. "Now the bad news."

"I'm ready," she said, looking toward the group.

"As I said, they identified the ship that may have brought Sofia," he slowly began, problem is it docked yesterday. The Mexican authorities had no reason to search, and if there were illegals, they've been off loaded already."

"Which means their headed to the border," Janice said looking toward the others.

"The worst is that we're on our own," he continued. "The bureau cannot commit resources without hard evidence."

"In three of four days, they will be across the border," Sofia blurted out as if to remind them, "and then be gone forever."

"Even by leaving now," Carson suggested, "and driving straight through, we'd be too late to help."

"Right," Janice replied while taking out the number of the nameless young man. "Let's pray for a miracle."

"Well, did you get the miracle we need?" Carson asked as she walked out from the bedroom, "Or do you have another plan?"

"Can't say," she said with a puzzled expression. "Told him what we needed, and all he said was, 'is that all?'"

"We could find a place near the studio," Carson suggested, "and watch for the trucks to come in."

Less than an hour later a large limousine pulled up outside, then a man wearing a black suit knocked on the door.

"Please come," he said without introduction, "we've little time."

"Where are you taking us," Janice asked. "We've not packed."

"All necessary arrangements have been made," he said, turning as he spoke. "Please hurry."

"You heard him," Carson replied while shrugging his shoulders. "I have my .45."

Within a half hour, the entire group arrived at an airport where a small private jet waited on the runway.

"Hello," a large man having silver hair greeted the group, "please hurry. The tower cleared us for takeoff 10 minutes ago."

"Janice, I don't know who you know or pray to," Carson said as he buckled in the comfortable seat, "but you got your miracle."

Chapter Twelve

W "Everyone comfortable?" the co-pilot asked, walking to the rear of the jet. "We'll be landing in about an hour. Unfortunately, we've no food but water."

"Water would be nice," Janice said, unsnapping her safety belt. "I had no idea we'd be treated to such extravagance. May I ask who arranged all this? I would like to thank him personally if possible."

"I assumed you spoke with the gentleman," he seemed shocked by her remarks, "who arranged all this."

"Can you tell me his name?" she said, wanting to know.

"Really don't know his name, but been told he's some rich kid," he explained, "made millions designing video games. However, was told he would do anything for you, something about his future sister in law."

"Sister in law?" she said, expressing doubt.

"Didn't you save some young lady soldier?" he replied. "That was you, right?"

"Yes, that was me," Janice said, remembering the young woman. "It's a small world."

When they finally landed at a small private airport, they found a camouflaged Humvee waiting in one of the hangers.

"Believe that is your ride." A lone man walked over to Carson and said, "Your partner called in some favors."

"The vehicle?" he said looking toward the modified vehicle. "Thanks."

"Nothing to do with that," he said, handing him a leather pouch.

"What's your name?" Carson asked, taking the pouch from his hand.

"Never here," he replied as he walked away.

"Janice, it's a Hybrid," Randy blurted out as he began reading the manual left on the driver's seat, "gassed and ready to go."

"Might want to see this first," Carson shouted. "Got satellite photos of the area."

"How in the world did you come by these?" Janice asked.

"Can't say," he admitted, "but the photos show tractor paths. There are several small buildings, probably used by those harvesting the crops."

"Look at this!" Randy came out wearing night vision googles. "They even have supplies stored in the back."

"He thought of everything," she said under her breath. "Quiet vehicle with supplies for a week."

"We could use these buildings to hide," Carson suggested. "No one would be using them until harvest time."

"We need to get going," Janice began ordering, "have to be there before sunrise."

"This is the quietest Humvee I have ever drove," Carson said as they drove down the road. "It's been modified and done well."

"When Sofia identifies the farm," she began while studying the photos, "we can use the batteries and goggles to travel along the tractor paths."

"I was thinking the same thing," he said, agreeing with her. "Just hope I'm right about people not living in those buildings."

"A little late to be worried about that now," she replied in a humorous tone.

"There it is!" Sofia shouted from the rear seat. "The farmhouse."

"Here we go," Carson said, turning off the engine and lights. "Hand me those goggles."

Following the narrow tractor path, the Humvee slowly plowed through the field toward the small buildings.

"Looks deserted," Janice said as they passed two. "Need to find a place to hide this vehicle and then a place for us to stay."

"Want to use the one furthest from the owner's home," he said, pointing to it, "and put this behind it."

Once they parked the vehicle behind the building, they entered to find two old metal beds and a dirty kitchen area with running water.

"Well, this is no hotel with room service," he said while touching the mattress that released dust, "but could stand for a little house cleaning service."

"Thank God we can sleep in the Humvee," Randy replied, "or the floor."

"I'll find a broom," Sofia said looking in a closet. "We'll clean the floor, and make it good."

"Sun's rising," Carson said while watching Sofia sweeping. "We can't stay in this mess. Let's get out of here and find a store where we can get what we need. Might consider putting up at a motel until tonight."

"We'll make a list," Janice added. "Plastic for the floors and air mattresses."

"If we're leaving," Randy replied, "a nice meal maybe."

"Better than the military MRE's," Janice reminded them. "May need them later."

"Let's go," Carson blurted out. "We know they won't be here today."

Within minutes, they were on the road and unobserved.

"Randy, I haven't asked before," Carson began, "are you certain your camera can take pictures without a flash or lighting?"

"Trust me, I can film by moonlight," he said as if defending himself, "or low light. Got the right film and speed. Understand you will not see faces clearly, but figures. If Sofia is right about the farmer turning on lights, we should have a great picture of the house."

"Depending on you Randy," Carson spoke up. "Won't speak of it again."

"There is a large sporting goods store and city with motels," Janice replied while checking her computer, "about 35 miles from here."

"Good," Carson said as he continued to drive, "far enough away from here that no one will notice us."

After shopping with a long list of supplies, the group ate at one of the many restaurants in the small city.

"Alright, I'll be waking everyone up around 8:00," Carson said as he handed each one a key to their motel room. "Get some sleep because, starting tonight, we go back."

"There're several fast food places here in town," Janice pointed out, "so we'll pick up dinner on our way out."

As scheduled, they were on the road by 9:00 with enough food to last until the following morning. Once again, they drove through the cornfield, using the tractor path.

Spreading the large sheets of plastic on the dusty floor, and then placing black plastic over the windows they began inflating the mattresses.

"Well, it's not perfect," Carson said after surveying the room, "but it's better. We now have to set up watch times, four hours outside."

"I can take the first watch," Janice volunteered.

"My idea," Carson spoke up, "Randy follows me then you."

"I watch after her," Sofia said while standing near the door. "I came to help."

"Just make sure when leaving," Carson said, pointing to the small battery lantern, "you turn it off before opening the door."

Once outside, Carson walked around the building to ensure no light was visible. After four hours, he entered the darkened building and woke Randy.

"It's after 2:00," he whispered, "your watch until 6:00."

"You know they won't be here for another two days," Randy said, rubbing his eyes while sitting up, "just saying."

"Can't afford taking any chances," he reminded him. "We need to stay alert and keep in mind there's a farmer who knows he's breaking the law."

"Right almost forgot about that," Randy said, standing up. "No need to speak of this again."

For the next two days, all went well; no sign of movement at night and the farmer seemed uninterested in either the crops or buildings.

On the afternoon of the third day, Sofia entered the building in a rush.

"Señor, someone's coming," she said, closing the door behind her. "A man and woman in a truck."

"Take the plastic off the windows," he ordered, "and I'll see where they go."

For several seconds the group could hardly breathe, hoping the vehicle wasn't out to inspect each building.

"They seem to be awful quiet," Janice said, while giving them a quick glance.

"What we have are two married people," Carson said while watching the two carefully leaving the truck, carrying blankets, "not to each other, getting together."

"Would like to film what they're doing," Randy blurted out. "Could put it in our movie."

"Well, for now, everyone relax," Carson said as he sat on one of the mattresses and took out his notebook. "Got his license plate number, just in case."

"They come out here a lot," Janice said while sitting beside Carson. "Look how prepared they are."

"What is important," he whispered to her, "is how long they stay."

An hour later, the two carefully exited the building and quietly drove away.

"Well, that tells it all," Carson replied. "Both married to someone else."

"Could be married," Janice said, trying to defend the two, "and just getting away."

"If it makes you feel better," Carson said while laughing at her observation.

"Like to think better of people," she replied while standing up.

Later, Janice said while entering the building, "They're coming! Saw people crossing the road and the farmer turned the lights on."

"Fifth day," Carson blurted out, "right on schedule."

"I'm ready," Randy said while taking hold of his camera. "Shall we?"

"Got a full moon tonight," Carson said while pointing to it, "and don't forget to film the farmhouse."

"Just let me do my job," he whispered, "and you'll have pictures."

While Randy began filming the group running toward the cornfield, Carson noticed all the small lights on the camera tapped over.

"Looks to be around 40 or more," he whispered to the group as Randy continued to film, "only four guards."

"Now what?" Randy asked as he stopped filming. "Can't see them now that they're in the cornfield."

"We wait," Carson said, as if relieved they had come. "Need to know where those guards go."

"You're wanting to follow them?" Randy asked, as if assuming his intentions. "And find out where those tunnels are."

"Correct," he replied, "and once we know, you will film it."

Within an hour, the four were walking back.

"You ready?" he asked Randy.

"Maybe we should go along?" Janice asked.

"No," Carson said, "stay here and watch. We should return in an hour or two."

After two hours, the two returned, both breathing hard.

"Found the tunnels," Randy whispered to her. "The maniac found the opening, and we went down to film it."

"Well, start filming the farmhouse," Janice said, ignoring his comment. "Two semi-trucks pulled up while the two of you were gone."

"They leave in the morning," Sofia replied as Randy began filming. "We must stop them."

"Can't do that," Carson quickly replied. "Got to let them go."

"We need them to deliver the people first," Janice replied, "to the studio."

"They suffer, and some may die," Sofia warned her.

"It's our only chance to arrest Zone," Janice reminded her, "by rescuing the people while they're on his property."

"I pray for them," she said, clasping her hands together.

"Well, while you pray…" Carson stood up. "I'll go down and put a tracker on one of their trucks."

With an hour, Carson had returned.

"Don't know how many times they've done this," he said, entering the building, "but enough for them to think no one's watching."

"They weren't watching the trucks?" Janice asked.

"Getting careless," Carson said with a smile as he spoke, "makes it easier on us. We'll be 10 miles behind them, and find out who's helping when they stop."

"The signal carries that far?" Randy asked.

"Up to 25 miles away," he replied, "and it's on a frequency no one uses."

"I have everything on this flash drive," Randy said, handing him the small item. "Can have your people see what I filmed."

"Appreciate it," he replied, taking the item as he spoke. "Let's see what they have to say now."

Having given his report over the phone and sending the information by computer, his superiors had instructed him to wait.

"Señor," Sofia carefully spoke up. "The trucks, they're leaving."

"Five in the morning," he said, looking at his watch. "Get everyone up."

"Thought you said we had to wait for instructions?" Janice asked while deflating the mattress. "What's the plan?"

"Follow the trucks," he answered. "Randy, you drive while I make a phone call."

Having made the phone call, Carson said nothing while monitoring the trucks ahead by computer.

"Maybe we should get closer?" Randy asked while driving.

"Doing good where we are," Carson said without looking up. "Twelve miles behind them, so just keep going."

By afternoon, Carson received the call he waited for, instructions.

"Got good news," he began. "When they stop for the night, we're to meet agents that will take our place. We've been ordered to rest up, then proceed to Hollywood."

"What else did they say?" Janice asked, knowing the length of the conversation.

"The Mexican authorities will not allow the ship to leave port," he explained. "They have unloaded the cargo and are not loading. In four days, authorities will board the vessel. A combined law enforcement operation is in the works, raids on homes and business belonging to the Columbian cartel are scheduled."

"Four days," Randy blurted out. "What if these trucks haven't delivered the people to the studio?"

"Be stopped by local authorities," he admitted. "Raids on the farmhouse and tunnels will go as planned."

"This is my story," Janice yelled out, "and now you want us to leave?"

"Hey, we've been doing all the work," Randy, in an angry tone, reminded him. "You wouldn't have anything without us."

"Look, call your Mr. Acorn," he suggested, "give him the information, and I'm sure arrangements can be worked out."

"Doesn't matter," Janice replied, showing her disgust and intentions. "Because we're not leaving you."

"Never intended to leave any of you behind," he replied as he wrote down all the important information he would need. "We started it together, and we will finish it. Now, have Mr. Acorn call those numbers, with the information given. The Mexican authorities might give him a little grief, but use my name. That should help."

Without questioning him further, Janice made the call.

As instructed, they turned over the tracking to two different agents, and finally got a restful sleep in a five star motel.

"Now on to Hollywood," Carson said, walking out of his room as the group assembled, "and got the call from my boss. Your network with camera crews will be present at all locations, including on the Mexican side."

"Thank you," Janice whispered to him.

"Be a helluva breaking story," he began, laughing while walking out of the motel.

"Let's hope we're broadcasting it from inside the studio," she said as if hoping.

"If all of you agree," Carson spoke while looking over each person, "we keep on the road stopping only when needed."

"Sleep in the car?" Sofia asked. "Stop only for food and bathroom."

"Yeah," he answered, "by the time we arrive, my people will have a place for us to stay. It will be near Zone's studio. We want to be close when those trucks arrive."

"Just make sure the place has decent food and showers," Randy said as he drove. "All of us be looking forward to a nice hot meal and shower."

"Promise, the place will meet your standards," Carson said, making a joke.

Within two days the group arrived in Hollywood and were given directions to a safe house overlooking the studio.

"Agent Hayseed." A young man wearing blue jeans and a polo shirt came out as they pulled up in the back of the brick structure. "My partner and I brought everything you might need. Been watching the place for the last three days, lot of activity but no trucks.'

"Is one of those for us?" he asked while looking over at the three garage stalls. "And what about food?"

"Use the middle one," he suggested, "the garage door works, but pull hard. Filled a freezer, and refrigerator."

"Ah, you're here," a second agent strolled out. "It's all yours, Agent Hayseed, and here are the keys to the place."

"Got the run of the entire building," the first agent pointed out. "Real sweet place."

"Janice, before we get settled," he said before she drove the vehicle in the garage. "We need to good shopping for clothes and other essentials."

"Good idea," she said, realizing all their clothes were unwashed.

"Buy anything you need," one of the agents said, taking out a black credit card, "on the government."

"Finding a mall," she replied, and he allowed the group to enjoy a day shopping.

Knowing the group had their fill of fast food, Carson had them enjoy a nice sit down meal at one of the restaurants in the mall.

"Now that's the way to spend a day," Janice said as they entered the building with sacks and boxes, "shopping and a fabulous meal."

"Well, let us not forget why we're here," Carson said while moving over to all the surveillance equipment that lined the windows. "Waiting again."

"Yeah, but look at this place," Randy replied as he strolled through each room. "Large beds with showers."

"A bathtub," Janice shouted out while looking into the room, "large enough to stretch out in!"

"Told you," Carson said while looking through one of the large camera's resting on a tripod, "you might need body shampoo."

"Well, in that case," she said, opening one of the packages, "do not bother me for an hour. Sofia, when I'm finished, it will be your turn."

"Gracias," she replied with a wide smile.

"Don't know how much that shampoo cost," Carson said as Janice came out wearing a white robe with wet hair, "but by the smell, worth every penny."

"Might share a little of that charm on Sofia," she said walking over to see the front of the studio. "She'll appreciate it."

"If I were 20 years younger," he replied, "and unmarried."

"Twenty years ago," she said, teasing him. "My mother would be tucking me in for bedtime."

"Point taken." Carson and the entire group began laughing.

On the afternoon of the third day, like clockwork, the trucks arrived.

"Can't believe it," Carson shouted as the trucks entered the studio without even being stopped by the security guard, "right on schedule."

"Now what?" Janice asked with interest.

"Call my boss," he said with excitement in his voice, "and tell him to make ready for tomorrow. At 9:00 tomorrow, teams from both sides of the border will raid businesses and homes."

"Then I'll have to call Mr. Acorn," Janice announced, "to arrange schedules."

"Make your phone call," he suggested, "while I make mine."

"My God, you seemed to be on that phone for hours," Carson said as she entered the room. "Why?"

"Each person will be given time," she began explaining, "and when to introduce them into the story."

"Now they must prepare dialog, so they can explain their segment," Randy continued, speaking quickly and to the point.

"Which means I must prepare myself," Janice said while taking a deep breath.

Just as the studio was to close for the night, the trucks left. It was a sleepless night for both Carson and Janice, both preparing for the morning activities.

"Wonder what they're doing here," Carson replied while looking at his watch. "Three older ladies entering the studio."

"It's only 7:00," Janice replied while folding a large sheet of paper.

"Doesn't matter," he replied, "in two hours we move."

"Just hope we find the people there," Janice began pacing.

"Morning everyone," the two agents that occupied the house first strolled in the back way, "Agent Hayseed, got eight agents ready to go."

"Good," he replied, "once the security guard is in custody, get to the office. Every building checked, and under no circumstances is anyone to make a phone call. The warehouse is my responsibility, and I'll call for more agents once I'm inside."

At 9:00, they descended on the studio, and within minutes entered the warehouse where they found the people.

"Please ladies," Carson in a calm tone spoke to the terrified people, "FBI."

"Maybe I should speak to them?" Sofia said, taking his arm.

In Spanish, she began speaking, and instantly, the people stopped screaming.

"Agent Hayseed," Janice said walking over to him. "Might want to come with me."

"These ladies gave up," Randy said while filming them, "they're cutting heroin."

"Film it," he ordered, "and then start filming the ladies in the other room."

"This is Janice Gardner reporting live," she began as Randy began recording, "I'm here at the Zone studio in Hollywood. I am proud to report that a human trafficking and drug operation has been exposed. Behind me are 47 young woman, some as young as 12, who have been rescued by the FBI. This is a joint operation between our country and the Mexican government. I can only say at 9:00 this morning, multiple raids were conducted by authorities from each country."

Throughout the day, Janice made reports of the progress with the investigation and always introduced those reporting the events in the different locations.

"Well how are we doing," she asked Carson, who had disappeared for several hours then reappeared, "long day?"

"Six thirty," he replied, looking at his watch, watched the 6:00 broadcast and as usual did a fantastic job. You can tell your 11:00 that we did well. However, three of the five Columbian leaders of the cartel have escape capture."

"How is that possible?" she asked. "And Mr. Zone, where is he?"

"Apparently, the three left for a resort five days ago," he began, "leaving relatives or girlfriends to watch the home. They didn't announce where they went, but over 200 associates were arrested. Our Mr. Zone was with an actress at her home during the raid. However, all his accounts are frozen and his photo given to all law enforcement officers."

"I'll report arrests are forthcoming," she said with a smile, "but stress the number of apprehensions."

"Just a matter of time before they're captured," he replied as if reassuring her. "They've no place to hide, which includes Zone for sure."

"Any casualties?" she continued to seek answers. "Need to know."

"Couple wounded," he reported, "but most gave up without a fight."

"Thank God," she said, relieved knowing. "It's surprising they gave up without a fight."

"Hard taking on tanks," he added, "and combat helicopters."

"Yay for the army," Janice shouted.

The story captivated the interest of the people, allowing Janice to broadcast the daily and nighttime special report. On the third day, she introduced a young Mexican female reporter, working the story concerning the seizure of the vessel.

"Anna, what have you learned?" she asked while viewing her on the large screen.

"First let me say what an honor it is working alongside you," she began, "but our wonderful officers having searched the vessel have found over $20 million in cash. Along with the money, 40 stolen high-end vehicles, valued around $6 million. They have located containers of weapons, and drugs. It's believed the weapons were meant for terrorist organizations in the middle east."

"A fine report, Anna," Janice said, giving her credit.

"Just following in your footsteps, Ms. Gardner," she said with a wide smile.

One the fourth day, the heads of the three Columbian leaders were found with a warning to stay out of Mexico. Then finally, on the fifth day, they discovered the body of Mr. Zone in an alley, having two bullets to the back of his head.

With interest waning and other news breaking, Janice watched as Carson gave the press a final update.

"Watched the interview," she said as Carson strolled in her office, "you were impressive. Got a little heated, will you get in any trouble telling off that reporter?"

"Little shit accusing me of working for you," he said as he sat down, "just put him straight, that's all."

"Told him to get off his lazy ass," she began laughing, "and then try working as hard as I do. Appreciate the compliment, but what will your boss say?"

"He called as I came here," he replied with a smile. "Said it was the best interview yet."

The following morning, Janice received word: "Return to New York."

Before leaving, Janice arranged one last dinner with the others.

"Real fancy place," Carson said, waiting outside of the restaurant. "You look beautiful."

"You clean up good," she replied, noticing the tuxedo he wore.

"Been through a lot together," he said, taking her by the arm, "wanted our last night to be special, so yeah I cleaned up."

"Got some good news for Sofia," she replied as they entered.

"Yeah?" he said, walking her over to the table where she and Randy sat. "So do I."

"Hello everyone," she began, "tonight is our night, so enjoy."

"Sofia you've been so helpful," Janice began after enjoying one of the most expensive but wonderful dinners. "Mr. Acorn has awarded you a full scholarship."

"I'm going to college?" she asked as tears began to flow down her cheeks. "And costs nothing?"

"That's right," she said, handing her a napkin and a contract. "We hope you'll study journalism and join our network. Additionally, Mr. Knows is your mentor, he will be there for you."

"Which means Sofia," Hayseed added while opening his coat, "you're eligible for student deferment. There is one more thing, while going through Mr. Zone's paperwork we found this."

"What is it?" she asked, taking the envelope from his hand.

"A $100,000 life insurance policy," he explained. "Apparently Zone insured all his people. You will notice he's the beneficiary, when next of kin cannot be determined. In this case, you are entitled to the money."

"I…" She was unable to catch her breath, "Do not know what to say."

"Thank you," Janice whispered in his ear.

"Been a night all of us will remember," Carson said with a smile. "You're leaving for New York, and I'm heading to Washington."

"Back to your family?" she asked.

"Yes," he said, squeezing her hand, "and a month of paperwork."

"Agent Hayseed," Randy said placing a small camera on the table, "maybe we could get someone to take our picture?"

"Want double copies," Carson insisted. "One copy to show my family and the other for the office."

After a lengthy jet ride, Randy and Janice arrived in New York. The two were then escorted immediately to the network's building, where everyone seemed anxious to shake their hands or congratulate them.

"Come in, Janice and Randy," Acorn yelled out as they walked toward his staff of people, all standing.

"Afternoon, Mr. Acorn," they said while closing the door. "Didn't expect all this."

"Did you see our ratings?" he said while spinning around in the chair. "Phenomenal!"

"Happen to see Agent Hayseed's interview?" she asked as they sat down.

"Where one of the jackals accused him of being a sponsor to this network?" he replied while laughing. "And his answer, of course!"

"Think that helped with ratings?" she replied.

"Mostly, it was you," he admitted, "giving the other reporters credit for their hard work and always mentioning the FBI and other agencies working the case. Even gave your Randy, and the other camera operators a shout out."

"Have to give them credit," she said. "They delivered some fine footage."

"Especially when they blew the hell out of those tunnels," he continued. "Too bad we could not show the heads."

"Would have been a bit much," she responded, shaking her head and chuckling.

"Now let us talk about you," he said, turning his attention to her. "What would you say if I offered you nightly anchor for all national news?"

"Maybe I should let the two of you talk about that," Randy said, standing up, "where she goes I follow."

"Randy, great work out there," he said as he left the office.

"First, I would point out you have some wonderful people doing it now," she began, "and their ratings are better than any other network."

"Change is good for that slot," he said in a calm tone, "and right now, our viewers want to see you there."

"Not interested in pushing good people away," she explained, "especially when they do the work that keeps people watching. Remember when you're climbing a ladder, one should never pull someone off."

"People retire all the time," he mentioned. "You are ready."

"Haven't heard a thing about retirement," she added, "and right now I'm still not ready to anchor a nightly broadcast."

"People want to see you," his voice insisted in a solemn tone. "They voted you the most trustworthy reporter above all the others, and that says a lot."

"Appreciate it," she said, shaking her head, "but I like reporting stories of interest."

"Fine," he said not wanting to argue. "You are hard headed."

"Which is why you love me," she told him with a smile.

"What would you say about special broadcast reports?" he began. "An hour time slot maybe twice or three times a month?"

"That would be something I'd consider doing." She seemed pleased by the offer.

"Give me a day or so," he said, relaxing in his chair, "and I might have something."

"In the meantime, I'll spend time with my family," she replied, standing as she spoke.

"It's been a long while since my last visit."

"By the way," he said, stopping her from leaving the office. "Got word that the sanctuary is doing quite well with over 1,000 patients. The army they formed located the insurgent's home base and training ground. Apparently, they killed or captured nearly 1,400, which means they no longer exist. Word is they intend keeping the army in place and are securing their borders."

"That is wonderful news," she said, remembering the destruction.

"All the leaders have agreed to work with the current government," he continued. "You started something there."

"No the people started it all," she said with a slight smile. "I just reported how a few courageous doctors kept the peace."

"Well, you had a hand in it," he replied, "by showing them how to do it."

"I'll leave a number where you can reach me." She could say no more without breaking down.

CHAPTER THIRTEEN

Surprising everyone when she arrived, the children quickly surrounded her as did Linda.

"Why didn't you call first?" Linda asked, trying to fix her hair and seeming to scold her. "I could have had dinner prepared and not looked like a mad woman."

"Wanted to surprise you," Janice said, holding Susan in her arms, "and what better way than this? So where're Frank and Leone?"

"Oh dear," she said, grabbing Lisa as she spoke, "Leone is in the hospital, and Frank's there to keep him company."

"Why didn't you tell me?" Janice asked, placing Susan down. "Is it serious?"

"You know Leone," she said in a calm tone. "He wouldn't admit pain if it were killing him. He checked himself in without telling us, saying he had a slight pain in his stomach. Anyway, two days ago they removed a piece of shrapnel. The doctor says it was successful but wanted to keep him for an extra day or so."

"Would you mind if I go now to visit him?" she asked.

"Mommy, can I go with Auntie?" Susan asked, almost pleading with her.

"Maybe she would rather go alone," she replied.

"I'd enjoy the company," Janice quickly replied. "She won't be any trouble, and I know Leone would like seeing her."

"Please Mommy?" Susan said, folding her hands as if praying.

"Alright, you can go," she said as if surrendering to their wishes, "but mind your manners when you get there."

Walking in the hospital brought back memories when her mother was sick, and the time she shared with Russell.

"Well, I come down to visit..." She strolled in the room where Leone lay and Frank sat, "And have to learn you're here?"

"I wish you called first," Leone said, sitting up in the bed and covering himself. "Don't like you seeing me like this; it's embarrassing."

"You said we're family," she said, walking over and giving him a quick kiss, "and Frank, I'm holding you responsible for not telling me."

"Daddy's in trouble," Susan said while jumping up on the bed. "Isn't he, Uncle Leone?"

"Think we both are dear," he said, giving her a hug. "Think she'll forgive us?"

"Yeah," Susan replied when watching Janice giving Frank a hug and kiss.

"What would you say about ice cream?" Frank said looking toward Susan. "We'll let Auntie and Leone have some private time."

"Okay, and we'll bring some back," she said, jumping off the bed.

"How do you really feel?" Janice immediately asked while alone.

"Fine, really," he replied. "Doctor said they removed the shrapnel that gave me trouble. Be going home tomorrow, so there is no need to worry."

"Linda said you wouldn't admit being hurt even if it killed you," she said, but in a tone showing concern.

"Then let's talk about you," he began with a wide smile, "been watching television, and what a great job saving all those young girls. You definitely pulled the stinger out of the Columbian cartel. What nearly $500 million lost?"

"Truthfully, they say the money isn't important to the cartel," she explained. "Losses like that are the nature of the business they're in. What is important was the organization, they made millions for a very long time. Most know they will return, but more careful."

"That may be," he admitted, "but tonight, they're gone."

"Coming over here..." Her tone became somber. "I've come to love all of you like family and the thought of anyone of you hurting...

"You know what the greatest pleasure we've had is?" he asked, gently placing his hand on her face, "Was the day you came into our lives. You are family, and we all love you."

"Was a great day for me, too," she replied.

"Alright," Frank entered the room carrying ice cream cones, "we had a choice of vanilla or chocolate, but they ran out of vanilla."

"Did you make Auntie cry?" Susan asked while wiping Janice's cheeks.

"They're happy tears," she said while placing Susan on her lap, "just happy tears."

"You know one of the nurses said there was a new restaurant opened downtown," Leone began while accepting the cone from Frank, "what ya say we all go there tomorrow night? My treat."

"Oh no," Janice said while licking the cone, "my treat. Got a nice raise, and a company credit card that hasn't been broke in yet."

"Well, there you have it," Leone said as if rejoicing, "and this week, let's get all dolled up for a family portrait."

"Can I have my own?" Susan asked, nearly falling off her lap.

"Sure." Frank seemed delighted by the idea. "I'll make the arrangement and have them put in a nice frame for everyone."

"Like a wallet size one," Leone suggested.

"Good idea," he blurted out. "Let's get going and let Leone sleep."

As Janice prepared for bed, she noticed Frank sitting alone as if deep in thought.

"Frank, please tell me the truth." She began walking toward him. "What's Leone's condition?"

"You know Leone was wounded overseas," he slowly began, "by some type of personal round. There's a lot of little pieces of shrapnel in his back. The doctors think any operation to remove them would cause more damage. The piece they removed was against his stomach, it was sharp, but they got it out. Right now, everything looks stable, so we just have to wait."

"What about a second opinion?" she asked while sitting.

"Seen a great many doctors," he admitted. "All say the same thing."

"If you really care for me," she said, touching his leg, "you'll call me if anything changes."

"Promise," he said, patting her hand then crossing his heart, "you'll be my first call."

"Thank you," she replied, standing up. "Can't explain, but I feel close to him and all of you."

"We're family," he replied while looking over and noticing Linda listening.

"Good night, Frank," she said, turning and entering her room.

"She's a fine young lady," he whispered.

The week went quickly, but the family portrait arrived before having to leave.

"Wish you could have stayed longer." Linda came in the room as she packed. "But I'm so happy you spoke to her before going to school."

"She's my little sister," Janice said, looking at the portrait in a well-made frame. "Going to put this in my new office."

"Now promise to call," she said, holding back the tears. "We now have that computer set up."

"Every night," she said, walking over and giving her a hug. "I love you."

"Love you more," she said as tears began to flow.

"Now come on." Frank and Leone walked in. "She's not leaving forever, and we can talk and see her on the computer."

"Be careful," Leone replied while giving her a hug, "we all love you."

As hard as it was to leave, Janice looked forward to a new adventure. Entering the office, Mr. Acorn stood waiting.

"Janice," he yelled out, startling everyone, "come with me."

Walking past a secretary, he entered a large office with windows.

"Well, how do you like it?" he said touching the dark green desk. "Your new home here near my office."

"Beautiful," she responded, looking at the handcrafted wooden bookshelves and desk, "and so large, I don't know what to say."

"Got your own personal secretary," he added, pointing to the young lady. "She's been with us for about a year and have heard good things."

"I don't know what to say about all this," she continued to view the room, "I mean…"

"You're my best reporter," he interrupted her thoughts, "and brought advertisers wanting to join us. Even Randy was given an office, along with equipment he asked for."

"Office, a raise and secretary..." She turned to him. "So what have you arranged for Randy and me?"

"What about an interview with the Mexican president," he blurted out, "who never allows any American to attend his news conferences?"

"He hates Americans," she added, "and makes it known by his speeches."

"The man has never allowed an American journalist to interview him," he said taking her by the arms, "yet he has asked for you. The staff at this very moment is preparing all the arrangements, and it appears he will be available in a week."

"A week?" she said as he released her. "Make sure he understands I'll be asking hard questions. Questions I'd like him to answer, without any advisor being there."

"I'll inform the staff," he said walking out, "be good having you so close to my office."

"Maybe we should introduce ourselves if you're working with me," Janice said to her new secretary while walking out of the office, "I'm Janice, and you are...?"

"Ah," she sat up as if in shock, "Carolina Dell.

"Good," Janice said, walking over and taking her hand, "come along."

"WOW, you've a great view," she said while following Janice inside the office.

"Now my door is always open to you," she began, "and Randy."

"Mr. Acorn gave me a list of my duties," she said, walking back to her desk and showing her the list.

"Just remind me of my appointments," taking the list and tearing it, "and normal stuff that you've been doing for others."

"I can do that," Carolina said with a smile while watching her place the list in the trash basket.

"One thing," she continued, "if any of my family calls you're to let me know immediately. I'll give you their names, and remember..."

"Call you immediately. no matter where or what you're doing," she blurted out while laughing. "Understood."

"Now they say I'm to interview the president of Mexico," she said while strolling back into her office. "Could you collect all of his speeches? Also, bring up any information on the economy, and any data I could use about the conditions there."

"Mr. Acorn has already assembled that information," Carolina said while pointing to several large boxes. "If you wish, I can organize all the paperwork and catalog it."

"We've an hour interview," she explained, "so we don't want to waste it on trivia."

For three days, the two reviewed all the material, and finally after hours of discussion, 20 questions were written out.

"Can't believe we did it," Carolina said while reading over the questions. "These are really good. You do know some of them might end the interview quickly, or land you in a jail somewhere in Mexico."

"Maybe," she began laughing at the very thought, "but I'm prepared."

"Wish I could come with you," she said, knowing it was impossible, "but even if there was a way, I couldn't."

"Why couldn't you?" Janice asked.

"Live with my mother," Carolina informed her, "she's disabled and needs me. Oh, it's not that bad," she continued explaining, "her back gave out years ago, and she can't stand or walk much."

"If you need anything," Janice said, touching her shoulders, "just ask, okay?"

"You're about the best boss I've had."

Her face turned a slight red.

"So, when I'm gone," Janice said, handing her the key to her office, "you're in charge. If you need me for anything, send a message on phone or computer."

With Randy, they entered the palace of the president and immediately were escorted to a large room.

"Ms. Gardner, we hope this room is agreeable," the man said while looking around the elegant room. "It's used for formal recitals. Please be careful when placing the equipment, the floors are pure marble."

"Great room." Randy began filming the entire area having murals with gold inlay. "Must have cost a fortune to decorate."

Within minutes, the staff laid several large handmade rugs down, then two comfortable chairs and small tables were brought in.

"Ms. Gardner," the president said. He was a strikingly handsome man who stood 6'1" with jet-black hair and beautiful green eyes. "May I say how wonderful it is to meet you."

"Mr. President," she said, standing then giving him a quick curtsy, "it is I who is honored to be here with you. This is my camera operator, Randy Kemp."

"Yes, I have admired his work," he said, sitting down, "along with yours."

"Thank you," they both spoke up.

"Shall we begin," he said while crossing his long legs.

"Certainly," she began. "Mr. President, you've been quite vocal in your speeches toward the American people. Could you explain such hostility, many would like to hear your views on the matter."

For 10 minutes, she allowed him to explain his position without interruption. He expressed his frustration by the American government treating Mexico as it were a stepchild in need of scolding, American farmers and businessmen treating his people as slaves, along with the wealthy believing his people were merely servants or gardeners. Then the overdependency to drugs, where so many are willing to pay.

"Understand," he said, finally finishing his criticism, "I wish only to provide my people with a sense of pride to be a citizen of this country. Our country has a rich history, equal to your own, and I intend it not be ignored."

"Everything you say is somewhat true," she began. "Many transgressions are committed against the Mexican workers. However, most Americans have no servants and work hard, which includes tending their own property. I applaud your efforts to instill pride in the people, but wonder why you can speak so harshly of America. You seem comfortable accepting our generous foreign aid, which I believe, is over $20 billion yearly."

"The aid which you refer to," his tone revealed a controlled anger, "has been use to improve the lives of my people. It has built schools and hospitals, new highways and better housing. Many citizens have been educated with those funds, who labor in those businesses. No one can accuse my administration of withholding money, or using it to make themselves rich."

"I would never accuse you or your government of wrongdoing," she spoke up. "The funds have greatly improved the living conditions of your people. I'm just pointing out you're quick to criticize, but fail to mention this to your people. Such was the case concerning the Columbian cartel. Your police and military did a superb job. However, no mention of FBI or DEA, who gave significant information to them. Evidence, which led to the seizure of the vessel and tunnels that your army destroyed."

"It was necessary to instill confidence in my people," he replied, defending his actions, "that our law enforcement officials and military are capable to fight such cartels."

"True," she said, looking into his face. "Last year in the southern provinces, there was an earthquake. An American relief organization sent over $3 million in food and necessaries to those towns effected. Your army was shown delivering and passing out those items, and there was no mention of where it came from."

"Yes, I am aware of the oversight," he admitted. However, the organization sought no notoriety."

"It was a religious foundation," she informed him, "that wished to avoid conflict. It was a gesture of good will, which you ignored."

"I must conclude this interview due to state business," he said, looking down at his watch, "but if you are willing to begin again tomorrow at the same time."

"If you must go," she realized only half an hour had passed, "we can finish the interview tomorrow."

"Before I leave," he said as he remained seated. "You have learned what is important to me," he began, "what is important to you?"

"Family comes first," she quickly answered, "and truth is second. Third is my country, and forth religion. Finally, my job, believing in the first four allow me to be a better reporter."

"Until tomorrow," he said with a slight smile as he removed the wires, "same time."

"Did you get all of it, Randy?" she asked once he had left.

"Oh yeah," he blurted out, "especially your answer about what is important."

"We have to include that," she said with a wide smile.

"I wonder if he'll even show," Randy said while helping her with the wires. "You pressed him hard.

"Find out tomorrow," she said, helping him with the equipment.

The following day the two entered the room and found it prepared for them.

"Ah, Ms. Gardner." He strolled in alone. "I must say yesterday you somewhat shamed and embarrassed me during the interview."

"It was not my intention," she admitted, "but if you're wanting an apology, you'll not be getting it from me."

"No, I expect none," he said, walking toward the chair, "your questions were to the point and truthful, which is why I've agreed to return."

"Is this where we start hearing El Deguello, or is it A Deguello?"

"El what?" Randy asked quickly.

"Give no quarter," she explained, "or slit the throat of the invaders."

"Very good, Ms. Gardner," he said, sitting down laughing, "a sense of humor and a knowledge of our history."

"I don't like the part about slitting throats." Randy's voice seemed to quiver.

"Antonio Lopez de Santa Anna," she said, turning to face Randy, "the Alamo."

"Oh yeah, I saw the movie," he blurted out, "the music they played."

"I must commend you on the collect use of his name," he said in a soft but calm tone,

"Unlike most," she said, sitting down and adjusting her wires, "I've read and enjoyed history of different countries."

"Let me begin by saying," he said, waiting for Randy to begin filming, "I've called the director of both FBI and DEA. I apologized for having neglected to mention their valuable information, which led to the elimination of the Columbian drug cartel."

"Maybe it's a good start," she added, "to ease some of the tension between our two countries and governments."

"Our two countries share many common beliefs," he admitted, "and similar problems. I cannot say I can resolve any of these concerns with your government; however, there are those in my government willing to try."

"Always good to know some are willing to try," Janice added.

For the next half hour, he seemed to shy away from criticizing America, and spoke of problems his government faced and how they were dealing with it. When the interview concluded, Janice realized much of what he spoke up could involve America. She also noticed his demeanor appeared to suggest a willingness to collaborate, with, of course, his officials.

Before leaving, he stood up.

"May I show you a room I am quite proud of?"

"Certainly," she agreed. Can we film it?"

"Of course," he graciously agreed, "an inspirational room, as my staff calls it."

Inside they found every wall covered with portraits of famous Mexican citizens, dating back hundreds of years.

"Maximillian," Janice walked over to study his portrait, "seems out of place here."

"He set in motion a pride in the people," he began, "that they could defeat tyranny and a great European country. Great men from Benito Juarez to Poncho Villa, along with poets and musicians."

"It is inspirational," she said, allowing Randy to film the room, "but I am sure some of these great people have crossed the border to extend their hand in friendship."

"Especially some of the musicians," Randy blurted out. "Got their albums.

"Yes, I believe you are correct," he admitted while looking over the many portraits. "It has been my honor having met both of you."

"Been our privilege being allowed this honor," she replied, allowing him to kiss her hand.

When the two returned to New York, they were greeted by the knowledge the interview was a success.

"Janice," Edgar Acorn shouted out as she walked toward her office, "did you see the ratings on your interview? In case you didn't, through the roof!"

"How's your mother, Carolina?" she asked as if ignoring his excitement.

"Better now that she knows I'm working for you," Carolina responded with a smile, "and thank you for asking about her."

"We girls have to stick together," Janice said with a smile. "Yes, Mr. Acorn, saw the ratings."

"Well, got another surprise," he said, walking over to her. "You've been invited to the White House where the president would like to speak with you."

"The president wants to sit down with me?" she said, looking down at Carolina, who seemed in shock, "And be interviewed?"

"Correct," Edgar replied, taking her by the hands. "Janice, pretty soon the entire world will be asking for you."

"When?" she asked as if out of breath.

"In a week," he replied. "Making all the arrangements now. Apparently, he watched your interview and decided to share his opinion."

As before, Carolina and her began researching everything related to the president, and especially his policies.

"By the way," Carolina said while walking over to her desk, "Randy mentioned you had some trouble with your computer while in Mexico."

"Something about the wrong connections," she said while watching Carolina turning on the computer.

"Well, I had our tech people fix the problem," she said while stepping away from the desk, "and now..."

"Auntie, can you see me?" Susan yelled out from the screen. "I can see the window."

"Hello, sweetheart," Janice quickly said, looking into the screen. "I can't believe it."

"Mommy said some nice men came," she explained, all excited, "and fixed it right."

"We're all here," Linda shouted from behind, "and they all wish to say hi."

One by one, they greeted her, and said how proud they were of her.

"Mommy said you could help me with my homework," Susan rushed in before Leone said goodnight.

"Now, sweetheart," she said with a smile, "we talked about that."

"Let mommy help," Susan said, as if disappointed.

"That's right," she continued, "but before bedtime, we'll talk."

"They're so nice," Carolina said as they signed off. "They really love you."

"Yes, they are and do," she admitted, "and one day I want you to meet them."

Prepared, Randy and Janice entered the People's House, and unlike in Mexico were first given a personal tour of the White House by the president.

"Thank you, sir," she acknowledged his generosity, "it was so kind of you to show us around, and I'm so privileged having seen it."

"Wanted to make you comfortable," he said, guiding her into the interview room, "so, ready?"

"Yes." She quickly sat across from him.

"Been filming since we got here," Randy replied.

"Listened to your interview with the Mexican president," he quickly started, "decided to clarify a great many issues he asserted during that meeting. First, we've never considered Mexico a step child, we've always thought the government as our ally. Yet all we hear is harsh criticism, blaming America for all their problems. Frankly' after listening to his explanation, I decided to let the people know how we see things."

"Please go on," she said, encouraging him.

"We know there are businesses and farmers taking advantage of his people," he continued, "but we've been active in locating these people and bringing them to justice. It does our economy no good when people receive near slave labor wages. Concerning the drug consumption, yes, we have a big problem, but this administration has opened more clinics to deal with those addicted. Yet his administration allows those same drugs to flood across the border, without any effort to stop it. He's an eloquent speaker, but does very little. If it hadn't been for your reporting and the FBI, the Columbian drug cartel would still be operating, with drugs and human trafficking. You are aware the Mexican cartel murdered the Columbian leaders, not the authorities?"

"Yes, we reported it," she agreed, "it never came up during the interview."

"The FBI believes nearly 1,500 women crossed the border," he continued to express his views, "with the help of the Columbians. We've learned nearly 70 percent of them were sent to Europe or Asia, yet the president of Mexico has shown no interest in locating them. Several months ago, we raided a sweatshop in Florida, rescued 100 women from his county. He gave a speech claiming we were holding them hostage, and treating them like animals. Sixteen were in need of medical attention for having worked 16 hours a day, the rest suffered from malnourishment. Spent over a month getting them healthy, even had his ambassador inspect their quarters."

"I never knew," she admitted, "was overseas."

"You mentioned the earthquake in southern Mexico," he continued. "We sent his rescue people equipment that could help finding people still buried under the rubble. Fifty very expensive monitoring systems, his government returned 22 units all broken or damaged. They claimed the others were missing, no doubt we'll be seeing them the next time they have an earthquake. You realize his tariffs are three times more than ours, and our American companies in Mexico must employee 90 percent Mexican labor. Under their law, all American workers must train two citizens and have them prepared to assume the position in two years."

"That I didn't know," she assured him. "I do know Americans are not allowed to own property or vote."

Many things our people aren't allowed to do if they work in Mexico," he replied, showing his frustration. "They must register every year to obtain a driver's license. They must report all travel to the local authorities, which gives permission. Now everyone knows my opinion of giving foreign aid to countries that are not friendly, which includes Mexico. I've had long discussions with many senators, many whom are starting to think as I do. We could do a lot of good for America with that money, better roads, hospitals, and schools would certainly be included. I haven't done nothing yet, but times are changing."

"Have our relations with Mexico gotten that bad?" she asked.

"Maybe," he admitted, "our border agents have reported Mexican armed troops escorting people across our borders. I've given warning on this. If he continues the policy, I'll send Marines to the border. Their orders will be to apprehend the soldiers, and if they resist to use whatever force necessary to make the arrest. Having armed soldiers crossing our borders is invasion."

"Isn't that a little extreme," she asked, "an armed conflict?"

"A foreign army with weapons crossing our border..." He was defiant, "Is an act of aggression and most certainly will lead to war. In the strongest terms, I've given notice, cease using the military to escort people across our border. My oath of office states clearly, I will defend the American people against all foreign or domestic armies."

"Hopefully he will heed your call to action," she said

"We'll see," the president responded with a slight smile, "besides with 40 percent of his people living in poverty, he has his hands full. You know about the hospitals he built with our tax dollars, but what he failed to talk about is after care. Many of the drugs they need once they leave the hospital aren't available, and most of his people can't afford what few drugs there are. However, that's for another time, so let's talk about what Americans need, it's what the people need to know."

For the next half hour, he presented an agenda of policies that he believed would help all Americans.

"Mr. President, I do thank you for the time you spent with us," she said, allowing him to take her hand, "and you certainly brought out many interesting points."

"You're referring to our discussion concerning Mexico," he said, understanding her concern. "I wanted our people to hear the facts of what is really going on."

"I have to admit you had your facts ready," she responded with a slight smile, "and I'm always happy reporting them. However, I am hoping we can avoid conflict; they are, after all, our ally and have been for some time."

"I do not expect either one of us will be best friends," he began, "but he must know I am no fool, and now he understands my position. In time, cooler heads will prevail from both sides."

"Cooler heads meaning executives," Janice said, understanding how politics work, "who have an interest of making money in both countries."

"His people will call my people," he said, chuckling over the very thought, "and in time they will work to tone down his rhetoric and new policies written. By the way, send me a copy of the interview for my library."

"We will," she replied as his staff whisked him away.

"Man, that was one great interview," Randy replied while packaging the equipment. "You allowed him to speak freely. How did you know he wanted to blast the Mexican president, and even warning him with us filming it?"

"Love or hate him," she said as they were being escorted out of the People's House, "he's a no nonsense person that will tell you what he thinks or knows."

"I'm sure by tomorrow," Randy said as he began placing the equipment in the van, "the Mexican president will regret having given us that interview."

"Want people to know they should not lie or hold back," she said, opening the door as she spoke, "information that I'm aware of."

"You knew about those things the president said," he replied, stopping and walking over to her. "Why didn't you ask him about them?"

"Then we would have never gotten an interview with the president," she replied. "Besides I'd rather have him tell the people."

After reviewing the interview, Edgar had it broadcasted during primetime.

"Good morning, Ms. Gardner." Carolina was the first to greet her. "Everyone's been talking about the interview, which was great."

"Apparently Edgar wants to see me," she said while noticing him waving as he spoke on the phone. Walking in, she sat without speaking until he ended the phone conversation.

"My God, what an interview," he began while standing and walking around the desk. "Had people cheering the president while praising you."

"Does that mean ratings were up?" she said as he sat on the edge of his desk.

"Doubled over your interview with the Mexican president," he began laughing. "Damn near called the nation to arms with you filming."

"It was a warning," she reminded him, "that his government will take serious."

"A feud between two countries," he blurted out, "and we have it on film."

"I'm just happy," she said with a smile, "you're happy."

"Got you something," he said, walking behind his desk and opening a drawer. "Know you're living in a small studio apartment."

"It's not small," she said, justifying her apartment. "Just right for me."

"Well, now you have a penthouse," he said, handing her a key. "Corporation just had it remodeled and wants you to have it."

"I've heard about this," she said, not wishing to touch the key just yet. "Taxes alone would take my salary. Besides, I'm never home, my studio suits me fine."

"Which is why we've given you a new contract," he said, taking it out of his coat pocket. "A five year extension with increase salary and bonus."

Taking the contract from his hand, she began reading it.

"You're including stock options and benefits?" she could hardly catch her breath with reading the amounts.

"Tell you what," he said while placing he key in his pocket. "We just purchased another building that we intend renovating. The rooms will be slightly smaller, but I'll allow you to meet with the designer and make what changes you want."

"Design my own apartment," she said, thrilled by the very idea, "and it's mine?"

"I'll write down the address where it is, "he said taking a pad, "and the name of the interior design company that will work with you."

"Can't believe you're doing all this for me," she said, taking out her pen and signing the contract, "I mean, it's like a dream."

"You've earned this and more," he said, taking the contract from her hand. "I was hoping to put you on the evening news desk but..."

"But what?" she knew something more was coming.

"Some very important people have asked that you interview them," he began. "Two former presidents that have not spoken to the press since leaving office. Foreign leaders have contacted us, along with of course Hollywood stars."

"Guess I'll be earning that raise," she said while standing.

CHAPTER FOURTEEN

"Ms. Gardner," an elderly black male wearing a polo shirt and blue jeans came running toward her as she entered the large room having several people working, "Mr. Acorn called that you might stop by."

"I just came by to meet with you," she said as the man gently took her hand, "and learn what you have in store for my new apartment."

"Well then, you must meet the man working on that," he said, standing straight to show his muscular body. "Just call me Vinnie, and I've assigned Liam Stewart, our top designer, to that task."

"How many people have you?" she asked looking over the man who stood 6'3" with graying hair.

"Ten total, but all are extremely talented." His brown eyes seem to brighten while he spoke of those he hired, "And Liam's one of the best."

"If Mr. Acorn selected you," she replied while following him through the different design desks, "you must be good."

"Liam," he called out to a young man wearing shorts and a half shirt, "may I present Mr. Janice Gardner?"

"Honored," he said, standing up showing his flat mid-section and nearly perfect physique. "Just knowing I am to be in the presence of such a beautiful and talented lady is reward enough. Trust me, I will be a most humble but loyal, servant catering to your every taste."

"I'm not looking for a servant," she said, looking into his brown eyes and handsome face. "Even a humble or loyal one. However, I do need a designer that can transform a very large room into comfortable living space."

"Then, my lady," he said, taking her hand and kissing it, "you've found such a person."

"Liam, may I say, you look like some handsome movie star," Vinnie said while laughing, "but do not let all that charm fool you. He is a great designer, who will make you a dream castle and much more."

"His attire does suggests he enjoys attracting attention," she said while rolling her eyes, but looking over his strong light brown legs and arms, she added, "and yes he does remind me of a young actor, but just can't remember who."

"Maybe by the time I'm finished," Liam said with a wide smile showing his white teeth, "you will remember."

"I've been to very few movies lately," she said, as if trying to ignore his comment, "and since my interests are elsewhere, I suggest we think only of the apartment."

"Liam, don't try outsmarting her," Vinnie said, shaking his head with a smile. "She's far better than any of us."

"Believe you're so right, Vinnie," Liam said, looking her over carefully.

"So, what is the first step," she asked, "in making my dream castle?"

"First I need to know more about you," Liam began in a soft but genuine tone. "Your favorite colors and likes or dislikes."

"I've duties to attend today," Janice replied while removing her day planner. "However, I can give you one maybe two hours tomorrow to discuss the matter."

"Unacceptable," he immediately blurted out, "come here at 11:00 tomorrow and be willing to spend three hours with me. Lunch will be on me, and I'll dress appropriately."

"Please, Ms. Gardner," Vinnie said while looking toward the man. "The time you'll spend with him is important. Mr. Acorn has been very generous with the renovations, and I believe the time spent will be most useful."

"Fine," she said, agreeing reluctantly. "Be on time, and for God's sake, no half shirt or shorts."

"Even wear shoes," he said, looking down at his sandals. "So, until tomorrow."

The following day, she arrived five minutes early and found he was in full dress with polo shirt and blue jeans.

"You look lovely," he said, looking over her light blue dress that revealed her slender body and legs. "Fine taste in color and fit."

"Ms. Gardner." Vinnie came over to her. "I've warned Liam to be on his best behavior today."

"You have nothing to worry about, she said in humorous tone, I'll buy a collar if he gets out of line."

"Kinky," Liam remarked aloud. "I like it."

"Be a choke collar," she blurted out, as everyone listening began laughing.

Once outside, Liam quickly opened her door and then gently closed it.

"Where to?" she asked as he slid into the passenger side. Hope you made reservations at a nice restaurant."

"Just follow the directions," he said while dialing the location on the vehicle's computer, "and please do not say anything."

After following the directions given to her by the voice, she exhaled.

"The zoo," she said, pulling up to the tollbooth.

"Five dollars, miss," the large man in uniform replied, "for parking."

"Here you are, sir," Liam said, reaching over with the bill in hand.

"Have a great day with us," he replied while raising the gate.

"You said we would be having lunch," she said, parking the vehicle, "and discuss what you're to do about my apartment."

"Come along," he quickly said while opening his door. "We've much to talk about."

Having paid to enter, his first stop was the bird sanctuary.

"Birds of the world," he pointed out the many species, "such vibrant colors."

"I love the light blue and yellow." She strolled over to view several chirping on a tree branch. "Or the gold on the wing of a butterfly and the soft brown of the lion."

"The lovely white fur of a polar bear," he calmly replied as if studying her, "only if I could capture the essence of your eyes and create the perfect color."

"Remember what I said about that collar," she began, laughing. "We're here to discuss colors."

"Yes, of course," he said as if snapping out of his thoughts. "Colors. What of the grey of an elephant, or brown of a giraffe?"

"Beautiful colors for them," she said while walking around the many trees and pointing, "but not for the apartment or me. Maybe a light green, like that."

"I have to say you're a beautiful lady," he said, gazing upon her. "Just watching astounds me, and I'm breathless."

"Appreciate what you said," she said, turning to face him, "but we've a lot to see and time is short. Besides, you promised lunch, and I'm hungry."

"Lead the way." He stepped aside. "Lunch is on me."

"Of course," she said while trotting toward the door, "it is."

For the next two hours, they journeyed through the zoo, speaking of color or admiring at all the different animals.

"Had a great time," she admitted while leaving the zoo. "Been a long time, but lunch was a little disappointing."

"Hamburg with fries," he began, "slaw and coke. What's disappointing about that?"

"You're right," she said, opening the car door, "a perfect meal for a wonderful time."

"One more favor," he said, sliding into the car. "Would you show me your apartment?"

"Absolutely not," she replied in a livid tone. "I don't invite anyone there."

"Please," he continued to insist, "it would give me a better understanding on what you consider comfortable. Five minutes, that's all."

"If I find you stalking me," she said, starting the engine, "I'll call Mr. Acorn and Vinnie."

Why she allowed him to enter, she would never know but found his interest only in the furnishings that surrounded her.

"Rocking chair," he said allowing it to sway back and forth, "old and not very comfortable, and your bed's so small."

"Yes, I know, she admitted while walking over and touching the bare wood, and the sofa is old, but they were my mothers. When she passed away, I sold our home. The high cost of living, and wasn't earning much."

"Do me a favor," he recommended. "Put tags on what you would like to keep.

"Fine," she agreed, "pictures of her and those I call family."

"This is a nice loft," he admitted, "but the new place will be so much better. The former owners spent over a million updating the electric, and all plumbing. They had great ideas, but failed to budget money, which drained them financially.

"How much money?" she asked.

"Five million," he replied, "Vinnie knew the architect who did the work. When it went up for sale, he called Mr. Acorn."

"They say he bought it for seven million," she said, surprising him, "a real bargain."

"Yes, it was," he said, walking to the door. "My five minutes are up."

"In two days," she said, following him, "I'll be leaving on assignment."

"Before you leave," he said, stepping out and watching her lock up. "I'll make up a quick design and show it to you."

"Well, I guess this was the first step." She turned to him. "Can't wait to see what the next step is."

"One can only hope it will get better," he said.

"In two days, since I'm leaving for three months, maybe I could treat you to dinner tomorrow," she asked.

"Be my great privilege to dine with you," he said, taking her hand and kissing it.

The following evening, Liam arrived wearing a well-tailored suit, along with 12 roses.

"WOW," she said, looking him over as he approached. "You look different."

"My grandmother always said," he said handing her the roses, "when attempting to impress someone, dress appropriate."

While they ate, she spoke of her mother, and the adopted family she loved.

"Oh my," she said, realizing she had consumed the entire conversation. "I've been so impolite by not allowing a word from you."

"I've enjoyed every word," he said with a smile. "Your enthusiasm when speaking of Susan or Leone. A kind heart speaks well of others, never themselves."

"Truthfully," she said, taking a deep breath. "I'm a little frightened by you."

"I'm not dangerous or a brute," he said, looking into her eyes, "so you need not worry I would do you any harm."

"You're charming and extremely handsome," she admitted, "but one day you may break my heart."

"To do such a foul thing," he began, "would certainly be the end of me."

"Please forgive me for mentioning such things to you," she said, being a little embarrassed. "We hardly know one another."

"No, you should express concern," he said, taking out a note pad, "and we could get to know one another by computer."

"Each night Susan and I talk," she told him, taking the small sheet of paper from his hand as she spoke, "and you may need my advice on the apartment."

"If there are changes," he agreed, "you could approve them."

"Yes, that would be nice," she said, relaxing somewhat. "We could find that we just want to be friends and no more."

"On the other hand, that you hate all my ideas," he began, laughing, "and want someone else working on the apartment."

As she and Randy were waiting at the airport, for the flight she saw Liam running toward them.

"Thank goodness, you haven't left," he said, out of breath while handing her a large envelope. "I finished the designs this morning and wanted you to look them over."

"But they're starting to board." She looked over toward the open doors.

"Take your time with them." He stood frozen. "And let me know when your free by the computer."

After reviewing the design, she could hardly contain herself with excitement. Once she signed off with Susan, she immediately sent a message to Liam.

"Hello Janice," he instantly said as the screen of her came on, "so how was your trip and did you have a chance to look over the plans?"

"Yes, and they're wonderful!" she nearly screamed into the computer. "But it must be late there."

"Not to worry," he replied. "Was hoping you would be on tonight. I slept earlier."

It was the first, and as days passed, she began looking forward to speaking with him about things unrelated to the apartment. But her days were filled with interviews of two ex-presidents, and retired western and comedy stars of old that never spoke to the press since leaving Hollywood.

"Well, Miss Gardner," one said as she was riding a beautiful white stallion alongside of a western legend. "What do you think of my ranch and animals?"

"They're beautiful," she said while patting the animals.

"A rare breed," he began, "called Andalusian."

"What makes them so special?" she asked, but she knew the answer, having researched his background.

"At birth they aren't white," he explained, "but by seven, pure white."

"Rare like you," she said, wanting him to open up, "a legend in Hollywood."

"Made over 50 films," he began, "made the studio and me rich. My favorite part was praise from the people that paid to watch me on the silver screen. Now I'm a legend, a name on a sidewall or wall with so many others."

"Some people only have their names on tombstones," she reminded him, "even after living a full life. You're a legend that will live forever in the films you made that future generations will see."

"I cried because I had no shoes," he said looking toward her as he spoke, "until I saw a man with no feet."

"I did not mean it that way," she said, assuring him.

"No," he answered, "but I did. I am so happy you came here. There's no reporter in the world that would have reminded me just how lucky I am."

"I'm the lucky one," she replied with a smile. "One of the fondness memories was watching your movies on the sofa with my mother."

With each passing day and interview, Janice was looking forward to returning and spending time with Liam. By the end of the three months, ratings were high, and her reputation as a fair reporter known to all.

"There is my girl!" Edgar Acorn came running over to her. "Number one in the ratings for the last three months. We have telegrams from just about every important person in America, congratulating us or asking for you."

"So does that mean I can have a couple days off?" she asked while taking her coat off. "To see my new apartment?"

"Wish I could clone you," he said, taking her by the shoulder and walking into her office. "Let one of you rest while the other makes us rich. But, of course, take time off, and enjoy your new apartment that I must say is marvelous."

"Carolina, you heard him didn't you," she yelled out, "make a note."

"Certainly, Ms. Gardner," she said laughing.

"Alright go," he said, releasing his arm around her shoulder, "and enjoy." Without waiting for him to reconsider, she fled from the office.

Entering the apartment, she found Liam inside placing vases of flowers around the room.

"Janice, you're home," he said, almost in a startled tone. "All your admiring fans set flowers, and I wanted them place just right."

"I'm so happy you're here," she said, walking over and removing her coat. "Been thinking about you and hoped you'd show me around."

"Good morning, Janice Gardner," a voice came over the many speakers, "I am Kim and so happy you have arrived. I have set the temperature at a comfortable 70 degrees, and have programed all machines for your instructions."

"Thank you...?" she replied while looking around the room.

"If you wish, I can begin running your bath water," the voice continued. "Having such a long journey, a warm bath might help ease the strain of work."

"No, thank you," she now said with excitement in her tone. "Maybe later."

"Kim, please allow me to show Ms. Gardner around the apartment," he replied while taking her hand.

"As you wish," the voice replied. "Sleep mode on."

"First, you've six large rooms," he said, leading her by hand. "The master bedroom the largest with walk in closets. An office room with desks and computer, and an entertainment room. All having cable televisions, along with stereo systems. The kitchen and dining room for 12 are open."

"Bath and shower in each of the guest rooms?" she asked.

"Yes," he replied, opening one of the rooms, "and I have taken the liberty of having your mother's bed placed here in a guest room. Now before you say anything, I decided to reward you with your own bed."

"Oh my God," she said, opening the master bedroom door. "Look at the size of it, and my mother's rocking chair and sofa."

"The bed is adjustable, and you determine the comfort level," he pointed out, "my gift to you."

"You bought this for me?" she asked, laying down on it. "It's so soft."

"Has over 50 comfort levels," he said handing her the remote. "Experiment a little."

"You padded the rocking chair," she said, jumping off the bed and sitting on it.

"Added something," he said while pointing to a lever. "Pull it."

"A padded footrest," she nearly screamed out.

"Wood is hard on the body," he said with a wide smile, "and your sofa re-padded and new springs that were showing wear."

"You did all this for me?" she asked, walking over to him while looking into his eyes.

"In every room, a picture of your family and mother," he continued in soft tone.

Giving him a long kiss, which led to another, finally she could restrain no further and began undressing him. All the built up passions erupted by his very touch, and the warmth of his body only intensified her desire.

Liam, a man who enjoyed the companionship of women throughout his life, began to use all that he had learned to pleasing her. His hands and lips moved to the tender spots releasing all qualms of doubts but allowing only ecstasy. For hours, the two make passionate love; nothing forbidden, only the need of desire. At times, she found it difficult to breathe but refused to allow him to stop.

Throughout the three days, they remained together ignoring the outside world. They bathed together and never dressed, so as to allow spontaneous lovemaking.

"Oh my God," she said, strolling over to the answering machine. "I've 30 calls!"

"Would you rather spend time answering them?" Liam said, kissing her neck while his hands cupped her breasts that came alive, "Or make love?"

"What do you think?" she asked, turning and wrapping her legs around his muscular body.

"You know we're running out of places where we haven't made love," he whispered in her ear. "What you say to a second time around?"

"What's wrong with right here on the floor?" She began sliding down.

"No matter how many times we make love," he said, out of breath while holding her, "it's like the first time."

"Do you think it would always be that way?" she asked. "I mean, if we stay together."

"Yes, it could be," he said, giving her a kiss, "if we're willing to give it a chance."

"Guess if you're ready for a second time around the apartment," she said, returning his kiss."

"Be ready for a second and even a hundredth time," he replied, embracing her.

"Think I need a shower," she whispered in his ear, "and maybe you could treat me to lunch. And a hamburg with french fries isn't going to cut it."

"Italian," he replied as they began standing, "or Chinese?"

"Italian," she said while running toward the shower, "so get dressed."

"If we're going out," he said, racing toward her, "I need a shower, too."

As they were preparing themselves to leave, the buzzer sounded.

"Mr. Acorn?" she said after opening the door. "Did something happen?"

"Don't you ever answer your phone?" he said walking over and noticing the number of unanswered phone messages. "And yes something happened."

"What is it?" she quickly asked. "Someone from my family."

"Nothing like that." His tone showed controlled frustration. "Tim Gaze suffered a massive heart attack this morning, and I need you to replace him. He's in critical condition and may not recover."

"I'm not ready to take over an anchor chair," she insisted. "What's his condition?"

"This time, it's not a request," he said in a firm tone, "but an order. You're the only one that can replace him. The people trust you, and I know it's time."

"People just might come to believe I'm taking advantage of a bad situation," she replied, sitting down, "while he's in the hospital fighting for his life."

"We've known about his heart condition for the last six months," he began to inform her, "medication and physicals every month provided. However, he knew this could happen, and he recommended you as his replacement."

"Hello, Mr. Acorn." Liam came out of the bedroom. "I'll leave so you two can talk."

"You heard." She turned toward him. You think I'm ready to anchor the evening national broadcast chair?"

"Like he said," Liam replied, walking over to her side, "people trust you, and apparently so does Mr. Gaze. Truthfully, you are ready, but the decision is yours alone."

"Two conditions," she immediately requested. "One, it's temporary until Tim returns, and secondly, I approve all broadcast news reports."

"Board members want some control," he spoke up, "certain reports given out."

"People need to know we report the news." She remained seated while explaining her position. "That we're not making it up with opinion or unknown confidential informants."

"You run it your way," he said, as if giving a warning, "but remember it's all about ratings."

"Means you're stuck here," Liam said while giving her a quick wink.

"Now, you've six hours to review tonight's broadcast," Edgar said, looking at his watch. "Suggest you get going."

"I guess a sit down Italian dinner is out of the question." She stood up and took Liam by the hand. "Forgive me."

"Go," he said, kissing her on the cheek. "I'll have something sent over."

"By the way, Liam," Edgar said while walking toward the door. "Vinnie's been looking for you, so you might want to let him know you're available."

"Thanks, I'll give him a call," he replied while shaking his head as if in disbelief.

The hours needed to review the vast material needed for the nightly broadcast went quickly, even with a staff of 10 people. But as the seconds ticked by, Janice had been to makeup was ready.

"Good evening," she began as several cameras began focusing on her. "Most of you already know my friend and colleague cannot be here tonight due to a heart attack. Our prayers will guide him through this, and rest assured, in God's hand, he will one day return. However, I, Janice Gardner, will keep this chair warm until he returns, and at that time will most happily leave the nightly reporting to Tim."

From that moment, the ratings began to climb, as all watching knew she would not take advantage of a man's misfortune. For the following few days, Janice carefully reviewed each report that her staff felt newsworthy. Working

14 hours a day, the half an hour news broadcast was gaining popularity and high ratings.

At work, Carolina and Randy were the two she depended on, but it was Liam catering to her every need when the apartment door closed.

"Good morning," Liam entered the bedroom with a breakfast tray. "Two months have passed and you still want me around."

"Without you, I don't think," she began as he placed the tray beside her bed, "I would have survived."

"WOW," he said, taking his fingers and lowering the sheet that covered her breast. "I guess the only way to keep you alive is by marrying you."

"Liam," she said with a smile as his fingers began touching her small nipples. "Get serious, and my breakfast is getting cold."

"So, you wouldn't want to wear this then?" he said, taking a ring from the tray and placing it on her finger. "It was my grandmother's, and I had it fitted for you."

"You're serious?" she said, looking at the large diamond ring as tears began to form.

"Yes, very," he admitted while sitting on the edge of the bed. "Now the ring is hers, but I decided you deserve a larger diamond."

"I love you," she said while lifting his polo shirt over his head.

"Hey, what about breakfast?" he said while the shirt dropped to the floor.

"I'm not hungry for that," she said, unbuckling his belt. "Later."

After making passionate love, the two lay in bed, allowing her to gaze at the ring.

"Janice, you know I'm crazy in love with you," Liam said in a soft voice, "so why not go down to the courthouse and get married?"

"Liam, I want a church wedding," she began, "with my family there and a few friends watching as I come down the aisle in a beautiful wedding dress."

"I've no family," he said, pausing for a brief moment, "but a few friends and clients that say they're my friends, so why not?"

"It doesn't have to be a large wedding," she said, hugging him. "A small church with just family and a few friends."

"Make the arrangements," he said, giving her a kiss on the neck.

"You'll come with me to meet my family," she said releasing him from the hug, "and I know they'll come to love you as I do."

"If it will make you happy," he said with a smile, "of course."

That night she announced to everyone of their engagement and gave a promise they would come to visit.

Having the responsibility of being an anchor for the nightly news, she began delegating tasks to each staff members, which allowed her to concentrate on the most serious news reports.

"Your staff seems to be a well-organized group," Edgar said while standing by one of the many cameras, "had to come down from my ivory tower to show you this."

"Must be important for you to come in person," she said, giving him a hug, "so show me."

"Voted the most trusted news anchor on television," he said, handing her one of the most popular magazines, "and giving the network all the credit."

"Credit goes to you," she said, looking down at her picture on the cover. "You gave me a chance and I just tried to please."

"Always been you," he replied. "Natural talent with a charm that most see immediately. I must admit since your engagement, you have a certain glow."

"Now that the prime time ratings are over," she said as they walked toward the elevator, maybe I could take a couple days off.

"Why not?" he conceded to her request. "With everyone in Washington on recess, it's a slow news week."

"Great, I can tell the staff I'll be gone," she near shouted, "along with Randy and Carolina, who will be thrilled to death."

She gave the news to Liam, who at first seemed concerned having to tell Vinnie he was leaving for a week.

"Can't believe it," he said after getting off the phone. "Vinnie said to have fun and come back refreshed."

"Well, maybe knowing you're about to marry," she began, giving him a hug, "the most trusted news anchor on television."

"Maybe one day people will consider me the most famous designer in America," he said, giving her a kiss.

"Vinnie and I already know that," she responded, giving him a passionate kiss.

"He also knows how much I love you," Liam added, unbuttoning her blouse.

"We've a lot of packing to do," she said, almost out of breath as he began kissing her neck.

"Packing can wait," he said, lifting her up in his arms and walking into the bedroom.

"Now, Liam, don't take anything Frank or Leone say personally," she began warning him as they made their way to the terminal. "They love making fun of people."

"Please relax," he replied with a smile, "having listened to you talk about them I'm prepared for anything."

"Janice," Susan screamed out over the crowd of people, "we're here!"

"Then why are you just standing there?" she said, reaching out her arms. "Come here!"

"I've missed you," she shouted out while running into her arms.

"Janice!" Linda came up to greet her. "We've been trying to make her act more lady like."

"She's my little sister," Janice replied, giving her a hug. "I never want her to act lady like around me."

"You must be Liam," Linda said with a smile, "so happy you came."

"Alright everyone," Janice said, looking over the group. "This is Liam Stewart the man I'm going to marry, so be nice."

"Janice has told me so much about all of you." Liam stepped forward with his hand out. "I feel that I know all of you personally."

"We don't shake hands," Linda replied while hugging him, "just hugs."

"Well, we're old fashioned," Leone said while Frank took his hand. "Hugs are nice but still like handshakes."

"Firm," Frank said, rubbing his hand. "Good sign."

"Grandmother always said a firm handshake is important," Liam said, taking Leone's hand, "but never vise like."

"Grandmother sounds like a wise lady," Leone said as he released his grip.

"She was," Liam said before looking down at the other two children. "And you must be Frank and Lisa, right?"

"Uh-huh," little Frank replied.

"It's 'yes, sir,'" Linda said, correcting him.

"It's all good," he said, kneeling down to face the young boy, "maybe we could become friends or even brothers."

"Like Susan," he said looking toward Linda.

"Why not?" Frankie said, taking his hand and gently shaking it.

"Alright, now that we've adopted Liam into our family," Linda said looking at the group, "we should find a nice restaurant."

As the days passed, Liam made every effort to fit in and even took time out to sketch the entire inside of the house as what it could be.

"WOW," Leone said while looking over the drawing, "you did this?"

"What I do for a living," Liam replied with a certain amount of pride. "Look at a room or space and see all the possibilities."

"Liam is a genius when it comes to designing rooms," Janice added.

"Thank you, dear," he said, walking over to her and giving her a hug, "but truthfully the smartest thing I've ever did was asking you to marry me."

"Well, if you don't let us women get back to it," she said, giving him a quick kiss. "There won't be a wedding."

"Then by all means," he said, releasing her, "back to work."

Having arranged for the local church to conduct the ceremony, they began the work of who should attend.

"So, Frank and Leone will escort you down the aisle," Linda said while looking over toward the two. "Susan will be the flower girl, and Frank the ring bearer."

"Mommy, he'll drop it and loose it," Susan announced.

"Will not!" he immediately shouted.

"He'll do fine," Linda said, placing her hands on each of them.

"Hon," Frank spoke up, "think I should help Liam, having only one best man."

"With college and work," Liam spoke up, "never had time to socialize."

"Maybe not with men," Janice whispered in his ears, "but women…"

"Don't think you'd want them to attend," he whispered back.

"I'll stand with Vinnie," Frank replied, "Carolina and you bridesmaids. Which means Leone, you're escorting her."

"Be my great honor," he said, looking toward Janice.

CHAPTER FIFTEEN

Picking a day for the wedding, the two were required to speak to the networks staff of attorneys.

"Mr. Stewart, as you know," one of the men began, "Ms. Gardner has signed a multi-million-dollar contract with the network. Your present contract and salary is far less, which brings us to a prenuptial contract."

"That's enough," Janice blurted out, "and we're leaving."

"This contract protects you, Ms. Gardner," he added, "and shows the world that Mr. Stewart wants nothing to do with your money."

"Janice, you know they're right about what people might say," Liam said while reading over the contract. "I love you not your money, so we live on my salary."

"Ms. Gardner, were not suggesting you can't spend the money you earn," one of the men spoke up, "the two of you can remain in the apartment rent free, which is a benefit. This contract doesn't hamper your life style, at all."

"I just don't want money to become an issue," she said looking toward him.

"It won't," he quickly began signing by each arrow, "and besides, one day I may make enough to ask you to sign such a contract."

"What would you do if I refused?" she asked, giving him a smile.

"Just sign the darn thing," he said pushing the contract toward her, "so we can leave and go home."

"Liam, if we're in this together," she said while holding the pen, "and you're serious about living on what you make, then I'll match your salary."

"Deal," he said as she began signing, "and boys make sure all that money she earns goes directly to her, not in your pockets."

"Quarterly audits required by law and sent," another spoke up as if defending their honor, "and if you need us, please do not hesitate to call."

"Thank you, gentlemen," Liam said while reaching his hand out to Janice.

After six weeks of planning, the wedding took place in the small church where over 100 attended. All went as planned as Susan cheerfully placed flowers on the floor, and Frank carried the ring without dropping it.

"What a day," Frank began as he strolled beside Leone, who watched Janice and Liam dancing together, "be a day to remember."

"Never thought I would wear this tuxedo again," he began with a slight smile, "but she makes a beautiful bride."

"Didn't think so many would attend," he replied, "and having Randy film it all."

"It was nice of him to do it," he admitted, "but I can't wait to see the pictures from the photographer we hired."

Each member of the wedding party danced with the couple, and then they rushed off for a honeymoon.

"Name's Rubin Quill," he said walking up to Leone and Frank, "wanted to say hello to the proud father of the bride."

"Thanks for the compliment," Leone said taking the man's hand, "but don't have the right to claim that title. Name's Leone Pegasus, just the person who escorted her down the aisle."

"I'm truly sorry," he said with surprise. "You looked so proud, like a father should be."

"Janice is family," Frank spoke up, "maybe not by blood, but family never the less."

"Well, I'm friends with Liam," he said while gulping down his drink, "who designed several rooms for me. He's a genius when it comes to design, but can't pick a winning team if his life were on the line."

"Never known him to gamble," Leone replied as the man ordered another drink.

"Nearly paid for the room with the winnings," he said, gulping down the drink, "but as I said, he's a genius when designing rooms."

"Rubin, you've drank far too much," she walked over and gently placed her hand under his arm, "now go sit down and enjoy the music."

"Yes, dear," he said, turning toward Leone. "Gotta follow the boss's order."

"Excuse my husband." She stood six feet and was a lovely lady in her late thirties. "He embellishes every story, especially when he wins."

"Just surprised that Liam gambles," Leone said, looking at her fair complexation and bright blue eyes. "What business is he in?"

"Rubin is a financial advisor and analyst," she said looking back toward him, "from time to time, he analyses some teams. He's not a gambler, mostly small friendly wagers, like with Liam."

"Liam never mentioned he enjoyed watching sports" he said while looking over her trim figure, "or betting on them."

"We've known Vinnie for years," she replied, chuckling as she spoke. "Liam was new to the company, and Vinnie wanted to see how he worked around a small budget. The entire project was $4,000, and we paid over half. Now the second room Liam designed cost an arm and leg."

"Thanks for clearing it up," Leone said, as if relieved.

"Liam married a beautiful woman," she continued. "No doubt that's all behind him."

Spending time at Niagara Falls made their honeymoon perfect, being one of the many newlyweds and just blending in.

"Well, my love," he said, laying on one of the large circular beds. "We've been under and on top of the falls, so what now?"

"Let me think," she said, snuggling him, "on top and under... Is there anything else?"

"You know come to think about it," he said, turning her over, "I like being under the falls."

"So why is that?" she asked, laying on his chest.

"Because I can see your beautiful face," he said, giving her a passionate kiss.

Finally, it was back to work, and both seemed eager to begin their new life together working together for a future.

"Hello," Janice entered the apartment holding a large bag. "Got dinner."

"Great, I'm famished," Liam said coming out of his workroom. "Had to bring work home and lost time."

"You've been working so hard," she said while placing the cartons on the table, "for the last two months you've been bringing work home."

"Vinnie's been telling everyone what a genius I am," he said while looking over each carton, "and that I'm married to you. I'm not sure if they want me, or you."

"It's you, my love," she replied, giving him a kiss, "and Vinnie knows it."

"Well, I'm making him rich," he said, opening one of the containers as he spoke, "signed on two new clients today."

"That's my genius of a husband," she said, opening a bottle of wine, "but you tell Vinnie I have needs and want my husband here ready to fulfill my contract."

"Just what are those needs?" he said while she poured the wine. "And you're right that I'm required to enforce that contract.

"Then eat quickly." She began nibbling on his ear.

The year passed quickly; Liam was becoming the genius Vinnie hoped for, and Janice continued to sweep the yearly ratings.

However, as with others, problems began to appear in the marriage. Strained by all the extra work, Liam began drinking and complained about the many clients he brought to the office without reward.

"What a day!" she entered with soaked hair from the snow. "People sick and others couldn't come to work because of all the snow. Anyone listening? I'm home."

"Yeah, I heard you," he said, walking out of his workroom, "but I'm on a deadline here."

"Come on," she said in an angry tone, "we've been through this 100 times. You're busy because people are starting to recognize your work."

"No, I'm busy because Vinnie is making money on my talent," he said while opening the wine refrigerator, "sitting behind that desk thinking I'm too stupid to know."

"Liam, I'm going out to bring back dinner," she said, ignoring his complaints. "When I come back we'll talk more."

As each month passed by, Liam openly spoke disparaging of the way Vinnie treated him, but Janice always found ways to tone his remarks down. With work consuming so much of her time, she began to worry, knowing Liam left alone could create an unamendable riff. .

As the new year began, Janice saw the change in Liam, heavy drinking, even while working, and one very disgruntled employee.

"Why don't we take a short vacation?" she asked, sitting on the sofa while watching all the people celebrating. "We haven't gone anywhere since our honeymoon."

"No mood to go anywhere," he snapped. "Just give it a rest."

Realizing she could never speak to him when drinking, Janice simply surrendered and began devoting more time to the nightly broadcast. For over three months, Janice went to work early, and came home late.

"Liam, I'm home," she said, entering the apartment finding all the lights on and the smell of something cooking.

"Thank God, you finally came home," he yelled from the kitchen. "Another half hour, and this sauce would be glue."

"Smells good," she said, walking and getting a warm hug from him. "What's the occasion?"

"Did what I should have months ago," he said, twirling her around, "I quit."

"You what?" she said, stepping away from him.

"Quit," he repeated, "and starting tomorrow, I am my own boss. Figure once I've located an office, clients will flock to me."

"But Vinnie just offered you a raise," she could hardly speak, "almost $50,000."

"Brought in over two million," he said, surrendering all excitement in his tone. "I deserve much more."

"Vinnie runs an office," Janice said, trying to explain. "Pays wages and all the expenses."

"Now that will be my responsibility," he continued to justify his decision.

"If that means you'll stop drinking..." She said, looking over at the empty wine bottle, "And no more arguments then, okay?"

"Deal," he promised while lifting her up and giving her a passionate kiss. "And the empty bottle went in the sauce."

For a month, Liam searched for the right location, but as with all plans, a letter arrived to dampen any celebration.

"He can't be allowed to do this!" Janice listened as Liam nearly screamed to the attorney. "I'll sue!"

"Mr. Stewart, I've read the contract you signed," the man began in a calm tone, "you're forbidden to conduct business within 150 miles from Vinnie's office. It further states you're forbidden to contact any client of his, otherwise he'll sue you."

"Can they put that in a contract," Janice asked, "depriving a man of his livelihood?"

"Standard practice," he continued, "protecting the business that someone started."

"I'm sure your contract has a similar clause, making it difficult for you to go elsewhere. Honestly, the year will go quickly, and financially, money shouldn't be an issue."

"What would you suggest I do for the year?" he asked.

"You're an interior designer," he replied, "prepare a resume of drawings."

"My ideas come from clients," he said, shaking his head, "learning how they live and what colors they enjoy."

"Look, just find a way to keep active for the year," he recommended, "and after that, you can start your business in the same building if you wish."

Knowing it was pointless to contest the contract, they accepted it reluctantly.

"What the…" Janice replied as she entered the apartment, "Liam?"

"Yes, dear?" He came out of his room, unshaven.

"Kim, would you turn off all the televisions?" she yelled out.

"Yes, Mrs. Stewart, if you wish," the voice came over the speakers.

"Why did you do that?" he strolled over to her.

"Sports channel," she said laying down her large purse, "all different games."

"Just keeping up with the outside world," he said calmly, "while working."

"You're wearing the same clothes you had on yesterday," she pointed out, "and every day the trash can is filled with half drawings."

"You forgot to mention I'm drinking again," he said, walking away from her.

"Liam, I love you," she began as if giving warning, "but this has to stop."

"A threat," he said, entering his room and slamming the door.

"It's a warning," she said under her breath while tears began flowing.

As if attempting to cope with his inactivity, Janice accepted his behavior as temporary to avoid arguments. After two months it appeared such acceptance was working; there were fewer arguments, and his mood began to change.

"Janice," he said, walking in the bedroom as she prepared for bed. "I know over the last few months, I've been acting crazy. With nothing to do, I'm worthless, but my love for you remains strong. How would you like taking a vacation, for about a week?"

"Sweeps are over," she said, looking into the mirror as she spoke, "and in a couple weeks begins our slow news time…"

"Got a call from Rubin Quill and his wife," he said while sitting beside her. "They own a large ranch in Texas and have invited us to stay there for a couple days."

"Yes, I remember meeting them at our wedding," she said, picking up a hair brush. "Seem like a nice couple and very generous."

"Get away from here," he said, looking around, "forget our troubles and maybe Rubin could help me find work."

"Be two, maybe three weeks before I could leave," she said, thinking aloud while brushing her hair. "We haven't been anywhere since our honeymoon."

"Look I'll call Rubin and tell him to expect us," Liam said, his voice filled with excitement.

It took an entire month, but they finally arrived at the home of Rubin Quill.

"Come on in," Rubin yelled out as he strolled toward the large double door. "Been looking forward to your visit."

"Mrs. Stewart, you're as beautiful today," Mindy said as stood waiting, "as you were on your wedding day."

"You're too kind," she replied while taking her hand. "Liam and I wish to thank you for asking us to visit."

"Know you must be hungry," Rubin said after greeting the two with hugs and kisses. "Damn airlines charge a fortune and serve peanuts."

"Come, you two," Mindy said taking Janice by the hand, "you're just in time for lunch that will be served on the veranda."

Janice was amazed at all the food laid out, lobster and steak along with wine.

"Now don't be shy," Rubin said while placing a large steak on his plate along with prepared cracked lobster. "Eat up."

After lunch, Mindy said sitting beside Janice, "We'll go four wheeling around the estate for fun."

"You own land beyond the wall?" Janice said looking at the 12-foot high wall that surrounded the home.

"Wall's for privacy." Rubin swallowed his food before speaking. "Got another 1,000 acres."

"It's mostly prairie," Mindy said jokingly, "but it's ours."

"Heard about you troubles, Liam," Rubin began while taking a sip of wine. "Damn people making it hard on others with contracts."

"For a year," he answered, "just have to hang in there."

Janice began to relax having feasted on such food, but noticed Liam enjoying himself for the first time in months. But there was nothing like racing around the prairie on four wheelers, that thrilled them more.

"Oh my God," she screamed while stopping for a moment after going airborne, "that was awesome."

"You must have hit that hill at 80," Mindy said driving up to her, "eight, maybe nine feet in the air."

"It was so much fun," she said, laughing at the very thought of flying through the air.

"There's my little daredevil," Liam yelled out as she pulled the four-wheeler into the garage, "maybe we should think about getting one of these."

"Liam, why don't we go into my study and enjoy a nice glass of wine," Rubin said while placing his helmet on the seat, "and a fine cigar."

"Fine, while you two bond," Mindy said walking over to Janice, "the two of us will be enjoying the pool."

"Won't it be a little chilly?" Janice asked as the sun was setting.

"It's a warm night," Mindy whispered, "and pool is heated."

"Oh, I didn't know," Janice said, somewhat shocked while strolling out to the pool.

"Come on dear," Mindy said, pulling her naked body from the water. "You're among friends, and no one can see you."

"Guess it will be alright," taking off the two-piece bikini. "Quite liberating."

"That's the spirit," Mindy said, plugging into the water.

For a half hour, they swam around the large pool, and finally relaxed on the side of the pool talking.

"Such a beautiful body," Mindy said looking toward her breasts, "so natural."

"You have a nice figure," Janice admitted, "at the wedding, I saw lots of men staring."

"Boobs are starting to sag," she said looking toward them. "Having to watch what I eat and work out more, but age is catching up."

"You're still beautiful," she said, giving her a compliment.

"Thank you for saying that," she said, giving her a quick kiss on the lips. "Sorry I didn't..."

"Please don't," Janice said, startled by the show of affection. "I know it didn't mean anything."

"Rubin and I have an open marriage," Mindy explained to her. "Belong to a group that gets together every month or so."

"Does Liam know?" Janice asked, surprised by her admission. "Not that I think it's wrong."

"Yeah, he knows," she said, admitting it to her. "Came with us a couple times, but don't worry; you're too high profile to be asked. Trust me, Liam loves you, and would never share you with anyone."

"Did you and Liam..." she began, needing to know, "ever...?"

"No never," she quickly responded to the question, "mostly out of fear it might destroy his relationship with Rubin."

"Maybe we should go inside," she said, relieved by her answer, "and see how their doing."

"Morning." Rubin was sitting at the table where several breakfast items lay. "Got some business in town, so thought Liam could come with me."

"In that case," Mindy said, walking out in sheer white gown revealing her slender figure, "Janice and I will go shopping."

"Wonderful," Liam spoke up. "Never pass up an opportunity to meet clients."

"Shopping sounds nice," Janice agreed.

Driving into the small town, they were taken by all the shops and advertising signs directing all to the local casino.

"A casino," Liam said looking toward the large billboards. "Maybe we should try our luck there."

"Don't bother," Rubin replied in an angry tone. "Nothing but a bunch of thieves working there. Owned by the damn local tribes, games are rigged. Not about losing my money to them, filthy animals all of them."

"Rubin doesn't like the way they do business," Mindy explained, "use only members of the tribe and avoid dealing with locals when possible."

"Shops all seem to have customers," Janice pointed out. "Many American natives."

"These shop owners would deal with the devil," Rubin blurted out, "to keep their doors open."

"Well, you can drop us off anywhere," Mindy insisted, "then go and finish what business you have."

For hours, they shopped and talked, always avoiding of the conversation they had while they swam.

"Liam, your wife seems very happy," Mindy said while packing the vehicle with boxes, "and for your information she likes turquoise jewelry."

"Bought a few necklaces," she admitted, "as a keepsake."

"Keepsake," Liam said shaking his head, "has a jewelry box filled with jewelry she never wears."

"Family heirlooms," she explained. "Diamond wedding rings and pearl necklaces that mother kept."

"Even ruby rings," Liam added, "along with other expensive pieces."

"Mother couldn't part with them," she calmly replied, "nor will I."

"Liam made some calls today," Rubin said as he drove along the dusty road. "Know the owners of a dog track near the border. Their building another one in Florida, told them about you, and they'd like to meet you."

"When?" Liam asked with excitement in his voice.

"We could drive down there tonight," he continued, "and meet with them."

"What do you say to that?" Liam asked, turning toward Janice, "A chance to get a feel for the place?"

"I'm tired," Janice said after having walked for hours, "maybe tomorrow."

"Truthfully, Janice, this might be a great opportunity for Liam," Rubin said in a business like tone. "They're willing to meet with him tonight. Strike while the iron is hot, come tomorrow they might be gone."

"It's a business meeting," Liam almost pleading with her. "Rubin and I can go down there and meet them. Later if things work out, we can all go."

"Remember," she said, giving him a quick kiss. "Dress for success."

"Of course," he said with a smile, "if you wish to impress."

Allowing the two to leave, Janice and Mindy had dinner together.

"I'm going to call it a night," Janice said after watching her replacement. "It's been a tiring day."

"It is getting late," she said, looking toward the large grandfather clock.

After a warm bath, she lay in bed hoping Liam would come back with good news.

"Janice, you still up?" Mindy said while opening the door. "May I come in?"

"Sure, come on in," she said while noticing Mindy wearing a sexy shear nighty.

"You're worried about Liam." She carefully laid beside her. "He seems to be preoccupied lately."

"More like old married couples," she said trying to cover her naked body with the sheet, "dealing with a husband out of work."

"Men complain when working," she moved forcing the sheet to drop slightly, "and become lost without it."

"Yeah," Janice agreed, pulling the sheet up.

"Janice, you're not afraid of me, are you?" Mindy asked, moving closer and forcing the sheet to fall. "I'm just trying to be a friend."

"No," Janice replied, allowing the sheet to remain under her breasts. "I enjoy your company."

"We do have much in common," Mindy said, touching Janice's face with her soft hand, "being alone while our husbands abandon us."

"For business," Janice said, in a soft tone as Mindy moved toward her.

"You're so beautiful," Mindy said, giving her a soft passionate kiss on the lips.

Maybe it was the wine during dinner, or the need to feel someone's touch but she returned the kiss. Janice's entire body began to quiver as they kissed; no longer could she think as desire controlled her every move. The knowledge Mindy knew was now used to break down any barrier, her soft hands cupped Janice's breasts while she slowly kissed her neck.

"This is so wrong," Janice, trying to control her breathing, spoke, "but…"

"Nothing we do is wrong," Mindy in a soft tone replied as she began kissing her breasts and flat stomach, "two souls needing and wanting each other."

"Oh my God," she said, feeling Mindy's hand between her slender legs, "that feels so nice."

"Janice, I've never felt so close to anyone," Mindy whispered while kissing her flat stomach, "and maybe you could feel the same in time."

"Please you must stop," Janice said, gently taking her hands and placing them on her face, "if you really care."

"Alright," she said while stopping, "because I do care."

"Mindy, I love Liam," she said, allowing Mindy to move to her side, "and I can't betray him by being with another."

"You seemed to be enjoying yourself," she said while Mindy moved up to face her, "and it's not like being with a man."

"I did," she said, looking straight into her eyes, "which is why it was wrong. I have only room in my heart for him and cannot share it with anyone."

"Hope Liam knows how lucky he is having you," Mindy said as tears began to flow, "and will this hurt our friendship?"

"No," she replied with a smile. "I've come to trust and admire you."

"Would you care if we just cuddle for a little while?" she calmly asked, "Just hold one another."

"I'd like that," she said, placing her arm around her neck, and within minutes both were fast asleep.

As her alarm rang, Janice woke to find Mindy gone.

"Good morning," Mindy said as Janice entered the veranda, "did you sleep well?"

"Slept wonderful," Janice said, taking her hands with a smile. "They're not back yet."

"Good sign," Mindy replied, releasing her hands while walking over to the table to pour her a cup of coffee, "had they returned last night, that would mean talks stalled."

"Then good news," Janice said, taking the cup from her hand.

"Maybe," she replied.

By two in the afternoon, the two returned all excited.

"Honey, they want me to design their restaurant," Liam said picking her up and twirling her around, "and if all goes well a second one."

"That is wonderful news," Janice said, almost screaming in his ear, "but where?"

"Florida," he replied, "eight months of work."

"But that will mean," she quickly stepped away, "you'll be gone for all those months."

"It's a great opportunity," he explained, "I'll be super busy, and every couple weeks fly up to celebrate."

"By the time he finishes the two restaurants," Rubin pointed out, "the year will be over, and he can use the money to start his own company."

"Think about it," Liam said, taking her hands, "come back start my company and put Vinnie out of business."

"Eight months will go fast," she said, squeezing his hand, "but when do you start?"

"They want to meet with me in two weeks," he added, "going over designs and colors they want."

"Guess our little vacation is over," she replied. "Got to get you ready to leave."

It was difficult to let Liam leave for such a long time, but he was once again the man she married. With all the pressure placed on her shoulders from the network, she at times was happy Liam was not around to see her questioning every decision made.

"Janice, I've cleared your schedule," Carolina said, running toward her after the cameras were tuned off. "Enjoy the weekend with your husband."

"Two visits in over three months," she said with a smile, "but we have the entire weekend to ourselves."

Without waiting for someone to interfere with her plans, Janice quickly grabbed her small coat and left.

"Liam, are you here?" she asked, rushing inside the apartment, "I'm sorry not meeting you at the airport, but you gave me such short notice."

"I'm a big boy," he said, walking out to her, "and can find my own way home."

"Oh my God what happened to you?" she asked, noticing his black eye and taped up nose. "Are you alright?"

"Careless accident," he replied, walking over to her and giving her a kiss on the cheek, "ran into a door that a worker opened. Wasn't paying attention, and not wearing my helmet or goggles, which made it a safety violation."

"Maybe you should have our doctors check you out." She began examining his wounds. "I can call them."

"Nonsense," he snapped, "just let me be, okay?"

"Liam, talk to me," she began after making love, "you seemed so distant and acted so cold as if you wanted nothing to do with me."

"Damn union called for a slow down," he began. We're already a week behind, and they want either overtime or for me to hire more men."

"What do the owners say?" she asked while covering her naked body with the sheets. "You did tell them."

"They understand," he admitted. "One told me if they were in Texas, illegals would have finished the job at half pay."

"Now that's the truth," she began, laughing.

"You're so right," he agreed, and for the first time he began laughing. "But they still want me to stay on and design their next restaurant.

"Four months down," she said, frustrated knowing he would be away, "another four to go."

"Promise to make it up one day," he said, giving her a passionate kiss. "You're my lucky charm and know I can't miss."

"You're my love," she said, looking him in the eyes, "and I just want you to be happy."

Throughout the weekend, she felt something was not right; his behavior would quickly change from distant or cold to loving.

"Liam, I can take the day off," she began while watching him pack, "and see you off."

"Airline leaves at 11:00," he said, stopping and walking over to her, "you said yourself how busy things are at the network. Just go now, I'll be fine and tonight call you."

For over three months, Liam spoke to her regularly by computer, but made excuses why he could not leave.

"Edgar, what are you doing down here?" she asked while noticing him standing by the exit door. "Something wrong?"

"Just came down to watch my favorite anchor in person," he began.

"Ratings off?" she asked, knowing he had never came down to watch her broadcast.

"All fine," he admitted. "Noticed you're more serious and smiling less."

"Lots of bad news," she explained, "not much to smile about lately."

"Maybe you could add more uplifting news," he recommended.

"Rescuing puppy dogs or cats," she smiled, "instead of showing people murdered in the streets or foreign countries."

"I'm just worried about you, that's all," he said, touching her shoulder, "but if there's anything I can do, just ask."

"I know," she said, placing her hand on his. "I'm fine, and things will get better."

Entering her apartment, she opened a bottle of wine when the doorbell chimed.

"Mindy," she said, opening the door, "what are you doing here?"

"Been wrestling with the decision for over a week," she said, removing her coat, "to come or not."

"Have you eaten?" she asked while hanging her coat up, "I can call down and have something delivered."

"No, thank you," she said, looking toward the bottle of wine, "but I will join you."

"Of course," Janice poured the liquid in a wine glass.

"You may come to hate me," she said, drinking the glass dry, "after hearing what I have to say, but you have to know."

"Mindy, you're my friend," she said, filling the glass as she spoke, "and no matter, what we will remain friends."

"Then you need to know how I came to have these," she said, opening her purse and handing her a small silk bag.

"My keepsake jewelry," she said while trying to catch her breath, "my mother's wedding ring and grandmother's ruby ring."

CHAPTER SIXTEEN

"Liam got himself in trouble," she began to explain, "gambling."

"His injuries weren't from an accident at work," Janice said, realizing he had lied.

"No," Mindy replied as if ashamed, "a warning for him to get the money. He came to Texas looking for Rubin, who was in California on a business trip. Liam needed $15,000, and gave the jewelry for collateral."

"Did he say how much he owed?" she asked wanting to know.

"Forty thousand," she added, "he had $25,000."

"Have you spoken with Rubin about this?" she asked.

"Rubin's been keeping company with a younger woman." Tears began to flow as she spoke. "Guess our open marriage wasn't such a good idea after all."

"I'm so sorry, Mindy," Janice said, giving her a gentle hug, "is there anything I can do?"

"No, not really," she replied, wiping her tears. "I've been preparing for this and have opened my own bank account."

"You're going to need that $15,000," she said, opening her purse and taking out a check book, "and if you need more, please don't hesitate."

"Janice, I'm sorry having been the one to tell you," she began to cry once again, "I should have told him no, but..."

"Mindy this was not your fault," Janice told her, taking a tissue from the table and wiping the tears. "You did what any friend would have given the situation, and I thank you."

"Will this hurt our friendship?" Mindy asked with concern.

"No," Janice said with a smile, "have you a place to stay tonight?"

"I've a return flight at 11:00," she said, "I'll find a hotel for tonight."

"Nonsense," she immediately replied, "it's getting late, so stay here tonight in our guest room."

"Are you sure?" Her voice cracked. "I don't want to be a bother."

"Pick any room," she said with a broad smile, "and make yourself at home while I order dinner for us."

"Thank you." For the first time a smile came to her face. "Let me clean up first."

"Chinese or Italian?" Janice yelled out as Mindy began inspecting each room.

"Kim, we have a guess tonight," Janice began speaking, "would you adjust the room temperatures and dial the numbers of my favorite restaurants?"

"Yes, Mrs. Stewart," the voice answered, "all numbers available."

"Thank you," she replied, "and please, a little mood music."

"As you wish," she said as the music began.

"My goodness, I've not eaten this much in months," Mindy said while relaxing on the sofa, "but the meal was magnificent."

"You can thank Kim," she said while listening to the music and sipping on wine. "She knows the numbers of all the five star restaurants."

"This is a beautiful apartment," Mindy said while looking around, "and I want to thank you again for everything."

"You have an early flight," Janice said, standing up, "maybe we should call it a night."

"Night, Janice," Mindy said while standing.

"Kim, please turn off the music," she ordered.

"As you wish." The music stopped playing. "And lights on manual."

Thinking of Liam's betrayal, Janice rose from her bed and walked down to the guest room where Mindy slept.

"Mindy, are you up?" she asked, slowly opening the door.

"No, I can't sleep," she said from the darkness.

"May I join you?" Janice asked, allowing her robe to fall to the floor,

Janice would never speak of the night spent with Mindy, but remember it fondly. As they parted the following morning, both seemed to know they would never again meet.

Preparing for Liam's return, Janice carefully planned every word or action needed to confront him.

"I'm finally home, my love," he said, entering the apartment, "and it's the weekend."

"Liam," she said walking from the bedroom and placing the bag of jewelry on the table. "Care to explain these?"

"Where did you get those?" he blurted out as his eyes seemed to bulge. "I should have known that bitch couldn't be trusted."

"Trust," she said while handing him a sheet of paper. "Eight months of work and nothing to show for it. However, $25,000 was withdrawn last week from our account. You talk of trust to me, knowing you told the bank manager to send all monthly statements to Florida."

"Janice, let me explain," he began, clasping his hands as if in prayer, "had a winning streak going, and then it got away from me. I thought just one big win, and all would be set right without you knowing."

"How much did you lose?" she asked with a glaring stare. "And don't lie to me."

"Ninety thousand," he said, slumping down on the chair. "Please forgive me, and I promise to do whatever it takes to make things right."

"I've packed all your things," she slowly began, "and there on the bed. You're to be out of here in an hour, if not I'll have Edgar bring in someone to escort you out."

"Please, Janice, give me another chance," he said, standing up, "I love you."

"When you find a place to live," she said, turning toward the door. "My attorneys will serve you with the divorce papers. I will be back in an hour, please be gone."

Returning, she found him gone, and realizing he had chosen to leave without out a fight, she began crying.

As the lawyers dragged the divorce through the court, the tabloids began printing rumors how she hoarded money and that her fame destroyed the marriage. For months, she refused to comment on any rumor, even when finding three or four reporters standing in front of her door demanding a response.

"Morning, Janice," Edgar said while sitting behind his desk with several tabloids scattered over his desk. "Undisclosed sources say you sent him to Florida in order to spend more time here."

"You forgot the part where I wanted him to make more money," she said, sitting down in front of his desk, as if exhausted, "because I didn't want to spend mine."

"Maybe you should confront all these rumors," he suggested. "Tell the people what really happened."

"Confronting a rumor," she began, "makes it a fact in people's mind."

"Our competition thinks this is a wonderful opportunity to bring you down," he added, "which helps their ratings."

"Liam and his attorney's aren't trying to destroy my reputation," she explained. "With the prenuptial, he walks away with nothing. With over three years of marriage, they'd like a third of my salary for those years."

"Give them the money, and be done with it," he recommended. "If you're right about his gambling trouble, he'll be broke in five."

"I've already spent a million to say no," she said, shaking her head, "and it's not about the money, truly it isn't."

"Then what is it?" he asked, wanting to know.

"We made a promise not to make money an issue," she continued. "Now it's all about money, not love."

"Love," he said, leaning back on his chair, "so many empires and people destroyed over that small word."

"Had I heard him say the only thing he wanted," she said with a single tear flowing down her cheek, "was to earn my love back."

"He would be walking out with a sizable check," he said, understanding her position.

"Don't know about sizable…" She began to laugh for the first time.

"By the way, I know you moved back to your old loft," he said while leaning forward in his chair. "Are you sure you don't want the apartment?"

"The apartment is much too large for me," she informed him, "and has many memories. My loft is perfect, three bedrooms, and a reminder of what I almost lost."

"I want you to understand," he said, standing up. "No matter what, the network is behind you 100 percent."

"My attorneys say my divorce will be final in a couple weeks." She stood to face him. "And maybe then I can tell everyone the truth."

"You do what you think is best," he said, reaching his hand out, "and if you need anything just ask."

"Just knowing you're here," she replied, taking his hand, "means so much to me."

"Know I love ya," he said, "and will always."

When the news that the divorce was finalized and that the signed agreement was valid, all parties signed the papers.

"Janice, heard the news about your divorce." Randy came running up to her as she prepared for the nightly broadcast. "Are you okay?"

"I'm okay, and relieved it's finally over," she said, giving him a kiss on the cheek. "Have you had dinner yet?"

"No, why?" he said, surprised by her concern.

"Maybe after the broadcast," she said, "we could have dinner together."

"Sounds great," he said walking toward his camera. "You paying?"

"Hello America," she began her broadcast, "this is Janice Gardner reporting..."

"Janice," Carolina came over while the makeup team finished. "We've another 10 minutes of air time, and you crossed off everything."

"Just have the camera ready when we get back from break," she said calmly.

"Alright," she replied while walking toward Randy and the others, "I'll tell them."

"You ready in one, two, three," said Randy, speaking from behind the camera.

"Tonight I wish to speak to you as a woman, having finalized my divorce. I married for love and built that relationship on trust. That trust was broken, unable to reclaim. I now travel that road so many others have, a divorced lady knowing loneliness and heartache. Many nights, I've wondered what if? Could

I have done things differently? One day my journey will end, making me stronger and wiser. Your prayers and well-wishing have assured me of this, I will forever be in your debt. Let me say, I will never betray your trust, and will continue to earn it each day. God bless all of you, and America. I am Janice Gardner saying, good night."

"That was beautiful Janice." Carolina came running over after the men turned the cameras off. "I saw your pain."

"Thank you," she said, turning so she could not see the tears falling. "I need a little time to be alone, please understand."

"Of course," Carolina said, allowing her to walk away.

The following morning, she entered her office, finding the entire room filled with flowers and two large stacks of letters on her desk.

"Admirers," Edgar said, walking behind her. "That big one's from me."

"People deserved to know," she said, walking in and smelling the different flowers.

"Last night, they interviewed Liam," he said remaining by the door, "said every word he heard was the truth. When they reminded him he walked away with nothing, his reply was having walked away from a woman who loved him."

"Who still does," she said under her breath while looking out the window.

For the next six months, her broadcast hour remained number one, and each night the ratings increased. While surrounded by her loyal team discussing what news item they needed, the door opened.

"Am I interrupting you, Janice?" his words slow but clear.

"Tim," she said with surprise. "Not at all."

"Maybe this is not the right time." Again, his words were slow but clear. "I could come back when you are not busy."

"Break time everyone," she replied. "Please, Tim, sit, and we'll talk."

"My right arm's paralyzed," he began as she sat beside him, "and I speak slow, but people say my words are clear."

"You want your anchor seat back," she said while touching his hand. "Let's go tell Edgar and make it happen."

"Edgar knows already," he said, standing behind the two. "I'm afraid that's not going to happen anytime soon."

"I gave Tim my promise." She stood as if defying him. "And he deserves it."

"He speaks so slow," Edgar seemed to point out the obvious. "He couldn't report 30 minutes of news."

"Then we'll give him 20 minutes of important news," she added, "which he'll do in 30 minutes."

"People expect to see you doing the news" Edgar said in a controlled tone.

"They expect me to keep a promise," she shouted.

"Please, I did not come here to make trouble," Tim said, stumbling as he tried to stand.

"Now, look what you did," she said, grabbing him by the arm.

"Let me help," Edgar said, taking his other arm and sitting him down. "The board won't allow it."

"Screw the board," she said, sitting beside him. "We can do this."

"Trial basis," he reluctantly agreed, "but if it doesn't work, you're back. Understand?"

"Edgar, thank you," she said. "We'll make this work."

After hours of preparation, the cameras began operating.

"Good evening," Janice sitting alone began. "Tonight, as promised, I will be turning over this chair to a man I trust and admire."

She stood up and walked away, while Tim walked over and sat.

"Good evening America," he slowly began, "I am Tim Gaze, reporting for duty."

As expected, the rating began to fall, and many believed it was just a matter of time before they ordered her back. However, Janice each day stood helping Tim, looking over each news item carefully with the staff and allowing him to speak to it. Every night she would walk through several news reporters, all wanting her comment on Tim's condition and ratings.

"Ms. Gardner," he came through the group with a cameraman, "when might we see you back on the nightly news?"

"If you hadn't noticed," she began to chuckle at his question, "Tim's anchoring now."

"People say he speaks so slow," he continued while showing the microphone. "They would prefer someone else."

"Yes, he speaks slow," she said, looking straight into the camera, "but understand every word that comes out is the truth."

It seemed all needed to hear her speak of it, and over the following weeks, his speech improved, as did the ratings.

"Edgar," Janice began after knocking on his office door. "Seen the ratings?"

"Yes, he's number two in his time slot," Edgar said, laying down his pen. "So you told me so."

"Have an idea about him being number one," she said sitting down. "Let me do an interview with people struggling after a heart attack."

"Show our audience how hard they work to get back," Edgar said, turning to look out his window, "and the reason they want to return."

For a week, Janice worked tirelessly with so many patients, always asking them why and learning so much. The broadcast was one of her best; however, her interview with Tim Gaze made it perfect.

"Tim, you listened to all those recovering from heart attacks," she paused for a brief second, "all saying they worked to regain what they had lost. What motivated you? I know how hard it was for you to come back."

"Yes, physical and speech therapy was difficult." Tears began to fall as if remembering those long hours. "But I trusted you to honor the promise given."

"Tim," she said, kissing his cheek. "I loved working to keep your chair warm. However, my biggest thrill was the day you came back."

"Your documentary last night was a hit," Edgar greeted her as the elevator door opened, "and if Tim isn't number one by the end of the month, I'll be surprised."

"So, what's next?" she asked with a wide smile. "I need work."

"Thinking of sending you to a new African nation," he said walking with her. "New Zana. They discovered large deposits of natural gas, and they want to be a member of the United Nations."

"Been reading about the country," she began, which surprised Edgar. "Terrorist group calling themselves Mansa, 'king of kings,' are threatening the elected president."

"They want nothing to do with the United Nations," Edgar spoke up, "but have formed a large army against the government's smaller one. Their one advantage is General Abebe, who by all reports is a brilliant commander."

"Well, when do I start?" Janice seemed anxious to move on.

"Need a week to arrange things," he said while walking into her office, "which will give you a week of vacation that you need."

"You know, you're right," she admitted. "For the last few years, I've neglected my family and need to visit them."

"Family will forgive you," he said as if giving a warning, "neglecting them for years."

"Yeah, they will," she said with confidence. "They're great."

After calling Linda, Janice took the first jet out and arrived before 3:00.

"Linda, look who finally found her way here," Frank said while opening the front door. "Not a word in years, but there she is."

"Frank, am I forgiven?" she asked, laying her suitcases down as the limousine pulled away.

"Of course, you are, my dear!" Linda came out running to her. "We all heard about your divorce and troubles."

"I wanted to tell you," she replied, tightly hugging her, "but didn't want any of you to get involved with the tabloids or gossip. My marriage fell apart so quickly, I wasn't prepared."

"Just like a woman," Frank came over and picked up the suitcases, "believing they can handle it all by themselves."

"Hush your mouth," Linda snapped. releasing her hold on Janice. "You have no idea how you'd handle a divorce."

"Because you'd shoot me if ever I'd want one," he began laughing.

"Never had it so good," she whispered, "and he knows it. So how long can you stay with us? Hope more than a few days."

"A week, maybe a couple extra days," she said following her to the house. "In the meantime be waiting on an assignment. So when will my little sister Susan be here? I'm anxious to see her after all this time."

"She called earlier." Her expression changed completely. "Said her friends were meeting after school and asked if she could stay overnight with one."

"Did you tell her I was coming?" Janice asked, disappointed by the news.

"Of course," Linda reluctantly replied, "but you know how teenagers are."

"Tell me the truth," Janice said, needing to know. "She's mad at me, right?"

"She's hurting right now," Linda said, walking toward the door while speaking. "For a year, she waited by the computer, hoping you'd appear. She no longer watches the news and had Frank take the computer out of her room."

"Oh my God, she hates me," Janice said, realizing the truth, "and I can't blame her."

"She's just confused, is all," Linda said, standing by the door, "believing you forgot all about her."

"What have I done?" She began to cry. "Coming here thinking all would be like it once was."

"Janice, we're adults and understand the hardships of marriage, little Frank and Lisa were so young. Susan was different, she came to love you as an older sister."

"Tell me what I can do to makes things right," she said, almost pleading, "anything."

"The only person she opens up to now," Linda said, taking a deep breath, "is Leone. Maybe you could talk with him, he might be able to suggest something."

"Think maybe it would be better," she said, hardly able to breathe, "that I just leave."

"Oh my God, no," she quickly replied. "That would be the worst thing you could do. Susan would never forgive you if you left."

"Would you mind putting my things in the room," she began, looking toward Leone's home, "while I go and speak with him?

"Not at all," Linda said with a smile. "Susan does have to come home sometime."

"Was just leaving," Leone, in a surprised tone, said while opening the door.

"I can come back," Janice said, standing by the door.

"Was coming to see you," he replied, giving her a hug. "Save me a walk."

"How are you?" she quickly asked. "Feeling okay?"

"On top of the world having you here." he stepped back to look her over, "And more beautiful than ever."

"I am so sorry having not called or even written," she began, "I've no excuse."

"Janice, told you," he said, taking her into his arms. "You're family, and nothing would ever change how we feel about you."

"Susan hates me," Janice said, her face buried on his chest, "and I am so afraid that I can't make it right."

"Come on in," he said, taking her by the shoulder. "I'll put coffee on, and we'll talk."

"Lots be happening around here," he began while making coffee. "Universe World Corps. is now in the movie business having bought a studio. They came in and emptied the entire mansion, anything of value gone to their movie prop warehouse. They've been putting the mansion in movies, three horror and one romantic. Been busier than ever, making sure no one wants pieces of it or the copper."

"It is a beautiful mansion," she admitted. "Sad they see it as something ugly."

"Times have changed," he replied, placing a cup in front of her, "so let us talk about Susan."

"Think it would be better if I just left," she began. "Linda said it would be a mistake.'

"I know you care deeply for her," he started, "but if I might ask what hurt you the most during your divorce."

"Liam never fought to save our marriage," her voice quivered. "He just left without speaking a word."

"So are you prepared to do that to her?" he asked after sipping on his coffee. "Or are you willing to face her and listen?"

"Yes," she admitted.

"Then sit down with her," he continued. "Show her you're not leaving and how much you love her."

"What if she doesn't believe me?" she asked.

"If you're there speaking from the heart," he said, touching her gently, "she'll believe because in truth she's hurt but loves you."

"Oh, Leone," she said, giving him a warm hug. "You're like the father I never knew."

"You will never know how much that means to me," he said. Tears rolled down his cheek.

"Look, I got your shirt all wet," she said, wiping her tears, "and made you cry."

"Just happy tears." He quickly wiped them away. "Just knowing how much you care for all of us."

"Never again will I neglect you," she said, kissing him on the cheek. "I promise to call or write every week, no matter where I am."

"Keep you to it," he said with a wide smile. "I'll walk over with you."

"Susan's on her way," Linda said meeting the two at the door. "She's not happy with me. She can't go to school in the same clothes. Besides, it's a school day."

"Hello Susan," Janice said, sitting at the table when she entered.

"Hi," Susan replied, walking past her, "got tons of homework."

"Susan, get back here," Linda said in a harsh tone while crossing her arms.

"No." Janice walked over and touched her arms. "We need alone time."

"Told you," Frank spoke up as Janice entered her room, "we should have used the belt instead of talking."

"Best we all go outside," Leone suggested, "and let them be."

"Maybe we should stay," Linda appeared worried, "just in case."

"No, everyone outside," Frank spoke up. "They have to work it out, and there's nothing we can do."

"Susan," Janice said, sitting on the edge of the bed as Susan lay reading. "I was a little disappointed you didn't come straight home from school."

"Was with my real friends." She continued to ignore looking toward her.

"I'm sorry having ignored you for so long," she began. "Can you forgive me?"

"Fine," she continued silent reading. "You're forgiven. Now go and leave me alone."

"No, I need you to know," she said, inching closer to her, "that I need you as my little sister."

"Mom said you divorced your husband," Susan said, turning over and dropping the book to the floor, "and now you need me to replace him."

"That hurt, Susan," she admitted.

"What would you know about hurt?" she asked, sitting up. "Sitting at the computer every night for over a year waiting just to talk to you?"

"I'm so sorry," she said, moving closer to her.

"You're sorry," she yelled out. "I cried every night knowing you lied and didn't care."

"Susan, I've never stopped caring," she said, attempting to hug her.

"I hate you," Susan responded, pushing her hands away, "just leave me alone and go away."

"No, I won't leave," she said, again attempting to hug her. "I do care and love you."

"I hate you," Susan began pounding her fist against Janice's shoulders, "I hate you."

With all the strength she had, Janice wrapped her arms around Susan.

"Please just go away." Susan began crying as Janice pulled her closer. "I hate you, so just leave me alone."

"I'm not going anywhere," she said in a calm tone while tears began to flow. "I've hurt so many. Liam, the man I love, this family, and you."

"You hurt me bad," she continued to cry. "I needed you, and you weren't there."

"I've made so many mistakes," she replied, holding her tight, "believing I could do it all and letting work become more important than family. Susan, you must know I love you, and I need to know you'll always be my little sister."

"I can't be hurt like that again." Her body seemed to collapse like rag doll.

"Oh, Susan," she said, kissing her on the head. "I promise never to hurt or ignore you again."

"I really don't hate you," Susan admitted, wrapping her arms around her. "I love you. I was so angry, and missed you so."

"Susan, you don't know how happy I am right now," she continued to hold her, "that my little sister forgives and loves me."

"I didn't hurt, you did I?" she asked, looking up while resting on her chest. "Are you alright?"

"I'm fine just to know your pain is gone," she said, releasing her.

"Maybe tonight you could help setting up the computer," she said looking over at the empty space, "so we can talk."

"As sisters, we keep no secrets," she said with a smile, "and every night, we'll remind one another how important sisters are."

The entire family joined in to help with the computer, and by 11:00, they completed the task.

"Eight o'clock," Janice said as they watched the machine operating, "every night we'll talk. Now if for some reason I'm unable to use a computer, I'll write letters. Now for some reason there isn't mail service, the letters will be bundled together and sent later.

"Alright, young lady," Linda said, looking at the clock, "its bath and bed time."

"Will you stay with me?" Susan said while holding Janice's hand, "Until I fall asleep?"

The following morning, Janice sat at the table, looking tired.

"Was nice of you to volunteer to speak to her class," Linda said walking in after seeing the children off.

"Don't believe Susan would have gone to school," she began, laughing, "had I not volunteered to speak."

"What's wrong with your shoulder?" Linda asked, noticing her expression of pain. "Let me see."

"It's nothing," Janice replied as Linda gently pulled her robe back.

"Did Susan do that?" Linda asked, looking at the bruising. "Frank, get in here."

"What is it?" he said, rushing into the room.

"Look what your daughter did," she said, showing the bruises.

"Call Leone," he immediately replied, "tell him we're coming over and why."

"Now, you get dressed," Linda insisted. "You'll be fine."

Within an hour Leone had arranged her to see a doctor, who ordered X-rays.

"Ms. Gardner," the doctor said, walking in while turning on the light to examine the photos, "no broken bones, but you have some nasty looking bruising."

"She seems to be in pain," Leone said, looking the young doctor in the eye.

"Typical football injury," he began explaining. "Heating pad along with warm showers and in a couple days, all better."

"Thank you, doctor," Janice said taking his hand. "Now I want all of you to promise not to say anything to anyone about this, especially you-know-who."

"Promise," Leone and Frank spoke up. "Thanks, doc."

After a warm shower, she was prepared to speak to Susan's class.

"Ms. Gardner," an elderly lady greeted her at the door, "I'm Mrs. Pier, principal."

"Is there a problem?" she asked. "Susan said her teacher would like me to address the class."

"When we heard you were willing to speak," she said, with a wide smile, "we were wondering, would you mind speaking to all the students?"

"Certainly," she said, surprised by the request, "only if Susan can join me on stage."

Standing on the stage of the auditorium, with Susan sitting beside her, Janice began speaking of the importance of family and job. After a half hour she allowed questions, knowing most would be simple.

"Is Susan really your little sister?" someone yelled from the back.

"Yes, she is," she said, looking toward her in a loving manner, "and keep in mind I have friends with the FBI, DEA, and Army. So be nice to her. We keep no secrets."

"The president of the United States," the principal spoke up, "is a friend."

"Man, if I had all the money you make," another voice from the back shouted out, "I wouldn't need any family or friends."

"Please," Janice said looking toward the principal, trying to see who yelled out, "let me just say, you could possess a mountain of gold, but without family or friends, be the loneliness person in the world."

"Ms. Gardner," a young girl stood up, "I've admired you forever, but are you no longer interested in finding Mr. Shakespeare?"

"I've heard he's published another novel." She admitted she continued to keep up with his work, though she had been preoccupied over the last few years. "I intend to continue chasing Shakespeare, no matter how long it takes."

"Why?" the young girl asked. "Been so many arrested for impersonating him and how would you know it is really him?"

"I'm on a quest among the stars," she began, "searching for the brightest, but along the way I've discovered others. Each discovery an adventure, meeting people that I would have never known. If we were to meet, I think he would prove himself to me."

"Any idea why he shuns notoriety?" the principal asked.

"Maybe having a family and friends is enough for him," she answered, "and he wants to have a simple life."

"Let's give Ms. Gardner a big hand for coming here." The principal began clapping, "And for speaking to us."

"Oh Janice," Susan ran to her after leaving the bus, "it was the greatest day ever. Had everyone talking, even the teachers."

"Now, little sister, don't let it go to your head," she said, hugging her. "Remember what is the most important thing we share."

"Being sisters," she replied, returning her hug.

For the following week, the two were inseparable, but they spent time with everyone.

"Well, you're off again." Leone stood as her limousine driver waited. "You know how I feel about you, but promise to be careful."

"Love you, too," she said, giving him a hug and kiss on the cheek. "Eight o'clock every night on computer if you get lonesome."

"Alright, get over here and give me a kiss," Linda demanded.

"Linda and Frank," giving both a hug and kiss, "love you."

Janice then bent down and kissed little Frank and Lisa goodbye.

"Susan, maybe this summer," she said, walking over to her and giving her a hug, "you could stay with me for a few weeks."

"Mom," she yelled out, "could I?"

"Of course," she said with a smile.

"Now I don't live in a real big apartment," she explained, "but a nice loft with enough room for two of us. We can shop, and go see a Broadway show."

"Oh that would be wonderful," she blurted out, "just the two of us."

"Of course," she said, giving her a kiss. "Maybe have Randy tag along, as long as he doesn't bring a camera."

"Maybe he could film us together," she said with excitement.

"Good idea," she said with the same enthusiasm, "and one day have him film all of us together."

"I'm going to miss you." Tears began to fall down her cheeks.

"No more tears," she said, wiping them. "Sister be back before you know it."

"Okay," she said smiling, "and we'll talk."

"Every night," she said, kissing each cheek, "but no boyfriends until you're 25."

"You've been talking to my dad," she said, looking toward Frank, "and Leone."

"Love you all," she said, waving as she entered the vehicle.

CHAPTER SEVENTEEN

"Janice, I'm a little reluctant to send you to New Zana," Edgar slowly began, "after hearing that the Mansa's tried to assassinate His Majesty King Gatura."

"Any idea on his condition," she asked, "or where he is?"

"We know he's alive," he continued, "and with his family at a secure location."

"I assume General Abebe has mobilized the army," she continued to question him.

"Yes," he replied, shaking his head as if unsure of the situation. "A total of 400 or 500 soldiers against maybe 1,200 to 1,400."

"Well, that's where the story is," she said while standing. "You arranged transportation for me and Randy."

"Yes, all arrangements were made," he said, standing up to face her, "but promise me if things go sideways, you'll get back here, story or no story."

"Not to worry," she said crossing her heart. "I'll come back with a story."

"I mean it, Janice," he told her in a stern tone. "Get out of there if shooting starts."

"Love you, too," she quickly turned and left.

"Damn girl's going to give me ulcers," he said, slamming his body onto his chair.

As the jet landed on the runway, Janice looked out to see several hundred people waiting by the single building.

"Look at that, Randy," she blurted out as the jet came to a stop. "A welcoming."

"Thank God there're soldiers with them," he pointed out.

"Just have your camera ready," she said, walking toward the exit.

"Ms. Gardner." He stood under six feet but wore a well-fitting uniform having five stars on his collar. "I am General Abebe, and the people wish to thank you for coming."

"Thank you for meeting us," she said, looking over the crowd. "Please tell the people how honored I am to be here."

"Many of these people," he said, turning toward the cheering people, "have walked hundreds of miles to be here."

"Hello." Janice walked over to a young child and knelt down to speak. "You're so pretty, and is this your mother?"

"Yes, she is the mother," Abebe replied after translating her words. "They have traveled here to see you."

"I'm a little embarrassed," she said, standing up and smiling. "I hadn't expected anyone to know me."

"We are a small country," he said, standing erect to show his slender frame, "but we have made great strides modernizing our communications."

"I met no disrespect," she continued. "May I say a few words to them?"

"Of course," he said in a gracious tone. "I will translate."

While Randy filmed, she spoke how humbled she was by knowing the long journey each had taken to come here.

"Are you taking me to see the King?" she asked after having given a brief speech.

"No," he said as he escorted her toward several waiting vehicles. "Your presence might place him in jeopardy. We will be going to my headquarters, and there you will remain safe."

"I came here to get a story about the Mansa," she said, entering the vehicle, "not to be a captive on a military base."

"My orders are clear," he replied as the vehicle began moving. "Keep you safe and not allow you out of my sight."

"Fine," she whispered under her breath. "I go where you go."

For two days she stayed inside the camp, and was told spies watched her every move. Which was why it was impossible for her to meet the King, who remained safe.

On the morning of the third day, several trucks began arriving, and the soldiers with packs and rifles began lining up.

"What's happening," she asked Abebe, dressed in camouflaged uniform.

"We've received a report," he explained, "the Mansa are attacking a village."

"Randy, get the camera ready," she yelled to him.

"You are not to go," he said, shocked by her willingness to come along.

"So I'm to stay behind," she pointed out, "where I might be kidnapped? Besides, your orders were not to let me out of your sight."

"Sergeant," he yelled out, "Ms. Gardner and cameraman will ride with me."

"Thank you," she said, smugly walking past him.

"I tolerate you," Abebe said, sliding into the seat, "by order of His Majesty."

"We can live with that," Janice replied while looking toward Randy.

Entering the village they found only the dead; they butchered everything including the animals.

"Randy, no close up shots," she said leaving the vehicle while surveying the surrounding area. "Show the bodies from the hill over there."

"Where are the women," Randy asked while looking around, "and children?"

"Get the camera ready," she said, trying to straighten her hair.

"So much blood," Randy said while walking toward the small hill. "How anyone could kill like this…"

"Most killed by machete," Abebe said while walking toward them. "They wish to make an example for others."

"Janice Gardner here at a small village in New Zana," she began. "Behind me are the bodies of those who once lived here. Murdered for no other reason than hate, by those calling themselves Mansa. Is the world prepared to accept such people as leaders, murderous and cruel? Their barbarian ways must be stopped, slaughtering innocents so they can rule. Let the world in one voice condemn those responsible, and help bring justice to those that lay dead."

"That was great, Janice," Randy said, turning the camera off, "especially with the village in the background."

"When the soldiers begin burying them," she said, looking toward the village, "film it."

"General, look," Randy yelled out as several people walked out of the jungle.

"Survivors," Janice yelled out. "Get your camera going."

"Any idea what they're saying?" Randy whispered while filming.

"They say women and children taken," one of the soldiers spoke up. "They sell for guns from slave traders."

"Is there any way to stop that?" she asked.

"Only if we find camp," he continued, "kill all, and bring people back."

For several hours the soldiers silently buried the dead while Randy filmed it.

"Recommend they cut the burial scene to 20 seconds," she began while reviewing all that he filmed, "and then show the soldier playing taps."

"Janice, you're different somehow," he carefully began, "like an actor performing for the camera showing emotion and concern."

"Maybe," she said in a soft tone, "but how else can I sleep?"

Once at the camp, Janice turned on the computer and found no connection.

"They must have destroyed the tower," she said, looking toward Randy. "Better get started on a letter."

For a week, she wrote every day, but was unable to find anyone going into the capital for supplies. Rumors began to circulate that a young woman had escaped from the Mansa camp and had marked her escape route.

"Ms. Gardner," a young soldier knocking on her door said. "General Abebe has asked you come."

As she walked toward his office, several hundred poorly clothed men having machetes entered the camp.

"Who are they?" she asked the young man. "And why are they here?"

"They're a tribe of the village," he explained, "come to kill all Mansa."

"Machetes against a rifle," she blurted out, "be a slaughter."

"They gave word," he continued. "Fight to death."

"Ms. Gardner," he began as she entered his office. "Tonight this young woman will lead us to the Mansa camp."

"Hello," she said, looking over at the young woman who sat quietly near his desk.

"I intend to do battle," he continued. "By what she has given, we will be out numbered two to one. Therefore, I intend sending you to the capital for your safety."

"No, I'm coming along," she said, defying him. "If you lose the battle, no one will be safe, including me."

"The American many talk of," the young woman spoke up, "they trust."

"They'll be shooting," Abebe explained, "and people killed."

"General, you're going to need every soldier," she reminded him, "to fight while I help get the hostages out."

"If killed," he snapped, "I'm responsible."

"Then have your soldiers kill them first," she simply replied while walking over to the young woman. "Do that, and we'll be fine."

"Insolence," he shouted. "Typical American."

"So are we riding with you," she asked, strolling over to him, "or some-one else?"

"We leave in 20 minutes," he said, turning and walking out.

"So, what is your name?" she said, turning toward the young woman who seemed paralyzed by the conversation. "You know mine already."

"Mirani," she replied. "No village woman ever speaks to man like that."

"Maybe it's time they did," Janice replied, taking her by the hand and lead-ing her out. "Come on."

Entering her quarters, she immediately ordered Randy to get ready as she explained the situation.

"You volunteered me?" he asked, sitting down. "What, you trying to get me killed?"

"Randy, it's why we're here," she continued. "If you want stay here and just give me the camera…"

"You know one day," he said, picking up the camera. "They'll be giving out crazy medals, and we'll get nominated."

"Hurry up!" Her reply was more of an order.

Once on the road, Abebe said nothing then turned around.

"Here," he said, handing Randy a Colt .45 pistol, "just in case."

"Hey, man, pacifist," he said, speaking quickly. "Besides, never shot a gun."

"Reporters," Janice spoke up, "can't take sides."

"I'll take it," Mirani said, taking the pistol from his hand, "and I'll use it."

"At least one has the good sense to take it," he said, turning around.

Mirani began pointing out the different spots she had marked and remembered the different locations where she found fruit or water.

"The lake where I found fish…" She pointed to a large lake. "I walked three days from camp to here."

"No more road," he said, looking around as his vehicle stopped. "Be on foot, and Mirani, you remember this place?"

"Come, camp's not far," she said, jumping out, "maybe five, six miles."

As they cut through the dense jungle, all were surprised to see their camp.

"Old military base," Janice replied, "and look how the trees have grown around it."

"German or British," Abebe replied. "Built well, and jungle vines have camouflaged all the buildings"

"Jungle grass, eight feet," Abebe began to survey the entire complex. "Two guards watching from the trees."

"My people in that large building." Mirani pointed to it. "Leaders stay in two buildings, and others in tents."

"Stay here while I make plans," Abebe ordered as he began moving back.

"It's getting cold," Randy said while looking toward the camp. "Should have known we'd be here so late."

"Shh," Mirani said with her finger over her lips. "It will be hot soon when shooting starts."

Suddenly two villagers wearing nothing but loin cloth crawled by, both having their machetes. They watched as the two crawled toward the camp, and then slowly began climbing the trees where the guards sat.

With two swipes of their blades, both heads fell to the ground.

"Excellent." Abebe crawled up while watching the men dispatching the two guards. "Men are getting into position now."

"We'll follow you, General," Janice whispered. "Mirani will lead us to the hostages, and we'll take them to the trucks."

"I'll have three soldiers helping you," he whispered. "Take the hostages by truck to the lake we passed. Leave them there, and have the trucks return."

"Understood," Janice replied.

"It is time," Abebe said after looking at his watch.

Running through the tall grass, they realized the battle had begun.

"Randy, are you filming?" Janice shouted over all the noise of automatic gunfire and the eruptions from hand grenades.

"Of course," he shouted. "Why you think I came along?"

As they followed Mirani, they saw several wounded soldiers along with several half-dressed enemy troops lying dead on the ground.

From the side of the building that housed the hostages, several men with machetes charge the group. The three soldiers instantly shot and killed six, and Mirani with the pistol killed two others.

"Hurry," Mirani shouted as she shot the lock off. "They're inside."

"My God," Janice shouted out while looking toward the people huddled together. "There must be over 100 here."

"Soldiers say we need to go." She looked toward the man as he spoke. "Mansa's soldiers are coming."

"Why aren't they moving?" Randy yelled out while filming them.

"American reporter Janice Gardner," Mirani began speaking their language, "came to save all. Be thankful she came along."

Janice looked over toward Randy as the people began moving toward the door.

"Mirani, why are they touching me?"

"I tell them you came to save them," she said with a smile.

"Randy, start leading them toward the trucks," Janice shouted.

Outside they found the three soldiers wounded, but they had killed over 20 enemy Mansa's soldiers.

"Mirani," Janice shouted, "tell the women to pick up our wounded soldiers."

One by one each wounded soldier they came across was carried by four women, who themselves were in poor condition. As they entered the tall grass, the shooting within the camp continued.

"Hurry," Mirani yelled out while holding a rifle.

They finally arrived at the trucks, and the drivers immediately began placing the wounded and women inside.

"Does battle go well?" one of the drivers asked Mirani. "How many do you bring?"

"Cannot say," she answered as they brought the wounded up. "Need to leave now and not talk."

"How many rifles you have?" he asked, looking toward those carrying the rifles.

"Six, she replied, showing the Colt, "and pistol."

"First three trucks have rifles," he explained to Mirani, "last three with rifles."

"Mirani," Janice came over to her, "tell him to get these trucks moving."

Following Janice's order, the drivers began moving the trucks once loaded. Within 40 minutes, they arrived at the lake, and quickly began unloading the hostages and wounded.

"Mirani, ask him if he has a radio," Janice said while helping the children off the trucks. "If so, have them send doctors and more trucks."

"They called, and trucks come," Mirani began, "with doctors."

"Great," she said walking toward the driver that she rode with. "Tell him we're heading back, and have the women care for the wounded until help arrives."

"I'll come," she replied.

"No, stay here," Janice ordered, "and see that everyone gets back safely."

Having Mirani order the drivers back to the trucks, Janice waved as they began the journey back.

"Randy," she replied as the trucks finally arrived back near the enemy's camp, "thought you might want to stay with Mirani."

"I'm your cameraman," he said, filming the trucks and drivers, "and crazy as it is, I'm not leaving you."

"Ms. Gardner, what are you doing back here?" Abebe came walking through the heavy jungle with his arm wrapped with a white sheet.

"You're hurt," she said, running over to him. "How's the battle going?"

"Caught them completely by surprise," he began while walking toward the drivers. "Once their leaders were killed, they could not organize. Over

1,000 killed, and 40 captured. Some have fled into the jungle. The villagers are hunting them now."

"Hostages and some of the wounded are safe," she began, "and the drivers ordered trucks and doctors to come."

"Very good," he responded, sounding exhausted, "but why are you here?"

"Told me to take the hostages by trucks to the lake," she began, "and afterwards to bring the trucks back."

"I believe the order was to return the trucks," he reminded her. "Not for you to come."

"Not the way I heard it," she said, walking with him.

"You are insubordinate," he said with a slight smile, "but daring."

"That go for me?" Randy said, filming him.

"Americans…" he said, walking away and shaking his head.

Abebe advised the drivers he had found a road into the camp, and once inside, they began placing the wounded and dead in the trucks. Once everyone, including the prisoners, were aboard the trucks, Abebe ordered them to leave after having the entire compound set fire.

"Randy, have you filmed everything?" Janice whispered. "The bodies in the camp and now the fire?"

"Got it all," he quietly answered. "Janice, you realize there were no wounded Mansa soldiers and only 40 prisoners."

"I know," she affirmed his concern, "best we not bring it up."

By late morning, they had arrived safely at the base, and they learned four of the wounded they had taken died. Yet there was good news, all 136 women and children hostages were well.

After several hours sleep, Janice, having not eaten in two days, made her way to the army kitchen.

"Ms. Gardner," the young officer came running toward her. "General Abebe would like a word."

"General Abebe," she said walking into his office and noticing his arm in a sling.

"I understand with the towers destroyed," he said, walking toward her with a large portable military telephone, "you could not contact family."

"Been writing letters," she admitted.

"Of course," he said, handing her the heavy unit. "Military channel, and you have only 10 minutes to talk."

"Linda," she said, listening to her voice, "it's me, Janice, and I'm on a military phone. I've only 10 minutes. Is Susan there?"

Within seconds, she heard Susan's voice with excitement.

"Hi darling sister," she began, "I'm fine but towers destroyed so haven't been able to use computer. Just wanted you to know wrote letters, be sending them when I arrive back at the capital. So good hearing your voice, and be looking forward to seeing you. Had Randy film some of the animals, be sending you a copy. General is pointing to his watch, have to go, but love you."

"Ms. Gardner, I know you have not eaten," Abebe said, taking the phone from her hand. "Please join me."

"Thank you so much," she replied, taking his good hand. "That phone call meant a lot."

"Like my soldiers," he said, walking her over to the table, "I've come to admire your bravery."

"Truthfully, General," she replied as two soldiers appeared with trays of food, "I was scared to death the entire time."

"Are all Americans," he began, helping with her chair as he spoke, "modest as you?"

"Not modest," she continued as he sat across from her, "truthful. It's easy to show bravery, especially when soldiers and someone like Mirani are beside you."

"Yes, a very brave young woman," he added, "and I'll speak to my soldiers of your praise. Shall we enjoy our last meeting, for I've received a message from your corporation. They will provide transportation for you and your cameraman to leave tomorrow morning."

"Our work here is far from over," she began to protest, "for we need to speak with the hostages and soldiers."

"I may delay your flight for a day," he said, filling his plate, "but you must obey."

"Would it be fine with you," she said, filling several plates with food, "if I were to start interviewing the hostages tonight?"

"Ms. Gardner," he said, standing up while she continued to pile food on plates, "we have fed the hostages and given medical attention."

"I'm sorry," she said, laying the plates, "I know they've been treated well."

"Escort Ms. Gardner to the hostage quarters," he said, picking up his plate, "and take all the extra food with her. I am sure they will appreciate the gesture."

"Thank you," she said, walking over and giving him a kiss on the cheek.

With Randy at her side, the interviews of the hostages began with the help of several women who spoke English. By the following evening with the help of a military interpreter, they spoke to the soldiers and villagers that took part in the raid.

"Well, we've enough to spend an entire week on," Randy said, walking into the building, "and tomorrow we go home."

"Randy, thank you for staying." For the first time, she said, "You know I can't do this without you."

"Don't get sentimental with me," he said, laying his camera down, "we're a team. Where you go, Randy's there."

As they walked through the airport, several soldiers confronted them.

"Ms. Gardner and Mr. Kemp, please follow us."

Entering a security area, they found several well-dressed men standing around the room. Then they notice the leader of the country sitting quietly at a small table.

"I could not allow you to leave," he said, standing up revealing his bright red coat and a large light blue sash over his chest with large medals, "without showing my appreciation on all the two of you did for my country."

Janice was taken how handsome he was, and young for a leader of a country.

"I wish to present you with this," he said, allowing one of the men to walk over holding a beautiful wooden box, "it is a medal of valor."

"I don't know what to say," she said, opening the box, "it's a great honor."

"Hostages returned safely," he began, while everyone stood at attention, "and our enemy destroyed. General Abebe relayed your bravery and concurs you be rewarded."

"Mirani was the bravest of all," Janice said, holding the box in her shaking hand, "and Randy."

"Amply rewarded, she'll be," he said while looking toward the others, "and become a national symbol of the bravery and courage of our people."

"We thank you," she said, bowing to him, "and humbly accept such a magnificent award."

"General Abebe did mention," he said, showing his perfect white teeth with a wide smile, "you were modest and always willing to give credit to others."

"It's easy to say when true," she said, looking toward Randy.

"My country will always be grateful," he said, taking her hand and kissing it.

The room cleared quickly, as the soldiers escorted His Highness away.

"Janice," Randy said as they began walking toward the jet. "Did you notice that the medal is pure gold?"

"How could I not?" she answered while walking out toward the awaiting jet. "But did you notice the craftsmanship of the box?"

"Beautiful," he admitted.

Once arriving back in the states, Edgar summoned Janice to his office.

"Afternoon Carolina," Janice said, walking toward her. "Any messages?"

"Ms. Gardner," Carolina said, jumping to her feet. "Mr. Acorn's been waiting."

"Was on a jet for two days", she continued to walk toward his office, "and I wasn't about to come here without a bath and sleep."

"It's about time," Edgar shouted from inside his office. "Been wondering when you would show up."

"The film and reports we sent," she said, sitting down. "Did you like?"

"Response was overwhelming," he admitted. "But you went too far this time. Could have gotten yourself and Randy killed. You're to report the story not get involved."

"Things happened so fast," she explained. "Didn't have time to think."

"Bullshit." It was the first time he ever used a foul word. "You could have waited outside the camp until the battle was over and hostages freed."

"Maybe," she continued, downplaying the event. "What were the ratings?"

"Ratings mean nothing if you get yourself killed," he blurted out, "but as usual, they were outstanding."

"Mr. Acorn?" Carolina entered the office. "There's a gentleman here to see Ms. Gardner with a subpoena."

"Ms. Gardner, you've been served," he said, handing her a paper. "Please present yourself to the Foreign Oversight Senate committee in two days."

"I'll call legal," Edgar said, picking up the phone. "Apparently they watched your report and have questions."

Having no recourse, Janice sat in front of several senators questioning her about the raid on the Mansa camp.

"Ms. Gardner, as you know, the government of New Zana has requested admission to the United Nations," one of the older senators began, "and American aid. However, it has been alleged defenseless soldiers, having surrendered, were killed. You were there. Did you witness any such behavior?"

"No, sir," she quickly answered, "I dealt with the hostages only. You've seen my entire broadcast and, as I explained, witnessed 30 or more Mansa soldiers attacking the compound where they held the hostages."

"Understand, Ms. Gardner," a much younger Senator spoke up. "The killings of innocent soldiers having surrender cannot be tolerated."

"Senator, I understand you were in the military," she slowly began. "What if an American city had its people murdered by terrorists? Your soldiers came late and buried the victims. Would you consider the terrorist innocent, or justified in killing them as they attacked your men?"

"A soldier could answer," he said with a smile, "as a Senator I cannot."

"Ms. Gardner," a third Senator spoke up, "would you have filmed such an event if it did in fact occur?"

"No," she answered, "I will never film killing. I film the destruction afterwards. Always from distance, and never close up to show wound or blood."

"Ms. Gardner," a fourth Senator spoke. "For over an hour, we've questioned you, and now, would you like to ask us anything?"

"Yes," she said with her most charming smile. "I wonder if those making the allegations are the ones who supported the Mansa soldiers."

"An interesting observation," the older Senator blurted out, "and this committee will certainly look into that."

"Ms. Gardner, you've been a most cooperative witness," the younger Senator seemed to speak for the others, "and we thank you."

"You're very welcome," she replied, "and if you need further please feel free to contact my office."

Several Senators afterwards gathered around her, knowing it was good press.

"Ms. Gardner," the younger Senator began once alone, "your testimony was impressive. I must say, you are more beautiful in person than on television."

"Thank you," she said, allowing him to take her hand. "You're very kind."

"You've dealt with hostages before," he continued. "If you're staying in Washington, I'd like for you to join me for dinner."

"Unfortunately, I'm to leave immediately," she said, taking her hand away. "Maybe next time."

"Until next time," he said, with a half-smile, "Ms. Gardner."

The following morning, Carolina and Janice were in the office laughing when Edgar appeared.

"So, what's so funny?" he asked stepping inside.

"Ms. Gardner said a senator hit on her," Carolina blurted out.

"Wonder what his wife would say?" Janice replied.

"They don't understand," Edgar began chuckling. "You're a good reporter that prepares for any situation."

"Ms. Gardner knew each one by name," Carolina continued, "along with wives and children's names."

"Janice, let me ask you a question," Edgar began. "I know you didn't witness the allegations that were alleged, but is it possible."

"When I watched, the soldiers burying the villagers," she explained, "I noticed their expression of rage. I can't say what happened, nor judge because it wasn't my country or people."

"Janice, God certainly created you," Edgar said with a smile, "and knowing it was perfection broke the mold."

"By the way," she said, changing the subject. "What'd the people think of my testimony?"

"Eighty-one percent believed you," he replied, "six percent think you withheld the truth, and the rest would not or could not answer."

"Six percent," she said in a condescending tone, "opposition viewers."

"Well, you've earned time off," he said, walking toward his office, "and take Carolina along because when you're not around she drives me crazy."

"I just ask him if he'd like my help," she said looking toward her.

"Carolina," she replied, "it's paid time off, so don't argue with the man."

For two days, Janice relaxed around her apartment, and as always left Susan messages on the computer. After a leisurely morning, she strolled around the apartment when the buzzer sounded throughout the rooms.

"Yes?" she asked, pressing the intercom button.

"Janice, it's me Frank," his voice came over the speakers. "May I come up?"

"Of course," she said, pressing the button to open the security door. She raced to meet him at the door and looked to see that he was alone. "You're alone." She could hardly catch her breath with concern, "What's wrong?"

"Yesterday, they admitted Leone to the hospital," he said while entering. "He was coughing blood. It's the shrapnel. Apparently it's moved and is cutting into his lungs."

"Is he dying?" she could hardly control herself. "Please tell me."

"They've recommended he enter a hospice facility," he continued, "but I know Leone, and he'll never agree to it."

"I'll call the office," she quickly replied. "Tell them where they can reach me."

"Janice, I need to tell you something important," he said, taking a deep breath. "You might want to sit down."

"Is it Susan?" she asked, believing there was more bad news coming. "She's been hurt?"

"No, nothing like that." He knelt down and took her hand. "What I'm about to tell you could destroy my friendship with Leone."

"Frank, please just tell me," she demanded.

"Leone," he began, pausing and swallowing deeply, "is your biological father."

CHAPTER EIGHTEEN

W "Frank, if it's money your needing," she said, pulling her hand away in anger, "just ask rather than come here with such a story."

"My coming here has nothing to do with money," he quickly informed her in a stern tone. "Because you need to know the truth."

"I buried mother beside my father," she said while stepping away from him, "and now you want me to believe he was a complete stranger?"

"Janice," he said, trying to explain. "Before you were born, your mother agreed with Leone to keep their relation a secret. The man who lays beside your mother was once a soldier, who served with Leone."

"I can't listen to this anymore," she shouted. "You come here with this preposterous story without any proof, so please leave."

"Linda said I have no right being the one to tell you," he began. "I'm breaking promises made years ago. Many times my friendship with Leone was tested, yet it survived. However, I know this may break that bond; if so, let it be. I'll leave, but first allow me to prove the truth."

"How can you prove what you claim?" she asked, folding her arms.

"If you want the truth," he turned toward the door, "keep the door open."

After 10 minutes, he entered the apartment with six boxes on a two-wheel dolly.

"I took these from Leone's home," he said removing them from the dolly.

"Letters from your mother and pictures. I'll leave now. Tomorrow, if you still don't believe, I'll take them back and never mention it again."

"Frank, who else knows about this?" she asked while opening the first box.

"Linda," he replied slowly, "no one else."

"How long has she known?" she continued to question him.

"Forever," he admitted. "When you've come to a decision, we'll talk."

Sitting down while looking into the box, Janice saw it was filled with bundled letters and several photo albums.

"Mother, why didn't you tell me?" She began crying.

Taking a bottle of wine from the cooler, she began reading the letters, and when tired, she began looking through the photo albums. When she fell asleep was unknown, but woke when hearing the buzzer blaring.

"Janice," Frank's voice came over the intercom, "am I still welcomed?"

"Of course," she quickly replied while unlocking the door.

"What would you like me to do?" he asked while entering the apartment. "Take them back or leave them?"

"I'd like more time," she said while realizing her appearance was somewhat disarranged from having fallen asleep on the sofa. "Please go home, and say nothing."

"If that's what you wish," she said, disappointed she hadn't made any decision. "I am sorry, and maybe Linda was right that I was wrong coming here."

"No one is right or wrong," she answered. "The wrong happened long ago."

"I brought pain," he said, taking a deep breath as if trying to control his emotions, "which will be my burden to carry."

"There's no burden to carry," she said, and for the first time, she smiled. "Just give me time."

"Alright," he said, "you'll send the boxes back when finished?"

"They'll be safe with me," she said, walking over and kissing him on the cheek. "Tell Susan I might be busy for a few days."

"I'll tell her," he said, touching his cheek, "and if there is anything, please just ask."

"Thank you," she said as he walked away.

Letter after letter, she read, and with it brought back memories of times shared and the fragrance of her mother's perfume. After three days of long hours, Janice went to the office to speak with Edgar.

"Edgar, may I speak with you in private?" she asked as he looked up from reading.

"Janice, I thought you were gone…" He immediately stood up, "Visiting family."

"Something important came up," she entered but seemed unable to sit, "and I needed to talk to someone about it."

"I'm listening," he said, sitting back down and placing his hands on his desk, "so?"

"All my life, I've believed in truth," she began, "and now my world's been scattered. The man, who I believe to be my father, isn't."

"Come and sit." He quickly stood and walked over to her. "You're shaking. I'm making you coffee, and start at the beginning."

After drinking the coffee, he made for her, she told of the letters and albums.

"So, Leone is your biological father?" he said, looking toward her. "And the letters all written by your mother somewhat assert that?"

"Yeah," she admitted, "she wrote of her love for him and always about me."

"She never wrote why she never married Leone?" he asked. "Or about the man who she claimed was your father?"

"Nothing," she continued. "She wrote about me mostly and things she and I did."

"Ha," he said surprising her using such a short word while folding his hands in front of his face, "interesting to say the least."

"Edgar, tell me what you think," she said, wanting his advice. "I do value your opinion."

"Having met the man," he slowly began speaking while lying his hands on the desk, "I've found him to be honorable. You speak fondly of him, and admire the man."

"As a friend," she instantly replied, "not as my father."

"You have many unanswered questions," he said, attempting to guide her to do what is right, "and the reporter in you knows what to do."

"What happens if he's unwilling to give the answers?" she asked.

"Then we both have misjudged him," he replied.

"My mother did love him," she admitted. "I just wonder if he felt the same."

"Whatever promise he made to your mother," he added, "was powerful enough to deny him the right to be a father."

"He never married," she said while giving his comment great thought, "I need to know why."

"I'll have our jet prepared," he said, reaching over toward the phone.

"Need to tell Carolina I'll be gone for a few days," she said, standing, "and Edgar, thank you."

"Janice," he said, moving his hand away from the phone and standing up. "The story you seek isn't for broadcasting, but one you will come to know as the most important."

"Important, yes," she said, turning toward the door then stopping, "but maybe hurtful."

Packing only what she needed for a couple days, Janice had the driver pack the limousine with all the boxes.

As the jet lifted off the runway, Janice began looking at each album again. Thumbing through the photos, she remembered asking why the need to have doubles for each roll. Yet the answer was always the same, that one day she would want a copy. Now she knew the truth; all copies sent to Leone, who carefully placed them in beautiful leather folders.

Once on the ground, she quickly ordered a van, and placing everything inside, she began her journey to discover the truth.

"Janice," Linda screamed as she waited outside for the school bus to bring the children home. "You came."

"Linda," she said, opening the door and walking over to give her a hug. "I had to come."

"I know all of this is a shock," she began as if apologizing. "Been thinking about it and know it's time for you to know the truth. I was opposed to it at first, mostly for Susan's sake."

"Nothing will change on my feelings for my little sister," she said, crossing her heart, "or you."

"Oh, Janice, you don't know how I've worried about that," she said, throwing her arms around her. "I don't know what I'd do if you ever left for good."

"Janice!" Susan screamed from inside the bus. "You're here."

"Hello, little sister," Janice said, catching her as she ran to her. "Missed you!"

"I told everyone you would come," Susan said, squeezing her. "I knew you'd come."

"You're growing up so fast," Janice said, kissing her on the head, "and becoming such a beautiful woman."

"Not as beautiful as you," Susan spoke with her head against Janice's body. "No one is as pretty as you are."

"Susan, help bring her suitcases inside," Linda ordered while wiping the tears from her eyes. "And tonight, we call out for dinner."

"Yes, Mother," Susan replied with a smile while running toward the van and opening the side door. "You want these boxes inside?"

"No, dear," Janice yelled out, "just the two suitcases; the boxes stay."

"I know you've a million questions." Linda waited for Susan to enter the house before speaking. "But wait for the children to be in school."

"Where's Frank?" she asked.

"At the hospital," she said as the second school bus pulled up. "And there's my little Frank and Lisa."

"Mommy, Janice is back!" Lisa came running up to her. "Is she staying with us?"

"I know," Linda said, bending down to give her a kiss, "and yes, she's staying with us."

"She'll probably spend all her time with Susan," Frank spoke up.

"Why would I do that," Janice said, lifting he young boy up for a kiss, "when there is a good-looking man around?"

"Mommy, Frankie is turning red!" Lisa shouted while laughing.

"Well then," Janice said, placing Frank down and lifting Lisa up then twirling her, "what about you?"

"Alright, inside now." Linda chuckled while speaking. "One cookie before supper."

"That go for me, too?" Janice asked while placing Lisa down.

"Good luck trying to eat," Linda said as the two ran toward the door, "with three hanging on you."

"You're so lucky," Janice replied while walking toward her. "Three beautiful children and a husband that idealizes you."

"Never forget," she said, taking her hand, "you're a big part of this family."

"Then what about that cookie?" She began laughing.

As predicted the three children surrounded Janice when Frank entered.

"You came," he said with surprise in his voice after giving Linda a kiss. "I hadn't expected you, but I'm happy you're here."

"How's Leone?" she quickly asked while walking toward him.

"Stubborn, but they're doing everything they can," he began as she kissed his cheek, "and they've come up with a plan to help."

"What plan?" Linda asked.

"Knowing he's refused to enter a hospice facility," he said while sitting down, "to help with breathing, he'll be on oxygen. They also want him to use a wheelchair to avoid unnecessary movement that might cause the shrapnel to move."

"Why oxygen?" Linda asked.

"They say it will help his breathing," he explained, "so he doesn't have to strain."

"We could send him to other specialist," Janice suggested, "that could perform the surgery he needs."

"They've consulted two specialists," Frank informed her, "and both agree surgery is out of the question."

"How long?" Janice's voice quivered. "Did they say?"

"Two, maybe three months," Frank replied, bowing his head while speaking. "If he does what they ask and limits activity."

"Can he leave the hospital?" Linda asked.

"Be released tomorrow," he said, looking toward the group as he spoke. "I'll bring him home."

Everyone stood silent as the doorbell rang.

"Frank, that's the deliveryman with our dinner," Linda spoke up. "Would you get it?"

After paying the man, the children set the table and all ate in silence.

"Maybe after school, I can visit Uncle Leone," Susan finally spoke. "He was worried when he saw your broadcast while rescuing those ladies."

"Think all of us were worried when we saw that broadcast," Linda reminded them.

"Homework," Frank said while taking his plate to the sink, "then a little television and bedtime."

With Linda's watching, Janice sat with the children while each read or wrote.

"I'm going to unpack," Janice whispered as the children began watching television.

"I can help," Susan, closing her book, spoke up, "and we can talk."

"Then afterward to bed," Linda said grabbing a towel as Frank washed the dishes.

"Mother said Uncle Leone is dying," Susan began as they began removing the clothes from the suitcase, "and no one I ever knew has died."

"Somethings are out of our hands," Janice said, placing her arm around her shoulders, "but let them know every minute how much you love them."

"Uncle Leone knows that," she admitted in a soft tone, "but he always seemed to know just what to say when we talked."

"Yes, he's a remarkable person," Janice said, kissing her head.

The following morning after the children left for school, Janice and Linda returned the boxes to Leone's home.

"Let Frank and Leone have time alone," Linda requested. "Leone will be furious when he learns that Frank broke the promise."

"No," she blurted out. "I'm the only one who should be furious.'

"Be right behind you," he said, taking a deep breath.

They watched from the kitchen as Frank wheeled Leone inside and into the living room where the boxes sat.

"What are these doing out here?" Leone asked.

Frank responded, "I let Janice see them," as stepping away from the wheelchair.

"You did what?" he yelled out as the oxygen nosepiece dropped away. "You had no right and betrayed my trust."

"You're right, Leone." Janice stepped into the living room. "He had no right telling me because that was your responsibility."

"Janice, I never wanted you to know," he said, placing the nosepiece back. "I gave my word."

"We've gone beyond that now," she said. "It's time for the truth."

"Leone, it's time she know everything," Linda spoke up.

"I need to know," Janice asked, kneeling beside him. "Did you love my mother?"

"As much as life itself." Tears fell from his eyes. "She was my soulmate."

"Let's start at the beginning," Linda recommended. "I'll put on coffee."

"This house is where Linda grew up with her parents," Leone explained, "I lived on a small farm a couple miles from here. My parents were share croppers, who sent me to the local school. Your mother lived with her father, a block from here."

"We were the four musketeers," Linda began remembering those times, "always together, no matter the weather."

"I knew the very first time we met," Leone spoke up. "She was the one and only."

"We had a great time," Frank said, "always together, never separated, even when playing sports."

"When your mother was 14, her father passed," Leone now spoke, "and afterwards was sent to live with her aunt. We kept in touch with letters, and during winter holidays, I visited them."

"Her aunt wasn't happy when we all showed up," Linda said, sitting down next to Frank. "She felt your mother was having a hard time adjusting, and we didn't help."

"My parents left the farm with I was 17," Leone once again began, "and knowing I needed money, joined the Army. Your mother at that time was working and going to college part time."

"You never asked to marry?" Janice asked.

"Several times," he admitted, "but her aunt thought it best to hold off until she finish school and for me to leave the Army. I was overseas when she passed away, and wrote asking your mother to consider marriage."

"Your mother quit school," Linda now spoke, "and worked full time. I visited her when Leone was overseas. She wanted to keep the house that her aunt left her, and try making it on her own."

"When I returned, they sent me to California," Leone once again began, "and the only time I could see her was on leave. The money from my overseas pay went to her, and she at first refused, but I insisted it go toward college. Afterwards, I began sending her money each month. I lived on base in the barracks and never spent much."

"Look at the time," Linda said, trying to control her voice, "the children will be coming home soon."

"Maybe we could start again in the morning?" Leone asked. "I'm a little tired."

"You haven't eaten either," Linda reminded everyone. "Get some sleep, and I'll bring over dinner."

"I'll help with dinner," Janice said as Frank began wheeling him into the bedroom, "and maybe Susan and I will come back with dinner."

Meeting the children at the bus stop, then helping with dinner, the two entered his darkened home.

"If he's sleeping," Susan whispered, "should we wake him?"

"Come on in," Leone yelled from the bedroom. "I'm awake and hungry."

"Uncle Leone," Susan said, entering. "You need to turn on lights when it gets dark."

"Guess I was a little more tired than I thought," he said while lying in bed. "Maybe I'll get me one of those clapper things."

"I'll put it on the list of things you need," Janice said, sitting on the edge of the bed. "How are you feeling? Ready to eat?"

"Feeling better now," he said with a smile, "and always ready to eat."

After helping him with the dinner, Frank entered and helped him into the bathroom and then bed.

"I'll be with him for a while," he said while walking them toward the door. "Tell Linda I'll be home shortly."

"I can stay with him," Janice said.

"For now, he'll be fine," Frank assured them. "He's weak from all the tests, and he'll gain his strength back in a couple days."

The following morning, after the children left reluctantly for school, the three entered Leone's home.

"Morning Leone," Linda yelled out. "How are you doing?"

"Coffee's on." He came out of the bedroom fully dressed but using the wheelchair. "And I want lunch."

"Let's see... Mother was making it on her own," Janice said, sitting on the sofa, "with your help. Now tell me about the man I believed was my father, and why."

"Bruce Collinwood," Leone began, "at age 10, they found him in a run-down apartment next to his deceased father a drug addict. Apparently no relatives, so they sent him to the county orphanage. People wanted babies, not a 10-year-old having a drug addict father. He ran away at 14, and for two years stayed clear of people. He signed up for the Army, and the orphanage, having no record of him, agreed that his age was 17."

"One moment," Linda yelled, out while serving coffee. "Janice, Bruce was so kind."

"That he was," Frank agreed.

"After he finish training," Leone started again. "They assigned him to my platoon. Unlike the other men, Bruce stayed on base even when given liberty. One two-week liberty, I found him alone reading, I was going to visit your mother, so I asked if he wanted to come along. We hit it off, and your mother treated him like a son. After that, when I visited, he came along."

"What did the neighbors think about two soldiers visiting her?' Janice seemed appalled by the idea.

"At first tongues waggled," he said chuckling, "but Bruce was a wonder around motors, and I knew how to use hammer and nail. Bruce became the neighborhood mechanic, and I their repairman. When we'd show up, people had lists, and we helped without charge. People stopped judging, and we fixed more cars and houses."

"I remember visiting your mother once," Linda spoke up, "and they asked if I could help fix a leaking roof."

"That had to be the time I was overseas," Leone said, looking toward her, "and Bruce signed up to go along. Having no real family, Bruce asked if I minded him sending money home to your mother, he knew I was, so he did."

"Your mother used it for college," Frank added, "and savings."

"Neighbors never said anything," Leone paused as if remembering, "but they never really knew your mother loved me, not Bruce. After serving overseas, he knew we would be split up and, with his enlistment up, decided to leave the army. It was then I learned your mother was pregnant, and once again, I asked her to marry me."

"She turned you down?" Janice asked.

"Yes," he replied in a soft tone. "Bruce left the Army and preparing to travel to New York for an interview. I told him everything, and asked he visit her to make sure she was alright. He visited her, and then began the drive. The State Police notified me that he died in an accident; the weather had turned and probably struck icy roads. I claimed his body, knowing no one else would. That's when I came up with the idea of giving you a father. Couldn't let you go through life without one."

"Why wouldn't mother marry you?" Janice needed to know.

"I can answer that," Linda quickly spoke up, "because she told me why. When her father died, for two years, she was alone with no friends and new schools. It was the worse time for her, and she never wanted you to feel that pain."

"She wanted you to have a home," Leone continued. "Friends, school, and a place you knew was there. I was in the Army, transferred to a different base every year."

"Your mother didn't want that life for you," Linda again spoke, "but she did agree to allow Bruce to be your father."

"I knew the Sergeant in charge of the print shop," Leone explained. "He owed money to a local loan shark over a gambling debt. I gave him money and never turned him in, and he printed up all the necessary marriage licenses. A year later, they found him hung, most say it wasn't suicide."

"No one ever questioned mother about her marriage," Janice asked.

"Your mother and I spent two weeks together in Florida," he said with a smile. "A wonderful time we had. Most people just assumed she was with Bruce, who had visited her two days before his death. Your mother made all the arrangements for his funeral, and we all promised never to reveal the truth."

"Over the years, we watched over you somewhat," Frank began to explain. "When you graduated or the first dance, one of us attended. I'm sure you noticed all the pictures in the album, when there were times none of us attended, your mother took pictures and sent them to Leone."

"Mother never changed her name to Collinwood," Janice seemed interested. "She placed his name on my birth certificate."

"Janet Gardner was your mother's maiden name," Leone informed her, "and she wanted you to carry on that name. Most understood why, and as time went on, no one cared. Janet never asked for any government assistance, schools were satisfied with the paperwork."

"Over the years, the neighborhood changed," Linda added. "People passed away or moved, so few were any knew about Bruce."

"Would you remember your first vacation?" Leone asked. "I mean the first real one?"

"Of course." Janice seemed to reminisce of that time. "We took a steamboat up the Mississippi River and visited so many towns."

"You wanted to go to camp with your friends," Leone remembered with a smile as he picked up one of the albums that lay near his bed, "and after two days, called crying, wanting to come home. I had planned the entire trip. Eight days alone with your mother aboard that slow moving steamboat."

"I ruined it for you," she realized, and for the first time her voice softened. "Had I known…"

"No, my dear, you brought joy to our lives," Leone assured her as he looked at the many photos. "The pictures of your smile and the fun you shared with Janet was worth every penny."

"We had such a wonderful time together." Tears fell from her eyes as she laughed. "And I think we ate our way through every town visited."

"Janet was so beautiful," Linda announced while bringing in sandwiches, "and being able to watch you blossom into a beautiful woman was a delight."

"When I learned about Janet passing," Leone said closing the album. "I decided to tell you the truth. I was at the cemetery, and when I saw all the people attending, I couldn't bring myself to do it. I realized she had raised you right, giving you a permanent home with so many friends and neighbors."

"In many of her last letters," Janice reminded him, "Mother regretted the promise she made but believed nothing could change it."

"We agreed to keep the promise," Frank began, "but when we learned about you wanting to meet this Shakespeare fellow, we came up with an idea to bring you here."

"Low and behold," Leone blurted out, "the wife of Senator Planterson arrived."

"Did you know about the investigation?" she asked.

"Now that, we did not know," Frank admitted, "but it did force you to stay longer to get to know us."

"Having you here was a blessing," Linda said, taking her hand. "Being able to talk with you instead of wondering what you thought in photos."

Leone began telling her of the many times they met and how they kept the secret from her. As before, they left to meet the children, and later Janice, with Susan, once again served Leone dinner.

"Look, Uncle Leone has all the lights on," Susan said joyfully. "Does that mean he's getting better?"

"He's regaining his strength," she admitted, "but he must stay in the wheelchair."

"Come in," his voice blurted out. "I'm hungrier than a wolf cub."

"Leone, what did the doctor say about you walking?" Janice replied while noticing him sitting at the kitchen table. "You best start listening."

"The best medicine is just having the two of you coming with dinner," he said with a smile.

"Uncle Leone, you're so funny sometimes," Susan said running toward him.

"How could it not help," he replied, giving her a hug as he spoke, "seeing the two most beautiful ladies in the world standing here?"

"Flattery will not get you out of trouble," Janice said, kissing his cheek. "After dinner, back in the wheelchair."

"Yes, dear," he said as he touched his cheek, as if wanting to remember her touch.

During dinner Susan did most of the talking, telling the two of school and the boys she thought were stupid.

"Susan, when is school out for the summer?" Janice asked.

"Two weeks," she quickly announced, "but we've already took tests."

"Leone, what are you doing out of your wheelchair?" Frank asked while entering.

"Already been shamed," he said, reaching over and grabbing it.

"Now, you get some sleep." Janice quickly stood and kissed his cheek. "I've some phone calls, so see you in the morning."

"Night, Uncle Leone," Susan said, following Janice.

After speaking with Linda, Janice asked for private time and called Edgar.

"You're not leaving?" Susan asked as she came out of the bedroom.

"No, dear," she said. "Had to call my boss to let him know where I am."

After breakfast and getting the children on the bus, Janice notice a vehicle parked outside of Leone's home.

"It's the visiting doctor," Linda explained. "He comes by before going to the hospital."

"Doctor!" Janice in pajamas and robe ran toward him. "Can I have a word?"

"Certainly," he said while meeting her at his car.

"How is he?" she quickly asked as Linda came out.

"Strangely enough, better," he admitted. "Seemed the oxygen is working, and without activity possibly has helped."

"Can he travel?" she asked. "Like, to take him to New York?"

"Air travel is out of the question," he quickly responded, "but travel by auto with comfortable arrangements, maybe."

"Janice, we talked about this last night," Linda reminded her, "stopping for meals and bathrooms."

"Doctor, what if we travel in a recreational vehicle," she blurted out, "large enough for all of us with a driver?"

"Well, that would work," he said with a smile. "I'll order a self-contained oxygen unit, so you won't have to worry about canisters."

"Please order whatever Leone might need," she ordered, "and thank you."

"I'll make a list," he said, "but might cost."

"Just give me the bill," she said, taking his hand. "I want the best, okay?"

"Are you sure about this?" Linda asked.

"New York, Linda," Janice said, taking her hands as the doctor drove away. "Family vacation."

"Fine, I'll tell Frank," Linda said, finally agreeing, "and start calling the school."

"Great," Janice said, walking toward the house. "I need to make some calls."

That night with Leone, Janice announced her plan.

"Leone, we're going to New York," she began, "all of us. Linda has arranged with the school, so they can go, and Frank is getting someone to watch the mansion while we're gone."

The children could not contain themselves with joy, while Leone sat quiet.

"Hon, I appreciate what you're doing," he spoke up, "but I'm not fit to travel."

"Not by air or van," she said, sitting next to him, "but trust me it will be great."

"Please, Uncle Leone?" Susan gave him a loving expression. "Say yes." Little Frank with Lisa gave him the sad expression, and knowing all eyes were on him, he began shaking his head.

"Fine," he said, finally agreeing. "I'll go, but remember, I tire easily."

All began cheering, as if they had won a grand game.

"You're not to worry," Janice whispered in his ear. "Let your daughter help."

"Sounds good," he said, looking up to her. "I'm all yours."

Everyone began preparing for the trip, especially Janice and Frank.

"Frank, there are two very large men at the door," Linda announced, "wanting to see you about hiring them."

"Groggin brothers," he quickly said while walking outside. "They're here to get the keys to the mansion."

"Hello," Janice said, walking out with Linda.

"Yep, that's her alrighty," one of the men said to the other, "she mighty pretty."

"Thank you," both Linda and Janice spoke up, "most kind."

"This is Hector and Willard," Frank said, introducing them. "They operate the local salvage yard and have agreed to watch over the mansion while we're gone."

"Ya knows we get paid for watching that big house," Hector spoke up, "$160 a day for two weeks."

"Mr. Groggin," Janice stepped forward. "That's $2,240, right?"

"If'in ya say so," he answered, "but we got dogs, too."

"We put them inside the fence," Willard spoke up. "No one with any sense would dare climb over that there fence."

"Twenty five hundred, gentlemen," Janice said, walking toward the two. "Dogs and your promise to protect the property."

"Got no cause to argue with a beautiful lady," Hector said with a smile revealing missing teeth, "especially when talking money."

"Shake on it," she said, taking his hand, "and take my check."

"Got our word," he said, shaking her hand, "and check from ya is golden."

"Never known those two to act so nice," Frank said as they left.

"Frank, the moment they shook hands," Linda began, laughing, "they were like putty in her hand."

"Their handshake is the bond," Janice informed them. "Better than a written contract by the best lawyers."

Two days later, boxes both large and small arrived, and inside was a motorized wheelchair and a portable oxygen unit.

"Great," Janice said while sitting on the wheelchair, "Father will love this."

"Janice, while were alone," Linda began. "Do you think we should tell the children about Leone being your father?"

"Let's keep that to ourselves for now," she said, operating the wheelchair. "Want nothing to spoil our vacation with questions."

"Well okay," Linda said with a smile. "We're all packed and ready to leave."

That night, Leone made full use of the wheelchair, giving each child a ride. At 8:00 the next morning, they were surprised to hear the blaring sound of air horns coming from outside. Everyone quickly ran outside, and there sat the largest recreational vehicle they had ever seen.

"Good morning, all." He stood 6'2" with a Stetson western hat over his long graying hair. "Name's Harvey and be driving ya to New York in my Entegra coach. Now before you ask, 50 feet long and 10 feet wide. Got all the power we need with a fine Cummings diesel engine, and enough room for all."

"Perfect," Janice said, walking out toward the man, "just like you promised."

"Little lady, when I heard your name," he said, bowing his slender body, "knew only the finest means of transportation was fitting."

"Ramp for the wheelchair?" she asked.

"Like I said, got everything," he said, taking her hand and kissing it, "and as you asked, got the entire route planned with fine restaurants and hotels."

"You know it's not that I don't want to sleep in the vehicle," she whispered, "but want this to be special for my family."

"Ms. Gardner," he said with a wide smile, "old Harvey will be driving while all of you just enjoy yourselves."

"Thank you." She turned to the group. "Alright, let's get going."

Chapter Nineteen

"Oh Lord," Linda said as they entered the luxury coach, "it's beautiful."

"Two bedrooms if you get tired," Harvey said, joining the family to show all the amenities the coach offered. "Two large screen televisions, satellite, of course. If you can't find something you're interested in, video machine on each. A full range of music, with speakers or headsets. Two bathrooms with shower, and plenty water. I've filled the refrigerator with cold cuts, and assorted soda or water."

"It's so elegant," Janice said looking over the fine workmanship, "better than some five star hotels I've been in."

"People who made this beauty," Harvey replied, "did it right by using only the best wood and flooring. Everything high quality, hand chosen by the builders."

"We can watch TV while you drive?" little Frank asked.

"Young man," Harvey knelt down to speak with him, "on this journey you can watch television and play music at the same time. Consider this your home, and I'll get you to New York safely."

"Know I shouldn't ask," Frank began while looking over the soft sofas and chairs.

"Wanting to know the cost?" Harvey stood up finishing the question Frank asked. "Tell everyone the same. When you enter a hotel, you never ask what it cost to build, you just enjoy the comfort, so let us keep it at that."

"Remember, Frank," Leone spoke up, "if you have to ask you can't afford it."

"Then I'll just enjoy the ride," Frank admitted.

"Well let's get this party started," Harvey said walking toward the door.

As he promised, they stopped only at the finest restaurants and five star hotels for the night.

With each stop, Janice invited Harvey to join them, but never would he allow her to pay for a room. One such night, Janice had to know why he accepted the meal but not hotel.

"Harvey, it gives us no pleasure knowing you're out here alone," she began, "when we're in the hotel."

"Ms. Gardner, having dined with you and the family fills my heart with joy," he began, "brings back good memories when the missus and I traveled the roads. But at night, got to attend my lady, and afterwards won't leave her."

"Just wanted you to know how we feel," she added.

"Never met a reporter," he said with a smile, "especially one as beautiful as you and so kind."

"I know we're close now," she continued. "When we get to New York, will you be alright while we're in the city?"

"Know a real nice truck and recreational depot," he said. "While waiting, I can catch up on old friends."

"If you need any extra money…" she began.

"Ms. Gardner, you've been more than generous," he continued.

"Harvey, please, if you need anything," she appealed to him, "don't hesitate, and from now on, it's Janice."

Knowing he could not drive such a vehicle into the city, Harvey made a call, and within a half hour had a large stretch van arrive.

"Janice, I'll be waiting," he said, giving her his card with telephone number. "My friend will take all of you to the hotel."

"Thank you," she told him, watching as a ramp came down on the van. "I'll call when ready to go back home."

It was late afternoon as they entered the Waldorf Astoria, having opened in 1893. The shear eloquence of the entire structure made one speechless. Golden figures graced the top of the beautiful entrance, and inside the art deco gave the illusion of a museum rather than a hotel. The children marveled at the shining bright black and white floors of marble, and the huge wooden cabinet clock with all its carvings. Overwhelmed by all the attention given to their every need, they felt out of place and a little embarrassed by being unfamiliar with such service or how to respond.

After receiving his card and doubling his normal service fee, the driver of the van promised to be available anytime she called.

"Ms. Gardner," the manager said, immediately recognizing her came running over. "We are so pleased that you selected our establishment."

"This is my family," she said, without introducing them by name. "I require three rooms on the same floor, executive or presidential suite, if possible.

"The presidential is on the top floor; that, I know you will find more than satisfactory, he explained while they stood waiting, "and two executive suites newly renovated on the floor below will meet your families every need."

"Linda, would you and Frank mind staying in the presidential suite, Janice asked while looking toward them, "with Frankie and Lisa? Susan and I will take one of the executive rooms, and Leone you the other."

"I don't know," Linda said with a smirk of a smile, "Susan, what do you think?"

"Oh, Mother…" She took in a deep breath with shoulders dropping.

"Fine, we'll take it," Linda said with a genuine smile, "Leone."

"Mister," Janice replied while looking at his nametag, "Norris."

"Yes, Madam," he said while straightening up.

"My family and I are here on a short vacation," she explained while carefully slipping him a $100 bill undetected, "and have chosen this wonderful hotel to make it memorable."

"Ms. Gardner, you need not worry," he said, palming he bill, "and it will be my honor to see to all your wishes."

"Please follow me," one of the two young porters wearing a blood red sport coat spoke up while lifting their luggage.

Entering the executive room, Janice handed the young man a $50 as he carefully laid the luggage down.

"Young man," she said, handing him two other bills, "please give these to the others."

"Thank you," he said, giving her the key to the room, "and I'll see they receive it."

"This really ours?" Susan said, running around the room having two bedrooms and a grand room. "It's bigger than our home."

"How would you like going with me to my office?" she asked while looking around.

"You sure I won't be a bother?" she said as if frozen.

"Now why would my little sister be a bother?" Janice replied, hugging her.

"I love you so much," Susan said, wrapping her arms around her.

Explaining to everyone the need to leave, Janice and Susan left but promised to return for dinner.

"Norris," Janice said walking up to him. "Can we have dinner reservations for 6:00?"

"Of course," he quickly answered. "May I suggest using our limousine service?"

"Thank you," she said while he instantly called and escorted the two outside.

Within minutes, a large black vehicle arrived, and as Norris opened the door, Janice once again carefully placed a bill in his hand.

"Janice, does everyone want money?" Susan asked in a soft voice after Janice told the driver the address. "At home we only give money to people bringing our food."

"This is New York," she responded with a smile, "you get the service you pay for. Besides, I think people come to expect me to pay a little more."

"Janice!" Edgar seemed pleased seeing her. "And Susan, right?"

"Mr. Acorn," she replied, giving him a slight curtsy.

"Janice, I see a future reporter," he said, taking Susan's hand and kissing it, "beautiful and extremely polite."

"Maybe one day she'll replace me," Janice said with a smile.

"Never," Susan instantly replied, "I'd never do that."

"Before getting ahead of ourselves," Edgar began, laughing, "your contract is ready for your signature and has everything you asked for."

"What about the other thing I asked about?" she said, following him into his office.

"Now that was difficult," he said, walking behind his desk and opening the middle drawer, "but my wife, having been an actress and model, made it happen."

"Tell her how much this means to me," Janice told him, taking the envelope from his hand.

"You can tell her yourself," he said, placing her contract on the desk, "when you come for dinner with us. Now about this contract, need your signature."

"Promise," she said while reading over the contract.

"This makes you a very wealthy woman," Edgar said after having waited the 20 minutes for her to read and sign, "and gives you five more years with me."

"Already wealthy." She handed him the contract, "That has nothing to do with money."

"Susan," he said, following them to the door, "I hope one day to have you sign such a contract with us."

"Don't let his charm fool you," Janice said, walking over and giving him a kiss on the cheek, "ask for double."

"Teaching her already," he said, touching his cheek while smiling.

"Ms. Gardner," Carolina came running in, "I didn't know you were coming in today."

"Be back in a couple weeks," she said after introducing Susan to her. "Anything I should know about?"

"Oh no," she replied, "I'm taking care of everything."

"Carolina has been helping me and my secretary," Edgar replied. "Just enjoy the time off."

Returning to the hotel, the driver handed her his card after receiving a generous tip for his service.

"Ms. Gardner," the maitre'd wearing a tuxedo standing by the entrance said, "your table has been prepared, please follow me."

"A fine bottle of wine for Linda and I," Janice began ordering. "Frank, Leone, what would you like to have?"

"Coffee for me," Leone said as Frank requested a light American beer.

"The children will have soda," Linda said looking toward the three.

"Mother, I can order for myself," Susan insisted, "but diet, please."

"Can I have pizza," Lisa spoke up, "with cheese and sausages?"

"Unfortunately, pizza is not on the menu," the maitre'd began as the head-waiter stood by, "however, I am sure Pierre can provide."

"Extra cheese and sausage," he stepped forward, "and crust."

"She likes thick," Linda admitted.

"I will make a call," the maitre'd saidwith a smile, "and young man, what would you desire?"

"A hamburger with tomato and bacon," he blurted out, "and French fries with ketchup on them."

"Our burgers are the finest in the city," he said with pride, "and our fries go very well with ketchup. Now, young lady, what may I provide for you?"

"May I order for all? Janice leaned over toward Susan. "Jumbo lobster tail with baked potato and salad for all of us."

Surprisingly, everyone agreed to her suggestion, even Susan, who had never had such a meal accepted.

"We have a wonderful lobsters bisque soup," Pierre announced, "if you wish."

"Pierre, have you ever served in the army?" Leone asked.

"Yes, Sergeant Pegasus," he said, standing at attention, "had the honor of serving with you."

"Family," Leone asked, "and things going well?"

"Very well," he replied, relaxing as he spoke, "married, two children, and attending night school."

"Fantastic," Leone replied.

"You, sir?" he asked, "All is right?"

"All is right," he answered.

"Pierre," Janice spoke up, "I'll leave dinner in your capable hands."

"Ms. Gardner," he calmly began speaking, "it will be my honor."

Every item was carefully prepared and served.

"My goodness, I never thought of eating so much," Linda said while looking at all the empty plates, "but everything is delicious."

"We even finished the wine," Janice whispered to her. "What about desert?"

Suddenly, out came Pierre, having a large cake with candles.

"Ms. Gardner, please accept this as a way for us to thank you," he began as the chef and others came out, "for bringing the man who saved my life."

"Corporal Pierre Lowell," Leone blurted out, "now I remember."

"Never had the opportunity to thank you," he said, laying the cake on the table, "but finally, tonight, I have."

Everyone from the chef to the maitre'd shook his hand, and several female waitresses kissed his cheek while those watching at the tables began clapping. As they were leaving, Janice turned to Pierre.

"Thank you for a wonderful evening," she told him, handing him $3,000. "Please, take this for your family."

"I don't know what to say," he began as his hand shook while taking the money, "but thank you so much."

"Ms. Gardner, it's been my pleasure having you as our guest," the maitre'd came over to her.

"Please have the bill sent to my room," she said, handing him $15,000. "Two thousand for you, and the rest divided equally among the staff."

"Ms. Gardner, thank you," he said, taking her hand and kissing it.

Finally with everyone settled in their rooms, Janice knocked on Leone's door then entered.

"Small world, isn't it, Dad?" she began while sitting by the side of his bed.

"Yes, it is," he admitted. "His squad was ambushed. My squad arrived just in time, got him off the path, and somehow stopped the bleeding."

"Like the hero you were," she said, kissing him goodnight.

"Uncle Leone's a real hero," Susan cried out as she entered the room, "and all those people cheering!"

"Yes, he is," she answered. "Did you enjoy yourself tonight?"

"Oh yes," she admitted with enthusiasm, "the food was wonderful."

"Got another surprise tomorrow," she said. "Now, to bed."

After ordering breakfast, Janice assembled the entire group in the presidential room to explain what she planned.

"The ladies and children are going shopping," she began. "Leone and Frank can remain here watching all the sports channels. However, I've asked the hotel tailor to come up, and Leone, he'll fit you for a nice light brown pinstripe suit. Frank, Linda ordered you a nice dark blue pinstripe suit, with matching shirt and tie."

"Got a real nice black suit," Leone replied.

"Of course you do," Janice answered, "but when going to the opera Friday night, I want you to wear something different."

"Opera," everyone shouted out with surprise.

"Now remember, it's in Italian," she warned, "but it's the music you'll enjoy."

"I know a little Italian," Leone admitted.

"So let's get going," Janice ordered.

"Janice," Frank said, taking her arm as the others began leaving, "I know you've been using your own money, and…"

"Frank, please," she said, turning toward him, "this is my treat, so let me do it."

"Alright," he replied, removing his hand from her arm, "but thought I could pay something."

"I want you to enjoy yourself," she continued, "and not worry about money."

For entire day, the small group using the limousine service of the hotel, shopped, and ate at small cafés that were scattered over the entire city.

"Ms. Gardner," the driver said while watching the children running toward the hotel, "I'll be here Friday, ready to drive you to the opera."

"Great," she said, handing him several bills, "you've made the children so happy having picked the right stores and cafés out."

"Know kids," he said with a smile, "got a couple myself. But in good conscience, you're paying far too much for my service."

"Truthfully," she said, noticing Linda waiting, "I think you're a bargain. So Friday, and the opera."

"Be all shined up," he said, tipping his hat.

"Father," Susan came running in as the staff carried the many packages, "I have the most beautiful dresses:

"Daddy, I got a train set," little Frank yelled out, "and Lisa a bike."

"Along with clothes," Linda said as Janice entered and handed each one a $100, "and what do we say?"

"Thank you, Janice,, all three yelled out as the staff began leaving.

"Well, we were fitted," Leone said, "and will be looking quite dapper come Friday."

"Mother, can I show father my dresses?" Susan asked.

"Maybe a couple," she replied while noticing Lisa laying down. "I think it's nap time."

"Been catching up on my reading,' Leone mentioned as he picked up the newspaper, "closing Twin Hills Advance Training Camp. Had some good times there, 12 hard weeks but learned a lot. Apparently, in a week the 120 soldiers will be the last class."

"May I see that?" Janice asked Leone.

"Not much news," Leone admitted, "must be a slow day."

"Posted the closings on page 14," she said. noticing as she read. "Army reports nine camp closings."

"Half a paragraph," Leone said. "sad how little they care about the importance of those bases."

"Yes, very sad," Janice said, placing the paper under her arm and noticing everyone had left, "so, how does my father feel today?"

"Feeling good" he said,, reaching over and taking her hand, "even ready for an opera."

"Promise to keep feeling good," she said, kissing him on the cheek.

As everyone began to return, Janice disappeared for an hour but returned.

"Let's order in," she said, walking out, "and watch movies."

By early Friday afternoon, the suits and accessories arrived, and by early evening, everyone looked forward for a night at the opera.

"WOW," little Frank blurted out as they walked out to view the limousine van.

"Ms. Gardner," the driver said, opening the side door having an electric ramp, "Mr. Pegasus, come on up."

"Worth every penny," Janice whispered in his ear, "thank you."

"Placed water in the refrigerator," he replied while operating the wheelchair ramp, "and after the performance, I know a nice restaurant."

Arriving at Carnegie Hall, several members of the staff escorted them to the Isaac Stern Auditorium.

"My goodness," Linda said as they sat on the plush seats that overlooked the entire stage, "I feel so out of place in such a beautiful place."

"No, you're precisely where you belong," Janice added. "This place should be honored by our presence."

"Oh Janice," Susan said, taking her arm, "what a wonderful night!"

"You look so beautiful in that dress," she began, "I know one day, some young man will be taking you to such places."

"But it will never be this perfect," Susan told her, squeezing her arm.

As the opera began, she reminded them to listen to the songs not words. It was an evening all would remember forever, even when Lisa fell asleep while sitting on Linda's lap. Waking Lisa with a standing ovation, they walked out to the waiting limousine.

"Never understood a single word," Frank said as they began entering the vehicle, "but it didn't matter with such great singing."

"Ms. Gardner, hotel or restaurant?" he asked before closing the door.

"Know where they serve pizza?" she asked.

"Best pie in New York," he replied, "mark my words."

Arriving at a small pizzeria shop, they ate what all agreed was the best pizza ever eaten. The following afternoon after having lunch with everyone, Janice announced to everyone to say goodbye to New York.

"It has been a wonderful vacation," Linda replied, "we have done so much in such a short time, but we must be leaving."

"I didn't say we're going home," Janice spoke up, "just leaving New York."

"So, what are you planning?" Leone asked, knowing she had made other arrangements and wished not to share them.

"Just be ready to leave in the morning," she said without further discussion.

As requested, the entire group was packed and ready to leave. The limousine was ready to take them to Harvey, who stood waiting.

"Ms. Gardner," the limousine driver said while watching the group waiting toward the large recreational vehicle, "it's been an honor being your driver, and if you ever come back, please call me."

"The honor has been mine," she said, handing him an envelope, "and if I ever need a chauffeur, you're the first person I'll be calling."

"Harvey, you have the route?" she asked while waving goodbye to the limousine driver. "Any problems?"

"None," he admitted. "Be there in two days and have it all planned out."

"Great," she said with a smile.

"So, are you going to tell us where we're off to?" Leone asked.

"No," she said in a defiant tone, "you'll just have to wait and see."

As promised, Harvey had the entire journey planned, and within the two days, they arrived at their destination.

"As promised folks," Harvey said while opening the door, "we're here."

"Leone, does this look familiar?" Janice asked while carefully wheeling him out of the vehicle. "Pretty country."

"Twin Hills," he said with surprise, "how and why?"

"That's what Mr. Acorn asked," Randy yelled out as he came running toward them, "wondered why you think this is a story people might be interested in."

"Randy," Susan screamed out as others began acknowledging him.

"Hello, everyone," Carolina said, walking up, "Randy asked Mr. Acorn if I could come along, and he said go."

"Carolina and I," Randy began to explain, "you see…"

"Shh," Janice said, placing her finger over his lips, "I know."

"We wanted to tell you," Carolina began while showing the ring, "but the right time never happened."

"Congratulations," Janice said, giving her a hug. "Now, the reason you're here."

"Camp is nearly deserted," Randy informed her, "the last class of 120 men with staff officers and kitchen support."

"For 30 years, this camp trained men for combat," Janice pointed out, "we have an audience of soldiers and family."

"I think it's exciting," Carolina blurted out. "They're so cute."

"Young lady," Leone said, wheeling over to her, "those are American soldiers, and 'cute' isn't in their vocabulary."

"Cute, maybe not," Frank said, walking over toward Leone, "but handsome."

"Handsome, yes," Linda replied. "Leone was so handsome in his dress uniform."

"Now that's enough talk about that," Leone said looking toward the two large hills. "They call them mother and father."

"Ms. Gardner." He stood over six feet wearing camouflaged uniform. "I am Colonel Kasper, commanding officer and have been instructed to see to your every need."

"Thank you, Colonel Kasper," she answered.

"May I say what a privilege it is having you here," he continued. "The men are quite excited having you and Master Sergeant Pegasus reviewing them."

"Sir," a young lieutenant stood at attention and saluting, "all arrangements made."

"Please follow the Lieutenant to your assigned accommodations," the Colonel continued. "There, you will find schedules."

All the accommodations were previously used as officer's homes, where they made all the furniture available.

"Well, Ms. Gardner, this is ours," Carolina said after opening the door. "Nice four-bedroom home with everything a family could use."

"Randy and Leone together," she began, laughing.

"Wonder what they'll be talking about," she questioned.

"Don't worry, Leone isn't much of a talker," she added, "and when Frank goes over, I would think Randy will be the butt of their jokes."

"They wouldn't hurt him, would they?" she asked, as if worried.

"Both harmless," she added.

With free access to the entire camp, Janice with Randy began filming.

"Hello, this is Janice Gardner here at one of the many bases preparing to close by the Army," she began as they toured the obstacle course. "Twin Hills Advanced Training Camp. The name comes from those two very large hills, called affectionately by the men who ran them twice a day mother and father. They spend 12 weeks here training, climbing over the 10-foot wall or crossing the rope bridge and crawling under the barbwire. Then they ran mother and father, sometimes more, every day."

For two days, Janice and Randy interviewed the officers, and several other members of the staff, including a cook who had served 20 years at the camp. On the fourth day, after a long day of filming and interviews, the commander requested they attend a special presentation.

Surrounded by all the soldiers and staff, the Colonel in a military manner walked toward Leone.

"Ladies and gentlemen," he said, standing tall in his dress uniform began, "we, the hundred and twentieth class, will soon graduate as the last. It has been the tradition for those leaving to present the camp sword to incoming class. For 30 years, this tradition has never been broken, and tonight, we intend to honor it. Sergeant Major Leone Pegasus, please stand."

They watched as a young lieutenant in uniform stood up, then handed the sword to the Colonel.

"Having read your service record," the Colonel once again in stern voice, "and with the consent of each member of this class, we wish to present you with this sword. Having graduated here, you have exemplified the integrity for all to follow. Having set a standard for all soldiers to follow, I take great pride handing this symbol of achievement to you."

"Thank you," Leone said as tears began to flow from his eyes as he stood to receive the sword, "I just did my duty as a good soldier and prayed it was enough."

Janice looked over at the others and found not a dry eye among them.

"Hoo-Ah!," all men began shouting.

"Randy, tell me you got that," Janice asked while tears flowed down her cheeks.

"Damn right," Randy said, wiping his eyes, "I got it all on film."

Each soldier paraded past Leone, shaking his hand.

"Colonel, how can I ever thank you?" Janice said while taking his hand.

"Read his service record to the men,' he explained while the men continued to shake Leone's hand and congratulated him. "This honor is long overdue."

When the last soldier made his way out the door, the Colonel stood in front of Leone and gave him a salute.

"Janice, did you have any idea this was going to happen?" Linda asked.

"No," she said as the Colonel walked out, "but it was wonderful."

The following day, Randy filmed the men leaving the camp.

"Today, these brave men will leave this camp," Janice began. "The camp will close but the tradition learned here will go on. I am proud to have been here, knowing such men are protecting us. I'm Janice Gardner, saying good night and God Bless America."

"Janice, we have five hours of film," Randy reminded her, "got a lot of work to get it down to 45 minutes."

"I know," she said with a smile, "it really doesn't matter because they honored my father."

"Ms. Gardner," Harvey said as they loaded the vehicle, "I watched when they presented the sword to Mr. Pegasus. Be telling all my friends to watch when your network broadcasts it."

"Just hope I can do justice to it," she said in a soft tone.

After arriving home, all began to settle in on their normal routine. Janice spent most of her time with Leone, and when he slept, she sat quietly on his porch as if thinking.

"Frank says he found blood on Leone's pillowcase," Linda in a soft voice said while sitting beside her. "He's getting worse but still has a twinkle in his eyes when you're there."

"I wish there was more I could do," she said, looking into the sky as she spoke.

".When your mother passed," Linda began, "Leone came back, and for weeks was in a dark place alone. After a while, Frank started spending time with him. Truthfully, it made me a little angry. Frank finally arranged for him to work at the mansion, and things got better. They went out there and cleaned, I think that's when they concocted the idea to help you some way."

"Just how did they know about my interest in Shakespeare?" she asked. "I never mentioned that to anyone."

"They went to New York while I stayed behind," she continued, "went to the bars where many of your people went and listened. From time to time, your name came up, they heard someone talking about your obsession with the man."

"Obsession," she blurted out, "is that what they think it is?"

"Some might," she admitted, "but Leone believes it's what energizes you to search for that farthest star no one can see."

"Only my father can make it sound less crazy." She began to laugh.

"How many people have you exposed as frauds," she asked, "pretending to be the great author?"

"Three or four," she said, as if remembering, "charging people for an autograph."

"If it weren't for you," Linda said, as if reminding her how important it is to expose such people, "they'd still be out there ripping people off."

Two weeks had passed when they received a call from Randy.

"Well, they've edited it," she said while walking toward the group, "and if all goes well they'll show it Saturday."

"It's so exciting," Susan in a modest scream, "I've told all my friends about it."

"Perfect," Janice said while crossing her fingers, "because we need all the people we know to watch."

Later in the evening, Janice found Susan alone in the bedroom, crying.

"What is it?" she asked, hugging her.

"Talking to Uncle Leone," she began, trying to control herself, "his lips had blood on them."

"Somethings are out of our control," Janice told her, wanting to cry but trying to be strong, "death is one of them."

"He was always there for me," she continued to cry, "and he had a way of explaining things."

"No matter what happens," Janice said, touching Susan's heart, "I know if we never forget, he will be with us."

As the evening ended, everyone said his or her goodnights.

"I'll watch him for a while," Janice said while entering the dark room where Frank sat, half asleep. "He looks peaceful.'

"Restless earlier," he whispered while standing.

As Janice sat beside him, and Frank strolled toward the door, Leone woke.

"Janet, I'm home," were his last words.

CHAPTER TWENTY

It was a week where all felt numb, without energy to speak but understood their obligation for Leone.

"Janice, I cannot tell you how sorry we are over your loss," Edgar said, with his wife standing beside him. "We must return tonight but wanted to be here for you."

"Just having the two of you here means a lot," she said, wearing black and attempting to hold back the tears, "and all his friends have helped all of us."

"The director said over 100 have come," he informed her. "Many soldiers and others who had known him."

"Just wished he could have watched the broadcast," she said. Tears began to flow as she spoke. "We weren't able to watch it."

"Did well," he said, taking her hand, "but let's not talk business now."

"Be another week before coming back," she continued, "and I'll bring back Randy and Carolina with me."

"Take what time you need," he said, kissing her on the cheek.

"Mrs. Acorn," Janice said taking her hand. "I never thanked you for getting those tickets for all of us."

"It was my pleasure," she said, holding her hand while speaking, "and I know it brought happiness to all of you."

"We'll let you get back to the others," Edgar replied while looking toward those waiting to speak with her.

"So, that's your boss." Linda walked to her side. "He's very handsome, and his wife is a real beauty."

"They're a beautiful couple," she admitted, "in so many ways."

For three days, they greeted the people, some having stories, others just wanting to say farewell to a neighbor or friend. Finally, they traveled with the coffin to the cemetery where her mother lay. Knowing the headstone was to be laid the following day, the children never questioned why they placed Leone beside her mother.

Janice, still suffering from the loss, went back to New York, knowing it was time to start again.

"Janice," Edgar quickly walked out of his office when she entered, "are you sure about coming back?"

"Yes," she said as Carolina followed, "it's time. Besides, Carolina left her mother in the care of relatives."

"I called every night," she admitted. "She's fine."

"Let's talk," he said, walking back to his office.

"You have assignments for me?" she asked while sitting down in front of his desk.

"Assignments, yes," he admitted while sitting down, "but Tim Gaze has asked if you would be interested in taking over the nightly broadcast."

"He's doing good," she replied. "There's no reason to replace him."

"Tim wants to retire," he quickly spoke up. "Wants to spend time with the family."

"Would he agree to stay on for a year or two?" she asked. "I'd like to travel a little before settling down for good."

"I'm sure he would agree," he said, surprised by her request. "I have some important interviews scheduled, if that's what you want."

"For now," she continued. "What were the ratings on the broadcast?"

"The Army sponsored the entire program with patriotic commercials," he said with a smile. "Even against primetime shows, it was number one in that time slot. Because of your story, the people voted our news network the most honest, trusted, and patriotic."

"That is fantastic," she said with satisfaction.

"Truthfully, I didn't think much of the idea," he admitted, "but you proved me wrong."

"Truth be known," she said, standing up, "I didn't think anyone would watch."

"Let's never have a conversation like this again," he replied. "Now, I'll get with Carolina and arrange your schedule."

Janice began fulfilling her obligations, interviewing political figures along with highly sought after stars of the movies. One such interview came by way of the United Nations, requesting her to interview the leader of a nation that proclaimed America as an enemy.

"You are the one who promotes hatred for my country," the man in a black silk robe and headscarf with aqel rope began with an interpreter, "reporting lies."

"I report only facts and truth," Janice said, defending herself, "which you claim are lies."

"You would not be welcomed in my country," he said in a warning tone. "The people would demand your arrest."

"Your army would arrest me," she continued to challenge him, "but the people for the first time would hear the truth."

"In my country, no woman would dare speak as you have," he said, standing up and removing the headset.

"Today, they may not have a voice," she said while the interpreter continued to report her words, "but one day they might."

Though the interview was short, it made all the nightly news broadcasts along with the late night comedians, who reinforced her reputation as a no nonsense reporter.

Having interviewed one of Chicago's great ball players, Janice decided to see the city at night. Wanting to avoid the high cost of a meal at the hotel, she walked toward the restaurant section of town.

"Janice?"

Hearing her name, she turned.

"Liam." Her heart nearly stopped as he approached with a young woman holding onto his arm.

"Tiffany, I'd like to introduce you to someone," he said rushing toward her. "Janice Gardner, one of the finest reporters in the entire world."

"Oh, Ms. Gardner, I'm one of your biggest fans," Tiffany said, nearly screaming her name, "You're my hero."

"I appreciate your kind words," she began, attempting to catch her breath, "and Liam, how are you?"

"Tiffany, would you mind if I have a minute alone?" he asked while leaving her side. "It's been a while and would like to catch up on old times."

"Had no idea you left New York," she began. "Things going well?"

"Better," he admitted, "and the family?

"Leone passed away nearly two years ago," she informed him, "but everyone else fine."

"I'm sorry, but I didn't know," he replied. "I know how much you liked the man."

"Wasn't national or even local news," she said, her expression showing the hurt. "Mostly family and his friends."

"I've been watching your interviews," he said, wanting to change the subject, "as always, great, and I have to say, still beautiful."

"Thanks," she said as a slight smile came to her face. "So, you're living here now?"

"Yeah, teaching at the local college," he said, wanting her to know, "the students like me, and I have 30 to 40 students interested in design."

"Thought by now you would be running your own company," she said, taken by surprise, "designing homes and businesses for the rich or famous."

"Got into a little trouble in New York," he said, showing her his hand which had two large scars. "Had a nice business going but couldn't stop myself betting on the wrong teams. But I'm in therapy, with sponsors that help."

"Your hand," she said, knowing it no longer functioned.

"Nail gun, and a warning," he began explaining, "hand infected but still there, and they didn't bother my good hand. Sold my business, paid off the debt, and came here."

"College know why?" she asked. "I'm sorry, just the reporter in me."

"Told them I got careless while constructing a wall," he began, laughing.

"They looked over my qualifications and offered me a job. Even have a place to live on campus, not fancy but nice."

"It seems to agree with you," she said while looking toward the young girl. "I'm happy for you."

"You're as beautiful today," he said, looking into her eyes, "as the day we married."

"And you're still the charming man I knew," she said with a slight chuckle.

"Told by friends I can't pick a winner if my life depended on it," he said in a serious tone as he spoke, "but one time, I did pick a winner. I messed up. Is there any…"

"Liam, we both know we cannot undo what happened," she said, interrupting his words. "Be best if we just let it go."

"If you're staying in Chicago," he quickly spoke up, "maybe we could meet for coffee?"

"Leaving in the morning," she answered, "on a schedule."

"Yeah," he replied in a solemn tone.

"Besides your young lady seems to want you to hurry up and finish," she said, looking toward the young girl. "She's probably hungry."

"Probably," he agreed. "Goodbye, Janice."

"Goodbye, Liam," she replied back, "and good seeing you again."

"Ms. Gardner," Tiffany said while grabbing Liam's arm and walking by her. "I can't wait to tell my dorm sisters that I met you."

Alone, Janice began walking. After several blocks, she entered a small alley. Leaning against the brick building, she began crying.

"Lady," a man said, speaking in a stern voice from inside the car, "you all right or is there a problem I can help with?"

"No problem," she said, wiping her eyes as the officer opened his door of his cruiser.

"I know you," he said, walking up to her. "Janice Gardner, the reporter."

"Feel more like a babbling baby," she replied, attempting to make light of the situation.

"Rough neighborhood, and no place for you," he said, gently taking her by the arm, "especially at this hour. Be my privilege taking you to the hotel. Watch all your interviews and like them."

"Thank you," she said, following him to his cruiser.

"So, if you don't mind me asking," he began while driving out of the neighborhood. "What's a beautiful reporter have to cry about?"

"Just realized how quickly people move on," she said, looking out the window as she spoke, "and forget."

"Ms. Gardner, you're one of the lucky ones," he continued while watching the road.

"I know I'm being foolish," she admitted, "given so many opportunities."

"Didn't mean anything like that," he said, wanting to correct her. "You work in television. Your entire career is on film, and one day may end up in some museum, where people will remember you forever. Where someone like me, not so lucky."

"I don't understand," she said looking over toward him.

"Been on the job for 28 years," he informed her, "always honest, but you know what will happen in two years?"

"You'll retire?" she replied.

"That's right," he began to chuckle, "be given a little party and be replaced by a rookie fresh out of the academy. Within a year, no one will remember me, but that's all right because I have a family and friends. My children and their children will remember me, by photos and stories I've told. I don't care about those who forget, just happy with the ones that don't."

"Thank you, Sergeant Hess," she said, giving him a quick kiss on the cheek.

"Well now I've another one that won't forget," he said, touching his cheek, "but unless you want to work my shift better tell me the hotel."

"You're right; I'm a little tired," she admitted, "but will never forget tonight."

Returning to New York, she entered her office before anyone.

"You're back." Edgar entered the brightly lit office. "Thought you wanted to stay away for another couple months."

"Decided it was time to stop living out of a suitcase," she said while walking out of the office toward him, "and settle down in one place."

"Best news I've heard all week," he said with a smile. "Tomorrow, we'll start informing the public of your decision."

"Let's allow Tim to tell the people he's retiring," she suggested, "and that he selected me to replace him, if that's all right with you."

"Better idea," he agreed. "Let him speak for himself."

After announcing his plan to retire, Tim gave a farewell speech to his staff and viewers. Then stood up and allowed Janice to sit. Everyone seemed to accept his retirement, allowing Janice to begin without controversy or drop in the ratings. For two years, she worked hard to maintain being the most watched news broadcast, and allowing the network to receive yearly awards.

"Going home for the holidays?" Edgar asked as they finished the last broadcast for the normal two-week vacation.

"Looking forward to it," she said walking toward him. "It's good talking to them each night, but it's not the same."

"Nothing like hugs and kisses," he blurted out. "What about Carolina and Randy?"

"When off camera," she began, laughing, "can't pry the two apart."

"Wish they'd just get married," he said, helping her with the winter coat, "and take it home."

"In time," she replied, watching him struggle with his coat. "Let me help."

"Thank you," he said. "Old age catching up."

"Stop that," she demanded. "You're too young to talk like that."

"Have a great holiday yourself," he said, standing up straight as if to prove her right.

Having taken the last jet out of New York due to weather, she was excited when it finally touched down on a dry runway.

"Janice," Susan stood waving, "I'm here."

"Where are the others?" she asked, giving her a hug.

"Home getting ready for you, of course," she blurted out, "and since I'm a responsible driver, I came. You won't believe all the news we have, but that's for later."

"I just can't believe how beautiful you've become," Janice said, admiring her as they walked to the van, "so grown up."

"Oh, Janice, we talk on computer every night," she replied. "Mother always says people look better in person."

"Just missed you, that's all," she replied, watching as the door automatically opened.

"I missed you, too," she said climbing in the driver's side, "and you helped, especially when I got on the cheerleading squad."

"How?" she asked, surprised by her comment. "You were so excited when they chose you."

"Every game, Father moaned about how short the uniform was," she began, laughing, "showed too much leg, but I reminded him of all your advice about boys."

"Your mother helped," Janice added, knowing Linda, "I'm sure."

"Of course," she said, driving the van out of the gate, "told him to watch the game instead of us girls."

"Now that sounds like your mother," both laughing. "Boyfriends?"

"Told you about them," she said with a slight smile, "but before you ask, I'm still a virgin."

"Thank goodness," she began breathing hard, "you actually listened to my advice."

"That," she said, looking over toward her, "and maybe they were so clumsy they couldn't even take off my bra."

"Thank you, Lord, for making boys clumsy," she blurted out the prayer.

As they arrived at the house, both were laughing.

"What in the world is so funny?" Linda came out when hearing the van arrive.

"Big sister was praying," Susan continued to laugh.

"Praying?" Janice said, giving Janice a hug. "That's no reason to laugh."

"Never mind," Janice said, returning the hug. "You look so good and happy being here."

"Janice," Frank came running to her, "now the family's all here."

"Hello," she said, giving him a hug and kiss on the cheek, "how are you?"

"Great," he said looking her over. "Linda, she's like you: more beautiful than ever."

"Hello, Ms. Gardner," Lisa and little Frank said standing by the door.

"Hello you two," Janice leaned down kissing each one. "You're both growing."

"We've waited for you," Linda announced, "and dinner is ready."

"Mommy and me have been cooking all day," Lisa said while looking over at the prepared table. "I made the rolls and potatoes."

"I'm starved," Janice said, removing her coat, "and would love a roll."

"Come along everyone," Linda ordered. "Let's eat."

After a quick prayer, everyone began to devour the food.

"Susan mentioned you have some big news," Janice said while wiping her mouth with the napkin. "Anything important?

"Well, as you know the corporation that owns the mansion is in the movie business," Frank began, "and having no further use of it has decided to sell it."

"They had stonecutters take away all the nice bricks," Linda explained. "All the windows and doors are gone."

"Took two murals," Frank interrupted Linda, "even some of the floors."

"Sad to see," Linda once again began, "such a beautiful mansion now an empty shell waiting for its destruction."

"What's going to happen with the town and people?" she asked.

"Sold the land to a company wanting to build a factory here," Frank added. "Be a year or so away, but coming."

"Where does that leave the two of you?" Her heart began to pound.

"Having worked with the corporation for so long," Frank said while pushing himself away from the table, "they offered Linda and me employment with their studio in California. They want us to manage workers' expenses, get bids. and write invoices."

"It's like running a household," Linda spoke up, "learn what they need then find the cheapest place to purchase the item."

"We'll be living in a gated community," Frank explained, "with other permanent workers and private schools are available for the kids."

"California," Janice said, looking toward Susan, "it's so far away."

"Well, little Frank is looking forward to it." Linda stood and began taking he plates from the table. "He's been reading all about the beaches. We talked with several people, and they assure us if Lisa is interested in music, California is where she needs to be."

"Been giving her piano lessons," said Frank with some pride, "and with her voice, she might surprise all of us."

"She has a wonderful voice," Susan added, "and takes her lessons serious."

"I'm really not that good," Lisa finally spoke up, "but enjoy singing."

"May not be real good on piano," little Frank said as if defending her, "but have to say she can sing."

"She's performing at her school Friday," Linda said taking the plates to the sink. "Would you come?"

"Love to!" Janice quickly stood and began helping with clearing the table. "But what about Susan?"

"A college in New York has accepted me," Susan said almost in a scream, "where I can earn a degree in journalism and broadcasting."

"It's a good college," Linda added, "private but has a great reputation."

"New York," Janice said with a smile. "How far from the city?"

"Couple hundred miles maybe," Susan said while leaving the room.

"Frank isn't fond of her living in New York," Linda said in a soft tone. "So far away, even if she is staying in the dorms."

"Here's all the information they sent about the school," Susan said walking in and handing her a large envelope. "Shows the campus and dorms then lists all the courses."

"My hands are a little wet," Janice said while wiping them. "Let's clean the table first, then we'll have time to look it over."

"The realtor has found a buyer for the house," Frank said as Susan placed the envelope on the table. "Offer was more than fair. While here, she made a fair offer on your home."

"Let me think about it," Janice said, sitting down and looking over the information on the college. "Campus and dorms look new."

"All the dorms remodeled last year," Susan said, sitting beside her, "and the courses are everything I want."

"Frank, I'd like to pay for Susan's college," she said while continuing to study the different brochures, with Leone's insurance policy and home."

"We appreciate the offer," he replied, shocked by her request, "but we've been saving for all of their educations."

"Think Leone would like the money to go for her education," she said, as if insisting, "besides I just signed a new contract. I've more money than I need, and with work don't spend."

"Father, you could use that money for little Frank and Lisa," Susan pointed out with emphasis, "and I'll be in New York."

"Since she wants to learn broadcasting," Janice said, attempting to convince him. "Summer break, she'll stay with me and work as my assistant."

"Susan will never come home." Linda stopped and turned toward the three.

"No, she will spend the first three weeks in California," Janice recommended, "then fly back to start work."

"Janice, with tuition and dorm," Frank said as if enlightening her on the cost, "over a hundred thousand a year, and that doesn't even cover books."

"Leone would be so proud," she said, looking over toward Susan, "knowing he did this."

"Janice, we have the money," Frank again repeated his concern.

"Has nothing to do with money," Janice turned to him in a calm tone. "It's about family and helping."

"Father, I could learn so much," Susan spoke up, "and earn money if they pay me."

"Hourly wage for assistants," Janice assured her, "and if she needs help with studies, whom better to help?"

"Against my better judgement..." Frank reconsidered. "Fine, but long holidays I want you home."

"Oh, Father, thank you." Susan jumped to her feet then hugging him around the neck. "I promise."

"We promise," Janice said, crossing her heart.

The weeks passed quickly, and Friday she watched Lisa perform in front of all the parents attending the schools musical. Lisa on stage was no longer the shy timid child, but a performer that could sing the high notes that most adults could not.

When the musical was over, Lisa received a standing ovation, and Janice, along with so many, was in awe of her ability.

"She was magnificent," Janice expressed what all must have thought. "Where did she learn to sing like that?"

"Can't say," Frank said while they waited for Lisa, "but the people in California produce musicals and maybe she could be in one."

"They have singing coaches and actors to help," Linda continued, "along with piano instructors that cater to the children."

"Whatever you do, encourage her," Janice said as Lisa ran toward them.

Throughout the night and next morning, all praise given to Lisa. Having decided to sell both homes, Janice and Susan packed valuables and pictures from the home.

"Are you leaving the furniture?" she asked while looking over the many boxes.

"No," she said, walking around and touching each piece. "Most was hardly used, so I'm donating it to the local veteran's organizations."

"I'm looking so forward to coming to New York," Susan said, almost out of breath with excitement, "working and living with you."

"Just remember our promise to your parents," Janice reminded, looking back toward her.

"We won't," she responded with a wide smile.

Once back at work, Janice prepared for Susan by creating a room of her own and then preparing everyone for her arrival.

"So, your little sister is coming to work here," Edgar said while walking out of his office into hers. "You seem excited."

"I'm worried something might go wrong," Janice admitted, "that she'll get homesick or we'll argue."

"Janice, you've handled presidents and dictators," he reminder her. "I'm sure Susan is more worried than you are. Besides that girl thinks the world rises and sets on you, so stop worrying."

When Susan arrived, the week was dreadful for both. Schedules were not followed, and long hours took their toll.

"Janice, maybe I should just go home," Susan came out of her room with swollen eyes from crying. "I'm getting in your way, and can't seem to do anything right."

"Susan, please don't give up on me just yet," she said, taking her into her arms. "Your first week of college went well."

"Oh God no," she began. "Late to classes and twice ended up in the wrong one. Can't tell you how many meals I missed, or people I bumped into or knocked down."

"However, here you are a year later," Janice said, in a soft tone. "Stop trying so hard and start enjoying yourself because my staff thinks you're great."

"They said that about me?" she asked, looking up. "Really?"

"Yes, because they all remember their first week," she began, laughing.

Within a month, Susan was part of the team, even giving small suggestions. The second year of college seemed harder than the first, professors demanding books written by them read. On one of the long weekends, Susan sat quietly reading and whispering under her breath.

"Okay, what gives?" Janice said while handing her a cup of tea. "You've hardly said anything but sit whispering to yourself."

"My professor demands we read his book about journalism," she said, handing her the book, "but hasn't worked as a journalist but thinks he knows everything about it."

"He lives in the ivory tower of education," she explained while thumbing through the many pages of the textbook, "and over the years has read many books of those who were in the field. He gives opinion, but mostly gives advice from those journalists that have made mistakes. If you wish to be a great reporter, read the reference books mentioned by him."

"Must be 30 or more," Susan answered.

"Don't have to read them all," she said, again laughing, but some. "Then remember things they suggest, and see if it works."

"Just more reading. I'm taking the book back. Learn more being your assistant."

"One day you will be the teacher," Janice said, gently clasping her hands around her face, "and I will be the student."

"Never," she said with a smile, "because you're my sister that won't give up on me."

"Susan, I will never give up on you," Janice said, giving her a hug.

The next three years seemed to go quickly and were some of best times the entire family had experienced in a very long time.

"Janice, can I have a word?" Edgar asked as she entered the office.

"Got a meeting with the staff in 10 minutes," she said, entering his office, "but if you need more time."

"No this won't take long," he said, opening his middle drawer. "By the way good story on that phony author claiming to be Shakespeare."

"Seems like for everyone I find," she said, sitting down, "another pops up trying to rip off the people who don't know better."

"Got a two-year contract extension for you to sign," he said, handing her the paperwork, "small increase over the last contract but a few more benefits."

"Two year?" she said, surprised by the offer. "Why not wait until my contract is up and go through the normal channels?"

"Got my reasons," he began. "You'll just have to trust my judgement."

"You're holding something back," she said, knowing he had asked for trust so few times. "Anything I can help with?"\

"Nothing you can do," he said with a reassuring smile, "but signing the contract would please me."

"Trust you with my life," Janice said while signing the places marked.

By the fourth year, Janice attended Susan's graduation, along with the entire family and a few close friends.

"Well, here we are," she said, taking her picture in the dark blue gown, "a degree in journalism and broadcasting."

"Don't forget," she said, giving her a wide smile for the camera, "minor in business."

"Can't believe my little Susan's all grown up," Linda began crying, "and ready to take on the world."

"Heard you accepted the offer from our competing network," Janice said while snapping several more pictures. "Edgar have anything to do with that?"

"He spoke with me," she admitted. "Felt I should strike out on my own. An offer was made, but with all the rumors..."

"I'm happy for you," she said, giving her a hug, "besides that network really needs you."

"Going to Chicago," Susan said, taking a deep breath. "Never been on my own."

"We'll talk on computer every night," she said, as if giving her reassurance, "and if you need me, just ask."

"There is always California," Frank spoke up. "I'm sure you can find work there."

"Thanks Dad," she said, turning toward him, "but time for me to leave the nest."

"Just promise not to do anything foolish," Linda said in a stern tone, "and come home when you can."

"Promise," she said, crossing her heart as all began laughing.

Janice once again found herself alone, but within weeks immersed herself in the work to keep the news relevant.

"Have you heard the news?" Carolina, out of breath, came running toward her.

"Slow down, Carolina," she said, taking her by the hand. "Now tell me what's going on."

"Mr. Acorn," she began, "they want him to retire."

"Nonsense," she said, releasing her and walking toward the elevator. "I'll find out what's happening real quick."

"Janice," he yelled out from his office as she appeared, "you've heard."

"What's happening?" she demanded, entering his office. "They can't retire you."

"Can and did," he said, looking toward the walls filled with awards. "Gave me a nice retirement package that I couldn't turn down."

"You never said anything," Janice began, wanting to scream but holding it.

"Offer made this morning," he explained. "Grandchildren are now in charge and given little choice."

"They don't know anything about running a news network," she blurted out. "I'll quit."

"You'll do no such thing," he said, standing up. "You've a two year contract. I knew this was coming, which is why I made you sign it. You're a professional, the people depend on you for their jobs."

"You think they'll destroy what you built?" she asked, realizing he was correct that others needed her, "And I'm here to stop it."

"Slow it down," he admitted. "Can't stop it. I've got until the end of the week, so we need to talk about our employees and their future."

For the rest of the week, they spoke in meetings and while packing his things. His final day was difficult for all, tears flowed, but when his wife arrived, the people began to understand his life hadn't ended but begun.

The following week the two young grandchildren met with everyone, and reassured them change was not forthcoming but to continue doing their job.

"Janice, you believe them about not changing anything?" Carolina asked in a concerned tone. "They seem sincere."

"No," Janice, in disgust, blurted out, "those two can't be trusted. There's very little they can do, Edgar saw to that."

"I'm a little scared," Carolina expressed her thoughts. "Randy and I were thinking about marriage."

"Great," she said, giving her a hug. "Just do it, and things will work out."

CHAPTER TWENTY-ONE

As time passed everyone noticed small but subtle rumors began to spread having to do with a more modern looking set for the news.

"Janice," Carolina came over to her while in a meeting with the staff, "the Dialers are asking for you."

"Alright, everyone," she said, standing up from her chair. "Go on with the meeting, and I'll be back shortly."

Entering the plush office of the Dialer brothers, she noticed several arcade game units and a large gumball machine.

"Nice playroom," she said while sitting without having been asked. "You actually get work done here?"

"It relaxes people, Ms. Gardner," one sitting at the desk remained silent while the other sat on the edge of the desk. "Not intimidating."

She noticed they looked like twins but different, having been born a year apart.

"The two-year contract is about to expire," he said, sitting comfortably behind the desk, "and I must say the ratings are good."

"Number one in the time slot," she reminded him. "Very good ratings."

"For now," he said, sitting on the desk, "an older generation who are slowly dying off are keeping those ratings high."

"The young hip generation wants to know what's new in fashion," he, without moving in his chair, explained. "They want to see technology that interests them. Gloom and doom news is important, but let's face it, they tune out."

"When did wars and starvation become unimportant?" she asked. "It's our profession to reveal such things along with monitoring government officials."

"We have no intention to eliminate such news," he said, removing himself from the desk, "just not dwell on it."

"What my older brother means to say," he said, looking toward him, "is for every such report we turn to a lighter side."

"Fluff news," Janice said, using the word they wished to avoid. "Dumb down the news."

"It's giving our viewers what they want." No longer interested in sitting on the desk or chair, he paced. "They understand there's nothing to be done short of becoming a soldier or minster."

"So what do you want from me?" she asked, wanting to get to the point of her being here.

"Over the years you've done wonders for our father's network," he said, leaning forward on his desk, "and we appreciate it. We would like to offer you a four-year contract, as a member on the entertainment board. Many of our programs haven't achieved the ratings we need, and with your help, that can change."

"Not the news?" she said, shocked by the very thought of leaving the news department.

"My brother and I will assume that responsibility," he said with a smile. "Got some ideas that we think will bring in new viewers."

"Is there an alternative?" she asked.

"Yes," he said, sitting back on his chair, "but you haven't heard our offer."

"Eighty million for four years," he said, pacing over to his seated brother. "All the perks you want in a contract."

"The other is a retirement package," he said, leaning back in his chair as his eyes widened. "Forty million with a 10-year health plan."

"May I see that contract?" she asked in a calm manner.

"Of course," he said, opening the middle drawer of his desk and handing her the paperwork, "the attorneys all said you would never retire."

"Your attorneys don't know me," she said, taking the paperwork and quickly scanning through the pages. "Two-week notice, that was nice of them."

"Eighty million," the eldest brother said, speaking in an angry tone. "Forty million difference, and you're prepared to walk away?"

"Walking away with forty million," she said, placing the paperwork in her handbag. "My lawyers will return the signed paperwork to you in the morning."

"You understand," the youngest jumped to his feet, "you cannot work in the news field for five years."

"Best you look over my contracts," she said, walking toward the door. "I had that section removed years ago."

"That Goddamn Acorn!" both began swearing his name. "He did this and now she's screwing us."

"Press is going to have a field day," she continued to listen, "claiming we forced her out after all she did."

Over the two weeks, Janice continued to anchor the nightly news, hundreds called to protest, even as she remained silent on the matter.

"Tonight will be my last broadcast," she began. "I've been honored to serve here while knowing of your support each and every night. I tried to bring news of importance, some brutal and heartbreaking. My intention was to inform all Americans on issues I felt were important, no doubt some disagree. News should be fair and impartial. Over the years, my bias revealed itself, hopefully forgiven by all. My future is unknown, but the time spent with all of you was one of my greatest pleasures. God bless you, and America. This is Janice Gardner saying goodbye."

"That was great, Janice," Randy said, giving her a hug. "Can't believe they kicked you out."

"What about you," she asked, "and Carolina?"

"I'm head cameraman," he said, "with a union, and Carolina will be working on the secretarial floor."

"So, marriage?" she said, watching as he removed his head gear.

"You know, in two weeks," he said with a smile, "you're coming right."

"Carolina handed me the invitation last week," Janice poking his stomach. "Wouldn't miss it for the world."

"Janice, you know I love you," he began, taking a deep breath, "not like I do Carolina but..."

"Back at you," she said, kissing him on the cheek. "Don't think I could have done it without you so many times."

"Greatest adventure any man could have had," he responded with a smile.

Over the next few months, many important interviews of prominent people canceled along with advertisers flooded with letters threatening boycott, yet Janice shied away from reporters, even when visiting the grave of Russell.

"Guys, I'm here to visit a friend," she said, holding several flowers. "Please go."

"Ms. Gardner, just one quick question," one of the men shouted out. "Did they force you out, so they could bring in a younger and more attractive anchor?"

"What, I'm old and wrinkled?" she began, laughing.

"No, Ms. Gardner, you're still beautiful," they all agreed.

"She seems nice," she answered, "and talented, so can I have my alone time?"

"Sure," the small group disappeared.

"Hello, Russell," she said, kneeling down to remove several leaves and placing the flowers vase, "well... got time to talk now."

For over an hour she spoke to him, of marriage, Susan, and Leone. The following day, she received an envelope under her hotel door, and inside, a photo along with negative of her kneeling at his grave with the caption "visiting a friend," not for publication.

Looking at the photo brought back memories, and a reminder of her loneliness.

After dressing and packing, Janice entered the lobby of the hotel.

"Ms. Gardner, I hope your stay was satisfactory," said the manager who stood behind the desk. "We appreciate you selecting our hotel and hope you will return."

"Service was wonderful," she said while he presented the bill, "and I will return."

"The staff and I will look forward to that day," he said, taking the credit card from her hand.

"Did I hear right," she asked, looking toward several televisions from the bar area, "Susan Ehlert and an accident?"

"A 20-vehicle pileup on some road in Chicago," he said while returning her card. "Fires with people trapped. It's been all over the news, that reporter refusing to leave the scene."

"Can you do me a favor?" she asked, looking toward the bar, "and copy the broadcast?"

"We've no way to copy it," he admitted, "but I can show you the entire broadcast in my office."

In the large plush office, the manager quickly turned on the large screen television and with the remote started the broadcast from the beginning.

"This is Susan Ehlert reporting on the Route 2, having over 20 vehicles involved in a terrible pileup. You're witnessing our courageous firemen and women battling fires where some are trapped. The main problem is a gas tanker having overturned and leaking. My cameraman and I are moving toward that tanker and will attempt to show it live."

Janice watched as the two moved toward the overturned tanker, and as the Fire Chief came running toward her.

"Lady, I want you and your cameraman out of here. You see those fires?"

"Yes, we do Chief," Susan answered.

"If those fires get anywhere near this tanker, just go."

"I'm not afraid, knowing you would never allow anything bad to happen to your men or me," she said, standing her ground. "When all of you leave, I'll go."

"Men, you hear that," he began shouting orders to his crew working around the tanker, "Can't make a liar out of her. Want more form and dirt on that leaking gas, and you men on the hoses get those car fires out."

"Heroes at work," Susan continued speaking as smoke covered the scene. "Men and women under terrible conditions saving lives."

"Sir, fires out, and we're getting those people tramped out," a young fire woman came running up to him. "Police say they have an empty tanker coming."

"Great," he shouted, "start moving those vehicles away from this tanker. All right young lady the fires are out, and danger over. So move back, you got your story."

"But they're still here," she said, looking at the crew still working around the tanker.

"Be here a while," he explained, "need to transfer gas to another tanker and afterwards clear this road."

"If you're sure...?" she asked as if disappointed.

"I'm sure young lady," he said with a smile.

"Wait until I see her!" Janice shouted while turning off the television. "Risking her life for a story."

"Is there anything I or the hotel can do for you?" the manager asked noticing her expression. "Please, we are here to serve."

"Would you call the airport and see when the next flight to Chicago is scheduled?" she said, turning toward him, "and arrange passage for me."

"We can make such arrangements," he said, walking toward the phone, "first class."

Once the flight landed, Janice was surprised to find a driver holding a sign with her name written on it.

"I'm Janice Gardner," she said, walking toward the well-dressed man. "You're my driver?"

"Chauffer, and anything else you may require," he said removing the sign, "and mostly your biggest fan, Ms. Gardner."

"Fine, Jeff," she said, looking at his nametag and handing him an address, "know this place?"

"Of course," he said, walking her toward the elevators, "local television network. We'll get your luggage, and in no time be there...

"Here we are, Ms. Gardner," he said while driving toward the guarded gate, "they check everyone."

"Hello," she said, opening her door, "Janice Gardner to see Susan Ehlert."

"Ms. Gardner," the guard immediately recognized her, "please proceed."

"Jeff, stay here," she said as he parked the limousine, "may need your services."

Entering the building, the word of her presence spread, and several people came down to meet or just see her.

"Ms. Gardner, I'm Mario Pratt broadcasting manager," he said while buttoning his suit coat, "and it's an honor meeting you."

"Thank you," she said, allowing him to take her hand, "but is Susan Ehlert here."

"She's in editing," he quickly replied, "please allow me to escort you to her."

"Janice," Susan screamed out. "Look, everyone, it's my big sister!"

"Thank you, Mr. Pratt," she said, turning toward him. "May I have a moment with my little sister, if you don't mind?"

"Of course," he answered. "Everyone out, and let the two have a moment."

"I am really upset with you," she said, giving her a hug when alone.

"Mother already called," Susan began, "but I'm so happy you came."

"Susan, you could have been killed," she blurted out, "or seriously burned."

"Mother and Father reminded me repeatedly," she replied, giving her an innocent expression, "and I spoke with the head of the network."

"What did he say?" she asked, attempting to show she was still angry.

"Said he along with the insurance company was concerned for my safety," she explained, "that I must be prudent and not endanger other workers. However, he felt that the fire chief had the entire matter under control and all went well."

"A man like that would feed you to the sharks," Janice taking a deep breath, "for a 10-point rating boost."

"He also said that he'd be watching how I do in the future," she said, expressing satisfaction. "Now tell me what you really thought of my broadcast."

"It was," she began, pausing for a moment, "a great broadcast especially with what the fire chief had to say."

"Come on," she said, taking her by the hand and leading her, "want to show you something that's in my office."

"A fire helmet," Janice said looking at the worn helmet.

"From the chief," she said putting it on, "and the note reads, 'If you wish to get so close to fires, best use this to protect that wonderful face.'"

"Susan, please just tell me you won't take such chances again," Janice asked while she laid the helmet down.

"Got me an invitation to interview the mayor," she said with pride. "Been in office for less than a year and has all types of problems."

"Have you researched him yet?" she asked.

"Since you're here," she began, "maybe you could help with that."

"Not in this small of an office," she said, looking at the room having bare walls.

"Hey, it's a small building," she said, defending the network, "and it's all mine."

"Fine," she said, taking her by the hand, "but first lunch."

Before leaving several asked for her autograph, along with group photos.

"Jeff," Janice said, walking toward the man. "Know any place that can serve two starving reporters by chance?"

"You're that reporter at the fire," he said, speaking directly to Susan. "Damn fine job."

"Jeff, don't encourage her," Janice quickly spoke. "Now about that restaurant."

"Hop in, ladies," he said, opening the door, "know the very place."

"Smells wonderful," Susan said as they entered the Italian restaurant, "almost like home when Mother cooked."

"Good afternoon!" A large man of 50 having a large white apron approached them. "We're closed now, but come back in two hours."

"Uncle, this is Ms. Gardner," Jeff came running in, "and Ms. Ehlert, the girl on the television reporting the fire."

"Ms. Gardner," a young girl in her teens came running from the dining room. "Father, she is very famous."

"If my Jeffrey bring you here," he began, stretching his large arm out as if inviting them to the dining room, "and my daughter says you're famous, come and enjoy."

Within minutes, the entire family of eight stood around them, and after taking several group pictures began bringing out bread and wine. After having a wonderful meal, the two walked toward the cash register.

"No charge, Ms. Gardner," Jeff said while walking toward the door. "We don't get famous people, especially ones that allow us to take photos."

"Nonsense," she said, opening her purse. "You can't give food away and stay in business."

"It's too much," he said, watching her lay down five $100 bills.

"Never too much for great food," she said, walking toward the door, "and service."

For two days Janice remained in Chicago helping Susan with the research and questions to be asked.

"Now tomorrow, I must return to New York," Janice said after having spent the entire day with Susan. "Let me suggest giving the mayor the questions a day before the interview is to take place."

"But he'll prepare," Susan pointed out.

"I know," she admitted, "but remember, he's only been in office less than a year. He inherited several city problems, give him a chance to explain, and one day he'll return the favor."

"Fine," Susan said, a little saddened by the advice and knowing she was leaving. "I'm going to miss you. I'll see you off, and let Jeff take me back."

"Of course," she said with a smile. "Don't know who will miss me most, you or Jeff."

"He's been great," Susan said, admitting his willingness to serve the two.

Saying goodbye was difficult, and as predicted Susan along with Jeff revealed admiration and love for her. When arriving at her apartment, she picked up the stack of mail left on the floor.

"Well at least the credit card people haven't forgotten me," she said, whispering to herself while looking over the many letters, "along with advertisers."

A week later Susan sent her a copy of the interview with the mayor, along with a note saying she was right about giving him advanced notice. Watching the video, she realized the mayor answered all her questions, admitting of having disbanded the drug unit due to indictments of the officers. Concerning the gang unit, it was determined they were understaffed and underfunded. However, he made it clear each a priority in his administration.

"Susan, your boss should be proud," she said turning the television off. "On your way to stardom."

After a week of cleaning the apartment several times and stocking the refrigerator with food, she sat quietly on the sofa enjoying a glass of wine when the door buzzer sounded.

"Yes," she asked, pressing the intercom button, "may I help you?"

"Ms. Gardner," a gruff voice came over the speaker. "The name is Brock Paxter, and I would like to speak to you about work."

"Mr. Paxter, I'm retired," she said, speaking into the box, "and have little need for work."

"Please, Ms. Gardner, hear me out," the voice replied. "Five minutes of your time."

"I don't receive visitors here," she continued. There is a small coffee shop a block away, and there, you'll have five minutes."

"My suit is gray," he began to describe himself, "with brown briefcase."

Entering the local coffee shop, she immediately noticed the large man sitting alone with brown briefcase on the table.

"Ms. Gardner, may I say how wonderful it is meeting you," he said, standing up and reaching his hand out, "and how foolish your network was by retiring you."

"You're wasting the five minutes," she said, taking his hand.

"Well, then, let's get right to the matter," he said, walking over and helping with the chair. "I represent several executives requiring your assistance."

"I can't see how I could help executives," she said while sitting, "unless they're in the broadcasting business."

"Natural gas," he said, sitting down across from her.

"May I take your order?" a young waitress came over to the table.

"Coffee, black," he ordered, "and Ms. Gardner?"

"Nothing, please," she said with a smile, "I may be leaving soon."

"Know anything about Native American or Canadian law?" he quickly began as the young girl vanished.

"Some," she admitted. "When purchasing land it must be documented that no native tribe resided on it for 200 years."

"Close enough," he said, pulling out several notepads. "Many tribes have used that law to take land from people. Now before defending it, I'm here to discuss a problem that pertains to that law."

"Go on," she said, mildly curious.

"My clients have discovered pockets of natural gas," he began explaining. "Some along the border of America and others on the Canadian side. Unfortunately, on the Canadian side, they unearthed skeletal remains. We've estimated the remains are at least 200 to 300 years old, and there in lays the dispute."

"What does this have to do with me?" she asked, unable to see why he called.

"Black coffee, sir," the young girl said, laying the coffee cup down on the table, "and ma'am, are you sure there's nothing I can get you?"

"Sure," she answered.

"Here, young lady," he said handing her a $10 bill. "Keep it."

"Thank you," she said, as if surprised by his generosity.

"There is a professor that has convinced the National Federation of Native Tribes," he began, pausing for a moment to sip on the coffee, "this discovery confirms his belief of a lost or forgotten tribe. As a result, the Federation filed court injunctions, and all work stopped."

"Again, why have you come to me?" she asked, still puzzled by his appearance.

"Both parties understand the cost of litigation," he said, showing her the initial cost thus far on one of the yellow pads, "and it takes years before final judgement. However, neither side will cooperate with the other, so I've suggested an impartial mediator."

"The human remains," she said, now becoming interested, "what were they?"

"Arm and hand bones," he said reaching inside his briefcase and showing photos of the remains, "a storm uprooted a tree and attached was the remains."

"Both left arm," she said while examining the photos.

"You've a keen eye," he complimented her, "most never notice."

"I assume they've dated the remains," she said, returning the photos to him.

"No, they have not," he admitted. "Still arguing what laboratory to send them to."

"Any idea just when those remains ended up there? she continued to question him. "I'm sure they have some idea."

"Tree rings," he said, chuckling as he produced another photo, "210 to 230 years ago."

"So the remains were there before the tree," she said, understanding the situation. "Tree grew, and the roots acquired the bones."

"Which brings us to the problem," he said while removing an large envelope. "Bodies were buried there over 200 years ago, However, the Federation is making the claim the tribe has never left the land."

"Having the people buried on the land," she saw the argument, "shows they never forfeited ownership."

"Crazy as it sounds," he said, shaking his head, "we have judges willing to rule in their favor."

"You do know the remains may just be two frontiersmen?" she said, pointing out a possible alternative, "Killed or died by injuries then buried by others."

"In 1815, the first white settlers wrote about crossing this land," he began, showing he had researched the history, "claiming land was poor and rock formations unsuitable for farming or raising livestock. Before you ask, no one died during the crossing."

"What conditions are there if I decide to help?" she asked. "And the budget?"

"Conditions, none," he assured her. "A million dollar salary and a budget large enough to get this matter resolved."

"Good terms," she said, almost bewildered by the amount offered, "but what happens if either side objects to the way I manage?"

"No one will object," he said, as if it were a promise. "However if such were to arise, call me."

"You promise to support me regardless?" she asked.

"My promise and an iron clad contract," he said, putting his hand out. "Deal?"

"Deal," Janice said, taking his hand. "I would like to meet with this professor if you could arrange it."

"I'll inform Mr. Throgmorton you wish an audience with him tomorrow," he said while finishing the coffee, "and have necessary paperwork with cashier check ready."

"Somehow I figure both parties agreed to this before you came here," she said, knowing such speed was only possible with prior meetings.

"Arm-twisting and threats," he began, laughing, "work better than idle chat."

"How did you know I would accept?" she wondered.

"It's a challenge," he admitted. "Your entire career is based on it with honest answers."

"Send me everything you have on Mr. Throgmorton," she said, standing up. "1:00."

The following day she arrived at the estate of Edward Throgmorton, whose family name dated back before the American Revolution.

"Ms. Gardner," said an elderly man as he opened the door wearing a black suit. "Mr. Throgmorton is expecting you and please if you would follow me."

Entering a large room filled with Indian artifacts, she noticed him behind a large oak desk studying an arrow.

"Ms. Gardner." He rose to reveal his oversized stomach while removing his glasses. "I am so honored having you here. May I get you a drink, or lunch?"

"Bottled water please," she asked, walking over and taking his outstretched, flabby hand. "Your collection of Native American culture is quite extensive."

"Miles, water for our guest," he said, looking toward the man as he began strolling around the room. "Three generations collecting such marvelous treasures."

"Madam," the man said, handing her a bottle, "your water."

"Thank you, Miles," he shouted from the far side of the room. "Why not take the rest of the afternoon off?"

"Sir," he spoke up, "given several days off, I have neglected my duties."

"Family comes first, Miles," he said, as if reminding him. "Your grandson just came out of the hospital and needs attention. Besides, Ms. Gardner and I have a lot to discuss. We'll be fine."

"Thank you, sir," he said, closing the door.

"Any problem?" she asked, "I can come back later this week."

"Tonsils," he said, laughing. "Miles is like family, and he worries about everything. I spoke with the doctor this morning, and the boy is fine."

"Apparently you must be close," she said while examining the many arrows. "Doctors normally don't speak to non-relatives."

"When my foundation supports the hospital," he continued, "and I support the doctor, they tend to speak to me. It's the advantage of having money, as you know."

"An archaeologist and professor at two universities," she began, revealing her knowledge of him, "here and Canada. You're also responsible for shutting down natural gas exploration, over a theory you wish to prove."

"To prove that once a great tribe lived on that land," he said walking toward her, "and for some unknown reason vanished."

"Tribes do not just vanish," she spoke up, "they leave in search of better land or break apart and assimilate with other tribes. However, they record such events in painting, and thus far nothing."

"This is proof they existed," he said, handing her gloves while pointing to a bow and several arrows in a fur lined quiver. "A ceremonial Seneca bow with arrows."

"What does that have to do with this?" she questioned him further.

"The history of my family goes back hundreds of years," he said, explaining their importance, "being both French and English, the family migrated to Canada during the American Revolution to avoid conflict between family members. Some opened supply stores, while others fur trapping. One of my great-great ancestors found these while exploring for beaver, possibly around 1785, maybe 1786. He described the location as a large razor back mountain, four man high stretching several miles. He understood if caught with the items, certain death. However, he could parlay them for his life, which is why he kept them. He remained fearful, but found no sign of their existence."

"Your ancestor wrote about this," she asked, "that the tribe had left?"

"Yes, in a journal," he said, walking over and showing her the ledger, "if you care to read."

"I would," she said, walking over toward the ledger encased in glass. "So, what is your theory on why they left?"

"Never left," he blurted out with excitement. "Have you seen the photos of the remains they unearthed?"

"Of course," she said, showing her knowledge, "two left arms."

"I noticed something," he said, walking over to his desk and removing the photos. "Each show signs of scorching on the finger bones. One has a small but noticeable cut on his upper arm, I believe from a stone knife or tomahawk."

"I can see that," she said, looking closely at the photos.

"I've two theories," he began. "The first is the village was attacked by an enemy tribe who started the fire, and during the chaos attacked. Taken by surprise the people were killed or captured, and those who escaped came back to bury the dead. Afterwards the survivors fled, maybe back to America or further into Canada.

"Possible," she said, pausing for a brief moment, "but the cut on the arm may be an old wound that healed."

"Which brings me to my second theory," he said, showing he had given this a great deal of thought. "A natural wild fire during the night. Sweeping through the village while they slept, people dying from lack of oxygen or flames. Again survivors returning to bury the dead, and leaving."

"So how did your bow and quiver," she began, challenging him to reconsider, "end up along this razor back mountain if it were consumed by fire?"

"That I cannot answer," he admitted. "Maybe it somehow survived the fire. Someone discovered it, and took it there."

"Had there been survivors of such an event," she said, using logic over theory, "they would have found a way to document what happened in either paintings or stories. Yet your research shows nothing of the sort. They just left."

"I agree they're just theories." His tone showed disappointment. "But there was a Seneca tribe and what happened is a mystery."

"We must deal in fact and truth," she reminded him of her philosophy. "You've involved yourself in this matter to prove a theory. As a result, you're knee deep in this conflict, so as of this minute, you work for me. Forget any theory you had. We search for truth."

"You're asking me to join you?" he said, surprised by her announcement. "I don't know what to say but thank you."

"Might want to save the thank you for later." Janice began strolling around the room. "I'll expect nothing less than hard work and loyalty. From this day forth, no mention of theory or speculation."

"I'm at your disposal," he said, taking her hand and kissing it. "Just tell me what to do."

"Starting tomorrow, the conflict between parties is over," she began, "and we need equipment to determine what if anything is under the ground."

"I can make up a list of equipment we could use," he recommended, "and I have graduate students who will volunteer to help."

"Good," she said with a smile. "This will be a summer job with hourly wages paid."

"Now I understand why they asked you here," he said, as if in awe.

"There will be some who will regret that decision," she said, laughing at the very thought, "but we will discover the truth."

CHAPTER TWENTY-TWO

"Good morning," Janice said with a wide smile as she entered the conference room where several men sat, including Throgmorton. "I hope everyone had a good night's sleep."

"Ms. Gardner." He stood over 6'4" with thinning brown hair and large muscular arms in a white shirt. "The name is…"

"Yes, Mr. Paul Ulanderson," she said, cutting his speech off, "contractor in charge of developing the land. Mr. Antoine Renaud represents the National Federation of Native Tribes, that includes the local Council of Indian Affairs. Of course, everyone knows Mr. Throgmorton, archaeologist."

"Alright, now that were all friends," Paul said, sitting down, "what now?"

"Having signed the contract that all of you signed," she began, stepping to the front of the table, "no more court action, and we proceed to learn the truth."

"The truth is simple," Antoine replied in a soft tone, "the land and mineral deposits belong to the Seneca tribe."

"You're clairvoyant?" she asked, looking toward him with interest for having soft tan skin and brown eyes with a handsome face that resembled a movie star of the forties. "I had no idea, but please continue."

"I surrender to your astuteness." His smile seemed to brighten up the room.

"Gentlemen, this feud must stop," she said looking toward each person. "It does no good and prevents any progress. You have agreed to accept my judgement, therefore any theory or speculation is over. First, the Smithsonian Institute will examine the skeletal remains."

"We can agree to that," Antoine spoke up. "What of the cost?"

"Shared," she continued to notice his slender features and thick black hair. "I will order what equipment we need. To avoid additional attention, we pay students from the university to help Professor Throgmorton excavate the ground."

"Union might not like that idea," Paul warned. "It's what they do for a living."

"Consider this an archaeological dig," she suggested. "Some heavy equipment will come in handy, but otherwise careful exploration."

"Can't believe this," Paul blurted out, "eight lousy trees and probably the only one that snagged those bones blew down. Should have taken those bones and placed them in a trash bag."

"What's done is done," Janice said, "so Edward, when can the equipment we need be here?"

"Two days, maybe three," he assured her, "if that's agreeable."

"Fine," Paul spoke up, "but let's not break the bank."

"I'll make arrangement for the remains to be sent to the Smithsonian," Antoine replied, "but understand I will remain here observing."

"If he stays," Paul said while standing, "so will I."

"This will be a fun week," Janice said, looking toward Edward as the two men walked out, "get that equipment and students here fast."

The following afternoon while at lunch, Janice noticed Antoine entering the restaurant and walking toward her.

"May I?" he asked, pointing to an empty chair.

"Not sure if that would be a good idea," she said, looking toward him. "Might appear I'm taking sides."

"I come in peace," he said with a smile, "and report the remains are en route to the Smithsonian. I haven't had lunch and would enjoy your company."

"Never let it be said that I deprived a starving person food," she said, motioning for him to sit, "but what of Mr. Ulanderson?"

"Paul listens to his boss, Brock Paxter," he said while sitting down, "a man I have come to admire as reasonable."

"Sir, would you need a menu?" a young man came to the table.

"Whatever Ms. Gardner ordered," he said, looking toward her plate, "smells delightful."

"It's our daily special," he quickly spoke up.

"Then I'll have it," he said, "with coffee, black."

"My mother adored an actor," she said, surprising herself by speaking of it, "and you remind me of him but can't for the life of me remember his name."

"My family claim I resemble Gilbert—" he began.

"Roland!" she blurted out his name.

"Give the beautiful lady a prize." He began laughing.

"I'm so sorry," she said, a little embarrassed by the outburst. "Just remembering the times my mother and I spent watching his movies."

"No apology needed," he said, taking her by the hand. "I'm thrilled knowing you see me in such a way. My people idolize you and think your one of the good ones."

"Good ones?" she said, wondering what it meant.

"Honest and truthful," he added, "a rare quality most reporters lack."

"Here you are, sir," the young man said, placing the plate down with a large container of coffee. "If you wish anything, please, just ask."

"Thank you," he said as he left. "So, shall we eat before it gets cold?"

"Unfortunately, I'm finished," she said, looking down at the empty plate, "but please."

"Then keep me company," he asked, "a man starving for conversation."

"Maybe a cup of coffee," she said, handing him her cup, "and I doubt you have little trouble finding someone to converse with."

"I would never turn down the opportunity to converse," he said, pouring her coffee, "with a beautiful and intelligent woman whom I admire."

"Such charm," she said, placing the cup down, "it must have come in handy while you attended college and work."

"I am pure blood," he explained while eating, "Dakota tribe. I can trace my family history back 500 years."

"Five hundred years," she said, shocked knowing such was possible. "I can trace my history to mother and father."

"Unlike most white settlers," he continued to educate her, "who wrote in

Bibles, tribes used animal hides. Yet they documented every birth, death, and event, including battles won or lost."

"So now they use computers," she said, "and your parents."

"My father served in the Marines, Purple Heart and Silver Star. Used the G.I. bill to graduate college and became chief land negotiator for several tribes. Also elected Head of Tribal Council, which he held for over 20 years. Mother, a princess, and became Superintendent of the school district."

"Must have made you a very popular student," she said, joking with him.

"Hardly," he laughed. "Geek mostly with studies and sports until college. Being the only Native American, seldom lonely and never needed a car. Law school was different, became an outsider among the well-to-do class. However, that allowed me to finish third in my class, and become the lawyer I am today."

"Married with children?" she said, as if needing to know.

"For another time," he said, looking at his watch. "I've an appointment, but allow me to buy lunch, all right?"

"Fine," she replied, watching as he picked up the two receipts. "How do you know there'll be another time?"

"Indian intuition," he replied while laying down a $50 bill, "besides you know a little of my life, and I know nothing of yours."

"I can sum up my life with one word," she answered.

"Which is?" he asked.

"Work," she responded.

The equipment needed finally arrived after four long days of waiting, and another three hours to set it up to work.

"Well, it's ready," Throgmorton said while looking into the monitor. "Bone finder is operating perfect."

"What the Hell does it do?" Ulanderson asked. "Besides costing us time and money."

"Radar sensor," he examined, "can detect bone and show it on the monitor."

"The depth?" Antoine asked.

"Up to 30 feet." He added, "Can we start?"

Within minutes, the students wheeled the machine over the area, and within an hour under the hot sun, a mass image of bones appeared on the monitor.

"This can't be right," Throgmorton replied in a surprised tone. "It just couldn't be."

"What couldn't be?" Janice asked, demanding an answer.

"It's circular, having animal bones," he said, stepping away from the monitor, "among human. Guys!" Throgmorton shouted out to the ones wheeling the machine, "it's a circular pit, so turn around and go slow over the next section."

"Circular," Antoine in a soft tone turned to Janice. "Never known any tribe to bury their people in that manner."

"Let's get down to it," Ulanderson spoke up in a loud tone. "How many human bodies are there?"

"Hundreds," he answered, "I've seen this only once in Africa where an entire village was massacred and buried in pit."

"This ain't Africa," he again spoke loud enough for all to hear, "so what now?"

"We start digging them out," he said while continuing to view the monitor, "and find out who they were because this isn't an Indian burial ground."

"How long will that take?" he said, demanding an answer.

"It will take whatever time needed." Janice stepped over to view the monitor. "Any objection from anyone?"

"We could speed it up by using some heavy equipment," Throgmonton spoke up, "if they follow my instructions."

"They'll do what you say," Ulanderson agreed. "Have them here within the hour."

"People," Throgmonton called his 12 students over. "We must tape off the entire area that needs exploration. Extend the circle another 10 feet, and after the heavy equipment is finished, bring shovels."

By nightfall, the heavy machines cleared over five feet of dirt, allowing the students with shovels to continue the following morning. More and more equipment arrived, along with tents with generators.

"Who ordered this?" Janice asked, looking at the refrigerators filled with bottled water and juices.

"Paul and I talked about it last night," Antoine said, walking over to her, "and we both want to know who's buried in that pit. There's little reason to let the kids suffer, so they need lights and special clothing."

"Gloves, masks, and white jump suits," she said, looking at all the items. "That was nice of you."

"When they get down to the remains," he said, picking up one of the suits. "It might get a little nasty, so we even have oxygen masks."

"You know, you're making it easy for us having another coffee," she told him with a smile, "unless there is a wife."

"No wife," he said, laying the suit down, "makes it that much easier."

"You do know this isn't an Indian burial ground," she said, walking toward him. "You could have just walked away."

"Smithsonian called yesterday," he said with a slight smile. "The two arms are white male. One in his early twenties, while the other late thirties. However when we spoke about the discovery, they wish to be involved so a representative is coming."

"Yet here you are," she said, feeling her heart beating faster.

"Maybe I'm curious," he answered, "or looking forward to our next coffee."

"Ah," she said, attempting to catch her breath.

"Ms. Gardner!" One of the young female students came running into the tent. "Professor Throgmorton said to come quick."

In a run, they followed the young girl and found they had uncovered most of the pit and exposing bones.

"Look," Throgmorton said, standing near the skeletal remains of a horse head. "This animal killed by pistol shot. We need those plastic tarps, to bring the remains out in the open."

"Before they start that," Antoine suggested, "get them in jump suits and masks."

"Yes, you're right," he immediately agreed, "everyone to the tents."

"Everyone, listen up," Janice shouted to the group as they began dressing. "Slow down and take water. There's much to do, so split up in three teams. One team will work for an hour, then rest for two while the other team works."

"Hot sun out there," Antoine spoke up to the group. "Come tomorrow, I'll have a tent here large enough to shade the entire pit and supply fans. If anyone feels nauseous, get to this tent lay down and remember, drink plenty of water or juice."

On the second day the representative from the Smithsonian arrived and began instructing and helping the group how best to remove remains.

"Your tent and fans are a lifesaver," Janice said as they stood watching the group. "They've unearth nearly 20 humans and several animals.

"Would that entitle me to ask that you have dinner with me tonight?" he asked, looking toward her in loving manner.

"Dinner would be nice," she replied, turning to face him. "Pizza and doughnuts are fine but…"

"Can't replace a fine wine with good food," he said, interrupting her. "Pick you up at, let's say, around 6:00?"

"At 5:00 would be better," she replied.

"Then 5:00 it is," he said with a smile.

Leaving the pit early, Janice was in need of a total makeover entered a beauty shop.

"My nails and hair are a mess," she said to the young attendant, "and I've a date."

"Girls," she yelled out. "We have a lady in need, and business is slow."

Within seconds, three young females surrounded her and began the work. After two hours of individual pampering by the three, she looked into the mirror.

"Oh my God, you performed a miracle," she said, touching her face having been given a facial. "My hair and nails."

"Ms. Gardner, we know who you are." The attendant came over with a smile while looking toward the others. "You're so beautiful, and we just highlighted it."

"Use this card," Janice began, handing it to the young attendant, "and authorize $4,500."

"Ms. Gardner," she said, somewhat dumbfounded.

"Five hundred to the shop," she said while taking the card, "and $1,000 dollar tip for each of you."

At the hotel she took a shower and unpacked every dress brought.

"Why didn't I bring an evening gown?" she muttered to herself. "Maybe he won't notice and not bring it up."

Finally, she settled on a light blue dress, which showed some cleavage and legs. While placing her shoes on, a knock came to the door.

"Breathe slowly," she told herself, walking to the door and opening it.

"My Lord," he said, looking toward her, "a princess of such beauty."

"Antoine," she said, breathing slowly as she spoke but noticing his well-tailored light brown pinstripe suit, "you look fabulous."

"Compliments are always welcome," he said, taking her by the hand and kissing it.

"They said you had to book reservations a month in advance to dine here," Janice said while entering the plush restaurant having statues and paintings.

"Antoine," a well-dressed man in his late forties giving him a bear hug. "Damn Dakota wanderer."

"Says an Apache sundowner," he replied.

"My God, what is wrong with this beautiful lady," he said, stepping away and looking her over, "being seen with the likes of you?"

"Told her we'd be meeting a scoundrel tonight," he said, slapping his back. "This is Jimuta Ferro, a friend of many years."

"Ms. Gardner," he said, taking her hand and gently kissing it. "An honor to meet you, and may I say you are more beautiful than Antoine said."

"Oh, so he mentioned me?" she said with a smile, looking over to him.

"All he talked about," Jimuta said in a whisper, "and what do you think of him?"

"That will be enough," he said, stepping to her side, "table please."

"We'll talk later," he said with a wink. "Come, I have your table ready."

"He's a real Apache," Janice began, watching as he slipped away. "Pure blood?"

"Apache, but not so much pure blood," he began. "Mother found him eating out of a trash can and brought him home. Father unknown and mother an addict, who abandoned him when he was six."

"That's terrible," she blurted out.

"Not so much," he said, watching as Jimuta come over with the menus. "He found us."

"Telling her my life story?" he asked, handing her the menu. "And does she know how many times I pulled you out of trouble?"

"Many more times than I'd like to think," he replied, laughing as if remembering those times. "We'd either fight our way out or ran like the wind."

"More running than fighting." He leaned down to speak to her, "And I've ordered a fine wine. May I suggest our special, which I will prepare personally?"

"Sounds good," she said, handing back the menu.

"Uncle says you've not called in while."

"Busy, Antoine," he said, taking a deep breath, "but I'll call tomorrow."

"Better," he seemed to warn him. "They will show up if you don't."

"An adoptive brother," she said as he walked away, "and close to the family."

"Family, what can you say?" he said, sipping the water. "You must have one."

She found herself speaking freely of her life, and about Leone along with the family she now had.

"I've taken the entire evening telling you my entire life story," she said, realizing he spoke very little as they ate and drank, "and haven't allowed you to speak at all."

"I regret not having met Leone and your mother," he began, which totally surprised her, "or Russell. People of Great Spirit, who even now watch over you."

"You're going to make me cry in front of all these people," she said, holding back the tears.

"Well, then," he said, moving closer to her, "I've no desire to meet Liam."

"Thank you." She began laughing.

"Well, Antoine?" Jimuta came over to the table.

"You outdid yourself," he said, picking up the check, "but remember..."

"Yes, I'll call uncle," he said, trying to take the check, "and Ms. Gardner, please come back."

"Food was so good," she said, kissing him on each cheek and whispering in his ear, "I stuffed myself tonight."

"Wonderful!" he shouted out. "Best compliment ever."

"Shall we walk?" he said while winking at Jimuta. "It's a nice night."

"So, married, divorced with children?" she asked, walking beside him. "Or are you saving yourself for just that right person?"

"Was married," he admitted. "My wife taught college. She was a pure blood Sioux, and the most beautiful woman I had ever seen. I was preparing for the State Bar Exam when I noticed her in the library. She seemed to float when walking, and her smile captivated me. From that moment on, I knew she was the one."

"You said was."

His entire expression had changed when speaking of her.

"We'd been married for a year," his voice quivered slightly as he retold the story. "I had just won a large settlement case, and she was coming to meet me. The county sheriff deputy came, she had been in an accident with a drunken driver and killed."

"I'm so sorry," Janice said, stopping for a moment, "but I now see why you defend your people."

"You're so wrong," he said, quickly wiping his eyes as he turned toward her, "the driver was Native American. He served time for DUI, and suspended license. The curse of my people is alcoholism, which is why I work with the casinos. Limited free drinks for hotel guests or high rollers. Others pay and monitored by money spent, then cut off. I've encouraged the casinos to open treatment centers and make sure the games are honest. I could not bring her back, but I know she would be pleased."

"I just assumed with all the time and money the Federation spent," she said taking his arm and began walking, "you've little time for others."

"My law firm has only 30 lawyers," he continued, "have white, Black, and even Chinese clients. My wife always said my best quality was never looking at a man's skin color, or size of his wallet, but justice."

"You must have loved her so," she said, remembering her love with Russell.

"Like the rain or sun against my face," he said, taking a deep breath. "Well, here we are."

"You could walk me to my room," she asked.

"Certainly," he said, opening the entrance door and escorting her to the elevator.

"Antoine," she said, opening the door to her room. "I don't want to be alone tonight."

Emotions overcame her, where she surrendered to him with a passionate kiss. She felt his strength as he lifted her in his arms and carried her to the bedroom. Janice felt his gentle manner and enjoyed his vast knowledge to satisfy her.

It was almost 5:00 in the morning, and they lay breathing hard, their energy exhausted and their bodies in need of rest.

"I never thought of finding someone like you," he whispered, "but the Great Spirits have brought us together."

"Antoine, I love every moment," she said, touching his face, "but we're from two different worlds, and…"

"Shh," he said, touching her lips. "When we first met, I knew our lives would be joined."

"It would be so easy to fall in love with you," she admitted, "but I'm afraid."

"The fear will pass," he said, kissing her, "changed by love."

In his arms, she fell in a deep sleep. They woke to the voice of a lady, claiming to be housekeeping.

"Antoine, it's after 10:00," she said jumping up and running toward the door. "If you could come back later…"

"Yes, ma'am," housekeeping answered from behind the door.

After a shower taking over an hour and dressing, they left the hotel.

"Sorry for being late." She walked toward Throgmorton as Antoine paid the cab driver and waited for several minutes. "Overslept, and Mr. Renaud was kind enough to bring me here."

"Ms. Gardner, we've a slight problem," he said walking over to and leading her away from the students, "so far not a single weapon found not even a knife."

"Any names or markings?" she asked while watching the students looking toward the two. "Who or what were they doing here?"

"Soldiers, no doubt," he said pointing to several remains having ragged or burnt green coats, we believe those with gold buttons were officers, and the rest regulars."

"An army without weapons?" she said, surprised by his findings, "That makes no sense. What else have you learned? I'm sure there has to be more."

"We found parts of wagons and barrels," he said, shaking his head, "which accounts for the explosions suffered by some of the men. But the vast majority of the remains we've uncovered show they were killed by arrows. Seneca."

"You're suggesting this army only brought powder and supplies with them," she began, pausing as if to gather her thoughts, "but no weapons, not even a knife among them?"

"Truthfully, it's a mystery," he blurted. "Over the years I've never known any soldier not having a knife or powder horn."

"Is it true about unarmed men massacred?" Antoine said, walking toward the two. "Soldiers without a single rifle or pistol?"

"Unfortunately, it appears so," he answered. "Nothing makes sense. The representative from the Smithsonian has been in contact with the Canadian government, and they've agreed to allow them to remove and examine the bodies for cause of death."

"You know what will happen," Antoine spoke up. "Reporters from all over will be here by tomorrow."

"Can't be helped," he admitted. "Canadian officials have authorized the removal."

"We need to make a statement," Janice suggested, "reminding people it's too early in our investigation to determine what occurred here."

After a long night of corrections, their prepared statement was ready. With several reporters now surrounding he pit, Janice repeated the statement word for word. However, their message ignored, historians gave interviews of past massacres by tribes over those they felt were invaders. Others gave theories, suggesting these men were traveling across the land to join with the French.

"Look at that," Janice said, placing a copy of the newspaper down, "'unarmed white men slaughtered by Seneca.'"

"Once again claiming we're nothing more than bloodthirsty savages," Antoine said, shaking his head in disbelief.

"Then let's prove them wrong," Janice spoke up. "We find out who these men were."

"May know where you can start," Throgmorton loudly replied. "Joelle, come here."

"Yes, Professor?" She appeared wearing the white jump suit that covered her body.

"Tell them what you told me," he said in an excited tone but calm.

"Well, the buttons," she began, as if embarrassed by the notoriety. "My thesis was buttons and how they influenced history. I interviewed the Button Man, Victor Crawl, who wrote several books on the subject. If anyone can identify these gold buttons, its him."

"Sweetheart," Antoine said, stepping over to kiss her on the cheek, "thank you, and where can we reach him?"

"I've his telephone number and address," she said, her face turning a slight red in color. "He's really nice and loves to talk about buttons."

Two days later Janice and Antoine arrived at the modest home of the Button Man, in the hope he could help. Entering, they met the man of 60, having thick silver hair and bright green eyes.

"I've read about your discovery." He seemed pleased having them in his home.

"Mr. Crawl," Janice began while looking toward the man of six feet. "We'd like you to look at a partial uniform found at the scene."

"Please, it's Victor." He stood tall and walked quickly. "Let's go into my study."

"Victor," Antoine said opening his briefcase, "some of the buttons were damaged by fire, but two are intact."

"Gold," Victor said, looking as Antoine removed the burnt uniform from a paper evidence bag, "most certainly made after the Revolution."

"How can you be so sure?" Janice asked.

"The American army could hardly afford food and equipment," he explained, "they would not purchase gold buttons for officers while men starved. No, this was after the war, and with initials HS on each proves it to be a special order."

"They say you're the expert on buttons," Janice asked with interest. "Why buttons?"

"Wrote two books on them, Ms. Gardner," he said, looking up to her, "and it's an honor. Buttons have been helping people for thousands of years, made of bone, glass, diamonds, and other rare gems. How many malfunctions are reported every year because of buttons, by design or poor construction? What would the world be without buttons, shirts, coats, even shoes?"

"Never gave it that much thought," she said, showing her lack of understanding.

"I've collected buttons all my life." He began to examine the gold buttons while speaking. "Some costing thousands of dollars while others pennies."

"The ones we brought," Antoine asked, "valuable?"

"Oh yes," he replied with a gleam in his eye, "especially with a proper story."

"Can you tell anything about them?" Janice asked, "When or who produced them?"

"Made by Pettrie Button Company," he said, showing them the initial on the back of button. "And they're still in business and have a wonderful collection of every one made."

"You're saying they can tell us who brought these buttons?" Janice exhaled with excitement, "Please say yes."

"Yes, they can," he said, handing the garment back, "but I have a huge request."

"Name it," Antoine spoke up, allowing Janice to catch her breath.

"May I have one of those?" he asked, pointing to one without gold and brown burn marks. "For my collection?"

"Take one of each," Antoine said, removing his pocketknife and cutting one gold then the burnt one off the garment, "and they'll be a great story behind them."

Presented with such valuable items, Victor served them lunch while making phone calls to the company.

With the help of Victor, they read the large sign: Pettrie Button Corporation.

"Nice building," Janice replied, looking toward the modern structure, "so let's go in."

"Janice, I know this may not be the proper place," he said, taking her hand, "but we've been together and need to know if this is more than a story."

"Dinners and nights are great," she said with a smile, "but it is a story that I sharing with you."

"You're not tiring of me yet?" he asked.

"After last night, you have to ask?" she said, kissing him on the cheek.

"Ms. Gardner and Mr. Renaud," a young receptionist met them at the door. "Mr. Pettrie is conducting a meeting, but asked me to escort you to the archives. Unfortunately, it's some distance from here, but I've arranged transportation."

"Clarence," the young receptionist, called out as they entered the large building, "I brought visitors."

"Yes, I've been told of their coming." An older man wearing a white shirt with dress pants in a wheelchair came out. "And asked to assist them."

"Good," she turned and started toward the door, "I'll leave them in your capable hands, Clarence."

"Well, Ms. Gardner," he said wheeling toward her. "I'm a fan, so what may I do for you and Mr. Renaud?"

"Would you have a record of who purchased this button," she said, speaking as Antoine opened his briefcase and showed the garment.

"Please follow me to my desk," he quickly turned and moved to the large desk having several machines, "time you believe it made?"

"Sometime between 1784 and 1786 or 1787," Antoine added.

"Let's see... Military design," he began typing while speaking, "gold."

"Your records," Janice asked, "how far back do they go?"

"From the time the business began," he said, looking into the screen. "Here it is, number 619 with mold. Eighty gold buttons, 75 cents per button, cash paid. There is another order for 1,400 plain green buttons, nine cents per button."

"Does it say who purchased the buttons?" Antoine asked as his heart raced.

"Hiram Schroeder, Colonel," he answered while reading the name. "Local militia."

"Hello," a young well-dressed man in his thirties came from behind. "Royce Pettrie."

"Mr. Pettrie." Janice walked over to the well-mannered and fit man. "Clarence has been extremely helpful."

"Ms. Gardner," he said, taking her hand and warmly shaking it, "it is an honor having you here. I assume this has something to do with the pit found."

"Yes," she answered, knowing there was little reason to avoid answering. "As you are aware there is controversy surrounding the discovery. We're here only to learn what occurred, not to make trouble or news."

"May I see your button?" he asked, looking down at the screen and placing gloves on. "Please, if you don't mind?"

"Of course," Antoine handed him the paper sack.

"Beautiful," he said, examining it closely. "Such fine work and time to produce."

"May I ask what something like that be worth in today's market?" Janice asked. "Not 75 cents?"

"Twenty-four karat gold twice dipped," he said, picking up a magnifying glass from the desk, "carefully dried and buffed, $1,000. Of course, if the story of its relevance in history revealed and rarity, priceless."

"Oh my, we didn't know," Janice said, remembering giving the two away.

"Yes, Victor told my father of your generosity," he began, laughing. "He's a fan of yours and expected no less from you."

"Going to have a lot of explaining to do," she said, looking toward Antoine.

"Nonsense," Royce explained. "Victor will return the gold button to the Smithsonian and keep the lead one."

"Thank you," she said, taking his hand.

"Now for our silence and help," he began, "when you've completed your story, we would like a news conference to be held here with Victor."

"Why not?" Antoine seemed to agree on the spot, "and bring any others that helped here to discuss what we learned."

"Great, and my father, who's away on a business trip," he said, pausing for a moment, "could met you Ms. Gardner."

"Deal," Janice said taking his hand, "but where to now?"

"I spoke with my father," Royce seemed willing to help, "and he believes if you're looking for a Revolutionary officer, Washington is where you should start looking."

"Back at the Smithsonian?" Antoine suggested.

"Father did say it would be there," he replied, "and check the foundations dealing with the Revolutionary War."

"Thank you so much," Janice said in a sincere tone. "You've been a big help."

"Just come back with a great story," he said with a smile. "I'll have my driver take you to the airport."

"Janice, we have a name," he said while they waited for the driver to appear, "and he's a military man."

CHAPTER TWENTY-THREE

While speaking with Susan, she learned the story of the pit was old news; however, it was her network fueling the conflict in an effort to discredit her.

"Well, what should I do about this?" Janice asked after showing him a news conference having Susan to defend her.

"Susan made it clear," he reassured her, "if there is a story, you'll find it and that she supports you 100 percent."

"Of course, she'd say that," Janice said, unnerved, knowing they had brought Susan into the fray. "Those grandsons that run the network are behind this."

"No doubt," he said, giving her a hug. "When you retired, they lost advertisers and audience. It's their way to sway some of the people back, supporting the story of unarmed men traveling to meet with the French."

"Making it look like my judgement is wrong, knowing their alternative motive, and justifying why they allowed me to retire."

"We continue the path given," he said, kissing her on the cheek. "Prove they were armed."

"They also want people to believe the Senecas are blood thirsty." She eased back into his body.

"Our appointment with the Smithsonian isn't for another two hours," he said, slowly removing her robe. "Can show you how peaceful we are."

"You keep showing me this way," she said, turning around as the robe dropped to the floor. "I may never make war."

Finally entering the Smithsonian, an assistant escorted them to the office of Keeler Flynn.

"Ms. Gardner and Mr. Renaud," said a man of 5'10" and totally bald, "I hear you've made some progress."

"We've a name," he began. "Nothing more."

"Just another piece of the puzzle," he said, taking her hand, "and having examined the bodies for injuries, we've added another piece."

"You discovered something?" Janice asked, excited by the suggestion.

"While determining cause of death," he said while shaking Antoine's hand, "we found pieces of whalebone and brass in the bones of several men. We all agree the men died when their powder horns ignited by the fire; however, it's what we didn't find."

"The powder horns," Janice quickly answered.

"Why carry powder horns," Antoine asked the simple question, "without a weapon?"

"One theory is to avoid capture by the British army," he said, repeating what he heard. "With weapons, the British would have arrested them."

"How many soldiers were there?" Janice asked.

"Three hundred and twenty-nine," he answered.

"With so many," Antoine explained, "they'd certainly forage for food with weapons."

"Answer to that," Keeler corrected him, "the tribe took the supplies and used the wagons for firewood."

"Vincent Groote, the historian who came up with this theory," Janice asked. "Would you consider him creditable?"

"Very," he said, confirming her worst fear. "Several books and many degrees."

"Then we really have our work cut out for us," Antoine spoke up.

"Hiram Schroeder paid for the buttons and probably uniforms," Janice informed him, "a colonel in the army."

"When the Smithsonian opened in 1846, they most likely took in anything involving the Revolutionary War. Use the office computers, I'm sure his name might be in there."

For two days, they searched every entry concerning the war and leaders, but nothing on Schroeder.

"Foundations," Janice began, remembering Royce's advice, "we've been researching major historical events and leaders collected. What if there were no major battle, and the information never put in the computer?"

"Let's go ask," Antoine said, deciding anything was better than wasting more time. "What happens when a foundation submits?"

Learning such submissions ended up in a large warehouse, they left for Maryland with hope. Inside, the entire building seemed to go on for miles, having crates and boxes stacked on large steel shelves.

"Ms. Gardner," an elderly lady having flaming red hair strolled out. "I rarely receive visitors, and never one so famous."

"Marsha Brooks," Janice said, reaching her hand out while reading her nametag, "you're the only one here."

"Like I said," she replied, taking her hand, "get few visitors."

"This place is huge," Antoine said, walking to her and holding out his hand, "and you alone care for it?"

"It's a job and quiet," she said, taking his hand and looking him over then winking, "and from time to time, I allow my husband to visit."

"Marsha," Janice asked while looking over the entire structure, "you're our last hope in finding a Colonel Hiram Schroeder who fought during the Revolutionary War."

"Come to my office," she said. She was a bit over weight, but she carried herself well. "Computer may have something on him."

"Janice, if there's nothing here," Antoine said, as if warning her, "I'm afraid we've failed."

"Strange, you said Schroeder was a colonel in the army," Marsha spoke while looking into the screen. "No mention of that but he is referred to in letters by a General Dodd after the war."

"What else," both retorted at the same time, "does it say?"

"Nothing," she continued. "Family presented the memoirs of General Dodd in 1947, a bad year for anything not pertaining to World War II. Looks as if someone read some of the letters, and referenced names of the people."

"So, the Dodd letters are here?" Janice asked quickly.

"Yeah, but," she began, pulling herself away from the desk while writing down numbers, "getting to them…"

"We'll help in any way," Antoine volunteered.

"You asked for it," she said, standing up. "Hop on my cart."

Riding in the motorized cart, Marsha raced around the steel shelves as if having done so many times.

"There they are," she said, stepping on the brake and checking the numbers against those shown on the shelves, "Dodd letters. Fourth shelf, near the end, so you wanted to help."

"How would I get up there?" Antoine asked stepping off the cart.

"Ladder down there," she said, pointing to it. "Just pull it over and climb."

Following her instructions, he stood high over the two watching.

"Four containers with Dodd's name," he shouted down.

"Air tight to protect the writing," she yelled back, "bring them all down and do not open any of them."

One by one, he brought the containers down and with help placed in the cart.

"Can only open them in the clean room," she explained while driving them back. "Gloves and clean jump suits worn at all times. One more thing, nothing leaves this building. Is that clear?"

As required, they entered the clean room with gloves and white jumpsuits.

"White room," Janice replied, "with matching table and chairs."

"Marsha," Antoine said, knowing she was outside monitoring their every move and listening, "there's a lot of work here. We may need more time, days in fact."

"Sweetheart," her voice seemed to surround the room, "I'm here five days a week."

"Tomorrow," Janice yelled out, "I'll have meals delivered."

On the second day, Janice found a folded letter among several drawings of men, including General Washington.

"Antoine, I found this," she said, handing him the letter. "It's in Italian."

"Let me see it," he said, carefully taking it from her hand. "It's addressed to General Washington."

"You read and speak Italian?" another reason to enhance her feelings,.

"Tribe calls me 'Man of Many Tongues,' I know Spanish and several tribal languages that are similar."

"So what does it say?" she asked, wanting to kiss him but holding off.

"Mentions a General Watts," he began reading. "Blue Coats responsible for massacre of settlements executed for their unsanctioned action. Wanted to assure the General his commander knew nothing, along with the British soldiers."

"Massacre," Janice whispered, "we must read his memoirs."

After five days, they read his memoirs of the battles fought, and of the settlements along with his letters. They found all written after the war, including ones to Colonel Tye and his assignment.

"Marsha," Janice said, walking out of the clean room with Antoine behind. "We placed everything back in the containers, but please, would you leave them here?"

"Are they that important?" she asked, realizing they found something.

"Battles and a settlements massacred," Janice repeated what she had read, "with a letter to General Washington. I know Mr. Flynn will want to read them, and contact others in the organization."

Immediately, they arrived at the office of Keeler Flynn, and after waiting 15 minutes, he entered the office.

"What's so important that I'm needed here?" he asked, sitting behind his desk.

"We've discovered documents from a General Dodd," Janice began, "a spy by the name Newton Young reported men paid by Schroeder entering Canada. Dodd assigned a man by the name of Tye to enter Canada, hoping he could warn the British."

For over an hour the two, using notes, reported what they had learned, and afterwards asked him to consider it.

"So this Tye crosses the border pretending to be searching for a murder suspect," Keeler began to recant the story, "but in truth hoping to convince the Mounted Police of Schroeder's intentions?"

"We found drawings of Tye and others," Antoine spoke up, "even one of this Peter Jameson who went by Peters."

"Brad Clark drew them," Janice stated his name, "even one of Washington."

"There is a reference to Blue Coats attacking settlements," Antione added, "and executed by the British."

"If what you say is true," he said, standing up, "it could create an awakening of our history."

"We've so much more to do," Janice reminded him, "and what we don't need now is more theories."

"Your right," he said, agreeing with her. "Besides I haven't seen a reporter in a week."

"For now, we need to find what happened to the Seneca tribe," Janice advised the two, "while collecting other information given to us by Dodd."

"I'll have all the Dodd files sent here to our clean room," Keeler began, "and personally read them. With the drawings, I'll have a very reliable friend come here. She's an expert in forensic facial reconstruction."

"The more people we involve," Janice warned, "the more likely press will find out."

"As an artist with family, she shies away from press," he assured them. "I'll do the Dodd work while you two discover what happened to that Seneca tribe."

"Think we need to speak with Throgmorton," Antoine recommended, "about that bow and arrow his ancestors found."

When notifying Throgmorton they once again needed his services, they found him anxiously waiting at his home.

"You've discovered much more, right?" he said without even waiting for them to enter the home. "Please, tell me everything."

For over two hours while they enjoyed a wonderful lunch, they updated him on all they learned.

"An invading army from America," he blurted out. "They had to be well armed."

"The answer to all our questions is finding where the tribe went," Janice said, leaning back on her chair, "and if they left a record of some kind behind."

"This bow and arrows with sheaf," Antoine said as he examined it. "Ceremonial items like this are highly regarded. Wherever your ancestor found this, the tribe was near very near."

"I've read every word he spoke many times," he replied, stepping toward the encased prize, "he spoke only of a razor back mountain three to four man high. He gave no other description, but near the Niagara River. Having explored that entire area, there is no such mountain."

"All of us know the entire landscape is unstable," Janice said, remembering her college days. "Earth tremors along with erosion."

"True, there were many earthquakes," he said, giving her suggestion more thought, "mountains buried years ago."

"Think your students are up for a paid field trip?" Janice asked.

"For money and a chance to be part of something?" Throgmorton said, excitement in his voice, "they'll come running."

"In that case," Antoine spoke up. "Call them, and I'll have everything prepared for the adventure of a lifetime."

After a week of preparation, the young students began exploring along the Niagara River. Each mile was photographed and documented by soil or rock contents. The nights were spent analyzing the makeup of the soil and comparing each rock sample with another.

"Soil samples show very little chemical differences," Edward in a disappointed tone. "Rocks show no similarity. Almost like the mountains were separate from the soil, it's as if each mountain was the product of different ionic compounds."

"Been only three days," Janice said while they tested each rock. "The falls are behind us, so maybe we'll get lucky."

On the fifth day, Janice began looking over the previous days photos, and noticed one of the students standing on a strange looking rock.

"Edward," she shouted out, "is this Gregory standing on this rock?"

"Yeah, that's Gregory," he said as if ashamed while examining at the photo of the young man, no shirt, yelling, "Top of the world!"

"Would you bring him here," she asked in a calm tone.

Several minutes later Edward escorted Gregory and a young female to her.

"Told you we'd get in trouble," the young girl replied as they entered the tent, "playing on those sharp rocks."

"We were just playing around, Ms. Gardner," Gregory said, defending himself and the young girl. "Coming back for lunch, and it just happened."

"Guys, I'm not mad," she said, laying out the photo. "Where did you take this picture?"

"About a mile from here," Gregory answered, "but it's not in the search area."

"Show me," she said, as if it were a demand.

On a run, the two escorted her and Edward to the spot, where Janice immediately began scrutinizing the terrain.

"Edward, what do you see?" she asked while climbing on the rock formation.

"Shark fin," he began guessing.

"Get up here," she said, holding out her hand to assist him, "and look around."

"Three maybe four protruding formations," he replied while looking, "but none three to four men high."

"What's all the excitement?" Antoine came running over. "Running around as if you're on fire."

"Step back and tell me what you see," Janice asked.

"You're thinking this is the razorback," Antoine replied after studying the entire rock formation, "all one mountain."

"It's not high enough," Edward pointed out.

"Only one-way to find out," Janice said jumping to the ground. "We have an expert come here while we keep looking."

"Rock Eater," Edward whispered as he climbed down. "He's the best."

"Who's this Rock Eater," Janice asked with interest.

"Read about him and his crew," Edward explained. "Miners in Mexico trapped after a collapse. For three days, experts made a mess of things, one collapse after another. He came down with his crew, and three days later, rescued them by going in the back way. His motto is, 'We do what others can't.'"

"Sounds like the man we need," Janice said with excitement in her voice.

"Know where they're out of?" Antoine asked, surrendering to her decision.

"New Orleans," Edward answered, "but expensive."

"Janice, you know this might not be anything," Antoine said, speaking softly while looking around. You sure?"

"We keep looking in the meantime," she said, grabbing his hand, "and if it isn't maybe, they could help."

Three days pasted, when two men drove up in a large military truck.

"Looking for a Antoine Renaud." He stood over 6'3", looking like a professional body builder.

"I'm Antoine," Antoine said, taking his hand and feeling a strong handshake, "and this is…"

"No need," he said, releasing his grip to take Janice by the hand. "Ms. Gardner, most pleased to make your acquaintance."

"Thank you," she said, surprised by his gentleness. "You come highly rated."

"This here is my partner and best friend," he said, turning toward the man of 40 with balding hair and bulging stomach, "Miles Rooseburg."

"Everyone, hello," he said while looking over the area. "So where is this mountain?"

"We're not sure," Edward spoke up. "Might be a series of small mountains."

"Please take me to it," he said. A strange expression came over his face. "Need to meet it."

As requested, the entire group, including every student, walked to the formation.

"Well, there it is," Edward began, pointing to it, "not much of a mountain."

"God and Mother Nature have their own timetable," he said, walking toward the rock formation, "and like a volcano erupting, man can do nothing but step aside and marvel."

"What is he doing?" Edward asked while watching the man touch it.

"Talking," said Rock with a smile. "Let him be."

"What could you have done to anger the Lord," he began speaking to it. "Did you boast of becoming the mightiest mountain of all by reaching into Heaven? Do not fear, for I will learn what secrets you hold."

"Nothing to do now but wait," Rock said while Miles strolled to the next formation. "Is that coffee I smell?"

"May I ask what Mr. Rooseburg is looking for?" Janice asked, handing him a cup.

"You want to know if it's all one mountain," he explained, pouring the coffee and handing her the filled cup. "He'll know."

"Thank you," he said, taking the cup and giving him another. "Is he a geologist?"

"He studied it," he responded, filling his cup, "but what he knows isn't in any book."

For over two hours they waited for him to finish, as he walked from one end to the other.

"Rock, it's all one large mountain," he said entering the tent, "maybe two miles long and broadens out by half or three quarter miles."

"There's your answer," he said, standing up and handing him a half drank cup of coffee.

"Sad mountain," he said, drinking from the cup, "been waiting for me."

"So, Mr. Renaud just what are you wanting to find?" he asked, turning toward him.

"Bodies," he said, getting straight to the point, "hundreds maybe."

"Something to do with the Seneca tribe," he answered. "Read about it."

"Yes," Janice spoke up. "We need to know what happened to them."

"Know some would prefer to leave it be," Antoine stood up and said, "only Indians that some reporters call savages."

"My ancestors came here by boat with $6," he responded, taking another cup and filling it, "worked hard for very little. They never met or seen a cowboy or Indian. My first meeting with one was in the Army wearing the same uniform. Built a fine company because my ancestors taught me to stay clear of bullshit."

The entire group began laughing, and all knew he was the man they needed.

"Need the entire team," Miles said, laying the empty cup down. "Special equipment to seal any entrance and pumps."

"Be expensive, Mr. Renaud. Around a million and a half," he said, pausing for several seconds. "You can find others to do it cheaper, but not better."

"If the Federation is unwilling to pay," Janice spoke up, "I will."

"Federation will pay," Antoine said, making a promise. "The entrance, where is it?"

"About a quarter mile from here," Miles said, pointing in the direction.

"Understand we may find nothing," Rock warned, "but if you agree, I'll have my people and equipment here in five days."

"Miles said the mountain waited for him," Janice spoke up. "Let's find out why."

"Five days," he said, taking Antoine's hand.

"I'll have a contract ready," he responded, shaking.

Members of the Federation had arrived to meet with Antoine, and they agreed to permit Janice to attend.

"Antoine we came to speak of this arrangement made with Rock Eater Mining," the one sitting at the head of the table spoke first. "It is a sizable amount without assurances."

"It is, but we seek truth," he said, speaking to the other six members, "to learn it, we must discover what happened to one of our tribes."

"Concerning this matter," another man began speaking, "we all have heard much."

"Theories describing the great Seneca tribe as savages," he said, again speaking to each man at the table, "killing unarmed soldiers."

"What proof do you have that this cave holds such truth?" the man at the head of the table ask.

"None," he admitted, "but we must try regardless of cost."

"Gentlemen," Janice spoke up, "if the cost is to great I will furnish the funds."

"Knowing it was your network that questioned your judgement," he continued, "creating doubt in many minds, and you wish only to prove them wrong."

"There have been rumors concerning your attraction to Mr. Renaud," another spoke up causing others to object, "clouding such judgement."

"I will not allow anyone to speak so ill of her." Antoine stood up and pounded his fist into the table.

"Antione, I can speak to it." Janice stood. "Yes, I am in love with him. We stand together as one, to discover the truth. His passion for truth has driven that love, and he has never wavered in that search."

"Gentlemen, I hereby resign from the Federation," Antoine taking her hand, "and will continued the path chosen."

"Antoine," the man spoke from the head of the table. "Please allow us a minute alone."

"Janice, did you mean what you said in there?" he asked, holding her.

"You know I did," she said, allowing a passionate kiss, "and you would resign for me?"

"Easiest decision ever made," he said, holding her tight. "I love you."

"Antoine," the one at the head of the table walked out, "you will received the needed funds. Understand if all fails, we will discuss your request to resign."

"Thank you," they both spoke.

With contract in hand, and funds the digging began.

"Miles?" Janice found him alone in the tent taking a bottle of water from the refrigerator. "How's it going?"

"Crews dug down 60 feet," he said, taking a drink, "another 30 or 40 will do it. Not to worry, that mountain wants us here."

"Janice," Antoine shouted as she lay in bed after a long morning.

"What is it?" she said, jumping up from the cot. "Did they find the entrance?"

"See for yourself," he said, taking her hand and running toward the men covered in dirt and sweat. "Everyone's coming."

"There she be," Rock said, scraping the dirt away from what appeared to be an arch. "The old mountain hid it well."

"So what now?" Antoine anxiously asked while the rest began snapping photos.

"Seal the entrance before removing the rocks," he said, looking at the obstruction. "Once it's cleared start pumping out the poor air. Then with air tanks and protective clothes, enter."

"Tomorrow," Miles whispered in her ear. "Told you she wanted us here."

The following day, five entered with Rock leading the group. Miles tied to Janice, and Antoine to Edward.

"Hold on," Rock said, kneeling down, "we have bodies, so need to back out. Looks to be a man and women, as if he tried to protect her from the falling rocks."

"Why leave?" Antoine blurted out.

"Need to place all bodies in plastic to avoid decomposing," he said, explaining, "and I want to build a walkway to avoid stepping on any others we find."

"How long will that take?" Antoine said, showing frustration.

"A day or two," Rock replied. "That's if you want it done right."

"Rock, were the two you saw Senecas?" Janice asked.

"Can't say about Seneca," he said, removing his tanks, "but Native American or Canadian definitely."

"Any bodies found can't be moved without permission," Antoine explained. "It's a Native burial ground, and Federation has rules."

"Figure you not wanting press," Rock began, "figure with wild fires out west and tornado brewing in the south, you have about a week before someone notices us. I'd suggest you make up your mind, waste time, or be prepared for the entire world to come looking over our shoulders."

"You need a day to get the walkway in," he pointed out, "and shore up the sides."

"Make it quick," he agreed. "My men work fast."

"I'll call Keeler," Janice spoke up, "you deal with the Federation."

With great care, the two bodies carefully place in steel container, and flown to Washington, where a spiritual tribe member joined.

Working with the men, Rock began as they dressed to enter the mountain.

"Found nine bodies all placed in plastic," he said. "We have lights now, so just stay on the walkway."

Entering the well-lit cave, the walls were covered in paintings.

"Janice, look, it's the history of the tribe," Antoine said, examining the paintings, "not sure what this one is about."

"Sent a picture of it to Keeler yesterday," Rock spoke through the mask, "said it's a prophecy from some person named Tenskwatawa. Something about an army of the dead, vanquishing an entire tribe."

"Doesn't make sense," Antoine replied as he moved to the next painting, "it shows that the tribe multiplied and live in peace."

"Antoine, look here," Janice yelled out from the mask. "White men in red coats with rifles inside the village."

"Many warriors left with the soldiers," he said while moving around her. "The chief left and his son became chief called Longteeth, or maybe tooth. Six returned, bringing death, many died of white man's sickness."

"They fought for the British during the war," Janice said with excitement in her voice, "and brought back diseases."

"Once again, they multiplied," he continued to move down, "living in peace. People happy, Chief marries Little Sparrow."

"That's the last painting," Miles came up to him, "think if there's more, it's behind that wall of rock. The bodies we found appeared running toward what's behind the rocks, mountain collapsed before they got there."

"More delays," said Rock in disgust.

"Got an idea," Miles mentioned. "Our tanks are emptying, so let's leave."

"Alright, what's your idea?" Rock asked while removing his air tanks.

"Need to speed things up."

"We can't take out the entire wall without the mountain coming down," Miles began while walking over and opening the refrigerator, but we can take out a section shoring it up as we remove each stone. We don't need much room, just enough to let us pass."

"Remove stone on the right..." Rock understood his idea, "Shore it up and move in with lights."

"Think we first seal it, recommending only, pumps still working. While we work on that, you two can start taking pictures."

"We can use my camera," Edward blurted out while taking a water bottle, "make for a great book for my students."

"I want photos of everyone," Janice said, walking toward him, "including the Rock Eaters who we can't thank enough."

"Of course," he agreed, "this is history in the making."

As they began working on the collapsed wall, roll after roll of film documented every painting along with the poor tribe members in plastic.

Leaving the mountain for another tank, Janice removed her mask.

"You haven't called me in three days," a familiar voice shouted out.

"Susan!" Janice exclaimed, running to her. "What are you doing here? I thought they sent you out west to cover the fires."

"Two days of eating smoke," she began, laughing, "and missed my sister, so I snuck away while no one was looking."

"So happy you being here," Janice said, hugging her.

"You discovered the lost tribe, right?" she said, excited as she returned the hug.

"Yes," Janice told her, jumping up and down. "Want to see?"

"Dark places scare me." Her expression changed, then she laughed. "Of course, I want to see."

After preparing her with protective suit and oxygen tanks, they entered.

"Antoine," Janice shouted while he continued to photograph the paintings, "I want you to meet my little sister."

"It's an honor to finally meet you, Susan," Antoine said, handing the camera to Edward. "Janice has told me so much about you."

"She talks about you, too," Susan said, taking his hand. "What's in the plastic?"

"They're the dead, Susan," Janice said looking toward one. ":Long story why we can't move them but tell you later."

"Who the hell is she?" Rock came over. "Don't need more visitors."

"My little sister, Susan Ehlert," Janice reported. "She's reporter but can be trusted."

"Hope so," he said, looking her over. "What, different family?"

"No, just one big happy family," Janice said, squeezing her hand.

"Be another couple of hours before we break through," he continued, "so best go out and get some rest. Once we've pumped the air out, think it might be an all-nighter."

"Let's do what he asks," Antoine suggested, "and grab something to eat."

"Well, what's he like?" Susan asked while alone in the tent. "Remember, no secrets."

"Kind, and I really care for him," Janice said, speaking honestly.

"How's he in bed?" she whispered.

"Susan!" Janice said in a slightly higher tone but still a whisper, then laughed. "Wonderful."

"I knew it!" she said as the two began laughing.

"Looks like the two of you are having a good time." Antoine came in with a pizza. "You need to eat, and I'll leave you be."

Finishing the pizza, the two fell asleep, only to be woke by Rock.

"Need to gear up," he said, gently touching their shoulders. "We broke through an hour ago and sealed the entrance."

"What about the air?" Janice asked while sitting up.

"Pump it out." He turned to leave. "You really need to come."

After placing the necessary protective gear on, they followed him inside.

"Turn them on," Rock ordered as the moved past the collapsed wall.

Suddenly portable lights lii up the entire cavern.

"Oh my God," Janice said in amazement.

"We counted over 90 tipis," Rock reported, "with five to six people inside each and a couple hundred scattered outside."

"Asphyxiation looks to be the cause of death," Miles said walking toward them. "Took us six hours to cut through a section of it with modern steel tools."

"Without oxygen, the people were entombed like you see in Egypt," Rock continued, "their bodies well preserved."

"There's more," Miles said. "Be careful and follow me."

"Look at all the painting on the walls," Antoine said while following.

"Entering what appeared to be a burial ground," Miles pointed.

"Found these two graves," he said kneeling down and picking up one of the saddlebags, crosses and saddlebags."

"White men," Edward blurted out.

"The rest are Indian," Miles stood and looked around, "and have symbols and jewelry on each one."

"What are they doing here?" Susan asked.

"Can't say," Rock admitted, "but nonetheless, they're here."

"Let's place the saddlebags in plastic like the bodies," Antoine suggested, "and send them to Smithsonian for examination."

"Good idea," Janice agreed. "Maybe they can make sense of this."

"They made an effort to bury them proper," Edward said.

"Two white men buried among the tribe," Janice softly spoke, "why?"

CHAPTER TWENTY FOUR

W"This discovery is much too large to hide from the public," Edward began as they entered the tent. "We must photograph and film every inch of the cave."

"Can we get additional lighting in the cavern?" Antoine asked while noticing the students placing the saddlebags in steel containers. "I need to examine the paintings."

"You wanting to start tonight?" Rock asked. "If so, just tell me."

"Sooner the better," he replied.

"I'll do the interviews," Susan spoke up, "and have my cameraman who's staying at the hotel come and film everything."

"You brought your cameraman with you?" Janice asked, taking a deep breath.

"He goes where I go," she said with a slight smile. "What can I say? He's loyal."

"Fine," she said with a smile. Janice could only admire her. "Call him."

With the entire cavern covered with lights, they reentered.

"Warriors discover an army that blinded the warriors," Antoine interpreted the paintings as best he could, "watch as they kill two white men, one wearing a red coat, the other buckskins."

"The two graves," Janice shouted out.

"They bring the bodies and saddlebags back to the village," he continued, "then brought them here for burial."

"Red coat," Edward spoke up, "either a British Soldier or Mounted Police."

"Oh my God, it has to be Tye," Janice said, taking Antoine by the arm. "Remember, Dodd asked him to go to Canada on a mission."

"Possible," he began, moving to the next painting. "Tribe begins to prepare for the army by cutting down fields and placing small pieces of wood under the dry grass."

"You're saying they prepared the field for a fire?" Rock asked. "Brilliant I can't believe the chief even thought of it."

"Army of green that shined entered with cannon and rifle," Antoine said with a smile, "the gold buttons on the uniforms would shine in the sunlight."

"They were well armed," Edward shouted out. "Hallelujah!"

"The soldiers began firing cannon and rifle as the battle began," Antoine said, closely looking at the painted scene. "Fires started with explosions. A white man leading the soldiers kills his horse by pistol, before dying."

"The horse's skull we found," again, Edward screamed.

"What's he talking about?" Susan leaned over to ask Janice.

"Found it among the dead," she whispered, "with a single bullet hole."

"Would have been better using it on himself," Susan said, thinking aloud.

"Probably," Janice said, laughing at her observation.

"With arrows and fire, all died," Antoine said, shaking his head. "Must have been a terrible sight watching the men die in such a manner. Once the fires cooled, they widened the pit, and bodies were placed in it."

"What happened to their weapons?" Edward asked, demanding to know. "Do they say?"

"Warriors gathered up all weapons," he said, trying to maintain his patience, "including the cannons and carried them to the great river. Taking nothing, everything thrown into it."

"Do you realize those weapons could still be there?" Edward the professor again spoke, but understood all thought it, "but buried under tons of sediment?"

"You're getting ahead of yourself," Rock spoke up. "What happened next?"

"Out of fear that another army would come seeking revenge," he continued, "they moved here. Spent at least one year here, maybe more. It's the last painting."

"We must find those weapons," Edward insisted. "It would prove everything."

"No, the first thing we must do is identify who the two were," Antoine replied, "then discover why this army came here."

"Once we film everything," Janice offered her opinion, "we could exhume the two bodies and send them to the Smithsonian."

"This being a tribal burial site," Antoine replied, "we cannot disturb any of the Senecas' bodies, but they're not part of it."

"You need to call the people from the Federation," Janice recommended, "while I call Keeler."

"I'll have my cameraman start first thing in the morning," Susan said with excitement in her voice, "and prepare to break the story."

"We promised to hold a news conference at the Pettrie factory," Janice turned to her, "Hope you understand."

"Fine," Susan seemed satisfied with it, "as long as I'm the first reporter to broadcast this wonderful discovery."

"Janice, this means you'll be our voice," Antoine spoke up.

"Susan, it's going to be a long night," she said, taking her by the hand. "We need to prepare."

Before entering the cave, Janice explained the importance of the discovery while Susan and her cameraman stood filming. Inside, she carefully pointed to the paintings, as Susan asked her to translate their importance. It was a solemn moment when filming the devastation caused by the mountain collapse, the silent village of tipis.

"Ms. Gardner." Keeler Flynn stood waiting as they came out. "I had to come and see this for myself."

"Keeler," she said, surprised by his appearance. "It's so wonderful having you here."

"They told me you were preparing to broadcast this discovery," he continued, "but I couldn't wait."

"Susan Ehlert, this is Keeler Flynn from the Smithsonian," Janice said, introducing her. "Her network will air the broadcast."

"Thought I'd have Miles take Mr. Flynn inside," Rock walked over as he shook Susan's hand, "unless you would prefer to do it."

"Miles would be perfect," Janice said with a smile. "Maybe he'll speak to the mountain about why it let his happened."

"No reason," Miles came walking up. "The mountain wasn't at fault, just happened. Mr. Throgmorton has asked to join us, got some questions for the man."

"Tell Edward he can gear up," Janice replied. "We have a few more things to do before sending this to her network."

"Satisfied?" Susan asked after reviewing the entire interview. "If so, we send."

"Breaking news at 12:00," Janice watched as she pressed the key on the computer. "Major discovery and complete story at 6:00."

"You have a copy," she said, relaxing on the chair, "and network theirs."

"It's not over yet," Janice added. "Need more than paintings to convince people."

After an hour Keeler and the others came out, saying nothing.

"So sad," Keeler replied while taking off his protective suit, "but a wonderful discovery that finally tells their story."

"Janice and Antoine," Edward yelled to them. "Keeler has an interesting theory where the army may have been going."

"After reading the letters and journal of Mr. Dodd," Keeler began, opening his briefcase as he spoke, "he made it clear Schroeder sought revenge against the Blue Coats. We know they had attacked several settlements, killing his daughter and grandson. I believe this army was intending to attack Kingstown, their line of march proves it."

"Why Kingstown? Susan asked while looking toward her cameraman.

"After the war, many of the Americans who supported England," he said, removing his computer and showing the settlement, "fled the country and settled there. Had he succeeded in destroying that settlement, Canada would have little choice but to declare war against America."

"These letters," Susan's interest intensified, "maybe you could show them to me and explain your theory."

"The saddlebags might have something of interest," Antoine pointed out, "take them back with you."

"Mr. Renaud, I understand this is a Federation project," Keeler said, choosing his words carefully. "However the two graves are not Native American. I'm asking they be removed, so we may examine them to learn their identity."

"I'll speak with the members," he promised. "No doubt, they will agree."

"When I learn something," he said, breathing normal, "I will call. Ms. Ehlert if you wish, there is enough room on the jet."

"Off to Washington," Susan told Janice, giving her a quick kiss on the cheek. "Call you later."

"You taught her well," Antoine said as she and the cameraman climbed into his vehicle. "She's a great sister and reporter."

"Sister and life savior," she added.

By day two, networks from around the country and world surrounded the entire area with news trucks, demanding an interview or entry into the cave.

"Your network has done it again," Edward entered her tent, fuming, "using Vincent Groote as their historian."

"Retired, remember," she said, turning toward him. "So what is he saying?"

"That I, Professor Edward Throgmorton, have a history of defending Native Americans," he began while pacing, "that the tribe fled to the mountain after having massacred the defenseless soldiers. He further insists Senecas, like many exaggerate, knowing they cannot omit defeating people who could not fight back. He continues to preach his theory, that they came to Canada to join the French against the British.

"Settle down," Janice calmly spoke, "come tomorrow, Mr. Groote might have to issue an apology to you."

"I don't understand," he said, sitting down on her cot. "Why?"

"Susan is releasing her interview with Mr. Flynn," she said, opening her refrigerator and taking out two bottles, "concerning the Dodd letters. They will also discuss the contents of the saddlebags, which will support everything we've been saying."

"What did they discover?" Edward jumped to his feet.

"Take a water," she said. "Keeler confirmed that one of the bodies is Tye."

"The other man?" he asked, taking the water from her hand.

"His name is Captain Zachary Pendle," Janice said, taking a sip of water. "Mounted Rifles, but we know them as the Royal Canadian Mounted Police."

For an hour she conveyed what Keeler had learned from Pendle's complete report, their meeting with the French leaders, and all their demands. Included was his instructions to escort Tye back across the border if Peters remained at large.

"I feel better now," Edward admitted, "so much learned, yet we still don't have a shred of proof concerning the weapons."

"Keeler mentioned he's working on it," she affirmed his concern. "Don't really know what he's planning, but something."

"We need to speak with all those news people," Antoine entered, expressing concern. "The Federation had the Canadian government proclaim this area as Native Canadian burial grounds."

"What's it mean?" Edward asked.

"No one can enter without tribal approval," he explained. "Bodies left untouched."

"Can't let them leave without something," Janice began to think of the consequences of such action. "What if we gave each network a copy of the cavern. We can explain why they can't enter, and that the decision was made without our knowledge."

Gathering the crews, they explained the changes and why. However, he allowed them to witness and film the removal of the two men, taken by an honor guard.

The following day, he handed each a video disc of the interior, and all seemed satisfied, and knowing the government was now involved, they began leaving.

"What happened to all those news vans?" Miles asked when they were sitting alone the kitchen tent.

"Government regulation," Antoine explained. "They can't enter, and we can't leave."

"Makes no sense," he said, admitting the obvious, "trying to make things right for them inside and the mountain."

"You're right," Antoine said in a strange tone. "We need to do something about that."

Two days, later several members of the Seneca tribe arrived, each dressed in traditional clothing with headdress.

"Who are they?" Janice asked.

"Spiritual Seneca leaders," Antoine said, informing her, "for the next day or so, they will perform rituals allowing the spirits of the dead to leave the cave."

"That's nice." Janice watched as they began singing and chatting.

"Had to be Miles to remind me," he said, as if disappointed having not thought of it.

"Maybe there's a little Native American in all of us," she whispered. "You do know he speaks to the mountain."

"Hello, you two lovebirds," Susan yelled out while leaving a military vehicle.

"You are so welcomed," Janice said, running to her arms. "How did the interview go?

"I'm fine, and how are you?" Susan said, ignoring her question. "What is going on over there?"

"Releasing the souls of the dead," Antoine said walking toward her. "How are you?"

"No camera allowed," she said, giving him a hug,

"Sacred," he answered, "no camera."

"Too bad," she said, releasing him. "Make for an interesting story."

"So, I'm okay, and you're okay," Janice said, expressing excitement. "How did your interview go with Keeler?"

"Great," she said, showing the exhilaration from the interview, "so good, your ex-network refuses to even mention this discovery."

"Sir," a young man standing waited behind them. "I've an important message."

"Oh right," he said, turning to him, "Private First Class Timothy Robes with the Canadian Royal Mounted Police."

"An honor, and we appreciate your service," Janice quickly acknowledged him.

"It's an honor," he said, handing Antoine a letter.

"Keeler arranged all this," Susan said, winking at the young man. "Handsome, yes?"

"Ignore her, Timothy," Janice said to him. "She flirts a lot."

"I am aware, Ms. Gardner," he said, his face turning reddish.

"The Commander wishes a meeting," Antoine blurted out. "Young man, any idea what he wants?"

"I am not privileged to that information," he said, standing at attention, "only to say if you wish, I could provide transportation."

"What are we waiting on?" Susan shouted. "My cameraman's inside."

"I'll tell Throgmorton we're leaving," Antoine said while walking away.

"What about clothes?" Janice asked.

"Command is in the center of the city," Timothy replied.

Without further decision, they entered the vehicle and proceeded to meet the commander of the Mounted Police. Passing through the gate manned by two armed police, Timothy drove directly to the Commander's office.

"Hope to see you later, Ms. Ehlert," he said, opening her door.

"Never know," she said, giving him a quick kiss on the cheek.

Inside they met the adjutant to the Commander and were immediately escorted in the office where he sat behind his desk.

Speaking at attention, he said, "Commander Otis Quinn."

"Welcome," he said, standing up from behind the desk. "Please make yourselves comfortable, and have some refreshments."

"Water?" Susan asked looking toward her cameraman and Janice.

"I'll see to it," the adjutant immediately replied then disappeared.

"Sir, may I ask why you wish to meet us?" Antoine questioned him.

"Captain Zachary Pendle," he stood over six feet having a slender firm body. "We are grateful you returned our companion to us. So much so that we wish to return the favor by helping to discover the location of the weapons."

"We'd appreciate such help," Antoine's heart began to beat faster, "but how?"

"Three constables are expert divers," he began, "and have volunteered. We've commandeered boats and equipment for only seven days."

"We need Throgmorton," Antoine said, thinking aloud. "He should give some insight on where to begin."

"Keeler thought so. too," he said leaning against his desk, "had his own ideas, but thought it best to keep them to himself."

"I'll arrange for him to be here tomorrow," Antoine promised.

Before the sun even rose, an officer found Edward sitting in one of the military vehicle working on his computer. Waking everyone, they quickly dressed and followed the officer to Edward.

"Morning," he said in a cheerful tone. "Wonderful news about our help."

"Strange man," the officer said while walking away. "Breakfast in an hour."

"Having spoken with Keeler," he began, as if everyone felt exuberant. "We both agree the warriors would use the cave as a starting point. Therefore, given terrain six miles east and west..."

"Search the banks six miles east of the cave," Antoine studied the line made on the computer, "and six miles west."

"Edward, that's a very narrow search pattern," Janice said, taking a deep breath of morning air. "Should we expand it to 12?"

"With only seven days," he explained, "a diver can search for a mile or mile in half but oxygen runs out and exhaustion."

"They are volunteering after all," Antoine pointed out, "but we could expand the search to nine miles east and west."

"Three miles a day," Throgmorton began, "six days."

"Let's find Commander Quinn," Janice suggested.

Having agreed to the nine-mile search pattern, the divers watched on the boats as they marked where to begin from the edge of the cliffs. For two days, the divers worked in sunny weather, but the third day spent waiting for the lightning storm to pass.

"Lost one day," Throgmorton said looking into the television broadcasting weather reports, "no storm tomorrow."

Fourth day, the divers found nothing; no longer were they optimistic about locating the weapons.

"Two more days," Antoine said while watching the divers entering the water, "then we go back empty handed."

"We at least tried," Throgmorton added to his misery.

"Hey," Janice said in a lively tone, "this search isn't over."

"My sister has faith," Susan said, taking her hand, "so let's wait and see how this day goes, alright?"

Watching for a half hour, the small group sat on the green soft grass enjoying the light breeze.

"Somethings going on down there," Janice began looking down as the boats began to close up.

A small balloon came to the surface, where the men on the boat began shouting. From where the balloon floated the diver surfaced, and held up a musket.

"It's a rifle," Janice shouted out. "They found them!"

For an hour, they searched for a place to climb down, and a cove where one of the boats could pick them up.

"You found the weapons," everyone said in harmony.

It was stuck on a rock ledge," the young diver blurted out, "just sitting there like over a fireplace."

"Need equipment to move the mud," another diver spoke up, "and heavy winches."

"Even larger boats," Throgmorton said while looking at the size of the boats. "Remember there may be cannons."

The discovery sparked interest by all the local merchants and was seen on national television, interviewed by Susan. Boats of all sizes surrounded the area, divers with pumps sucking up mud while others waited anxiously.

"Susan," Janice walked over as her cameraman filmed.

"Five minutes, we go live," she said. "Everyone wants to see a cannon come out."

Winches began dropping lines into the water, men shouting orders.

"This is Susan Ehlert reporting," she said, looking into the camera.

As the winch strained, the mouth of the cannon appeared then wheels.

"Hot damn!" Throgmorton shouted out as Susan continued to report to the world the discovery.

"Antoine," Janice said, grabbing him around his arms with excitement as the cannon came to rest on one of the barrages. "We did it and proved everything they said."

"Marry me," he said in a calm manner.

"What?" she said, releasing him as if stunned by his proposal.

"I love you," he said. gently holding her, "I don't want this to be the end, but the beginning."

"Are you sure?" she said, pausing before giving an answer. "You're pure blood, and I'm…"

"Please just tell me how you feel," he said, touching her lips.

"I do love you," she said, wrapping her arms around him, "and yes, I'll marry you."

"Good, but before telling everyone," he said, listening to Susan reporting. "Let's wait until she's finished. The world may not be ready for our news."

It seemed a lifetime before Susan stopped reporting the discovery, but Janice bursting with enthusiasm was able to suppress the urge to shout out the news.

"Everybody," Janice shouted out, "Antoine proposed, and I said yes."

"It's about time," Throgmorton said, taking his hand. "Thought a shotgun marriage may be needed."

"That is wonderful," Susan said, giving Janice a hug. "I'll be your maid of honor and…"

"Hold on," she said, stopping her from going on, I haven't even gotten a ring yet."

"By tonight," Antoine promised, "a ring will be on your finger."

For two days, they brought up countless muskets and knives of all shapes and sizes. The powder horns of all items became the topic of discussion, many hand carved from bone of whale or large animal such as walrus.

"Bet each warrior hated to toss these in the river," one of the captains of the vessels said while placing them in containers, "some damn nice."

"Along with the knives," Antoine said, looking over at the container.

"Well, the Smithsonian will have a fun week," the captain said, chewing on his unlit pipe. "Rifles with burnt stocks and knives blades. So, what's next? Got your proof."

"Don't really know," he admitted. "It's up to the Federation and government now."

"Well, good luck with those two organizations." He began laughing.

Having transferred all the weapons to the Smithsonian, they returned to the mountain to learn that the spiritual leaders had left.

"When did the leaders leave?" Antoine asked Miles, who sat quietly in the tent, "And what did they have to say?"

"Looked no worse for wear," he chuckled. "Claimed the spirits of the dead were free to leave. Only thing is, they all decided to stay."

"Miles, how do you know that?" Antoine joined by Janice and Susan.

"Mountain told me," he continued. "Apparently the Great Spirits came down and spoke to the dead. After a lot of discussion, they agreed to remain.

The mountain is their home and resting place. Mountain agrees, and has welcomed them to stay."

"Mr. Miles, mountains and the dead can't talk," Susan pointed out.

"So they say," he said, standing up and walking toward the entrance.

"He's a strange person in many ways," Janice replied as he left, "but I've come to believe him."

"Regardless," Antoine spoke up, "it's been decided that Chief Longteeth and Little Sparrow be placed in the cavern with all the others. The entrance sealed for good, and a wall built around the entire mountain."

"A wall?" Susan asked with surprise.

"To keep out grave robbers wanting to loot the burial site," he informed her. "Having the bodies, they were able to construct facial features. Federation intends to have a bronze statue made of the two, and along the wall, and all the paintings shown."

"Wonder what the mountain will say to that," Susan said, half-joking.

"What of the bodies from the pit?" Janice asked.

"Still in discussion," Antoine said, shaking his head. "Americans, but property of Canada."

"Well, every news outlet is clamoring for interviews," Susan began, "so we need to call everyone involved and arrange a date."

"Throgmorton has already told the students," Janice began, "Rock Eaters are still here, and we need to call the rest."

"Canadian Mounties can contact the people there," Antoine suggested. "Keeler, his staff and others."

"Can't forget Victor Crawl," Janice added. "The Button Man was helpful."

"Start making list," he recommended. "I'll call Royce and have him set the dates for the interview at the factory."

"What about Ulanderson?" she asked knowing all the trouble they had caused him.

"Give him a call," he agreed, "let him decide."

On the day of the interview weeks in the making, all arrived and greeted by Royce and the entire family of Pettrie.

"Look at all the people," Antoine said holding her tight, what started as a simple tree falling led to this."

"Every major news organization but the one that I worked never showed," she said, somewhat disappointed, "they must really hate me."

"No, they envy you," he said, kissing her on the forehead, "and are too stupid to admit it."

"Mr. Renaud," a young officer ran to his side, "the Prime Minister will arrive in 10 minutes. He was a little late."

"It's okay, just starting to introduce everyone to the press corps," he replied.

Finally, the Prime Minister arrived, just in time to take the stage.

"Ladies and gentlemen, he began as if having rehearsed the speech, we are here to celebrate a wonderful historical event. One that changed the course of history, and bounded by truth. Unbeknown to a great tribal nation, they alone averted a great war between our country and America. We now believe an American army seeking revenge, intended to destroy Kingstown. In a great battle, the Seneca tribe prevented it from happening. We know only through their paintings how the battle unfolded, but the efforts of all those here today confirmed the facts. We owe the Seneca tribe a debt of gratitude. Had it not been for their bravery, thousands of Americans and Canadians would have suffered death in war. It is my honor to proclaim the mountain where they now rest is a National Cemetery."

Everyone began clapping, joyful over the news.

The next speaker was Throgmorton, who spoke of the history surrounding Colonel Schroeder and Peters. He spoke of the loyalty of Tye, in pursuit of justice for the young British soldier Howard Deanery and the wife of Peters.

Keeler was next, surprising everyone by including faces in clay of all those identified by drawings.

"The drawings by Brad Clark allowed us to recreate their image," he began while walking over to the bust of Schroeder, "but the mistrust caused by the killing of two brave men is undeniable. Never knowing what happened to Royal Canadian Officer Zachary Pendle and Tye, a rumor began claiming the French settlers were the culprits. This mistrust fueled further hostiles, until war broke out. We have sent that rumor to rest."

Commander Quinn could only thank everyone for having brought back a brave man, who would now rest with other members of the Mounted Police.

As Commander Quinn left the podium, Antoine strolled up.

"I am a lawyer by trade," he slowly began, "dealing in fact and truth. All those you see here today, sought truth, not rumor or theory. After the battle of the Little Bighorn, the prevailing theory was thousands of bloodthirsty savages massacred General Custer's entire command.

"Few if any wished to understand the errors committed, leaving cannon and Gatlin guns behind. Failing to wait for General Crooks planned three-prong attack, and dividing his force into three different commands. Yet one man in 1908 by the name of Edward Curtis attempted, he interview many of the Native American survivors along with photos. Having shown President Theodore Roosevelt all he had gathered, and afterwards asked not to publish, which he agreed. We now know a great deal about the battle, and to Mr. Curtis's credit, he was factual but not brave. Today, I stand among the brave that have sought truth, and now face the world."

"Ms. Gardner, what would you say to those that besmirched your judgement," a reporter yelled out.

"May I speak to that?" Vincent Groote yelled out while standing in the aisle.

"You may," Janice sat back down to allow him to speak.

"I allowed my ego to overshadow reputations," he said, looking toward her and Edward. "Money and praise clouded my judgement. Promises given to prove how an esteem professor fabricated information, to support Native American claims. However, such proof never materialized. Given to me were documents, which if interested can be shown, claiming General Schroeder corresponded with the Canadian French."

Pausing for several seconds while producing the documents, he carefully handed them to Throgmorton.

"Forgeries that any person could easily see," he continued, "but my ego would not allow such thought. I come before you not to cast blame, but ask for forgiveness. Let others guilty parties plead their case, my reputation ru-ined,, but Professor Throgmorton and Ms. Gardner's remain intact."

Saying goodbye, he simply walked away.

"Professor, will you show the documents?" one of the reporters yelled out.

"Yes, he will," Royce said, jumping to the podium, "those forgeries like buttons are part of history now."

"Mr. Pettrie," another reporter shouted, "your buttons were found on men intending to massacre innocent people..."

"Don't forget Peters who murdered his wife," said an unknown voice as laughter began.

"Yes, unfortunately all true," he said with a slight smile while showing part of the uniform with the buttons, "but understand these buttons encountered flame and hundreds of years in the ground. Yet they weathered the test of time, and shine as bright today as they day made. Proof of quality, ladies and gentlemen, then and now."

"The man should run for public office," Janice whispered to Antoine, "has a silver tongue and is a quick thinker."

"Had he been alive back then," Antoine began, giggling, "probably would have sold buttons to all the tribes for 10 times what they were worth."

When the presentation was finished, they allowed the news people to interview any member they wished. Walking around greeting people, Janice overheard Royce, speaking to the press.

"We here at Pettrie Button Company would like the folks to own a commemorative button such as these," Royce said, showing the original buttons, "gold plated but beautifully restored place in a lovely presidential case. A constant reminder of our history, and the goods made here."

"Antoine," Janice said in a calm tone when she found him standing alone. "Everyone's now talking about how to make money. Victor is promising to write another book about buttons, to include what we discovered, Keeler wants to display everything we learned for a year at the Smithsonian, including all the documents."

"At least the students along with Throgmorton will return," he said, pausing for a moment, "to tell everyone of the wonderful historical adventure they worked on."

"Have you heard the remains of the soldier's returned to Canada," she asked hoping he had heard, "buried at the pit with some memorial placed in the center?"

"Yes, I heard," he said, admitting he did know. "Ulanderson agreed to it. Be making it a cemetery, circling all the bodies around the memorial."

"They heard Ulanderson saying it's just another historical eyesore," she said, laughing, "but he's happy construction can start in a week or two."

"At least the wall around the mountain has begun," he said. "They've asked that I arrange to have artists ready to paint the displays we found in the caves on the walls."

"I noticed the proposals submitted for the bronze statutes of Chief Long-teeth and Little Sparrow," she replied while moving against him. "I know they would approve."

"Still a lot of work ahead of us," he said with a smile, "but need to start making plans for our marriage and honeymoon."

"I can't wait," she said, wrapping her arms around him.

"Told the council my intentions to marry you," he began. "They've asked to meet with us sometime next week."

"Is there something you're not telling me?" she said, stepping back as her heart began beating faster, "about the marriage?"

"Just a formality," he said while hugging her, "something about being a pure blood."

"Why can't we just be left alone," she said, burying her head into his chest. "Everyone knows how much we love one another."

"Not to worry," he said, kissing her on the lips. "Nothing is going to stop me from marrying you, and that is a promise."

"We've been so happy," she said, taking a deep breath. "Can't the council see that?"

"My love," he said, lifting her face up with his hand. "They know."

"I love you more every day," she said with a smile as she spoke.

CHAPTER TWENTY-FIVE

"You've been on that phone all morning," Janice said, covering her wet hair with the towel, "and ignoring me"

"Got all the artists ready to go," he said, placing the phone down. "Now that the wall is nearly completed, we can start planning a date to dedicate the mountain as protected sacred land. When the bronze statues arrive, be a celebration."

"Wonder what they would think, seeing themselves in bronze," she asked while placing the towel around her shoulders.

"Might say never ignore loved ones," he said, removing her towel and allowing her robe to fall to the floor. "A very wise couple."

"The last couple of weeks have been wonderful," Janice began while lying under the sheets, "waking up with you and not having to leave."

"Wore me out," he said, laughing while holding her.

"You enjoy every minute," she said, squirming to move away. "Admit it."

"Not every minute, but second," he said, pulling her toward him. "I can't exist without you."

"I love you," she said, softly speaking while moving her body on top of his, "and make you a good wife."

Entering the village to meet with the council, Janice was spellbound by what lay in front of her.

"So tell me," Antoine asked while looking toward the many tipis and struc-tures. "My tribe as it was 300 years ago."

"They live and work here?" she said, surprised when smelling the different foods being prepared and looking toward the people dressed in ceremonial buckskin.

"No, once a year my people come together to rejoice our past," he ex-plained, "tell children stories and show them how we survived."

"Like a family reunion," she blurted out.

"Yes, exactly," he said, realizing she understood, "and the members of the council thought this was the perfect place to meet."

"Antoine, what if they think I don't belong here?" she said, questioning him.

"I know of no other," he said, taking her in his arms, "who deserves to be here more."

"It's just, I'm both excited and afraid," she said, admitting her feelings, "and don't want to disappoint you."

"Never could you or would you disappoint me," he said, holding her tight.

"Antoine," Jimuta Ferro came out of a sunken structure, "you ready for this?"

"As ready as I'll ever be," he said, admitting concern. "Will you be join-ing us?"

"No, I'm no member," he said with a smile. "Council wanted you to see a friendly face."

"Will you stay with Janice?" he asked.

"Of course," he said, placing his hand on his shoulder. "Remember you're not to speak unless asked, so hold that tongue of yours."

Once inside, the members, wearing long feathered headdress and cere-monial tribal dress, sat in a circle.

"Antoine Renaud comes this day to seek permission to wed an outsider," one of the members began, "and of pureblood, we must decide."

"Once pureblood were as many as leaves on trees," another spoke up. "Now so few one can count on one hand. We must protect such members for the sake of the tribe, we cannot allow anyone to contaminate what flows in his body."

Arguments began between members, some objecting to the word contam-inate, others believing the time of purebloods over.

Listening, Antoine's anger rose, and he felt the need to speak.

Suddenly, Chatan, the oldest and wisest of member, raised his hand, where all stopped speaking.

"Having lived for so many years, some believe the Great Spirits bless me. Our customs guide us, with the belief the spirits of our ancestors watch over us. I have watched Antoine grow into a man, strong. Purebloods, I have seen, sought fame and fortune for themselves. It is true, Antoine, has gained fame and fortune, but unlike others, took the path of truth and justice. A path depriving him of a loved one, allowing him to seek blame and vengeance. Yet he chose forgiveness, and worked tirelessly to help our people against the scourge of alcoholism. As he traveled that path, he found a traveler."

He began coughing, where several members allowed him to drink.

"Like Antoine," he began again, "she, too, sought truth and justice. She proclaimed her love for him, while all remained silent. When the white man cried massacre, voices rose wanting to abandon all further discovery. She stood beside Antoine, risking reputation and fortune. Is she unworthy to join our tribe, who among us can judge her?"

Pausing for several seconds, he waited to see if anyone objected.

"Does not the heart pump the blood," he continued, "making it pure? Would our people be better served having a pure heart seeking truth, or pure blood. You have heard my words. I will speak no more."

"Antoine, you may now go," another spoke up. "We now speak among us."

"So how did it go in there?" Jimuta asked while Janice followed.

"Don't really know," he admitted. "Chatan spoke for us."

"That's a good sign," Jimuta said, looking toward Janice.

"Antoine," a member of the council came out from the structure, "council approved to allow Ms. Gardner the rite of passage."

"Terrific," Jimuta yelled out as Antoine lifted Janice.

"What does it mean?" she asked.

"Cleanse your body and soul," he began, "to become a member of our tribe."

"Tomorrow, you're be sent to one of the special tipis," Jimuta explained. "The women will bathe and dress you. Four spiritual leaders sitting outside, east, west, north, and south, chanting or praying."

"For two days," Antoine spoke up, "they will introduce you to our departed ancestors. They will then greet you as a member of the tribe."

"Will I be able to see them?" she asked.

"No," he began to laugh, "only your spirit will speak to them."

"Only thing is," Jimuta warned, "you must fast for the two days. But tonight, I'll provide a feast."

"Water will be given," Antoine quickly spoke, "and it's not that difficult."

As predicted the ladies of the village bathed her and placed a soft deer robe over her for warmth. For two days, she listened to the chants of the spiritual leaders and began to remember or dream of her life. So real the visions, she could feel their touch.

Spending long hours alone in the warm, closed tipi made the dreams seem real, or the smoke from the fire that changed colors when the ladies entered. Janice would never know, but remembering was both frightening and joyous.

On the morning when the chanting stopped, the ladies brought in broth and allowed a breeze to enter the tipi.

They again bathed her, washing her hair and placing it in a ponytail. Three entered and began to dress her in a beautiful white royalty dress, embroidered by hand. Now, all escorted her to a large wooden building, where family and friends sat waiting for her arrival.

"You ready for this?" Susan asked, walking out from one of the rooms followed by Linda.

"You're here," tears began falling as they began hugging.

"Please stand," he stood by the podium wearing a white clergy collar.

"They said only family and a few friends," Susan explained. "Dad's best man and Randy is there with him along with Jimuta."

"Where's Lisa and little Frank?" she asked looking around. They did come?"

"Lisa is the ring bearer," Susan replied. "Frankie is the usher."

"Mr. Acorn's came," Janice said, almost out of breath, "Throgmorton and Rock came, too?"

"Are you kidding," she began laughing, "couldn't keep them away without a real good fight starting."

"So many others asked to come," Linda spoke up, "but we explained everything."

"Just having you guys here is more than I could ask for," she said, wiping her tears, "and your dresses are so lovely."

"They say they're maiden princesses' dresses," Susan said, twirling around to show all the handcrafting. "Pretty cool."

"Hello," the minister said in a calm manner. "You ready?"

Instantly, they began walking down the aisle, and everyone looked toward her.

"You look beautiful," Sofia Jabra leaned toward her with a smile.

Standing beside Antoine, the minister placed a white ceremonial belt over their outstretched hands and began speaking of love. He spoke for 10 minutes of their love, and the faith each held. When over, he simply looked to them, and after allowing for a passionate kiss, introduced the two to all.

All enjoyed themselves, even without alcoholic beverages forbidden by the people of the village. When over, the two entered a special tipi, having a large bed in the center.

"So, your tribe had beds?" Janice began bouncing on it.

"No, but would you prefer the hard ground?" he asked, sitting beside her.

"I'd lie anywhere with you," she said, giving him a passionate kiss.

"Guess this will do," he said. returning her kiss.

After an hour and covered in sweat, Janice, laying on his chest, listened to his beating heart.

"Antoine, what if," she began, pausing for a moment, "I can't give you children."

"If we're met to have children, then we will," he began, "and with the help of our spiritual leaders chanting, be patient."

"What do you mean by that?" she said, sitting up as the sheet fell from her body.

"Having a pure heart," he said, pulling her down. "They asked for the blessing of children."

"Does that really work?" she asked, lying on top of him.

"Maybe," he said, rolling her over, "but I enjoy trying."

The following morning, they spent the day at the hotel with everyone that came. During this time, it was Throgmorton that gave thought on her future, recommending teaching at the college level. Susan, however, insisted on coming with her and becoming a member of her network.

"Antoine, what would you say if I decided to teach?" she asked, entering their room after a wonderful dinner with everyone. "You think Susan would be upset?"

"Your little sister wants you to be happy," he said, closing the door and holding her, "as does everyone else. My largest law firm is in Nevada, I spend most of my time there, and there are several great colleges."

"They have journalist courses," she said, relaxing in his arms, "right?"

"For sure," he said, confident they had such classes, "but if they don't we'll encourage them by providing a building for it."

However, the building was unnecessary; several universities and private colleges having journalism courses were interested in having her teach. For 10 years, Janice would teach while giving birth to three children.

"Mrs. Janice Renaud," an elderly man said, walking toward her after having finished class, "may I have a minute?"

"Certainly," she said, placing her books in the briefcase, "but I must go to my office to meet with several students."

"We can walk," he said, taking her briefcase.

"You're not a student or faulty member," she said, looking at his suit and handmade shoes, "so who are you?"

"Names York, attorney at law," he replied while they began walking out of the large classroom. "Great pleasure meeting you."

"My husband's an attorney," she said, reminding him, "and he handles all legal matters."

"Janice, I represent a client that would like to meet you," he continued as they walked. "For years, my client has followed your career and believes it is time to meet."

"I'm just a professor now," she replied. "No more interviews."

"No interview," he answered. "Just a sit down to talk."

"So who is this client?" she asked, somewhat interested.

"Shakespeare," he responded, saying only one word.

"Wait, you're talking about A. Shakespeare," she said, stopping and turning toward him, "the genuine author?"

"Of course," he said, surprised by her reaction. "The publishing company has agreed to this meeting and here we are."

"Requirements?" she asked. believing there were more nondisclosure forms needed.

"No forms or promises," he admitted. "A sit down meeting, and afterwards you may do what you wish with the knowledge."

"Why?" she asked, needing to know.

"Your interest has helped sales for one," he explained, "and more importantly, saved the company financially by exposing frauds."

"No conditions?" she could hardly believe it. "When?"

"Your last class is Friday," he said, handing her briefcase back, "I'll have transportation arranged for your journey."

"May I bring my family?" she asked.

"I can arrange for them to come," he said, but in a firm tone continued, "however they cannot attend the meeting with my client."

"Then I'll accept," she said, her heart beating hard, "and we'll be ready."

"Great," he said, taking her hand," let's shake on it."

As promised, a limousine arrived at their home and transported them to a private airport where a jet waited.

"Now everyone," they were told entering the jet. "Put on these earplugs, you'll thank me later."

Her two daughters and son obeyed, as did Antoine.

"Hello, I am Mary, your flight attendant." A lovely young lady came out from the cockpit. "If you need anything, please ask, but for now buckle up."

"Know you're looking forward to meeting this Shakespeare, Antoine speaking loudly while the children watched a cartoon. "Have you made up your list of questions?"

"For the first time in my life, I don't know what to ask him," she admitted. "Meeting him means I've accomplished everything."

"Janice, he'll just be another person like the rest of us," Antoine said, explaining his view, "and you'll come away knowing our family is your greatest accomplishment."

"He'll be just a man," she said with a smile, "and I'll be disappointed."

"A man who wanted to write and avoid people interfering," he continued, "and spent a lot to achieve that goal."

"Simple," she admitted, "but probably true."

"On the other hand, he could be an ugly man," he said, laughing while exaggerating, "so ugly he frightens everyone who looks upon him."

"Now stop it," she said, laughing with him.

Once they landed, they placed the family in a townhouse with everything, including servants that catered to every need.

"Mr. York informed us of your family," a young girl wearing a pantsuit spoke up for the entire staff of three, "and that your every wish be attended to."

"We don't wish anything," Antoine spoke up, "just go about your normal business."

"Please follow me," she said, ignoring his request. "Lunch is ready."

Entering the dining room, they found assorted lunch items that included food for the children.

"You will find a list of items for dinner," she said, pointing to a pad. "Please fill it out, and we serve at 6:00."

"Look at the food on the list," Antoine said, reading the list, "lobster or steak."

"Hot dogs, hamburgs, and pizza," Janice pointed out. "Great list."

The family began to relax and enjoyed the special treatment given.

"It's as if this place was designed for us," Janice said, watching as the children watched television or sat on desks coloring.

"Kids' network," Antoine said while holding her, "and in our bedroom cable."

"It's almost as if he knew our family," Janice remarked.

"Mrs. Renaud, I've been informed your ride will be here at 10:00," the young girl stepped out from the kitchen. "Mr. York will escort you."

"Thank you," Janice replied, sitting with Antoine.

The following morning at 10:00, Mr. York appeared and waited.

"You've been waiting for this moment for a long time," Antoine said while kissing her. "You look great."

"I'm prepared and ready," she said, taking a deep breath. "Children, be good while I'm gone."

Arriving at a multi-story office building, Mr. York escorted her to a private conference room.

"Hello Janice," Linda replied while standing by the window with Frank.

"Hi," she said. walking over and giving both a hug. "What are you two doing here? They said I was to meet Shakespeare alone. I don't understand."

"I'll leave the three of you alone," Mr. York said while closing the door.

"We're Shakespeare," Frank spoke up, "as was Leone."

"The three of you wrote all those books?" she said, sitting down to avoid falling. "I mean, how?"

"Don't be mad," Linda said sitting beside her. "Leone asked that we not tell you until we thought the time was right. Even our children don't know, but we wanted you to be the first to hear it."

"Why did Father keep that from me?" Tears began to flow as if remembering him. "We spent so little time together, and he never mentioned it."

"We created Shakespeare to avoid publicity," Janice began. "And it was Leone's idea to use the name."

"We all have a little Shakespeare in us," Frank spoke up, "he always said."

"Leone saw that spark in you," Linda began, "that you'd search the world over to find us. In doing so, you'd find adventure and fame."

"Most say it's the fire in the belly that keeps people going," Frank added. "Leone never wanted to extinguish that fire."

"When you first came to us," Linda noticed Janice smiling as if remembering, "Leone was so proud of you and knowing you found him. Shakespeare brought you to us, and we became a family."

"But how did it all start?" she asked, wanting to know how they began.

"When Leone left the service he had met so many characters," Frank explained, "we started making up stories, and Linda did the dialogue."

"Along with the typing," she reminded him, "it worked beautifully."

"We'd work when the children were at school." Frank sat across from her, "or late. Leone and I became the characters, and Linda gave us the words to speak."

"They were wonderful times," Linda replied, "watching the two warmed my heart."

"Wrote over 20 stories," Frank said, taking a deep breath as if relieved, "so many rejection letters until finally one publisher took a chance."

"The first four books given honorable mentioned reviews," Linda continued remembering, "and overnight, people began asking for our stories."

"We begged him to tell you," Frank admitted, "but he wanted you to know him, not the author."

"He used the money for your college," Linda said, knowing it would come up, "and paying off mortgages, but the rest is sitting in a bank for you."

"To make it fair," Frank decided to explain, "it was hard dividing the money between three of us when two are married. The accountants came up with creative ways, where we divided the money fairly."

"Maybe it's time to call in Mr. York," Linda suggested.

Within minutes, the man appeared with a large folder.

"Now that the shock has settled in," he began while opening the folder, "we need to speak of your inheritance."

"Inheritance?" she said, surprised by his casual business tone.

"Yes," he said laying out several documents on the table. "Your father, Mr. Pegasus, arranged everything. Having invested wisely, as Mr. and Mrs. Ehlert have, there is a great sum of money."

"Father," she repeated the name, "yes, he was."

"Taxes and legal fees paid as requested by your father," he said, taking a pen out from the folder. "We've a check for $32 million."

"Investments and some sitting in the bank drawing interest," Frank informed her, "unfortunately interest is taxable and with legal fees."

"So if you would sign here," he said, pointing to the check and documents. "I'll have the funds transferred to your account unless you would prefer to have your attorneys review the paperwork first."

"May I have my husband look the papers over?" she asked, shaking while speaking.

"Certainly," he said, placing the items back in the folder, "I'll meet with him this afternoon."

"Janice, if you want," Linda in a soft tone, "we'll allow you to announce who A. Shakespeare really is."

"How many more stories are there?" she asked.

"Four," Frank replied, "but we want you to be the one to announce it."

"No," she said with a smile, "let Shakespeare remain a mystery. It's what father would want."

"Be more money for you," York spoke up, "because people love a mystery man."

"We keep doing what we've been doing?" Frank asked.

"Shakespeare continues to pay taxes," York began, laughing, "and my fees."

As an attorney, Antoine helped to secure the legend of Shakespeare. Five years would pass, and word spread quickly that Shakespeare had retired without revealing his identity.

Janice continued to teach, while raising a family. She was highly sought after by many colleges to give lectures of her time as a journalist. Attending a college as a guest speaker in California, Janice spoke to over 300 students on truth and justice as a journalist. When finished a young female student asked a question, would her life been better had she found Shakespeare.

"Would life be better?" She paused for several seconds to consider the question. "To answer that question is to understand the search. I looked into the night sky, and there I found the brightest star. My journey began that night, traveling from one adventure to another. My quest to seek that star allowed me to meet wonderful people, and a family that took me in as their own. I gained a sister, and learned so much from her. Many mistakes made, and corrected. Became a wife to a wonderful man, and children."

She paused as her voice began to crack and tool a sip of water.

"That bright star eluded me, but I discovered me. I learned to see the world one person at a time, and to believe in the good, not bad. My life was the search, and I enjoyed every moment. I can only say, find your bright star in the dark night, and follow it with all the energy and passion one has. Then many years from now, you will tell others of your wonderful adventures. Thank you."

For 10 minutes, the students stood cheering, many hoping to find their star.

"Beautiful speech, my love," Antoine said, giving her a kiss. "The kids even liked it."

"Where are they?" he asked while looking around.

"Sitting in my limousine with my kids," Susan said as she walked past the many students leaving. "Great speech, especially about all I taught you."

"Thought you were still in Chicago," Janice said, giving her a hug, "but so happy you came."

"Mother called," she said, returning the hug, "said you were coming to town. So Harvey and I packed the kids up and came out."

"Where is Harvey?" Antoine asked. "Heard he's been promoted and in charge of the FBI bureau in Chicago."

"More headaches for him," she said turning, "but he loves it. He's with the folks, probably swopping stories."

"Just got the new album from Lisa," Janice reminder her. "I can't believe she's doing so well."

"Planning on some world tour," she said, shaking her head. "Father's furious that she wants to drop out of college for a year. Told him not to worry, little Frank will take care of everything now that he's her attorney."

"We'll talk with her," she said, taking her by the arm, "and have her graduate first."

"Tell us about your new contract," Antoine asked. "Rumor is that it's big."

"Harvey has another two years before he retires," she began, and they begged me to sign a four-year deal, so I stay in Chicago to anchor the nightly news."

"Wish that Leone could be here to see how well we all did," Janice remarked.

"I still can't believe the three were writers," Susan said ensuring no one was around, "and making us believe money was tight."

"Then giving all of you millions," Janice said, laughing.

"Shameful how they made us get work," Susan began, laughing, "and earn our own fortune and fame."

"Too bad our children will never know what we went through," Janice looked toward Antoine, "and just hope the money doesn't stop them from finding their own way."

"Stop this right now," Antoine blurted out. "We're great parents, and the kids know it."

"You're right," she said, smiling, "we are."

"So let's get going," he insisted. "Don't want to be late for your mother's dinner."

"Now that Shakespeare is gone," Susan said, taking her by the arm and walking her out. "I was thinking..."

"About what?" Janice asked in a soft voice.

"Our husbands like us have stories," she whispered, "maybe it's time for a female writer of old to start writing again."

END